DRAGON THIEF

SKYSTONE CHRONICLES BOOK 1

BLAKE & RAVEN PENN

For Our Family

(And our teenage selves, who totally would have loved this book)

Contents

Dear Reader   VIII

The Land of Evgard Map   IX

Drakfell Map   X

The Ethereal Triad   XI

From the Authors   XII

Vision 1   1

Chapter 1: Executed   7

Chapter 2: Steel Rim   21

Chapter 3: The Drunken Drake   32

Chapter 4: Knights of the Torch   40

Fragment - Valla   52

Chapter 5: Karl   56

Chapter 6: Inquisition   68

Chapter 7: The Black Valkyrie   77

Chapter 8: Bait   95

Vision 2   108

Chapter 9: The Scar   114

Chapter 10: Mud Pots   131

Chapter 11: The Inventor   146

Chapter 12: Sandy 155

Chapter 13: Don't Mess With the Owl 172

Chapter 14: The Bridge 184

Fragment - Jaira 197

Chapter 15: The Dragonstorm Sea 200

Chapter 16: Keep Drakfell 215

Chapter 17: The Dragon Dens 230

Vision 3 240

Chapter 18: The True Dragon Egg 245

Chapter 19: Stone 260

Chapter 20: The Challenge 268

Fragment: Kheradok 282

Chapter 21: Stars 286

Chapter 22: Oh Great Skymage 305

Fragment - Aradan 320

Chapter 23: The Plan 324

Chapter 24: The Gala 338

Vision 4 350

Chapter 25: Betrayed 354

Fragment - Thorn 361

Chapter 26: Executed Again 363

Chapter 27: Mutiny 367

Chapter 28: The Duel 381

Chapter 29: Thief 399

Chapter 30: Skygard 408

Vision 5 424

Now, check out a sneak peak of: 429

Reflection 1 430

Chapter 1: The Dragon Chasm 435

Brief Guide to Evgard 450

Mystics 451

Sentinels 452

Archons 453

True Dragons 454

Dragons 455

Evgardian Creatures 456

Drekai 457

Acknowledgments 458

About the Authors 460

Dear reader,

In our travels across worlds,
we've gathered many stories of
heroes. Those heroes always face
an unseen enemy.
May this book help you face yours.

Sincerely,

Blake Penn

Raven Penn

THE SKYSTONE CHRONICLES

The Land of
EVGARD

the skystone chronicles

The Land of
DRAKFELL

the skystone chronicles

The Ethereal Triad

The chart below shows the nine types of etherarchy common among worlds. Your world tends to call these effects "magic" or "supernatural." We use the term etherarchy because it is the command of ether that accomplishes these mythic effects.

Any person who can command etherarchy is a magi. They fall into one of three groups:

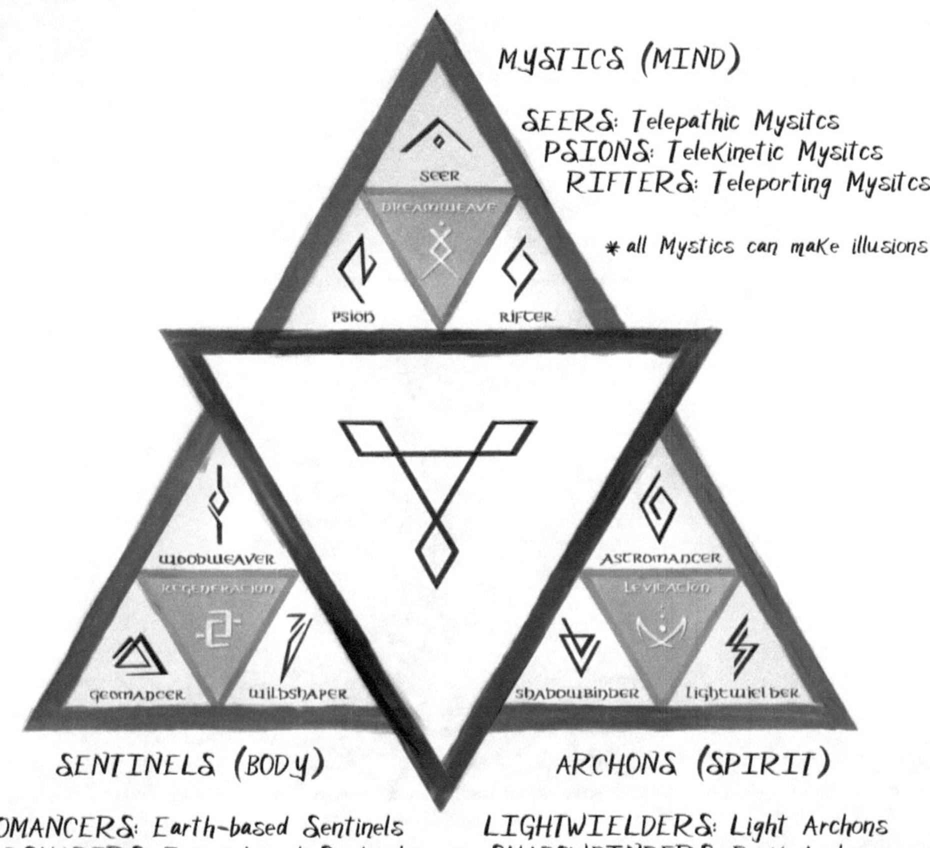

MYSTICS (MIND)

SEERS: Telepathic Mysitcs
PSIONS: Telekinetic Mysitcs
RIFTERS: Teleporting Mysitcs

*all Mystics can make illusions

SENTINELS (BODY)

GEOMANCERS: Earth-based Sentinels
WILDSHAPERS: Fauna-based Sentinels
WOODWEAVERS: Flora-based Sentinels

*all Sentinels can regenerate

ARCHONS (SPIRIT)

LIGHTWIELDERS: Light Archons
SHADOWBINDERS: Dark Archons
ASTROMANCERS: Ether Archons

*all Archons can levitate

*A note on silver: It is common knowledge that all etherarchy is nullified on contact with silver. This is why Mage Hunters wield silver weapons, and why Evgardian Keeps have silver lined cells designed to hold magi.

the skystone chronicles

From the Authors

Thanks for your interest in the land of Evgard!

If you want to know more about it, you can dive in deeper with the Brief Guide to Evgard included in the back of the book, or check out skystonechronicles.com for more.

Signing up for our mailing list will even get you a free short-story set in the world of Evgard!

Now, without further ado, we hope you enjoy *Dragon Thief*!

Vision I

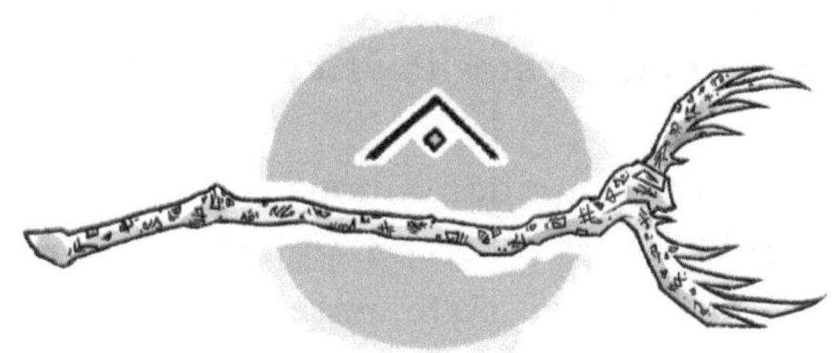

F ading stars.

In the last dregs of darkness as the dawn approached, a shower of emerald lights streaked across the heavens. The stars had been falling more often lately. Luckily, this skyfall would land far to the west. The stars brought both power and destruction—skystone and dragons.

A nomad's dragonhide hut stood concealed among the thick undergrowth. Only someone who knew where to look could find it.

Or someone who knew *how* to look.

The dying light of the moon reflected against the network of pale scars running up the woman's arms and across her face. It shone on the blades of her two long seaxes.

She paused, closing her eyes as she breathed in the scents of pine and raw earth. Glowing golden marks traced out underneath her angular eyes, flowing from the bridge of her nose over her high cheekbones.

Her eyes opened, her irises shifting from their usual black to the icy white of a polar wolf.

She was a Wildshaper.

Her enhanced eyes narrowed, honing in on the hut ahead.

Crack.

She spun around, her lupine eyes making her glare all the more intimidating.

"Sorry," her companion whispered, bringing a finger to his lips. His artfully-crafted goatee and spiffy nobleman's tunic made him look especially absurd out here in the woods. He too had a scar, though not from battle—the silvermark on his left cheek branded him as a Psion. He made a big show of taking stealthy steps to follow the woman.

She rolled her eyes.

Bringing up the rear was a mountainous canine of red and black fur. The bloodhusky held his ears erect, on high alert.

They reached the hut, a lavvu-style tent made from thick dragonhide. Painted in red above the door flaps was an icon of a beacon of light—the symbol of the Knights of the Torch.

The woman and man exchanged looks. Reverent. A little afraid.

The bloodhusky gave a low growl as it took a watchful post. The man and woman entered the hut.

A wispy layer of smoke hung above their heads, and the smell of woodchips filled the air. A bed of orange coals crackled at their feet.

Wings.

A black bird with silvery runemarks all over its feathers flew between them from behind, startling both the woman and the man. Starry violet light gleamed in the creature's eyes.

The Farseer's mythraven landed, perching atop the antler of a dragonstag which had been fused to the top of a gnarled wooden staff. There wasn't an inch of the staff that didn't have a rune scratched into it.

The travelers inhaled sharply as they saw who held the staff. He wore a pair of red dragonscale ascension gauntlets with intricate runes covering all but the back of his hands. A lone, ancient symbol stood out there, one that had been long forgotten. He blended into the smoky shadows in his dark red, hooded robes. All the woman and man could see within the hood were a pair of shining eyes and a small, glowing white stone suspended over his forehead. A skystone.

The man bowed reverently, his suave, light eastern accent apparent as he addressed the hooded figure. "Great Farseer, we have traveled—"

"I know why you are here, Solrac, Duke of Glacia. And you, Valla of White Cliff."

The woman straightened at the sound of her name. The marks beneath her almond eyes faded and her irises returned to their normal black.

Three runes on the Farseer's staff burned gold, and he pointed an armored finger at the bed of coals upon the ground. Valla and Solrac jumped backward as bright gold flames erupted from the coals and leaped as high as their heads.

"I have seen the omens in a pattern of three. First, the past. What do you see?" the Farseer's voice echoed through the wall of golden omenfire.

"Uh…" Solrac gazed hesitantly into the flames.

Within the fire, images.

Longships sailing east. At their head, a man wearing brilliant white ascension armor, forged from the shed scales of his bonded Lightwielder dragon. The dragon, a mighty, wingless drake, stood proudly at his side.

A crown adorned the man's head. Solrac recognized him.

"King Rodan of Drakfell," he murmured.

In King Rodan's hands shone an elongated orb with a pearlescent hue. Tiny crystalline scales covered its surface, and white light shone from within as it pulsed with life.

"That isn't…" Valla started.

"The egg of a true dragon," the Farseer confirmed. "One of the last. Stolen from the Dragon Isles."

"The King of Drakfell stole from the Drekai?" Valla shot a worried glance at Solrac.

"Perhaps to sway High King Magnus to send aid against the increasing skyfalls," Solrac said. "Though he may just be trading one type of war for another."

The Farseer swirled his staff. The mythraven cawed as it transferred to the Farseer's shoulder, and the vision in the flames shifted.

"Next, the present," the Farseer said.

Solrac and Valla peered into the fire. Flashes of men and women with horns and bright scales along their hairlines and cheekbones. Scales in all colors grew along the backs of their hands, shoulders, and tails. Many had wings.

They were the Drekai—the part-dragon people who lived on the Isles west of Drakfell. And judging by the fine battleworn bronze armor they donned, they were preparing for war.

"Now finally," the Farseer whirled his staff in a circular motion once more. "The future. Shadows of what may yet come. Take care, and remember that omens of the future are uncertain—filled with symbolism."

The vision in the fire changed again. A beautiful woman with harsh, midnight blue eyes and steely gray hair stood alone. A warrior in black, the emblem of a swan etched in silver on the blackened pauldron over her shoulder.

It was her.

Valla's gaze flashed to Solrac to gauge his reaction, but his face remained a blank mask.

In the flames, a gray mist swirled around the woman's feet, startling her. It crept along her black cloak, and Solrac and Valla watched with interest as the woman hurried to remove it. Wondering what the strange omen meant, Solrac frowned as the grayness leaped onto her pauldron.

The omen became even more confusing when the swan icon on her armor peeled free, taking flight. The black swan spread its wings, then burst in an explosion of hundreds of feathers to leave behind a single red rose.

One by one, each petal turned black, the image of the woman melting into the omenfire. Solrac took a step closer to the flame, and Valla took him by the arm to keep him from getting singed.

The vision shifted again.

A mighty, oversized frost drake lay dead against a backdrop of the starry night sky. Standing proudly before the creature was a young man in gleaming armor, a greataxe dripping with copper-colored dragon's blood clutched in his hand. It was none other than Mason Drakeslayer, the son of the High King over all the realm.

Vivid blue lightning crackled, flashing across the High Prince's regal frame. The omenfire burned higher, consuming the High Prince's face for a split second. When the flames pulled back, his young chiseled features had shifted into those of his proud, bearded father, High King Magnus. The nine skystones in his dragonforged steel crown glittered with eerie blue light.

But the omens weren't finished. Unsure what any of it meant, Solrac and Valla watched as the depiction of the High King disappeared, leaving behind only the starry heavens. Solrac stroked his goatee—that looked like the constellation of the Great Dragon.

Suddenly, each star in the constellation began to fall, becoming green-tailed comets as they shot downward toward an enormous map of Evgard. As the comets landed on the map, they morphed into sharp, jagged starglass daggers.

Without warning, more gray mists rapidly ate away at the edges of the map until they consumed it. The grayness swirled together into a massive, writhing gray dragon, who turned its head, electric blue eyes staring straight at Solrac.

Then, all at once, the flames died.

The image of those eyes lingered with Valla and Solrac, almost as if some unseen entity was watching them even now.

The hut was silent but for Solrac and Valla's breathing.

The quiet was interrupted as a howl from the bloodhusky outside pierced the air. The Farseer's strange, glowing eyes turned toward the door to the hut.

"Mage Hunters," the Farseer warned. "Too many to face. You must hurry. Get to the nearest safehouse. See if you can convince the rest of the Knights of the Torch to aid you."

Then he reached into one of the folds of his robes, pulling out a small hoop carved from bone. The circle was tied with gold threads running across it to form a star.

A dreamweb.

Tied in the center of the web was a chunk of white crystal. Not a skystone, but an ether-filled quartz. A series of tiny, carved runes decorated the crystal's surface.

The Farseer passed the dreamweb to Solrac. "Use this to consult me further in times of need. Now flee, before it is too late."

With that, the Farseer pounded his staff on the ground. Smoke billowed all around him, and in a flash of golden light, the Farseer disappeared.

Solrac gave a low chuckle. "The Farseer never misses a chance for a dramatic exit, eh?"

Valla's face was serious. "Where's the nearest safehouse?"

"Steel Rim. We'll meet with the Knights in the area there, regroup, then move on to King Rodan in Keep Drakfell."

"Keep Drakfell." Valla narrowed her eyes. "Do you mean what I think you mean?"

"Oh, yes." Solrac's eyes lit up with determination. "We have a true dragon egg to steal."

CHAPTER I: EXECUTED

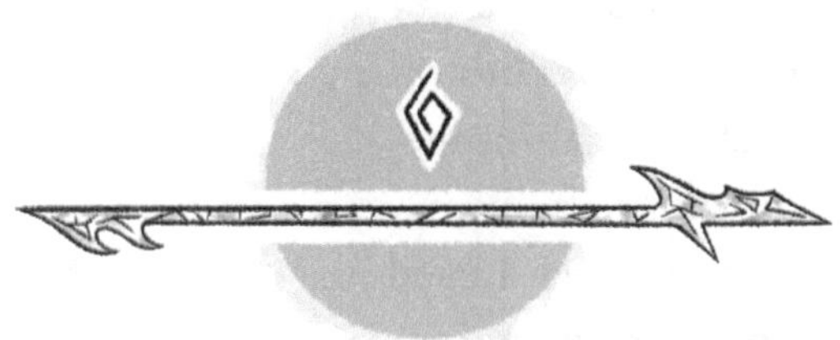

If I were a better thief, I wouldn't be leaping to my death from the top of a tower.

My desert tan cloak, stolen from a guard, billowed as I plummeted through the air. Behind me, the stark white tower reached skyward above the smokesage and junipers of the badlands beyond. If only I'd been wearing my signature turquoise bandana, I'd have looked even more epic.

Asher, what are you doing? Kai's voice sounded in my head. Kai's mirror gecko, Glint, was hiding in my boot, one of her scaly little feet touching my shin in order to form a mindlink between my best friend and me. I felt the gecko grip tighter as I fell—she hated heights.

What? I thought back. *You wanted a distraction.*

Instead of words, Kai's mind replied with a muffled mix of frustration and amusement.

Do I at least look cool? I asked in my mind.

No answer from Kai.

That was fair. Something else must've been taking the bulk of his attention—probably whatever great treasure he was trying to get away with.

As I fell, I looked over my shoulder at the guards crowding the top of Whitestone Hall's tower. An entire squad and a half stood together, looking down at me. I was honored to have so many on my tail.

I mean, I hadn't stolen three whole skystones for nothing.

The guards watched anxiously, as if deciding whether or not to waste any crossbow bolts on me. It looked like one of their squad captains had given the order to wait, figuring the fall would finish me.

They were wrong.

I breathed in deeply through my nose, ignoring the black strands of hair that had come free of my warrior's fangknot to whip me in the face. As I focused on my breath, I felt an exhilarating surge of energy. My eyes blazed gold as I accessed the ether within me.

The sun-baked town square below was rising fast. I let my breath out.

All at once, my descent slowed. I used just enough of my levitation power to keep myself from splattering against the square.

I hit the ground and rolled, nailing the landing completely unscathed and only a little dusty.

I wished I had time to enjoy the stunned faces of the guards above as I ducked for cover behind a stack of barrels.

"Three... two... one," I muttered.

Thump, thump, thump.

And there were the crossbow bolts.

Some thudded harmlessly into the ground, while others stuck into the barrels behind me.

"Magi!" I heard a guard shout from high atop the tower.

"Archon," another confirmed.

Soot.

Maybe they'd seen my eyes glow. Of course, no other kind of magi could survive a fall like that.

Asher, you okay? Kai's voice sounded inside my head.

Of course, I sent back. Glint the mirror gecko was practically squeezing the life out of my leg. *Did that get you the opening you needed?*

I think so, he answered. *They're sending everyone after you. I just need a few more minutes.*

Sounds like fun.

The thunder of guards' boots approached behind me, along with some mild cursing. They were fast.

But I was faster.

Leaping up from behind the cover of the barrels, I sprinted down the street.

The faded white adobe longhouses formed tight alleys, and before long, I came up against a dead end.

Behind me, I saw the quickest guards closing in.

Time for more etherarchy.

My eyes blazed gold as I used my archonic levitation to hover-run up the side of the wall. When I looked back, I could just make out a fading trail of gold light warping the air directly behind me. My feet skidded over the siding and up onto the roof of the longhouse, then right back over the other side and onto the street again.

I could hear the guards protesting as they searched for a way around.

I kept hover-running, levitating myself just enough to dash up and over more adobe longhouses. I dodged sporadic tumbleweeds as I darted around, over, and through alleyways and dead ends, leaving the guards scrambling to follow.

The gasps of random townspeople were music to my ears. Apparently, they didn't often see seventeen-year-old Archons racing through their streets, scaling the walls of their homes like it was nothing.

Probably because most magi in Evgard got sentenced to death.

Just then, I saw a cute, freckle-faced girl stacking thick, leathery agave leaves outside a shop. She was staring at me in disbelief, of course. I winked and gave her a salute.

She totally fainted... on the inside.

On the outside, her face was a mix of amused, annoyed, and a little afraid. She probably believed what the Mage Hunters said about magi—that we drew wild dragons to the realm.

Well, we *did* technically draw wild dragons to the realm. But it wasn't our fault we were born with ether in our souls, nor that ether just happened to be a wild dragon's favorite snack. And anyway, any dragons that were after her town weren't here for me. They'd have been after the ether-filled skystone I'd just stolen from her Keeper.

Really, I was doing her a service by robbing her town.

I hover-vaulted more homes, listening for guards around every corner. They were gaining on me, and there were more of them.

They'd seen me levitating, so they knew I was an Archon. But they didn't know which type—Shadowbinder, Lightwielder, or Astromancer.

Those who'd bothered to learn the differences between the nine types of magi would find out soon enough.

Without slowing down, I dug deep, my eyes glowing even brighter. Misty white, pure ether swirled together along my chest and back, hardening into semi-transparent, crystalline armor.

Starglass, a sure sign of an Astromancer.

Perfect. Assuming this shabby frontier town didn't have any silver-tipped mageslayer bolts, my armor would last at least until the end of the day. Not that I planned to need it for that long.

Right on cue, a guard stepped out from behind a stack of crates. He took aim with his crossbow, firing at me as I hover-hurtled an apothecary.

The bolt grazed my newly formed starglass armor and skittered harmlessly away.

"Good shot," I shouted to him as I ducked into the next alley.

You clear yet? I thought to Kai through our mindlink.

Almost, but I need Glint, he replied, his mental voice sounding distracted.

Sending her now, I thought back. I ducked to the side of a building and knelt down to let the dreambeast out of my boot.

Thanks, Asher. Stall just a little longer.

Glint the mirror gecko hopped to the ground, severing the mindlink as soon as we stopped touching. The rune-speckled gecko blinked her mirrored eyes at me in farewell, then disappeared into thin air, leaving little puffs of dust as the only evidence that she was ever there. She'd gone back to Kai through the dream realm.

Now I was on my own.

The sound of approaching guards was coming closer. I looked around, spotting a star-topped spire a street or two down from where I stood.

That'd do.

I hover-ran down the streets, then dashed up the side of an adobe chapel of Streya, the mind goddess. I channeled more ether to amplify my wild leap so I could catch hold of the spire.

I said a brief prayer to Streya, just in case there really was a mind goddess out there. Making sure every guard in Whitestone Hall would have time to see me, I theatrically scanned my surroundings as if deciding on an escape route.

"Three... two..." I murmured.

Before I got to 'one,' a crossbow bolt hit me in the shoulder, bouncing off my starglass pauldron.

"You're getting faster!" I called out.

The nearest wall was to the east. Once I was in the badlands' scrub brush, I could hide easily.

I jumped off of the star-topped spire just in time. Another couple of crossbow bolts buzzed past me. One hit the church spire, and I wondered if Streya would give that guard some kind of curse.

I slowed my fall before I hit the ground, rolling to soften the landing. Hopefully, my display had bought Kai enough time.

Within seconds, I hit another dead end. Here, two small, masked draccoons were fighting over a bone. They stopped and blinked their beady black eyes at me.

"Gentlemen," I nodded to them, then burned ether to hover-jump the next building. The safety of the badlands was just a few more alleyways, rooftops, and a wall away.

Almost free.

I checked my ether well. The source of my ether felt like a warm light in my heart. I'd used about a third of my day's supply.

Weightlessly, I hover-ran up the side of another building and onto the rooftop.

The distant guards cursed as they saw me.

I smiled and waved as I ran, tauntingly patting the skystone-filled satchel at my side.

A series of twangs sounded behind me, and more crossbow bolts buzzed past. Two bounced off my starglass armor, almost knocking me off balance. The starglass didn't shatter, though. Still no silver-tipped mageslayer bolts.

The town wall was now only thirty feet away.

I ran along the ridge of the last longhouse, putting on a burst of speed before making my final, ether-powered hover-jump.

I leaped.

It felt like time slowed as I neared the top of the wall. Freedom was within reach. Just a few more feet...

Then I caught a silvery glimmer out of my right eye. Someone in a dusk blue cloak and a gleaming, silver pauldron stepped out from within a tower on the wall. She expertly lashed out at me with a chain whip made of silver.

My escape came crashing down.

Well, I came crashing down.

The silver chain felt frigid against my skin as it wrapped around me and cut off my ether.

My exhilarating rush of power sputtered, and my glowing gold eyes flickered like dying embers. My levitation faltered, and I smashed into the wall before crashing onto the ground below, tugging the whip from her grip. The contents of my satchel spilled across the packed earth street below.

My starglass armor shattered and faded into starry oblivion wherever the silver had touched it. As I pulled the chain away, my fingers tingled painfully with every touch from the icy silver.

Stars, that was a good hit. And a silver whip like this could only mean one thing.

Mage Hunter.

Panic welled up inside me. Mage Hunters traveled in pairs, and if there were two here, then escape had just gotten a lot harder. The guards were closing in. If I was going to get out of here, I needed to make this next jump count.

I scrambled to recover the skystones that had spilled from my pack. Three chunks of pebble-sized, raw crystal. The crystals pulsed with glowing white energy—pure, unchanneled ether.

It dawned on me that the extra boost I could get if I used one of these would get me over the wall, regardless of the Mage Hunters.

I replaced two of the skystones in my satchel and cradled the other in my hand. Already I could feel the energy from the power it contained.

Then, out of the corner of my eye, I saw Kai.

He was a ways down the wall from me, a large sack slung over his shoulder. He was trying to be subtle, but the wall guards were heading his way, about to turn the corner and run straight into him.

Soot. If I didn't do something, they'd catch him for sure.

Without hesitation, I cried out and tossed the skystone back inside my satchel. It clacked into place against the other two. Ignoring the rush of freezing pain from the silver, I grabbed the whip and wrapped it back around me. The silver cut off my etherflow, and I knew I wouldn't be able to access my ether well while I was tangled up like this.

With a somewhat exaggerated yell, I clawed at the wall as if trying to climb it.

"Silver... too... much! Can't... climb!"

I fell to the ground in a melodramatic heap, the silver chain still draped over my shoulders.

My display did exactly what I'd hoped, grabbing the attention of every guard in range. Relief flooded me as the two guards who'd been about to notice Kai turned their gazes on me.

My relief quickly turned to panic when, within moments, several squads of guards had me surrounded. They had crossbows, seaxes, and spears, all trained on me. They'd finally caught up, and they'd sent everyone. Kai could now saunter away with the wealth of Whitestone Hall in his pack, whatever it was.

I braced myself for a skirmish. Most of the guards looked very sweaty and extremely annoyed. Maybe I shouldn't have made them run around so much.

I even spotted the town Keeper herself standing with the guard.

"Hold fire," came the Keeper's snide, snarling voice. Then she spat on the ground.

"Ethercursed," she muttered.

"Well, that's not very nice," I said, pretending to be shocked. But I'd been called the derogatory term for magi so many times before, it no longer fazed me.

The Keeper narrowed her eyes as she strode my way with hands clasped behind her back. She bent down to get a better look at me, her smug, oily face coming within inches of mine.

"Ah, a half-born."

I sat up a little straighter. Technically, it was my mother who was the full half-born, so I was three-quarters human. But nobody seemed to care about that distinction. We were all half-borns to people like the Keeper.

I proudly regarded her with my dragonfire green eyes, then tossed my hair back so she could get an even better look at the dark teal scales on the tips of my pointed ears. While I kept my hair long on top, I made sure to always cut it short on the sides to prove I wasn't ashamed of my heritage.

The Keeper smirked. I'd been sure they'd execute me before for being an unregistered magi, but now that she knew I was a half-born, I had no doubts.

The Keeper of Whitestone Hall kneeled down, utter disdain on her face.

"No wonder you were so interested in my skystone," she said, low enough that the guards couldn't hear. Then she added loudly, "We'll execute him tomorrow morning. Death by dragon."

I knew it.

Then she straightened up, and the last thing I saw was a triumphant sneer on her slick face before her heavy boot connected with my head and everything went black.

At least she hadn't kicked me in the nose. I really liked my nose.

I woke up in the dungeon of Whitestone Hall. Sitting up from a shabby bedroll on the stone floor, I pushed my hair out of my face.

I scanned my surroundings. I'd been in my fair share of prisons, and this one was surprisingly less dingy than the rest of the town. It looked like a repurposed cellar under Whitestone Hall's greathouse. Barrels of draquila sat in stacks in the shadows beyond my cell. The alcoholic beverage, made from red agave and a few drops of bronze dragon blood, gave the cellar a fresh spiced smell.

They'd left my pants and boots, but stripped my stolen guard's uniform. The burlap shirt they'd put me in scratched at my skin, and I shivered through the thin cloth. I couldn't quite see my breath, but it was cold down here.

Soot, what if they'd silvermarked me?

My fingers flew to the left side of my face, and I was relieved to feel only smooth skin. I'd made it this long without them branding me, and I wasn't interested in getting carved up with a silvermark now.

I rubbed at my temples, my head still sore from the Keeper's kick. The blood was dry, so I must've been out for a while.

I needed to escape. If I got executed again, my dad was going to kill me.

I stood, blinking in the dim candlelight of the cellar. No one was out there. There was a larger guy snoring in the cell next to me—definitely not skinny enough to be Kai. The other cells were empty, which meant that Kai must've escaped the city. Good.

Kai would have an escape plan for me, too. He'd probably know about the Mage Hunters being here now, so he wouldn't go with a jailbreak. I was probably going to have to wait for the execution.

Soot. Those kinds of escapes were always more risky, especially with Mage Hunters around. I wondered if I could get out on my own.

I held my breath as footsteps stomped above me. I waited for them to fade, then looked at the lock on my cell door.

It was now or never.

I crept toward the door and reached through the bars, feeling for the keyhole on the other side.

It was easy to find, and it was big. And this town was cheap enough that the lock wasn't silver, either.

I breathed in to focus as my eyes turned from dragonfire green to blazing gold. Holding out my hand, my palm shone with ethereal light as I carefully formed a small starglass key.

The key slid easily into the lock, but it was way too small. I rattled it around a little, getting a feel for the lock's interior.

I focused my breath, adding more starglass to the key until it felt right. I turned the key, and the lock clicked open.

I was going to tell Kai it had worked on the first try.

Carefully, I lifted the lock from the door.

From across the room, deep in the shadows, I heard a slow clap.

Soot.

My heart sank as a grizzled old jailer leaned forward into the candlelight. He casually trained his crossbow on me and smiled.

"Go ahead, half-born," he said, his thick eyebrows lowering. "Open the door so I have an excuse."

I slowly replaced the lock and smiled back at him. "Just testing the security here. I gotta say, you run a fine jail."

If only it'd been a girl jailer. Flirting my way out of prison had worked once before.

Not today.

The jailer leaned back and laughed, resting the crossbow on his belly.

"You here to silvermark me?" I asked, trying to sound fearless despite the growing pit in my stomach.

"Nah. Wouldn't waste the silver when they're just going to feed you to the dragons in the morning," he said, the candlelight dancing in his eyes.

I sat back on my cot, crossing my arms over the scratchy burlap shirt.

"You sure gave the guard a good run there," the jailer said, a look of amusement on his scarred face. "If not for my daughter snagging you with her whip, you'd have made it."

"Well, at least someone around here is taking their training seriously," I said, running my fingers through my long bangs. My hair band must've fallen out during the action.

"We have to when rogue magi like you keep running around unregistered."

"What can I say?" I shrugged. "Nothing like having a guard's seaxe at your throat every once in a while. Keeps me on my toes."

"It's pronounced *sax*," the guard said, pronouncing the word with a short 'a' sound and shortening it to one syllable.

"I've heard it both ways," I said. "Point is, I'd rather run than be killed."

"Killed? Who's been feeding you lies like that? Turn yourself in. My daughter just got back from the Mage Hunter Academy last week—says they've finally perfected the magi cure."

"Right," I said with a bitter laugh. "You mean the 'cure' where the Black Valkyrie drags you east, then kills you in cold blood?"

"Don't fall for that soot those Farseer-believers say. The Mage Hunters are just trying to do what's best for Evgard."

"By exterminating us?"

The jailer sighed. "I guess that means you'd rather endure execution by order of the Keeper over the chance to be cured of your magi curse."

"Yeah, if my choice is death or death, I guess I choose death."

The jailer glared. "At least when you die, the dragons who slaughter you will be the last you draw to our town."

"You know the dragons attacking Whitestone Hall lately aren't my fault, don't you?"

"Oh, I know. Unregistered magi are always 'just passing through,' right?"

"I guess they didn't show you what I stole from your Keeper, then."

The jailer furrowed his brow. I went on, looking him straight in the eye.

"She's been hoarding skystone. Three big crystals. That's what's been drawing your dragons."

His face darkened.

The keepdoms were supposed to collect the skystone from skyfalls and send it on to Evgard Capital. That way, High King Magnus could control how it was used. Most keeps didn't dare defy the high king, but the temptation to hoard a powerful, versatile resource like skystone was great. Rumor even had it that skystone kept the legendary Farseer himself from aging.

The jailer grunted, stroking his beard. "It's hard to trust a thief. Especially one with eyes like yours. But I'll ask my girl if what you say is true."

"And if it is?"

"Then we might need to replace our Keeper," he said, cracking his knuckles.

"Yeah, I'd say Whitestone Hall would be much better off without selfish, corrupt nobility in charge."

He gave me a sidelong glance. "Either way, you gave me a good laugh seeing this lot of guards get all turned around after neglecting their training for so long. You deserve some dignity."

He threw me a dragonleather cord for my hair. It had the crest of Drakfell engraved on it, a dragon's fang.

"Thanks," I said, pulling the top half of my hair back from my face and into a quick, messy fangknot. "Gotta look good for those dragons before they tear me to pieces."

The jailer gave a sad chuckle. "Stars be with you."

I was late for my own execution.

To be fair, it wasn't my fault. The jailer was right—most of the guards at Whitestone Hall weren't exactly on top of their game. And from the disheveled look of the Keeper, she wasn't used to getting up by dawn.

Standing out in a row of wrinkly guard cloaks and slouchy uniforms was the young woman in the silver pauldron and crisp, dusk blue cloak of a Mage Hunter. She must've been the jailer's daughter—the one who'd snagged me with her silver chain whip. Her silver pauldron bore an insignia of a sword stabbing through a triangle—the symbol of the Mage Hunters.

It kinda softened the blow to know that the only one who took her job seriously had been the one to take me down. Even her Mage Hunter partner beside her was lazily leaning on his silver sword as he watched them lead me out.

The jailer's daughter caught my eye, and I could see the resemblance between her and her father. She had thick, intense eyebrows, too, and her short hair was pulled back into a low draketail. She was a lot prettier than her father, though it looked like she'd never laughed before in her life.

I gave her a nod of respect, but the Keeper, who stood next to the Mage Hunters, thought the nod had been for her. The Keeper scoffed at me, and I barely resisted the urge to stick out my tongue.

A pair of guards looked around nervously as they led me through the northern gate of the city. An execution platform stood in a clearing a decent distance from the wall where the Keeper, Mage Hunters, and guards watched. Someone had scrawled the words 'magi not welcome' across the dingy white wall using bronze dragon's blood as paint.

With trembling hands, one guard tethered me to a post in the center of the platform. She tied one end of the rawhide rope to the post and the other end around my waist so that I had some range of motion. The other guard handed me a dragonhook spear, a grim look on his face. Drakfell saw it as distasteful to let me die without a fighting chance. Technically, their laws said that if I fought off the wild dragons and stayed alive, they'd free me after three days. But out here on the frontiers, most didn't make it more than three hours.

They saw it as justice, executing magi through death by dragon.

But I saw it as counterproductive. If they really wanted dragons to stop eating people, they should probably stop feeding them... well, people.

Though I guessed that in their eyes, unregistered magi didn't count as people. Especially half-born magi like me.

I was positive I could form starglass into something that would cut the rope. But one look at that row of guards and I knew I wouldn't get far before getting hit with a bolt from a crossbow. Silver-tipped mageslayer bolts this time.

To the west, the quarries that gave Whitestone Hall its name were the perfect hiding place for wild dragons. To the northeast, juniper trees and smokesage brush provided plenty of cover as well. It was only a matter of time.

"Any skyfalls last night?" I asked one guard as she finished securing the rope around my waist. "Just wondering if there'll be any dreklings out there today."

She stared at me through the visor of her ravenhelm and shook her head.

"Perfect. Thanks," I said with a wink and a lopsided grin.

She rolled her eyes, but I caught the ghost of a smile playing at her lips. I think she tied the rope a little looser around my waist.

With one last fearful look toward the wild badlands, both guards hurried back toward the safety of the wall. That left me alone and exposed.

Just then, a tiny sparkle of light caught my eye from underneath the platform. Between a gap in the wooden slats, I saw the shine of a little mirror gecko watching me. She licked her shiny eyes.

I smiled.

Bong. From high atop the platform, I heard the Keeper toll the execution bell. Did they realize it was basically a dinner bell for dragons?

I looked to the sky, and almost as if on cue, I saw a black silhouette winging its way toward me. That was fast. Too fast.

The wyvern gave a feral shriek as it dove toward me. At the last second, it swooped upward, flying past me toward the guards on the wall.

I heard frantic screams as the wyvern scattered the guards. To the Keeper's credit, neither she nor the Mage Hunters ran away. They held their ground as the wyvern swooped back toward me. The dragon knew where the easy meal was, after all.

I dropped into a defensive stance, aware of the tether around my waist limiting my range.

The black wyvern landed right in front of me and bared his teeth, as if daring me to take a stab at him. His two wide wings folded upwards and he leaned forward, menacing claws at his wing joints serving as forelegs. Angular bronze patterns wove around his dragonfire green eyes, long neck, and shoulders. Short, bronze antlers, each with three gleaming points, sprouted from his serpentine head. His tail whipped back and forth, a bronze, thornlike blade growing from its tip.

The wyvern roared again, and I could feel the hot air from his maw on my face.

I didn't stand a chance.

Chapter 2: Steel Rim

Time for a show.

I yelled, brandishing my spear at the black and bronze wyvern.

The dragon hissed, whipping his tail blade forward. He smacked the dragonhook spear from my grip and knocked me to my knees.

I could hear the Keeper's cruel laughter from all the way down here.

The wyvern swished his tail blade again, this time slashing through my tether.

Out of the corner of my eye, I caught the flash of the mirror gecko dashing onto the platform and into my boot.

The wyvern snatched me up with his powerful hind claws. Then, with a few mighty flaps of his wings, he carried me off into the sky.

Justice had been served. Or... I guess *I* had been served.

I screamed in terror as I watched Whitestone Hall fade away. Once I was out of earshot and certain that no one would hear me, I cried out.

"No! I'm too handsome to die!"

The wyvern gave me a little shake, and I hung limply in his talons.

Once we'd flown a little further, I perked up. "Nice one, Thorn. Let me put up more of a fight next time though, okay? They think I died a wimp."

From above me, Thorn, my bonded wyvern and best dragon-friend, let out a low chuckle.

We soared over the Drakfell badlands. The mirror gecko clung to my leg from inside my boot as scrubby junipers and black-stemmed smokesage passed beneath. The faraway smell of burning filled the air, either from a nomad campfire or a dragon buffalo in rut, snorting flames then fanning them with their vestigial wings. Antlered drakalope and scrub kirin scattered when they caught a glimpse of the wyvern gliding above.

We flew over several small outlander settlements that dotted the land east of Whitestone Hall. I kept playing dead as we passed by a few of them, just in case. Once we were in the clear, I climbed onto Thorn's back for a more comfortable ride.

As we flew, I opened a secret compartment that had been sewn into my belt. Kai's sister, Kari, had made it for me as a way to hide Thorn's heartscale when I was on a raid.

The heartscale was arrowhead-shaped and black, with copper patterns matching the ones that wove around Thorn's eyes and shoulders. I'd tied the scale to a leather cord so I could wear it around my neck. The heartscale softly thudded into place over my heart, and I felt the bond with my dragon bloom to life like a warm, comforting bonfire.

Thorn roared joyfully, and I let out a whoop as we flew over the smoky badlands toward home.

A tall cliff towered over the north side of my outlander hometown, glowing gold in the late afternoon light.

The town of Steel Rim spread out from the base of the cliff near the torch-lit entrances to the deep iron mines. The cliff face helped catch rain and funnel it into some old mine shafts that the town's founder had converted into reservoirs.

Just south of the sprawling longhouses of Steel Rim, Thorn's den was nestled between some ridges of sandstone. One tall ridge had tipped over to rest against another, forming a spacious cavern. A few junipers grew just right, blocking the entrance from view.

We landed in a small clearing at the mouth of the cavern. I dismounted from Thorn and let Glint out of my boot. She skittered across the dirt and disappeared into the den. A slight purple glow emanated from inside.

Oh stars. I rolled my eyes. Kai had set up his 'defense system' again. A glowing, semi-transparent wall of purple dream energy contained within a stone archway blocked my path. My friend had etched Mystic runes all along the stones to fuel the dream barrier.

Walking through it would knock me out. I'd learned that the hard way.

I rapped my knuckles on the cave wall, trying to remember the intricate rhythm that was Kai's absurdly long, secret knock.

No answer.

From behind, Thorn gave a low, draconic chuckle before settling down in a patch of sunlight and closing his eyes.

"Kai?" I asked. "Did I do the knock wrong or something?"

After a moment, Kai's voice sounded through the wall of dream energy.

"We switched to passwords, remember?"

Soot. I vaguely recalled a conversation about random, complex numbers and words.

"Uh... Four, One, Two, Pebble, Ring, Naga. Right?"

"No, that's the old one," Kai said.

"Stars above, Kai. It's obviously me."

"That's exactly what a Mage Hunter would say."

"No, a Mage Hunter would just cut through this wall with their silver sword."

There was silence for a second, then I heard a quill scratching against paper.

"Are you taking notes?"

"Don't know how I overlooked such a dangerous flaw. Remember the password now?"

"It's too complicated. Don't you have a backup way to verify it's me?" I asked.

"Of course," Kai scoffed, and I heard the rapid flipping of pages. "Security questions. How long did you have a crush on Kari?"

"What, like when we were kids?"

"More recently than that."

Soot, he knew about that?

"She's not in there with you, is she?"

Silence.

"Is she?"

"...No."

"Okay, like four months."

"Soot, wrong again. One more strike and I'll have to mindwipe you and find out who you really are."

"Hold on now, I wasn't really sure I liked her until the summer."

Kai paused, mulling over my claim. "Fine. Just one strike then."

I heard him scratch something out in his book.

"So can I come in now?" I asked, leaning back against the cavern wall.

"Next question. What was your mother's name?"

"Zerana of Moss Falls."

"Okay, now just one more since that one felt too easy."

"That's it," I said, my eyes glowing gold. I channeled my ether and made a shield of starglass, then held it over my head. I pressed the shield's edge into the glowing purple wall. The starglass stopped the dream field from above so I could walk through without getting drenched in dream energy.

I found Kai sitting on a rock near the entrance. As usual, he was wearing an excessive amount of full plate armor, custom made by Kari. Kai's dreambeast, Glint, perched on his shoulder as he furiously wrote more notes in his black leather journal.

"Soot, didn't realize astromancy would make it so easy to get in. Maybe if I add more runes coming from underneath..." Kai said. He kept writing with one hand, while he deactivated the dream wall with an absent-minded wave from the other. I let my starglass shield dissipate into starry ether dust as well.

Kai muttered to himself as he flipped through one of the many books he kept inside his pack. He scanned the pages, copying a few runes into his journal.

Mystics. The idea of having to memorize so many runes and trace them into the air just to use etherarchy seemed so clunky. I was glad I was an Archon.

"Ouch," I murmured, putting a hand to my head wound. As great as it was being an Archon, I knew all Sentinels shared the power of regeneration, which sounded nice right about now. Thorn was a Sentinel, and I'd seen firsthand how quickly he healed himself.

"We should just go back to knocking," I said. "Or, better yet, nothing. We've been hiding here for years and nobody's found the den."

"Maybe I could make it throw out some illusions..." Kai continued musing, ignoring me as I changed out of my prison clothes.

The first thing I did was tie my turquoise bandana around my neck. It was well made, with tiny, intricate patterns covering the square of fabric. Unless someone looked closely, they'd have no idea the pattern was really draconic writing. As the tight-knit cloth rubbed against my skin, I finally felt like myself again.

Kai thought the turquoise dust scarf was too flashy, and that I'd be better off wearing a brown or tan one like most others did out here in the desert. But I liked the way my mom's old scarf made me stand out just a little.

My dragon buffalo leather jacket was another design by Kari, with metal plates on the inside to protect me from dragon claws and bites. Buckles down the front allowed me to close it up and stay warm when Thorn and I flew high, but on hot desert days like this one, I liked to leave it open. The simple pauldron on my right shoulder and the fingerless, dragonleather climbing gloves both bore a small fang-and-anvil crest on the corner—Kari's signature. I finished it off by belting on my father's skyseeker dagger. It had a small guard, a long, clip-pointed blade that was perfect for fighting dragons, and a small curved chisel at the end of the handle designed to pry skystones from fallen meteors.

My stomach let out a low growl as I finished dressing. Getting executed always left me starving. I rummaged through the pockets of my jacket—I still had some leftover drakalope jerky from before the raid. I scarfed some down, saving a few of the best pieces for Thorn for later. Drakalope jerky was his favorite treat.

Kai finally put his journal down, and I gave him a look.

"Alright, are you ready to explain why you let your best friend get jailed and executed now?"

"Glint didn't get stuck in jail," Kai said smugly, walking over to the boulder that hid our hoard.

"So, you admit your best friend is an ethereal familiar that you literally created yourself? She has no choice but to like you."

Glint stuck out her tongue at me, blinking her mirrored eyes.

"Of course," Kai said, placing his hands against the boulder. "And your capture was part of backup plan four. Now, help me out so I can show you your capture was worth it."

I shook my head, joining Kai at the stone to push.

Thorn poked his head through the arch, then joined us inside. Whatever Kai was about to show me had him excited.

Kai and I pushed on the rock.

"It'll be enough to get us to Skygard, no more raids necessary," Kai said with a grunt. The rock gave way to a small hollow. We stepped back, and the opening revealed a whole trove of dragon eggs, each about the size of a fist.

My jaw dropped. Kai grinned.

"There are five drake eggs, three wyvern eggs, and four evren eggs," Kai explained, taking each of them from the hollow and reverently placing them on the ground in front of him. "At least six are mythic."

This was an even more valuable score than the skystone.

Kai animatedly pointed to various eggs. "I'm pretty sure this drake egg holds a stonescale. This one looks like a stormscale evren, and this is definitely a dreamhorn wyvern. Thought this one might be a skyskipper, but I'm less sure. The other two mythic ones look like Sentinels of some kind, but it's really hard to tell by their egg patterns alone."

Thorn shuffled deeper into the cave to sniff curiously at the eggs, and Glint climbed on top of Thorn's head to get a better look.

Kai arranged the scale-covered drake eggs to one side, the leathery wyvern eggs in the middle, and the spherical, crystalline evren eggs to the other side.

"I've tried bonding them all, but no luck."

Kai's face betrayed a hint of dejection. I knew just how badly my friend wanted to bond a dragon.

I tried to cheer him up. "Hey, when I found Thorn, he chose to bond me. Maybe one will pick you?"

"I don't think so. *Fjordan's Dragonium* says once a dragon has hatched, they can choose to initiate a bond with someone. But with unhatched eggs, in almost all cases, if a potential human bond tries to forge a connection with the egg by touching it, the egg will hatch. I've tried already with all of them. Nothing."

I shrugged. Kai was just being too analytical. Bonds weren't about logic and statistics.

Then it hit me. The guard at Whitestone Hall was definitely going to be searching for these. I was suddenly glad I'd faked my death so well.

"We have to move these fast," I said.

"I know. I've got it covered."

"How was this not as well-guarded as the treasury?"

"Well... it *was*. But your distraction was extremely effective. By the way, that was quite the jump off the top of the tower. How'd it look on your end?"

Kai raised a gauntleted finger and traced a rune in the air. Gold light trailed after his finger, and the same rune appeared over his forehead. I recognized this rune, the design reminiscent of an all-seeing eye. He was about to do what Seers like him did best.

He reached over and touched two fingers to my temple.

Time to mess with Kai.

I sent my thoughts racing, and imagined the scene just a little differently than it had actually happened.

I remembered my leap from the tower, but reimagined the looks on the guards' faces to be even more awestruck. In my mind, I smoothed out my landing, and even threw in a flip for good measure. I pictured myself offering a confident bow to the guard when I landed, which got them firing their crossbows.

From there, I imagined spinning behind the barrels and running right into Kai's sister, Kari. I wrapped my arms around her, dipped her, and was just about to kiss her when Kai broke his contact and dismissed his mind-reading rune in a puff of golden dust.

"You're an idiot," he said, shaking his head.

"Guess you can't read a mind that's not there," I said, winking. "Really though, it was pretty impressive. You should be impressed with me."

"I don't know. That fantasy about my sister was too convincing. You sure you haven't dreamed about that before?"

"Oh, every night," I said with a laugh.

That was it. Kai skirted around the dragon eggs and shoved me hard.

We hit the ground and started wrestling. Kai wasn't as used to hand-to-hand fighting as I was, but with his heavy armor on, we were pretty evenly matched. Thorn crawled protectively over the eggs, shielding them from us with his wing.

Just then, I heard an odd twang sound. The next thing I knew, a net was thrown over us.

Instinctively, I ignited my ether. I dropped Kai and floated up to the ceiling as the net fell off. I hovered there, glaring with glowing golden eyes down at the intruder.

Kari.

Thorn sent me an amused glow through our bond. He'd seen her come in but hadn't told me. I sent him a spark of annoyance.

Kari scowled at the modified crossbow in her hands.

"Still has trouble spreading the net at low angles," she muttered to herself. Her thick, curly black hair bounced behind her in its clip as she walked toward us. She picked up the net and reloaded it into the crossbow, finally acknowledging our presence.

"Thanks for the chance to test this," Kari said with a winning smile.

Kai's warning about fantasizing about his sister was for good reason. Kari had thick eyelashes and intelligent brown eyes; she even made a blacksmithing apron look good. But I'd learned long ago that Kari saw me as nothing more than her little brother's goofy friend. Besides, I had a rule not to go for girls two years older than me.

I floated back down, my eyes returning to their usual dragonfire green. Kari raised an eyebrow at Kai, who was still on the ground.

"So this is how you two always dent up the armor I make for you."

Kai and I shrugged as Kari returned her attention to the crossbow.

"Just saw your dad, Asher," Kari spoke as she fiddled with some levers. "Said you owed him for being late this time."

"I think he'll survive," I said, lightly pushing the crossbow out of Kari's line of sight. "Just wait until you see our haul."

Thorn pulled back his wing to reveal the dragon eggs, and Kari's jaw dropped as far as mine had. Her eyes lit up.

"Okay, how?" she asked.

We sat around the eggs as we told her about our heist. Kari half-listened, half-worked on her invention. When we finished, Kai pulled a bottle of scorchapple cider from a corner of the den to celebrate.

"What is this, the third time you've been executed?" Kari noted as we wrapped up our tale.

"Fourth, actually," Kai corrected. "Third death by dragon, though. They really need to fix that flaw in the judicial system."

"Well, maybe it's time to be a bit more careful. I've been hearing talk of more Mage Hunters in the area, and... and..."

She trailed off, casting a nervous look toward me.

"What?" I asked, leaning forward.

Kari gave Kai an apologetic, warning glance before going on. "Someone at the tavern mentioned the Black Valkyrie's in Drakfell."

I was on my feet in a flash, eyes burning gold as I accessed my ether. Before I was even sure what was happening, I'd used starglass to form a long, double-bladed dragonhook spear. The kind I used for hunting.

Kai and Kari stood, grabbing me by the shoulders to hold me still.

"Asher," Kai said in a calming voice. "Breathe."

I didn't want to, but the rational part of me listened. I inhaled slowly, then exhaled, dismissing my starglass weapon and cutting off my ether flow.

Kari looked apologetic. "I'm sorry, Asher. I didn't want to bring it up."

I shook my head. I hated that the mere mention of the Black Valkyrie got me so upset.

The Black Valkyrie was the powerful, ruthless leader of the Mage Hunters. She was a magi-turned-Mage Hunter who never failed to bring in a target.

She was also responsible for my mother's death three years ago.

She hadn't returned to Drakfell since. I knew the Black Valkyrie only went after the most powerful magi. Why in the void would she be here now?

I didn't care. All I knew was that if Kari was right and the Black Valkyrie really was in the Badlands Keepdom, this might be the chance I'd been waiting for. My chance to avenge my mother.

I looked back at the dragon eggs. If we could sell them, we'd have the money we needed to get my dad to Skygard. Once he, Kai, and Kari were safe there, then I could go after the Black Valkyrie alone.

We sat and chatted for a little while longer until the red light of the setting sun filled the front of the den.

Kari looked out at the sky. "Well, that's my cue. Gotta go before the badlands get real bad."

A troubled look flashed across her face so quickly I thought I'd imagined it. But Kai seemed to notice it, too. He squinted as his sister picked up her crossbow, and I caught the tiniest, reflective flash of a mirror gecko leaping up onto Kari's shoulder. Glint was stealthy, and Kari didn't notice.

We said our goodbyes, and Kari disappeared into the fading daylight outside the cave.

I immediately turned to Kai, who was dismissing a mind-reading rune as Glint padded back into the den.

"So, what was Kari thinking? I impressed her with my daring leap off the tower at Whitestone Hall, right? Or maybe she was thinking about my piercing, dragonfire green eyes—"

Kai dipped the tips of his fingers into his cider and flicked it at me.

"Okay, I deserved that," I said. "But really, what was she thinking?"

"About meeting with the Knights of the Torch tonight."

For a second time today, my jaw dropped.

"And she's the one telling us to be careful? Why's she meeting with them?" I asked.

"Don't know. Didn't have time to read that far back," Kai said, looking after where she had gone. "We have to follow her."

All I knew about the Knights of the Torch was that they were dangerous, and that they followed the legendary Farseer. Kai and Kari's parents had gotten mixed up with them right before they disappeared, leaving Kai and Kari to stay with my dad and me. If Kari was involved with them...

Kai was right. We had to follow her.

Chapter 3: The Drunken Drake

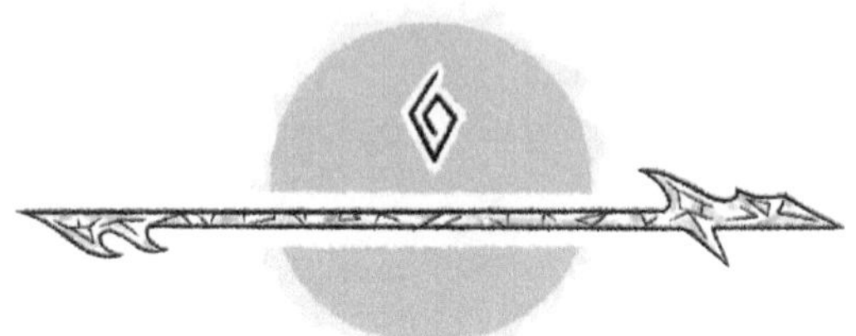

We left Thorn at the den to guard the eggs. Meanwhile, Kai and I followed Kari at a distance through the stretch of dusty badlands between the den and the town. Kai intentionally lagged behind since his excessive armor kept clanking.

Kari reached Steel Rim proper as the wash of glowing red light against the cliffside turned to gray. In the darkness of the early night, I caught sight of a distant skyfall. The emerald streaks were far enough to the south that we wouldn't see any dreklings from it tonight.

Kari passed the butcher's shop, a fireproof, dragon bone-decorated building on the outskirts of town. Cragchasers like Kai and I regularly dropped off our kills there.

She passed a small library with a star of Streya symbol above the door that had been set up by the Sisters of Streya in an effort to help educate—and hopefully one day 'civilize'—Steel Rim.

Next to the library was an oddly-shaped, somewhat dilapidated tavern, the Drunken Drake. The place had been built over the skeletal remains of a huge drake that must have grown impossibly big from some form of geomancy. Adobe mud had been plastered between the bones in the ribcage to form walls, and a thatched roof adorned the top.

Kari headed straight for the tavern. After a quick check over her shoulder, she went inside.

I ducked in after her.

The tavern was loud, and the bard was pitchy. The smell of spiced draquila and cheap ale filled the room.

I kept a low profile. Steel Rim was small and, as far as I knew, I was the only half-born. I wouldn't want to run into Baron Eidan here—he hated half-borns, and had already put me through the silver rod test to see if I was secretly a magi several times. I always passed, but he kept testing me out of spite.

Then again, someone like the Baron wouldn't be caught dead in a rough tavern like the Drunken Drake. He was probably in the town greathouse, showing off the mounted heads of beasts he probably hadn't killed himself, drinking mead with his semi-noble friends, and laughing at poor people.

I followed Kari to the bar, keeping out of her line of sight. I casually leaned against a post, which was actually an enormous dragon bone.

A girl about my age sat at a table beside me, loudly trying to sing along to the bard's song. She'd had a little too much draquila, and her singing was making it very difficult to focus on Kari. I was about to switch locations when the drunk girl grabbed me by the hand and laced her fingers through my own.

"You have nice hands for a half-born," she slurred.

Soot. I was missing Kari's exchange with the bartender. Time to get rid of her.

"Thanks," I said. "I just hope they last through the shadow wasting."

At the mention of the ethereal disease that turned flesh numb and gray, she quickly dropped my hand. Her glassy eyes widened. Many thought the shadow wasting was highly contagious.

"You know," I said with a smile. "The bard sounds like he could use some help with his song, and with a voice like yours..."

I gestured toward the musically-challenged bard crowing in his corner. The girl beamed drunkenly at me then scurried toward him. She actually improved the song.

Through our bond, I felt Thorn chuckle.

I turned my attention back to Kari, just barely catching her say, "The Hunter's Torch is lit again."

With that, the barkeep led her behind the bar and through a back door nestled at the base of the drake skeleton's skull.

I knew I couldn't follow her from here without a plan. I was bad at those. But luckily, I had a certain best friend who lived for them.

Outside the Drunken Drake, Kai was smiling. He held his black leather notebook in his hands, open to a page where he'd already taken notes on a new strategy.

Kai beckoned me to follow him down an alley behind the bar. Glint sat atop his shoulder, her shiny eyes reflecting back at me.

"I sent Glint in with you to sneak onto the barkeep," Kai said. "I read his mind, and I know exactly how we're going to sneak in."

As a Seer, Kai's telepathy was his primary power, but all Mystics could access the dreamweave to make illusion etherarchy as well. I'd seen Kai spend hours poring over texts on how to do them properly.

Kai traced a series of illusion runes in the air. They floated over his forehead in a row, then he made a mystical-looking gesture, first toward himself, and then at me. Twists of golden ether wound around our bodies.

Kai's illusion settled over us. When I looked at Kai, an illusory body had replaced his skinny frame and dark skin. He now had muscular arms and shoulders, and short, steely gray hair with a maroon bandana wrapped across his forehead. He looked just a few years older than us, and someone had torn the sleeves off his tunic, probably to show off his imposing biceps.

This guy definitely didn't have a life outside of working out.

Kai put two fingers to my temple to form a mindlink and showed me what I looked like. I noticed no runemark over his forehead, which meant he must've added an extra illusion rune into his disguise to mask the ones he was actively using. Clever.

Through Kai's mind, I saw myself. I looked like an older, wiry guy with stark white hair—a snowhead with roots in Evgard's northeast. He had deeply tanned skin, as if he'd spent his entire life baking in the sun, and a stubbly beard flecked with gray. The sturdy clothing he wore on his well-built frame made me think this was a man used to the roughs. His dragonscale cloak marked him as a dragonslayer.

Kai pulled back his hand, and the mindlink faded. I noticed Kai trying to cover a wave of fatigue—that was a lot of ether he'd just channeled.

"You just had to make me the old guy," I said, trying to help him laugh it off.

"Based on what I read from the bartender's mind, you'll want to use a more gravelly voice and a strong northern accent," Kai said, a little out of breath.

"Ya just had to make me the old guy," I repeated, using the roughest voice I could muster.

"I said gravel, not rockslide. And I made you the older guy because he was closer to your height. I'd have had to stretch out the buff guy to fit you, or hide the top of your head, which is much harder to pull off. Plus, Boone's an Astromancer, like you."

"Boone? That's my name?"

Kai nodded. "You're Boone, and I'm Jax. They're a pair of Knights of the Torch that the barkeep knows. They've been on assignment at Ghost Lake, but he wouldn't be surprised to see them return for tonight's meeting."

"Will they actually be returning for tonight's meeting?"

"There's a ten percent chance."

Kai winced and put his hand to his forehead. These illusions must've taken a lot of ether.

"What about the beard?" I asked, feeling my face and trying to distract him from the effects of ether overdraw.

"Well, I haven't learned how to make an illusion to fool touch yet. Besides, the chances someone feels your face are astronomically low."

He was probably right. But still...

I channeled my ether, forming dull, minuscule shards of starglass all over my chin to mimic a beard. I felt my face again. It was a little rougher than a real beard, but still pretty good.

"What now?" I said.

Kai looked down at his black notebook. "Now, you do your thing, and get us in."

"My thing?"

"You know, make up some dragondung."

I glared at him.

"Perfect, that's definitely a look Boone would make," Kai said with a laugh. It was weird seeing his voice come out of a different body.

"Shut up, Jack," I said, giving him a small shove.

"It's Jax, but yeah, I will. My voice isn't like Jax's at all. Your Boone voice is close enough. Just throw in a folksy saying or two and don't talk much. We'll be fine."

I nodded. This was gonna be fun.

We walked into the Drunken Drake, heading straight for the bar. I leaned onto the counter and grunted to get the barkeep's attention.

"Boone!" he turned to us, surprised. "Didn't think you and Jax would make it back so soon."

He looked at us expectantly. I leaned into my character.

"Look, I don't have time to dance with the drakalopes. The Hunter's Torch is lit again and all that, just get Jax and me back there before we miss too much, eh?"

The barkeep nodded and gestured for us to follow him behind the bar.

I fought to keep from smiling. Boone wouldn't grin like an idiot.

The barkeep led us through the door at the base of the giant drake skull. Behind the door was a steep set of stairs. At the bottom was another door, this one with a torch symbol carved into it at eye level.

The barkeep gave the door a rhythmic knock, and it swung open. He stepped aside, and Kai and I entered an illustrious hideout. While the rest of the bar was on the grimy side, the hideout was immaculate. Maps and tapestries and torches adorned the stone walls, as well as the heads of draconic creatures like ridgerunners, crag hoppers, and even dreklings.

A large table stood in the center of the room, with a detailed map of Evgard lying flat on top of it.

A group of Knights of the Torch stood surrounding the table. Kari was there. She noticed us and waved at Kai... or Jax. Was that a flirty wave? I fought back another grin. Kai and I might have to tease Kari about that later.

At the head of the table stood a man with mid-length black hair, a goatee, and more class than anyone I'd ever seen in Steel Rim. A stark silvermark on his left cheek marked him as a Psion, a type of Mystic. His sharp brown eyes shone with discernment as he surveyed the room. His clothes were well-tailored, with a silver-buttoned black vest and a pair of ornately-decorated bracers. He was a noble for sure.

To his right stood a woman with black hair pulled back in three braids on one side to reveal angular eyes and high cheekbones. She was really pretty, in an 'I-could-kill-you-in-my-sleep' kind of way. The polar wolf fur around her shoulders only added to her dangerous air. She had dozens of silvery scars and more weapons on her than anyone else in the room. Long seaxes hung from either side of her belt, she had a war sword slung over her back, and she'd strapped some smaller knives along her thighs and calves. And those were just the blades I could see.

Then I noticed the massive bloodhusky standing between the man and woman. As the man stroked the red mountain of fluffy muscle, I got a jolt of awareness from Thorn to keep an eye on him. Bloodhuskies were bred to fight drakes.

The man caught sight of Kai and me, and his face brightened. He gave a warm, welcoming nod, showing no sign of suspicion.

I couldn't say the same for the woman with the silver scars, who narrowed her eyes at me. She placed a hand on the bloodhusky's head and the beast made a low, throaty sound before padding toward us.

I wanted to run, but fought the impulse. I fumbled in the pocket of my jacket, pulling out some of my leftover drakalope jerky I'd saved for Thorn. The massive dog's expression went from suspicious to approving. He snapped it up and settled against my leg, relaxing a lot more than I did. Through our bond, I felt a burning sensation from Thorn letting me know he wasn't particularly pleased with that.

I felt Kai subtly lean toward me and touch his arm to mine to form a mindlink. He spoke to me in my head.

The nobleman is their leader. His name is Solrac. Kai must've been using Glint to read someone's mind. Again, I worried about how much ether he was using.

"As I was saying," Solrac addressed the group. He had a light eastern accent. "A war is coming. The Knights of the Torch are recruiting."

Soot. What had Kari gotten herself into?

Solrac continued. "We need every willing soul we can find. The Farseer has seen many omens of difficulty and woe. The Mage Hunters are watching, and our scouts have sighted the Black Valkyrie near Steel Rim."

My blood went cold, and I saw Kai's—Jax's—eyes glance nervously toward me. But I kept a calm exterior while my thoughts raced. Did the Knights know something that could get me to the Black Valkyrie?

"But we have more ill tidings," Solrac said dramatically, letting a hush fall over the room. He traced an illusion rune in the air, and the rune appeared in gold over his forehead.

There was a flash and a twist of golden ether, and a miniaturized, burly man appeared on the table, over the Dragon Isles on the map. The illusory man on the table was part dragon. A pair of horns stuck out from his hair, and scales covered his forearms, shoulders, and cheekbones. His tail lashed from side to side, and his eyes were a bright dragonfire green like mine. Murmurs rippled through the crowd. Some had never seen a Drekai before. It made me wonder how they'd react to a half-born like me.

"The Farseer has made it known that the Drekai are readying an assault on Keep Drakfell."

The group gasped. I made sure to add a Boone-worthy scowl to my face. As I did, I looked to Kai. The false face he wore looked exhausted.

We had to get out of here. If he lost concentration, our illusions would burst.

Solrac added more runes with a flourish, making a small army of Drekai on the map. Their ranks bristled with an assortment of long-handled scimitars, boomerangs, and warbows. "Even now, they're on our shores."

I grabbed Kai by the arm and began scooting toward the door. The bloodhusky startled at my feet, and I dropped another piece of drakalope jerky to keep him quiet.

Solrac went on. "The Drekai are after something stolen by King Rodan," Solrac said, adding more runes and gesturing to Keep Drakfell in the east.

A mini, illusory King Rodan appeared, with his stormscale drake, Rex, at his side. He was in his bright white ascension armor, holding his imposing dragonforged warsword. The blade was like a massive version of the one on my father's skyseeker dagger. The things nobles spent their money on...

I pulled Kai toward the edge of the crowd. The bloodhusky nudged me again, but I was out of jerky.

Solrac continued, adding a glowing, white egg to the illusion of Drakfell's king. "In a raid on the Dragon Isles, King Rodan stole one of the last remaining true dragon eggs from the Drekai. But Rodan's desperate act may yet be the answer to the Knights' empty coffers."

Solrac held the group enthralled. We couldn't break from the crowd just yet without drawing attention to ourselves. We just needed the right moment.

"It's up to us to steal back the egg," Solrac finished.

The room went abuzz with excitement. The bloodhusky whined at me. The woman with the silver scars looked my way.

The door was so close.

"So what's the plan?" Kari leaned in.

Just how involved in this group was she? We'd have to ask later. Now, we had to go.

"That depends," Solrac said, "on how our recent operation at Ghost Lake went."

With that, Solrac gestured my way. The whole room turned toward Kai and me.

I froze.

"Boone, Jax?" Solrac asked with a jovial grin. "Care to give us a report?"

Oh stars.

Chapter 4: Knights of the Torch

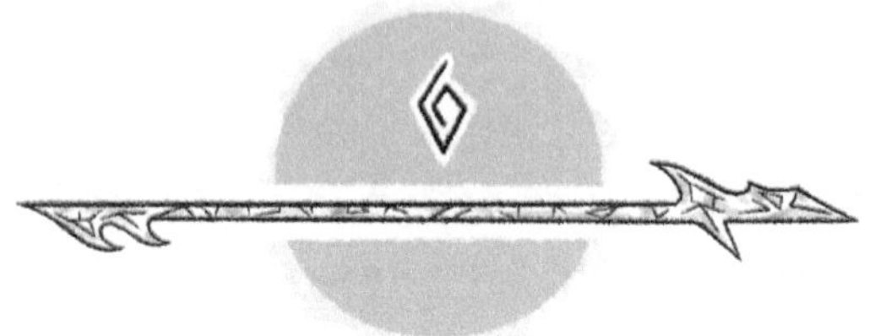

In my efforts to keep a look of panic from crossing my—well, Boone's face, I ended up just slowly raising an eyebrow.

The room full of Knights of the Torch watched us expectantly. Fiery skepticism shone in the scarred woman's eyes.

We should not have come here.

I sure hoped you couldn't sweat through an illusion. Kai cast me a helpless, tired glance. It was taking all his concentration just to keep the illusion up. He wouldn't be any help. But his hopeless look gave me an idea.

Time for a show.

I looked to the floor, squinting my eyes in shame, then spoke in my gravelly Boone voice.

"We failed. Miserably."

Crestfallen looks fell over the group. Kari tried to make eye contact with Kai's persona, Jax, as worry filled her eyes. Again, I couldn't help but wonder who this guy was to her.

I let a moment of silence linger, hoping that my cryptic explanation had been enough information. Maybe I wouldn't have to give any more details on our 'mission.'

But of course, that would've been too easy.

Finally, Solrac spoke. "It's alright, Boone. Go on."

I swallowed, saying the first thing I could think of. "Too many guards. Had to take a leap for my life off a tower. Barely survived, thanks to my astromancy. Mage Hunter got Jax here with a silver whip. Nearly couldn't get 'im out in time."

I watched the room out of the corner of my eye, gauging their reactions, but nobody seemed fazed by my report.

Except Kari, who looked confused. Stars, I probably shouldn't have made it sound so similar to our latest raid at Whitestone Hall!

The scarred woman was also still skeptical. What had Kai said about folksy sayings being a habit of Boone's?

I breathed deeply and accessed my ether to make my eyes flash gold for effect.

"But we gave 'em more soot than a wyvernhog in heat, I'll tell you that."

The group relaxed, and some even chuckled a little.

"Jax, you're awfully quiet," said the woman with the silvery scars. "You really fell for a Mage Hunter's whip?"

All eyes turned to Kai. The color drained from his illusory face.

"Come on now," I began, only a little defensive. "Them whips can be tricky. Happens to the best of us."

The scarred woman's fingertips lightly brushed the antler hilt of one of her weapons.

"And what about the assets? Were they where we expected them?" Valla asked.

Stars, they weren't making this easy.

"Ah, the assets. They'd moved 'em just before we got there. Tried to catch word on what town they'd taken 'em to, but like I said. We failed. Whole mission's a wash."

"Come on, Valla." Solrac put a hand on her shoulder, grinning widely. "At least they're back safely. And in time for our next mission."

The woman, Valla, narrowed her eyes to slits, but backed down. My muscles relaxed. Feeling pretty pleased that we'd made it through questioning, I gave Valla a wink. She folded her arms, not taking her eyes off of me. Maybe I shouldn't have winked.

The bloodhusky rubbed against my side, still hoping for more jerky. I rubbed him along the back of his head and neck. He wagged his tail contentedly.

Thorn sent me a pang of jealousy through our bond. I sent back a warm, loyal feeling, and that calmed him down a little.

Solrac continued outlining their plans. It involved the recruitment of lots of magi. The Knights of the Torch planned to outfit their own army that would lean more heavily on magi than the armies of Evgard. They'd protect the far-flung reaches of Drakfell to keep them from being overrun by the new skyfalls and dragons and Drekai, in turn earning the people's gratitude and more recruits. Their end goal was a society safe for magi to live in freely. Honestly, that sounded pretty good to me.

Plus, anything that undermined nobles like King Rodan and High King Magnus was fine by me.

The whole time Solrac was speaking, I kept watching for an opportunity to go for the door. We had to get out of there before our illusions gave out. But every time I moved a muscle, Valla's eyes snapped back onto me. Her hand never left the hilt of her seaxe.

After what seemed like an eternity, Solrac closed the meeting. The Knights of the Torch began filtering out the door and back into the bar, a few at a time. We couldn't all leave at once without drawing suspicion.

I tried to get us out first, but couldn't look over eager without attracting even more of Valla's attention. I patted the bloodhusky on the head in farewell, which he seemed to understand. Though I was out of jerky, it looked like I'd won him over.

We had to hurry. It looked like Kari was making her way around the table to come talk to this Jax guy. The last thing exhausted Kai probably wanted right now was for his sister to walk up and start flirting with him. That would be kind of hilarious, but the risk of being discovered was too high. Practically dragging Kai along, I took a step toward the door and freedom.

A hand clasped onto my shoulder.

"Boone, did you really think you could get away without talking to me?"

I turned to find myself staring directly into the pretty, yet murderous eyes of Valla. Why was she standing so close? And why had she slipped her hand onto my chest like that?

Before I knew what was happening, she leaned forward and kissed me right on the mouth.

My mind raced, trying to figure out how Boone would react to this. His short beard indicated he was married, but was he married to Valla? Or was he widowed? Or did he have a wife somewhere who would be very angry that this was happening?

While racking my brain for what to do, I noticed Kari over Valla's shoulder. She looked shocked.

So this wasn't normal.

I stiffened and made it clear I wasn't going to kiss her back. Valla pulled away, looking at me expectantly.

I narrowed my eyes.

"You done?" I asked with every ounce of gravelly gruffness I could muster.

Valla closed her eyes and let out a breath. Then she punched me in the arm.

"Thank Selene, it's you. I was worried the Mage Hunters had sent a mirage."

"I ain't no spy."

She rubbed her chin.

"Your beard's kind of rough. Might want to wash it out."

"Why don't you go see if Solrac's goatee is softer?" I said with a Boone-like chuckle.

Valla's face went bright red. She punched me in the arm again, and walked back toward the table. Apparently, that had struck a nerve. I pretended the punch hadn't hurt at all, but Boone was obviously tougher than I was.

"I still want more details on the mission later," Valla said over her shoulder.

I grunted in agreement, determined to make it out of there before Kari intercepted us. Valla's kiss had thrown her off, but we only had a few more seconds.

As I turned back to the door, I startled backward. Someone was standing in the doorway, blocking our exit.

Solrac.

"Boone," he spoke in a hushed voice. "What really happened to that skystone you were after?"

I tried to think fast, but poor Kai wouldn't last much longer.

"I already told you, we couldn't get to it," I grunted. "Now, I'm gonna go drink like a naga to drown my sorrows if that's alright with you."

Solrac pursed his lips. "What a shame. You were doing so well."

He drew a quick rune in the air, and with a flick of his wrist, the door behind him slammed shut. Simultaneously, he raised a hand and lifted Kai and me off our feet, suspended by our jackets. It wasn't like levitating—that was Archon etherarchy. Solrac's silvermark was a Psion's, and Psions couldn't use their telekinesis on anything living.

He traced another rune faster than I could register, and the illusions over Kai and me burst, dissolving into gold flickers.

I found myself standing there, once again looking like a black-haired, half-born seventeen-year-old.

Beside me, Kai no longer looked like an egotistical bodybuilder. He had a hand to his head as he hung limply in the air, exhausted from too much ether use. He'd let his ether well run too low, which always gave him a nasty headache. It was a Mystic thing.

Solrac seemed to recognize it too, using a hand to gently lower him to the floor.

Within seconds, at least a dozen members of the Knights of the Torch faced us, many of them brandishing weapons. Valla stood ready at the front of the pack with one of her seaxes.

Oh, soot.

At least the bloodhusky looked unfazed. Had he known the whole time?

With the illusion gone, I let my dumb starglass beard dissipate back into ether.

"How did you—" I started.

Solrac cut me off. "Boone and Jax weren't retrieving skystone in Ghost Lake."

Valla took that as permission to pin me to the wall by the door with one arm, the other holding a blade to my throat.

My eyes widened. This was not how I wanted to die.

Thorn sensed my distress and sent a signal through our bond that he was coming. But he'd never make it in time. I told him to stay away. A wyvern breaking into the bar wouldn't end well for any of us. We came to a compromise, Thorn promising to come halfway and stand by.

"Asher? Kai? Seriously?" came Kari's exasperated voice.

I slowly saluted and gave a half-grin, careful not to make any sudden movements.

"You know these imposters?" Valla asked Kari, pressing her blade harder against my throat.

"Unfortunately," Kari said. "The one on the floor is my little brother, Kai, and that's Asher, his idiot friend. They're stupid, but harmless."

Most of the Knights put their weapons away at that. Valla didn't.

Kari crossed her arms, not making eye contact with me. She looked something between embarrassed and angry. I didn't blame her.

Solrac put a hand on Valla's shoulder and smiled. "They look like promising new recruits, don't you think?"

Valla scowled. "They snuck into our meeting."

"Which is the best thing that could've possibly happened," Solrac laughed. "Now we know we could use better security."

He grandly gestured to Kai on the floor. "Though I must say, those illusions were truly top-notch. Far better than anything I could do. Despite the headache, you're quite the talented young Mystic. Kai, was it?"

Kai nodded.

"And you," Solrac gestured to me this time. "Not a bad performance at all. You had Boone's grumpy mannerisms down. We could use a brazen talker with no regard for sanity. And we don't have a half-born yet. Well, I do have a drop or two of Drekai blood on my father's side... Anyhow, we'd love to consider you for the team—that is, if Valla can ever find it in her heart to relinquish her hold on your throat."

Apparently, Valla could not yet find it in her heart.

"They know too much," she said, holding the blade fast.

"Hmm," Solrac put a hand to his chin. "Let's consider for a moment. If we kill them, what do we gain?"

Kari gasped.

"We would..." Valla hesitated. "We'd maintain our security."

"While also offending our own lovely Kari and ridding the world of one exceptional illusionist and one—possibly—half-decent Astromancer. I see a solution where we both maintain our secrecy and unite some useful magi to the cause. That solution? Recruitment."

Valla looked over her shoulder at Solrac, her seaxe pressing uncomfortably close to my jugular vein.

"How can you not see them as a problem?" she glared.

"Because His Majesty doesn't," Solrac said with a shrug.

With that, the bloodhusky barked happily, then trotted over and rubbed his nose against my leg.

"His Majesty is an impeccable judge of character," Solrac said.

His Majesty... was the dog's name. Despite everything, I grinned. I couldn't like this guy on principle, him being a noble and all, but he had picked a great name for his dog. And I'd never been more grateful for drakalope jerky.

Valla may've been the one holding me in place with her blade, but Solrac still kept me suspended in the air, the rune glowing strong over his forehead. He strode over to the table in the center of the room and pressed a panel on its side. A hidden compartment slid open, and Solrac pulled out a cluster of glasses and a large bottle.

"Now Valla," Solrac said as he poured. "You can obviously do what you like, but my vote is you cut the foolish, yet potentially useful, adolescents a little slack so we can discuss their joining the Knights of the Torch. And not at the edge of a blade."

Reluctantly, Valla backed off. Solrac finally lowered me to the ground with another flick of his wrist. I let out a breath of relief and rubbed my throat as the runes over his forehead dissipated.

"Thanks," I said. "I like my neck."

Valla glared and feigned a lunge at me. I yelped, and she seemed satisfied. Fine, I'd deserved that.

"Kari, join us, please," Solrac said as he psionically pulled several chairs to a lushly decorated corner of the room. A thick, red rug lay over the floor, and several proud, enormous drakalope heads were mounted on the wall. He set up the glasses on a short, intricately-carved side table and beckoned for us to join him.

I reached out a hand to Kai to help him up off the floor. I gave him a meaningful look as he stood. As usual, I had no plan, and for once, it looked like he didn't either. Apparently a recruitment chat and drinks hadn't been in his notebook of potential backup plans.

We joined Solrac, Valla, and Kari at the chairs in the corner.

His Majesty padded over, curling up his muscular mass of red fur between all of us and seeming perfectly at ease. I wished I could share the sentiment. Through our bond, I could feel Thorn's anxiety, too. I channeled my thoughts toward him, willing him to know we'd be alright and to stay put until we knew more. He begrudgingly agreed, staying perched atop a small hill nearby.

"First things first," Solrac began as he took a drink, his grip on the glass light and sophisticated. He was definitely a noble. "How did you know to impersonate Boone and Jax? I hope you haven't harmed my friends in their travels, as that would change my opinion of you considerably."

Kai looked at me anxiously. It was time to come clean.

"We never met them," I started. "And we have no idea where they are. Kai read the mind of the barkeep."

"Genius. We definitely need a good Seer on the team. We've got the Farseer, of course, but he's rather elusive and vague. Not much one for doing the nitty gritty work if you know what I mean." Solrac clapped and laughed, then looked to Valla as if expecting her to join in. She didn't.

"What prompted you to infiltrate our meeting tonight?" Solrac continued. "Wait, let me guess. Kari's been quite secretive about her involvement with the Knights. Perhaps because she, being the older sister, wanted to protect her younger brother from such worries. Especially after what happened with your parents. So you followed her, wanting to make sure she wasn't in over her head?"

He smiled wide, leaning back in his chair and taking another drink.

Kari, Kai, and I looked at each other.

"That's about right," I said.

"You know what happened to our parents? You mean, they're not dead?" Kai asked, and I couldn't be sure if he was asking Solrac or Kari.

"Oh no," Solrac replied, and for the first time since we walked into the Knights' hideout, he wasn't smiling. "The odds of that are quite slim. I wish I knew what happened to Kaidan and Kalari, but I'm afraid I don't know any more than you do."

Kai's face fell, and Kari put a comforting hand on his shoulder.

"Now Asher," Solrac said. "Just after Kai's illusion went out, I noticed you'd managed to produce some sort of makeshift beard made from what I'm willing to bet was starglass. Starglass so fine, it convinced Valla when she touched it. Not bad."

"Thanks."

"Not bad, but not terribly useful either," Solrac said bluntly. "Can you do anything of actual significance?"

For whatever reason, I felt a strong need to prove that I was just as valuable as Kai. We hunted and raided as a team, after all.

Alright then.

I leaned forward in my chair, breathing deeply and accessing my ether well. My eyes glowed gold as I felt the familiar rush of exhilarating power. I looked down at my hands and focused the ether into the shape of a cup.

I presented it to Solrac. He took it, examining it for a moment before pouring his drink from the cup in his hand into the one I'd just made from starglass.

He took a long drink, holding all of our attention.

"Ahh," he exhaled, holding up the empty starglass cup. "Is that all you've got?"

I thought for a second, imagining what I could make that would impress a leader in a lawless rebel organization.

I dismissed the cup from his hand and burned more ether. This time, I formed a starglass key in my hand, like the one I'd used at the Whitestone Hall prison. As Solrac and the rest watched, I morphed the starglass key, first adding more layers of starglass to make it large and old-fashioned, then removing layers to make it smaller with fewer notches. I formed and reformed it a few more times before dismissing the key as well.

Solrac leaned forward. "That's more like it. Boone could do with learning finer control like that. Remarkable."

"Can you make anything that would keep you alive in combat?" Valla said. Somehow, I wasn't surprised she was thinking about violence.

I quirked a smile at her and stood up. My eyes flashed gold, and I focused pure ether into white, crystalline starglass. It started over my heart, then grew to form armor all over my body. Then, once she and Solrac looked sufficiently impressed, I channeled more ether to form my favorite style of dragonhook spear.

Since starglass was lighter than steel, I always made the crystalline blade larger than it would normally be to give it enough weight to be effective. And since I didn't have to worry about the practicality of carrying it around, I added a second smaller, hooked blade on the bottom of the shaft.

And because I was sure Valla would want me to prove I could use it, I spun the spear a couple of times in my hand. I whipped the blade around as if fighting an enemy, ending in a defensive stance.

Solrac stood and clapped.

"Now that's something you don't see every day," he said, grinning widely. "That's far better than decent—that's excellent. Your teacher should be proud. Although being from Steel Rim... am I to believe you're self-taught?"

I nodded. Both my parents were magi—my father was a Rifter, and mom had been a Shadowbinder, but neither was an Astromancer like me. My mom had taught me a thing or two about levitation, since that was the one power shared by all Archons. But with magi being illegal, we couldn't exactly go around looking for a teacher. Everything I knew about astromancy I'd learned through trial and error.

"Okay, so he can do some tricks with starglass," Valla grumbled. "Can you manipulate raw ether? Like into ether darts or pulses?"

I dismissed my spear and armor, and they vanished into golden stars as I shook my head.

"No matter, " Solrac said. "All that is Boone's specialty, anyway. Perhaps the two of you can teach each other. Well, assuming he hasn't died a horrible death at Ghost Lake."

Solrac let out another resounding laugh. Kai and I looked at each other—This was an interesting guy. Again, I resisted the urge to like him, reminding myself to never trust nobles.

"I guess that settles it," Solrac continued. "I must say, between the infiltration and your etherarchy that was the best audition I've seen in a while. Truly top notch. I'll have to consult the other two heads, but I think these two would make excellent Knights of the Torch. That is, if you're interested in fighting for an end to magi oppression."

Kai and I shrugged. I wasn't *not* interested in ending magi oppression. I just wasn't sure about these Knights of the Torch, or Solrac himself.

Then I remembered what Kari said back in Thorn's den. I realized the Knights of the Torch must've been who told her about the Black Valkyrie being in Drakfell. After all, Solrac had mentioned her whereabouts again during the meeting. If the Knights could help me get to her, maybe I could finally get revenge for what she did to my mother.

Solrac went on. "Of course, we'll need Kari's full endorsement."

All eyes turned to Kari. She looked back and forth between Kai and me, and I got the sense she was worried. She probably didn't want us to get in too deep and end up getting in trouble. But she also knew us. We risked our lives constantly on raids. How was this any different?

Kari gave a single nod.

"Excellent," Solrac clapped his hands together. "More drinks while we brief them on—"

Suddenly, the door banged open, cutting Solrac off. A thin Knight burst into the room looking wildly around until he locked eyes with Solrac.

"Mage Hunters."

Kari, Kai, and I froze. Valla jumped to her feet, drawing her seaxes.

Solrac slowly stood. "How many?"

"Two enforcers. The Keeper of Whitestone Hall called for them, looking for a half-born thief who stole her dragon eggs. The Baron here directed them to the house of some half-born boy on the edge of town."

My blood ran cold. I was the only half-born in town. That meant the Mage Hunters had sent enforcers to my house.

Dad.

I was rushing for the door in an instant. I had to get to my dad. If the Mage Hunters found out he was a magi, they'd silvermark and execute him.

"Asher, wait!" Kari and Kai tried to hold me back, but Kai was too weak from ether overuse and I successfully wrenched free.

I'd almost made it to the door when I felt a yank from my midsection. Then I was skidding backward, being dragged by my belt.

I looked back and saw a golden rune glowing over Solrac's brow. His hand made a pulling motion, then a stopping motion as I came to a halt.

"Let me go!" I shouted. "You don't understand. My dad—he's in danger."

"Don't act too hastily," Solrac said calmly. "Rushing to your home now would be foolish. You'd only endanger your father further."

"He's right, Asher," Kai agreed, ever the planner.

"I say this is a wonderful opportunity," Solrac continued to hold me back with his etherarchy. "The Mage Hunters will be after you, not the Knights. That'll give us quite the upper hand. We need to strategize. Come up with a great story for why they have the wrong half-born thief."

Kari spoke up. "But they don't have the wrong half-born thief."

"Inconsequential."

"So, what do we do now?" Valla asked.

"We have Asher do what he does best," Solrac said.

"What?" I asked.

Solrac smiled. "Talk."

"Wait," Kai interjected, pulling out his black leather notebook and opening to a blank page. "First, we'll need something to convince them that Asher's been hard at work in Steel Rim the past several days, and that he couldn't've been in Whitestone Hall."

"What do we need for that?" I asked.

Kai was already writing. "We need to kill a craghopper. Not just any craghopper. The giant one that's been terrorizing Steel Rim for over a year."

My vibrant green eyes grew even brighter. "Karl?"

Kai nodded. "Karl."

Fragment - Valla

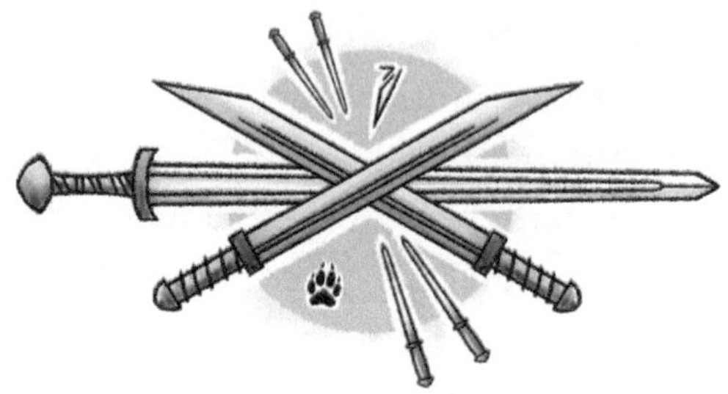

Valla used her seaxe to hack through the thick, tangled smokesage near Steel Rim's cliffs. She channeled her aggression into each swing, halfway imagining that the prickly brambles were the heads of her enemies. Mage Hunters, mostly. Decapitating things helped her relax.

Solrac had been foolish to welcome the infiltrators so quickly into their circle. Then again, Solrac was always assuming people had good intentions. That's why he needed Valla. She never assumed people had good intentions.

Either way, Valla knew she needed to hurry now. Her task was simple: track down the enormous dragon goat that lived along the cliffs. The craghopper the half-born had idiotically dubbed 'Karl.'

Valla took out the last smokey briar with a clean slice from her seaxe. As she stepped into the clearing, she found herself staring at the boarded-up entrance to an old mine shaft.

But not just any old shaft. This was the same one Valla had visited the last time she'd been to Steel Rim just over a decade ago. Her senses must've been kicking in, leading her to the familiar spot.

Valla could almost hear the screams from the miners echoing inside the cave as she remembered the last time she was here.

She'd been young, traveling with Solrac and the others for the first time. She hadn't yet become Solrac's personal bodyguard, but already she'd felt a certain protectiveness over him.

They'd come to Steel Rim to do what Solrac did best—recruit more people into the Knights of the Torch. They'd met Kari's parents in the Drunken Drake tavern to talk over the Knights' purpose. Kari's parents were excited to learn more, and they'd even brought a few friends to hear what Solrac had to say.

They'd just gotten their drinks when a man came rushing into the tavern covered in dirt and scrapes. He'd cried out, pleading for someone, anyone in the bar to help—there had been a collapse at the mines.

Without hesitation, one of Kari's parents' friends leaped to her feet. She was a half-born, with bright, dragonfire green eyes and scale-tipped ears. Zerana knew many of the people working in the mines that day, and was racing from the tavern within moments.

Zerana's husband, Akayto, had grabbed his scaleslayer crossbow before taking off after her. Solrac, Vidya, Elogan, Valla, and the rest followed close behind.

By the time Valla and the others had reached the mine's entrance, Zerana had already pulled out at least half a dozen miners. Zerana wasted no time, her eyes aglow with gold archonic power as she used her shadowbinding to eat away at the dirt and beams that held the last miner captive.

Valla remembered admiring how brazenly Zerana had used her etherarchy in front of her neighbors. She hadn't been initiated into the Knights, yet she was living their code naturally by putting others' lives ahead of her own.

Suddenly, a feral roar had erupted from within the collapsed mine. Zerana rushed to pull the last miner out. Once he was free, Akayto carried him to safety as an onslaught of dirt cascaded onto Zerana, burying her alive.

Valla had yelped, worried for the woman. Soon another roar sounded as a hulking stonescale drake climbed through the pile of dirt and debris blocking the mine entrance.

At once, Valla realized that the mine collapse had been no accident. And the wild drake wasn't about to let the miners go without a fight.

Solrac, Vidya, and a few others had tensed, unsure whether to fight the drake or flee with the miners. But before they could decide, a sharp, Drekai scimitar sprouted from the pile of dirt behind the drake.

Valla had all but given Zerana up for lost when the half-born woman came shooting out of the debris. Her eyes glowed once more as she used her levitation powers to balance as she ran up the creature's spiny back.

With a yell, Zerana used her Shadowbinding power to light the edge of her scimitar with black shadowfire. She swung at the stonescale drake's nearly impenetrable hide, slicing the thick horn on his nose clean off his face. The shadowfire along the edge of her blade had eaten through the bone, and the horn thumped against the earth as it fell.

The drake bellowed in rage, pounding the rocks with its massive feet and sending golden patterns across the ground wherever it stepped. Each step sent out a shockwave, and Valla remembered having to throw out her hands to steady herself.

Solrac and Vidya both drew their weapons, ready to join Zerana against the drake.

"Wait," Akayto had said, rushing back after getting the miners out of harm's way. "She'll never forgive me if I let you step in."

"Are you crazy?" Vidya replied. "That beast is too strong for one person to fight alone—even a magi."

Akayto gave a lopsided grin. "Then you haven't seen Zerana." He turned to his wife as she clashed with the rampaging drake. "How're you doing, honey?"

Zerana's scimitar arced through the air, slicing through the stonescale's thick hide. The beast roared, slashing back with a claw. Zerana's eyes burned an even brighter gold as she used her shadowbinding to phase shift—make parts of herself into semi-incorporeal darkness—through the strike. Valla's jaw dropped as she watched the drake's sharp talons pass straight through Zerana's torso, leaving her completely unscathed.

"I'm doing fine, my *rakaai*," Zerana replied, using the Drekai word for 'love.' "I'll be just another minute."

Akayto laughed and shook his head. "Soot, I love that woman."

Valla and the others watched in awe as Zerana finished off the drake with a final, graceful slash to its neck. Valla appreciated the instinct.

The chilly, desert night wind blew, shaking Valla from the memory. The mineshaft was sealed shut now, all evidence of the tremendous feat of

shadowbinding gone. Zerana may not have joined the Knights of the Torch in the end, but she'd certainly inspired Valla that day. Valla hoped to one day show that kind of bravery, selflessness, and skill in the face of danger.

No, not hoped—Valla *trained*.

The sound of howling pulled Valla's attention northward. Ridgerunners. The draconic wolves would know where the craghopper was. All Valla needed to do was ask them—and if they were stingy about the information, she could always take down their alpha to get them to comply.

Valla sheathed her seaxe, then placed a hand on the marked polar wolf's fang that hung from a cord around her neck. She felt a tug in her gut as angular, gold patterns glowed to life along her arms, legs, torso, and face. A golden mist surrounded her for just a moment as she shifted.

Valla let out a harsh snarl as she leaped from the dissipating golden cloud. She landed smoothly on the pads of her four paws, the white fur along her back catching the moonlight. Within moments, Valla, now in full polar wolf form, disappeared into the trees, heading north along the cliffside.

Chapter 5: Karl

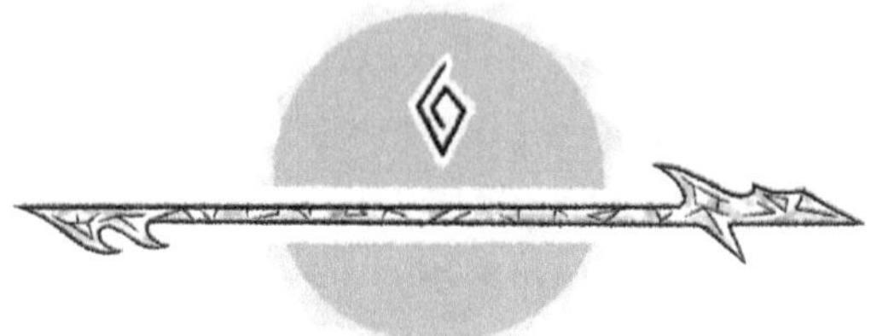

A pair of massive horns curled twice, sprouting majestically out of the beast's head. His thick, scaly back hunched intimidatingly over his front claws. Craghopper claws were something between a dragon's talon and a goat's hoof—good for keeping balance on cliffs, but sharp enough to tear through dragonhide.

Karl, the massive craghopper, stood majestically atop the cliff face overlooking Steel Rim. The full moon shone brightly behind him as he surveyed his territory, the light glinting off of the armored gray-and-white scales that grew along his back and joints. Even from the base of the cliff, I could tell it was Karl and not just any run-of-the-mill craghopper. Karl was twice as big—at least Thorn's size—and ten times angrier.

A craghopper running through Steel Rim every once in a while was no big deal. They had pretty big appetites, so a few farmers might lose some crops and maybe a wyvernhog or two. But the problem with craghoppers was that they ate everything. Everything. When they hunted in packs, the good folk of Steel Rim lost all kinds of livestock, fields, fences... sometimes even homes.

Karl was the worst one of all. He could eat as much as a pack by himself. Over this last year, he'd consumed several fields' worth of barley and almost all of Old Man Josef's herd of dragon buffalo, not to mention he'd bitten sizable chunks out of half the walls in town. Wood, thatch, adobe, stone...

Karl's digestive system didn't mind. He'd even choked down an entire wall on Baron Eidan's personal estate. For that, I had to give the huge draconic goat some credit. Part of me wondered if I could train him to only eat the property of nobility... but unfortunately, I had bigger things to worry about.

Normally, when Kai and I weren't out on raids, we were hard at work doing our cover-job: cragchasing. If we could claim we'd been out hunting Karl on the cliffs these past few days, there wasn't a citizen of Steel Rim who wouldn't vouch for the legitimacy of that story. They may've believed our story if we came home empty-handed, but showing up with Karl in tow would make it undeniable.

"Stars, Valla," I said in a hushed voice as we stared up at the beast. "Kai and I have been after Karl for months. You tracked him in a matter of hours."

By my side, Thorn let out a low growl of approval. I rubbed him under the chin. He appreciated a good hunter.

"I'm a Wildshaper, remember? Tracking a craghopper is nothing. Especially one this big," she said with a small glare my way. I guess she still hadn't forgiven me for tricking her with my Boone performance.

"It's perfect," Kai said, slipping off of Thorn's back as he finally looked up from his black leather notebook. He'd been riding on Thorn's back as we'd followed Valla, scribbling out his plans and backup plans. It honestly impressed me he was up to doing anything at all, after pouring so much of his ether into our illusions earlier. But Solrac had shown us a small ether vent through a door in the Drunken Drake's basement. Kai and I had refilled our ether wells there, and Kai even filled a quartz crystal Solrac had given him with a little extra. According to Valla, the real Jax was constantly running out of ether, so Solrac always pressured him to refill his ether crystals as often as possible. We hadn't had time to get Kai's ether well quite back to brimming, but the quartz crystal lent him enough ether to get back into the action.

Good thing, too, because we had to bag this craghopper as quickly as possible. I was itching to get back to my father to make sure he was alright. I hated the idea of him hosting Mage Hunter enforcers overnight, but the Knights of the Torch assured me they'd keep an eye on my home while we took down Karl.

"Why are you guys so willing to help?" I asked Valla.

Valla shrugged. "Beats me. Solrac said to."

"It's not because I'm so charming?" I grinned, and Thorn chortled quietly, sending me a warm, eye-roll feeling through the bond.

Valla didn't dignify me with a comment on that. Fair.

"Even if Solrac wasn't interested in recruiting you and Kai, you and your father are magi. The Knights of the Torch help magi. It's part of our code."

A wave of gratitude hit me. Despite what Kai and I had always believed, maybe the Knights weren't all that bad. And they had a code? I wondered what the specifics of that might be. At least Valla was here with us, not like some above-it-all noble like Solrac. They always managed to avoid doing the dirty work.

"I'll watch from the brush," Valla muttered.

"Wait, what?" I said. "You're not going to help?"

"She can't," Kai said, pointing to a page in his notebook that he and I both knew I wouldn't read. "It has to look like just you and I killed it. If Valla helps, questions could arise."

Valla nodded to Kai, then gave me another disapproving look before melting silently into the brush. Maybe the code of the Knights of the Torch wasn't so great after all.

As nice as it would've been to have Valla and her thousand-and-a-half weapons with us, I was sure Kai and I could handle this, especially with Thorn as backup. Plus, with Valla watching, maybe she'd see I wasn't bad in a fight. My impulsive charm wasn't getting her respect, but perhaps my combat skills would get me on her good side. Or at least off her bad side.

In the night sky, another bright green skyfall slashed across the blackness, far to the south.

I looked at Kai, ready for the plan.

"Armor up," he said, readying his crossbow.

My crystalline starglass armor caught the streams of moonlight through the clouds as I hover-dashed up the cliffside.

I weightlessly darted from foothold to foothold, zigzagging up the cliff. The clawed toes Kari had made for my boots mimicked a craghopper's claws, helping me find purchase on the nearly sheer surface.

I was honestly a little excited that Kai's plan involved me running up to Karl's overlook on my own rather than on wyvernback. Flying on Thorn was the best, but sometimes I liked to really experience the adventure with my own two feet. Although, according to Kai, the chances of death or serious injury were extremely high.

That made me smile.

His reasoning was that craghoppers were prey to the larger flying dragons and had experience in avoiding them. Karl would be far less likely to run from a lone human scaling the cliffside on his own.

I finally reached the top of the cliff, using one last burst of archonic levitation power to boost myself quietly over the ridge. I dusted off my pants, then scanned the flat clifftop for Karl the craghopper.

Unfortunately, he spotted me first.

Karl's beady, black eyes were murderous. His thick, muscular legs tensed, and his front clawed hoof pawed at the dirt.

With a wild snort, Karl charged.

My bright green eyes blazed gold as I conjured my starglass dragonhook spear. My instincts told me to run for my life, but Kai's plan called for me to hold my ground on the edge of the cliff.

I counted down in my mind as Karl got closer. His thick, reinforced ram's horns would hit me in...

Three...

Two...

One.

At the last possible moment, I fell backward off the cliff. I added a brief salute to Karl on the way down just for fun.

Wind rushed past my scale-tipped ears for just a second before I flared my ether, levitating myself enough to stop my momentum and gain my footing a little over halfway down the cliffside.

With an enraged roar, Karl followed, only he didn't lose control like Kai had hoped. Instead, he turned on his clever hooves and began pursuing the tasty magi half-born. The rocky terrain hardly slowed him down.

That was fine. I was sure Kai's plan two would kick in any moment now.

Thud.

Kai's crossbow bolt hit... the rock. His shot lodged harmlessly into the cliff, grazing some of Karl's armored scales, but narrowly missing his ribs.

Kai's shot had failed, but he had definitely succeeded in making Karl angrier. With a barbaric snort, Karl dove forward, horns poised to gore me.

I caught the horns around the spiral with my spear, which saved me from the attack, but allowed Karl to drive me over the edge. I hung from the spear, my feet dangling over pure nothing.

Then Karl began madly thrashing his head. My spear's hold slipped, and the next thing I knew, I was falling.

I slowed my descent with some levitation, but if I tried to land on the cliffside now, I'd be a sitting duck for Karl. Luckily, plan three came swooping in, catching me on his back as we soared away.

Thorn sent me a fiery, loyal feeling through our bond. Together, we swooped back around toward Karl and the cliff.

On the ground below, I saw Kai fumbling to reload his crossbow. Unfortunately, Karl noticed him too. He started down the cliff toward Kai. Soot. We'd have to adjust. Luckily, Thorn and I had an idea of our own.

Thorn, shoot! I thought through our bond. He gave a roar, then swung his tail toward the enormous craghopper.

The pointed blade at the tip of Thorn's tail released from the rest of his tail, launching a spike as long as my forearm right at Karl. I didn't give Thorn his name for nothing.

The spike hit true, lodging between the scales over Karl's hunched back. I felt Thorn glow with pride through the bond. Based on Karl's feral howl, that hurt.

But it wasn't enough to drop him. And even though gold Sentinel patterns were already tracing around Thorn's tail to regrow the spike, it would take a minute or two to fully regenerate, so another shot from him was out.

"Thorn, get me closer!"

I needed to get back onto the cliff to keep Karl's attention off of Kai.

Thorn did his best, getting me as close to the cliff and Karl as his wingspan would safely allow. It was close enough. Thorn sensed my plan and turned, angling so that his long tail faced the cliffside.

My eyes glowed gold as I burned more ether. Then I hover-ran down Thorn's back and made a wild, flying leap off the end of his tail.

My legs pedaled through open space as I launched toward the cliff. I used my dragonhook spear to stab at the cliffside to help me stick the landing as I gained my footing on the cliff face's narrow footholds.

I landed right where I wanted to, just a short distance down-cliff from angry Karl.

From the ground below, I heard Kai yell something about that not being part of the plan.

I brandished my spear, gesturing with one hand for the craghopper to come at me.

Karl obliged.

I rushed to meet him, aiming my spear at his chest. But Karl's head was so enormous that when he ducked at the last second, my spear once again got tangled in his horns. He thrashed once, wrenching the spear from my hands and tossing it off the cliff.

Another benefit of forming them from starglass. It hurt less when I lost them.

Karl seemed pretty happy that I was weaponless. He pawed at the ground and backed up along the narrow path, preparing for another charge.

"Kai?" I called out. "Got any more backup plans?"

I could just make out some curse words. Below, I caught a tiny flicker of gold light, which must've been Kai runetracing.

Suddenly, another me—down to the messy, black fangknot hairstyle and turquoise bandana—appeared directly in front of me.

I caught onto Kai's idea quickly. Leaving the illusory Asher standing there, wide open, I skidded over the edge of the cliffside, dropping down to another shallow outcropping below. Both the real me and the illusion of me conjured a new spear out of starglass.

I looked up as Karl ran, horns poised, toward the illusion of me. Illusion-Asher swung his spear in a windmill motion, fearlessly facing the beast. I wondered if the real me looked that fierce.

I didn't get to consider that for long, because illusory Asher promptly got gored by a pair of giant craghopper horns. I jabbed with my spear from the outcropping below, catching it on one of Karl's patches of armored scales as illusory me disappeared in a shower of starry golden ether dust. My spear didn't do much, but it threw Karl off balance and sent him skidding.

Karl looked confused for only a moment before he caught sight of me down below. He snorted, then began another descent toward me.

"Give me another one!" I yelled down to Kai. He understood, and by the time Karl got onto my level, two more illusory Ashers flickered to life on either side of me.

The Asher on my right went first, rushing at Karl headlong. The Asher to my left ducked, rolling off the side of the cliff and shimmying down to the next lowest foothold. Karl looked between the three of us, unsure which to pursue. In his anger, he chose the nearest threat—the illusory Asher who was now only a few strides away. Karl dashed to meet him.

The distraction gave me the opportunity to get around to Karl's side. Just as Karl struck illusion-me, I jabbed him with my spear. Another gash appeared on Karl's side, and coppery, draconic blood poured from the wound.

Karl bellowed in rage, and I swiped my weapon in a wide circle along the ground. The hook caught on his front hoof, and I yanked hard, causing Karl to stumble.

Meanwhile, Kai made the other illusory Asher levitate back into Karl's view, and Karl turned on him. Illusion-Asher made a face, sticking his tongue out and crossing his eyes.

Come on, Kai. I wasn't that juvenile.

"What now, goat-breath?" I taunted as Karl readied himself to chase fake me.

At the sound of my voice, Karl skidded to a stop, turning on the real me.

Uh oh. That was faster than I'd expected.

I didn't have time to dodge. When Karl's horns hit, it knocked the wind out of me and cracked my starglass chest plate. Luckily, he hadn't been far enough away to build the speed to do more damage.

I barely caught myself on a small foothold a few feet away.

Thorn tried to get in to help, but the cliff-face was too tight and I was too close to Karl for him to attack clearly.

Karl came at me again. With nowhere else to go, I rolled off the rock and out of his way.

Just then, a crossbow bolt stuck into Karl's shoulder. He bellowed, turning down the cliffside toward Kai.

Karl rushed down the cliff, straight at him.

Scorch, he was fast.

I tried to keep up, but it was no use.

I stumbled down the nearly sheer cliff-face, barely faster than falling, while Karl gracefully thundered toward Kai. I could just make out the faint traces of warped, golden light trailing behind the hulking beast.

I tried my best to direct my descent toward an outcropping below. When I got to it, I flared my ether and launched myself out and into the air away from the cliffside.

Thorn could feel what I needed him to do. Before gravity had the chance to pull me down, Thorn swooped in underneath me, catching me mid-flop on his back.

Thanks, buddy, I thought through the bond. He sent back a feeling as warm as the sun's rays.

Karl was so fast, it was no wonder he'd never been caught. I thought of the way the air behind him warped and tinged gold as he ran, and realized he must've been using some form of archonic etherarchy to propel himself forward. Maybe I could do the same.

I scrambled to sit up as Thorn flew downward. We had to intercept Karl before he got to Kai.

At the bottom of the cliff, I saw Kai standing wide open, crossbow at the ready. Karl had just reached the bottom. It only took him a moment to regain his footing, which was all the time Kai needed to take his next shot.

Karl roared as a new crossbow bolt sprouted from the side of his thick neck, right next to Thorn's tail spike.

But the giant craghopper still didn't go down.

Thorn and I were close, but not close enough to catch Karl. He charged toward Kai with renewed gusto.

Kai reached for another bolt to reload, but there was no way he'd have time.

So, I did the only natural thing.

My eyes burned with golden etherlight as I flung myself off of Thorn's back. I willed my ether to propel me forward, like Karl's charge. This was new. I felt the breakthrough as I accessed my ether in a new way. It drained a lot more of my power than I'd expected.

While my usual hover-dashing left a warped golden trail in the air behind me, this extra-fast use of my levitation abilities left a jet of misty, white ether in my wake.

Like a shooting star, I sped forward through the air and slammed into Karl's back.

Karl was livid, but at least it threw off his momentum. He flailed, bucking his hind feet into the air over and over again. It was all I could do to hold on to the spike Thorn had lodged between the scales in Karl's hunch.

I rode the craghopper with everything I had. Out of the corner of my eye, I saw Kai finally get his next bolt loaded. He took aim.

I had to give him a clear shot. I grabbed Karl by his massive horns and grunted as I pulled backward with all my strength, adding in some levitation for good measure.

Karl reared back with my movement, exposing his massive, goat-like chest.

Kai took the shot, hitting the beast right in the heart.

Karl went down instantly, and we fell together. I rolled to avoid getting crushed by his body and slammed right into a large rock. With a groan, I wished I'd had the forethought to reform my broken starglass chest plate. That was going to leave a bruise. At least the kick to my head from the Whitestone Hall Keeper didn't seem so bad anymore, and wouldn't stand out alongside my fresh injuries.

Slowly, I staggered to my feet in time to see Valla emerging from her hiding place. She gave three slow claps.

Despite my wounds, I took a bow.

"Well done," she started as she looked over the fallen craghopper. "Kai."

I looked up from my bow, brow furrowed.

"Fantastic shot," she went on. "And brilliant illusion work."

"Thank you," Kai beamed, looking only a little shaken up.

"What about me?" I said, a little exasperated.

"Asher," she said, not bothering to look at me. "You made an excellent distraction."

"Distraction? Is that all?"

"A valuable position. Gives the true warriors the opportunities they need to strike at a foe," she said, patting Kai on the shoulder and nodding to Thorn. Kai beamed even brighter while I felt Thorn glow through our bond.

Was she saying she didn't think I was a 'true warrior'? Had she not seen me riding Karl?

She took in my indignant face, then closed her eyes. I could've sworn she muttered, "Selene, give me peace."

Kai shot me an apologetic look. "Hey, that hover-charge you did to land on his back was cool. New breakthrough?"

I nodded.

"I'll have to keep that in mind for future plans," Kai said, already scratching down notes in his book.

I smiled as Valla glanced over toward the distant mountains to the east.

"Sunrise is soon," she said ominously. "We need to get this thing back to your father's home before the Mage Hunters get antsy."

Getting the gargantuan craghopper home was no easy task. Valla helped us put together a makeshift sledge using two long, thick branches, with another tied perpendicularly between them. It took a lot more of my levitation power than I was happy with to load Karl onto the contraption. I could feel that my ether well was over halfway drained.

We harnessed the sledge onto Thorn's back. There was no way he'd be able to carry Karl while flying, so we trekked back into town the long way.

As we walked, I felt the fatigue setting in. I hadn't slept since my night in Whitestone Hall's dungeon. My head throbbed from the Keeper's kick to the head. That pain was still there, but it hardly compared to the recent injuries from Karl. Whitestone Hall felt like a lifetime ago.

But I had to be alert and ready. Kai was in the clear, but it was up to me to convince the Mage Hunters that I'd been nowhere near Whitestone Hall these past few days. Then they'd move on, and the Knights of the Torch could move forward with their plans.

Most importantly, my dad would be safe. We'd be able to pawn the stolen dragon eggs, and he'd have enough funds to relocate to Skygard and the promise of safety. The journey from here to Skygard was difficult, but Kai had done some research on ways we could get in—for the right price.

As for me, I planned to take Solrac up on his offer to join the Knights. But not because I knew all that much about their code of honor or whatnot.

It was because they could get me to the Black Valkyrie.

We made sure to have Thorn drag Karl through Steel Rim to make sure others saw our prize and could vouch for our story. We passed the last few homes before arriving at my family's longhouse at the edge of town just as the first rays of day began shining over the cliffs.

Our home was on the humbler side, just a squat, brown adobe hovel with a roof we'd thatched and fireproofed ourselves. A small, blue bramblevine cactus garden grew along either side of the wooden front door, though the garden was not as well-tended as it once was. The flowering plants grew wild, tangling as they climbed up the front wall of the house.

The garden had been my mom's idea. When I was eight, she and I had hiked the desert mountain trails, searching for just the right sprigs to bring home. I'd been so excited, I'd pricked my fingers on the sharp thorns so many times I started crying. Mom had used her shadowbinding powers, patiently wrapping each finger in shadowsilk. She then explained to me that the plants, while beautiful, had a sharp side. The thorns were the cactus's way of protecting itself. You had to be careful how you approached, but once you got to the flower, it was worth it.

Even years after her death, looking at the cactus garden was painful. But not as painful as it would be to get rid of the garden altogether.

With a nod to me for luck, Kai and Valla disappeared around the bend in the road. This part, I had to do on my own. I was the half-born, after all.

I ran over the plan in my head.

The Knight who'd relayed the message told us that Whitestone Hall had sent for Mage Hunter enforcers, which were regional agents brought in for specific operations. The ones in Whitestone Hall who'd been present at my execution were a locally stationed team. That meant the ones here wouldn't recognize me.

Now, I just had to get these highly-trained enforcers to believe I'd spent the past few days nearly dying, taking on this giant craghopper. I inhaled deeply, then exhaled.

Time for a show.

At my prompting, Thorn let out a roar, alerting anyone who might be in the house that we were here. I climbed on top of Karl's giant body, one leg on his side, the other proudly atop his hunched back.

Momentarily, the Mage Hunter enforcers came hurrying out of the house, their silver armor crisp and shiny. The silver pauldrons on their right shoulders bore the Mage Hunter's insignia—a sword thrust through a triangle representing the ethereal triad. When they looked out to see what was the matter, they saw me standing majestically atop my kill. The morning sunlight streamed behind, silhouetting Thorn, Karl, and me.

I jumped down from Karl's back, my boots disturbing the dusty earth as I landed. The pair of Mage Hunters looked at me, and though their silver enforcer helmets hid their faces, I could tell they were surprised. And their body language told me they were more than a little impressed.

I locked eyes with the more confident-looking of the two, my dragonfire green eyes bright and challenging.

Trying to keep any nerves out of my voice, I called out across the yard.

"Heard you were looking for me?"

Chapter 6: Inquisition

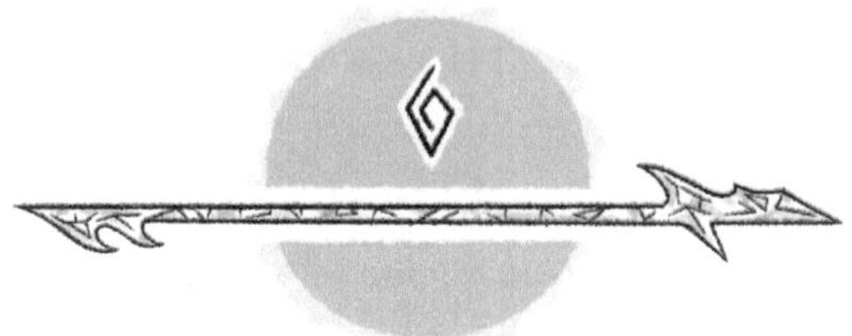

When the Mage Hunters finally stopped gaping, the more con-fident one removed her helmet to reveal long, blonde hair. A small wave of relief washed over me—she was definitely not the jailer's daughter.

"You're Akayto's half-born son?" she asked.

I gave her a winning smile, slightly turning my head to show off the dark teal, scaly tips of my pointed ears. I winked to emphasize the dragonfire color of my eyes.

"What do you think?"

The second Mage Hunter took off his helmet to get a better look, confirming that neither of these enforcers had seen me in Whitestone Hall. I didn't get too comfortable though—they still looked intimidating with their gleaming silver plate armor, silver shields, and rich, dusk blue cloaks. Most Mage Hunters wore lighter armor, but these two must've specialized in bringing in targets by force. So much silver made them all but impervious to etherarchy.

They still looked nervous about my wyvern though. Silver stopped dragonfire too, but not the claws of a dragon three times their size.

"Thorn, give us some space, eh?" I said, patting him on the nose. Sending my dragon away would show these two that I wasn't afraid.

Thorn snorted and gave the enforcers a warning look before he flew off into the hilly, juniper-covered wilderness that was my backyard. He'd wheel around behind the house, out of sight, but near enough to help if need be.

The enforcers visibly relaxed. Good.

The woman was a little shorter than I was and a lot older, probably in her mid-thirties.

The other Mage Hunter had thick red hair and was closer to my age, and seemed to have a lot of nervous energy. If I had to guess, I'd say this was his first real-world magi interrogation.

The older Mage Hunter gave her partner a meaningful look, and the newbie cleared his throat.

"If you don't mind stepping inside, we have a couple of questions."

The older Mage Hunter jabbed him with an elbow, and her partner's tone shifted from shaky to something slightly sterner.

"Uh, I mean, step inside for questioning, half-born."

"Ah, yes," I said, striding past them toward the front door. "That was much more intimidating. Come on in then. Let's get this over with."

"Wait," the older one said.

When I looked back, I saw a slender, silver rod in her hands, about the length of my forearm.

"Right," I said. I held out a hand and braced myself.

She pressed the rod harshly into my palm, and a painful, icy sensation rushed through me from the point of contact. I felt a sort of internal block, cutting me off from my ether well.

I kept my face even through the pain, raising an eyebrow just to emphasize how little the silver bothered me. I'd passed the silver rod test at least a hundred times now.

"Not a magi," the older enforcer grumbled, sounding a little disappointed.

I shrugged. "So no interrogation necessary then?"

The Mage Hunter shook her head, clearly annoyed by my casual attitude. Maybe she'd get thrown off her game if I got under her skin.

"Fair enough," I smiled. "Come on in."

I led them back through the front door and into my home. It wasn't much—other than the two tiny bedrooms in the back, it was just the one room. A humble kitchen filled one corner, and an intricately carved dining table and four chairs stood proudly beside the only window.

"Asher!" Dad stood up from his place at the table when he heard me come in. He carefully made his way toward me from across the room, his unseeing eyes unfocused.

With the Mage Hunters here, he had to hide his etherarchy, which meant he was totally blind. Dad lost his sight the same day the Black Valkyrie took Mom. It made things more difficult for him, but still I envied him. At least he'd fought back that day.

Dad stumbled a little, then reached out, feeling through the air until he clasped onto my shoulder. I bit back a laugh. Dad and I both knew he could navigate our home with ease. But Dad loved to overplay the blind-guy routine when we had company. It was smart, actually. Made him seem less threatening. In reality, if he used his etherarchy, I was pretty sure my dad could take both these Mage Hunters down without even breaking a sweat.

"I'm glad you're back. It's been so long since you went out..." Dad trailed off, giving me a look.

"Cragchasing," I supplied.

"Cragchasing, of course. That's what I was telling these fine en-forcers. My son's one of Steel Rim's best cragchasers, you know."

"Aww, stop it, Dad," I said, stifling another chuckle. Dad needed to rein it in before he laid it on too thick. These Mage Hunter enforcers probably weren't as easy to fool as Baron Eidan's idiot guards.

"We finally brought in the big one who's been eating up the buildings all over town," I bragged. "He's outside now. I'll need to bring him into the butcher's shop just as soon as we're done here."

I turned to the Mage Hunters. "How long is this whole questioning thing gonna take?"

"Uh..." the new Mage Hunter left his mouth hanging open.

"Think you're funny, half-born?" The older Mage Hunter crossed her arms across her chest.

"Me? Nah. But I am hungry. Anyone else want a sandwich?"

"I'll take one," Dad said.

The young Mage Hunter looked like he was about to say yes as well, but his partner gave him another elbow-jab and he promptly shut up.

"Just two then," I said, making my way toward our meager kitchen. "Don't just stand there, have a seat. Did my dad mention he carved the furniture himself?"

"Obviously, not recently," Dad said, gesturing toward his blank, brown eyes.

The Mage Hunters hesitated, but begrudgingly sat down. My dad took a place at the table too as I rifled through the cupboards for a loaf of bread.

"So what brings you to Steel Rim?" I asked, infusing each word with as much casual energy as I could.

"We ask the questions," the older Mage Hunter said.

I used a bread knife to gesture toward her, offering her the floor.

"Where have you been over the past two days?" she said with as much authority as she could muster while sitting down.

I sliced bread. The pieces turned out a little slanted—I was never much use in a kitchen.

"We just told you, I've been out bagging craghoppers. Did you not see that massive beast lying outside the house? Took me all week to track and nab him."

"Ever been to Whitestone Hall?"

"Hmm. That name rings a bell. Isn't that one of the outlander towns near Keep Drakfell? On the east side of the Scar, right?"

"No. Whitestone Hall is southwest of Steel Rim," the newer Mage Hunter said, earning another glare from his more experienced partner.

"Oh, thanks, I don't get out much," I said, organizing my sandwich materials.

"We've just come from Whitestone Hall after the Keeper there called us in. Seems she lost something valuable," said the woman.

"Dragon eggs," added the redheaded Mage Hunter, trying to be important. His partner looked like she wanted to murder him.

"What a shame," I lamented, slicing up some cheese and dragon buffalo meat. "I hate it when obscenely rich nobles lose valuable things."

"Don't test me, boy." The older Mage Hunter stood up.

"That's right, Asher," Dad stood up as well. "Don't test the nice woman. She's come all this way from her post miles away from here. Speaking of distances, let's think about Whitestone Hall. That's what, at least a two-day journey from Steel Rim? Hmm. And wasn't the Keeper robbed yesterday? Call me crazy, but I don't see how anyone could rob Whitestone Hall yesterday, travel back to Steel Rim, track and capture the biggest craghopper in the badlands overnight, and be home in time for breakfast."

"Speaking of breakfast," I said, walking over to the table with a large plateful of sandwiches. "I made extras in case the two of you change your minds."

I stood in front of the table's fourth chair, my eyes daring the Mage Hunter to sit down first. She wasn't backing down. With me, the Mage Hunter, and my father all standing now, the nervous Mage Hunter slowly rose to his feet as well so as not to feel left out.

I shrugged and grabbed a sandwich.

"The wyvern outside," the older Mage Hunter said. "As the dragon flies, Whitestone Hall's only a half a day away."

"Thorn?" I laughed, and I was glad Kai had had the foresight to make me hide my dragon's heartscale inside the secret compartment on my belt. "That's not my wyvern. It used to belong to one of the old ranchers on the edge of town before he died. Thorn still hangs out by the cliffs and helps me tow my larger kills back into Steel Rim. He's a good dragon, but he's not mine."

The Mage Hunter narrowed her eyes. I saw them flash to my collarbone for a moment as if checking for a heartscale under my turquoise dust scarf. I rolled my eyes and lifted the scarf to prove there was nothing there.

"Besides," I said, taking a huge bite, then talking with my mouth full. "Even if I somehow managed to fly back from Whitestone Hall that quickly, then what? You think I hurried and flew back to Steel Rim, stashed the Keeper's treasure in a cave somewhere, went out and tracked a giant craghopper, killed it, and lugged it back here just in time to meet you two?"

I laughed heartily at the almost completely true story I'd just told. It was how I always could trick Kai's mind reading powers—it wasn't about trying to block out the truth from my mind. It was by remembering the truth, but with a few key twists.

The Mage Hunters both looked stumped and frustrated. Finally, with a sigh, the older one stepped away from the table.

"So maybe you were in Steel Rim," she said. She took a few steps toward the doorway, then nodded for her companion to join her. The younger Mage Hunter scurried after her.

"Sorry to disappoint you," my father said. "I did tell you the thief couldn't have been my son."

"Thank you, Akayto," the older Mage Hunter said, opening the door with a creak.

"Hope the rich Keeper finds their super valuable dragon eggs," I called as they left. "Got to keep that wealth and power where it belongs."

The redheaded Mage Hunter paused in the doorway, spinning to face me. His companion turned to see what was the matter.

"Ha!" The newer Mage Hunter pointed at me. "Caught you. Who ever said the Keeper's treasure was dragon eggs?"

There was a moment of silence as I blinked back at him.

"Um... you did," I said.

"That's true, you did," Dad added.

"Did I?" the Mage Hunter looked at his older companion.

"Yes, you did. Come on Lothar," she grumbled.

The young Mage Hunter looked dumbfounded. His partner grabbed him by the scruff of his dusky blue cloak and dragged him back toward the door.

"Sandwich for the road?" I offered. The redheaded Mage Hunter looked tempted, but he was too busy being hauled away.

I closed the door behind them, counted to nine, then let out a long breath of relief.

That relief was short-lived.

"Asher of Steel Rim," Dad's voice, so playful and light during our interrogation, was now colder than the Mage Hunters' silver rod. "You and Kai were out stealing dragon eggs?"

Oh soot.

"To be fair, the dragon eggs weren't the original target," I turned back to Dad. Stars, for a blind guy, he sure was glaring daggers at me.

Dad raised a hand and runetraced, gold light following his finger in the air. The Rifter's rune for the Sight appeared over his forehead, and the smallest fleck of gold light appeared deep in Dad's eyes.

He marched over to me, staring down at my very soul. Literally.

I knew he was staring at my soul, because that's what the rune for the Sight did. Dad said the Sight let him see people's souls, or auras. Everyone's spirit had a different color and texture, clinging close to them. Dad didn't need his physical eyes to see. In fact, Dad saw more in Etheria, the Spirit World, than any of us saw without the Sight.

Although right now, I kind of wished Dad was still blind. Then I could hide from his scolding.

"I thought I told you to lay off raiding with Kai after you almost got killed in Naga Bay. They tried to execute you!" Dad said, angry eyes boring into mine.

"So did Whitestone Hall, technically."

"Asher!" He threw his hands up. "This is exactly the kind of reckless behavior that's going to get you killed."

"Dad, I'm fine."

"This time. But what about next time, eh? One of these raids is going to end poorly, and your mother would never forgive me if I let that happen."

"Dad, Mom isn't here."

"That you can see," Dad said, looking over my shoulder.

I looked behind me, but of course, saw nothing. That made me angry.

Dad swore he could sometimes see Mom's spirit, still with us, in Etheria. But every Mystic book Kai had that mentioned the Sight only noted how tricky it was. How little we could really know about Etheria, and how sometimes Rifters could go crazy from the things they saw.

Researching the Sight wasn't easy. Almost every reference to rifting, along with the vast majority of Rifters themselves, had been destroyed during Mad Queen Frida's Great Rifter Purge decades ago. Dad was one of the few Rifters still around in Evgard. He had nobody to teach him the intricacies of the Sight, or how to keep from losing himself in it.

Since going blind in his fight with the Black Valkyrie, he used the Sight almost constantly. He sometimes saw things and said things that just didn't make sense. He talked to himself a lot at night. But whenever I asked him about it the next day, he said he didn't remember talking to anyone.

I wanted to believe that Mom's spirit was still around. But the longer Dad spent looking for her in Etheria, the more worried I became.

I worried I was losing him too.

The Black Valkyrie took my mom away from me that day three years ago. In some ways, I felt like she took away my dad as well.

Dad sighed. "I can't lose you too, Asher."

I folded my arms. "Well, lucky for you, I won't be going on any more raids."

Dad raised an eyebrow, the same way I always did. "Oh really? And I suppose Thorn won't be eating any more drakalope, either. And Kai won't be making plans in his notebook. And Kari won't be inventing any more thing-a-ma-whats."

"Really. This last haul—the dragon eggs. Once we sell them, it'll be enough to get you to Skygard. You'll be safe. No more Mage Hunters."

"That's wonderful. But I can't help but notice you said 'it'll be enough to get *you* to Skygard.' You don't intend to come along?"

I shuffled my feet.

"Asher," Dad said, lowering his tone in the way only a father can.

"It's just... I might've found some people who know something about where the Black Valkyrie might be."

"No."

"But—"

"Absolutely not. You can't go off chasing the most dangerous woman in Evgard."

"But Mom—"

"Mom would want you to stay safe. That's why she died protecting you."

"Safe," I spat. "This is what you call safety? Constantly hiding from Mage Hunters. Always avoiding the guard. Nowhere is safe until the Black Valkyrie is dead."

Suddenly, my dad looked past me and, using the Sight, beyond the door. He signaled for me to be quiet. I froze.

"It's the Mage Hunters again—I recognize their auras. They've brought someone new with them."

A few seconds later, a knock at the door made me jump.

My dad let the rune over his forehead go out, then sat back down at the table. I took a few deep breaths to calm myself, then swung open the door with a smile.

That smile instantly died.

"Hello, half-born," the older Mage Hunter said with a wicked grin. Her junior partner looked at me, an excited smirk on his face.

Behind them stood a third Mage Hunter. A girl with a short black drake-tail and a silver chain whip strapped to her belt. A pair of intense eyebrows lowered over smug, brown eyes.

Oh soot.

It was the jailer's daughter from Whitestone Hall.

Chapter 7: The Black Valkyrie

"Thank the goddesses, you found her!" I said, throwing the door wide open and gesturing for the Mage Hunters to enter.

They paused, confused.

"Found her?" asked the younger enforcer.

"This is my ex," I cupped a hand around my mouth as if I were letting him in on a secret. "She's been stalking me for the past several months, accusing me of being a magi and trying to get me jailed. Haven't had any death threats or long-winded love letters in about a week, so I was starting to worry she'd been kidnapped or something."

Through his helmet, I could see the redhead, Lothar, was almost buying it. His older companion wasn't. The jailer's daughter looked amused, as if she wanted to see what I came up with next.

The seasoned Mage Hunter held a hand to her chin, thoughtful.

"What's her name?" she asked.

Without a moment's hesitation, I said the first name that came to mind. "Helga."

I was pretty sure Helga was the name of one of the elderly Sisters of Streya who used to work at Steel Rim's sorry excuse for a library. I wondered why my brain picked that now.

The jailer's daughter scoffed. The older Mage Hunter shook her head, turning to the young woman.

"What should we do with him, *Jaira*?" she asked.

"Oh, no," I said, shaking my head. "She's lying about her name again? Real original, Helga. Come on."

None of them were buying it now. Not even the newbie.

"Take him," Jaira commanded, her tone cool and superior. The two enforcers each grabbed me by an arm, pulling me out of my home and holding fast. Thorn signaled me through the bond, ready to come at a moment's notice. I hesitated to get him involved. Any wounds he got with a silver sword wouldn't regenerate when he used his Sentinel etherarchy. Their cold silver gauntlets stung my arms, even through my jacket, and I fought the urge to wince. Jaira took a few slow steps closer, looking me over from head to toe.

"Nice try, but you're not my type. Even if you weren't a half-born. Besides, you talk too much."

"But that's part of the charm. It's what you used to love about me, Helga honey." I winked.

"Enough," she said with a flick of her wrist. On that signal, the older enforcer expertly kicked me in the back of the leg, sending me to my knees. She held me there by the arms as Jaira reached into a small bag clipped to her belt and pulled out a thin, silver writing stylus and a bottle of silver ink.

Soot.

That was a pen for silvermarking. Pen wasn't quite the right word—it was more like a small knife used to brand magi by marking their left cheek with a silver symbol of their magi type. For me, they would cut an Astromancer's silvermark.

So much for passing the silver rod test.

Jaira sneered. "They should've marked you as a magi back in Whitestone Hall. You'll obviously be executed—properly this time, but in the meantime, don't think you'll avoid silvermarking again."

"Wait," Dad spoke up, feeling his way out the front door. "Silvermarking my son? That can't be right. I think I would've realized by now if my own son was a magi."

"I saw him use etherarchy with my own eyes," Jaira said flatly. "My studies at the Academy tell me he's an Archon—subtype Astromancer."

"But—"

"Save your breath, blind man."

Dad didn't know what to do. He hadn't used his etherarchy in combat in a long time. I squirmed in the Mage Hunters' grasp, wondering if I should just summon starglass and fight them off before they could mark me. They already knew what I was. Stars, I didn't even know if I could access my ether with the enforcers' silver gauntlets cutting off my ether at my wrists.

There were three of them, each with an arsenal of silver weapons. If it were me alone, I still might go for it. But with Dad around... he'd refuse to let me fight them off by myself. He'd use his etherarchy to try and save me, and in doing so, he'd reveal that he was a magi too.

No, fighting the Mage Hunters would only get us both killed. Instead, I was forced to do my least favorite thing in the world.

Nothing.

I closed my eyes, and thought I heard some kind of commotion from down in the center of town. I was sure the Mage Hunters could hear it too, but they were focused on the task at hand.

Through the bond, I could feel that Thorn was through with waiting. Despite my protests, he sent a torch-like flare to my heart to let me know that he was coming. But I knew he'd be too late.

Jaira placed her hand on my cheek, silvermarking pen ready. I braced myself for the chilling silver touch.

Thunk!

All of us turned our heads to stare at the crossbow bolt that had just lodged itself into the wall of the house amidst the tangled cactus vines. Jaira lifted a hand to her cheek, where a faint line of red blood showed the bolt's path. Finally, our gazes followed that path to another home just down the way from us.

"Why, hello there!" a voice called. Of all people, Solrac smiled as he leaned against the side of the longhouse. "Yes, that was me. Don't worry, dear, I don't intend to harm you, truly. I just wanted to get your attention to let you know that Steel Rim is under attack by a Drekai raiding party. You might want to take a look, as the battle is practically on your doorstep."

He had the audacity to blow an over-the-top kiss before ducking away behind the other house.

The three Mage Hunters looked at each other. I'd hoped they'd let me go in their haste, but instead, they dragged me along by the upper arms down the path toward town. The sound of a commotion grew louder as we turned the corner to get a better look behind a row of homes.

The sight before our eyes was pure chaos.

It honestly surprised me to see that Solrac hadn't been lying. When I looked down the street toward the heart of Steel Rim, I saw a horde of Drekai, at least a dozen expert raiders. Many wielded two long-handled scimitars each, their strikes like fierce, graceful ocean waves in comparison to the unrefined efforts of the townspeople. Others hurled telekinetically powered boomerangs, Drekai *kalaata,* through the air to strike at unexpected angles before returning to their throwers. Even hardened outlanders like the folks of Steel Rim didn't stand a chance.

Steel Rim's sorry excuse for a town guard was made up of a handful of volunteers wearing the tan cloaks of the Keepdom of Drakfell, joined by some cragchasers. I was sure there were more—both guard members and Drekai—that I couldn't see from here.

I checked in with Thorn through the bond, telling him to hurry down here to see what was going on, but to be careful. I felt his faint acknowledgement like an ember in my soul.

My heart raced. I knew that a raiding party of the half-dragon people from the Dragon Isles had hit Steel Rim once before, about eighteen years ago. They'd severely damaged the town and taken a lot of our resources. But it was also how my father had met my mother, so I couldn't complain much.

Why were they raiding our small outlander settlement now? On the same day our little stunt in Whitestone Hall brought Mage Hunters to my doorstep? At the same time the Knights of the Torch had gathered here for a big meeting? What were the odds?

I could almost hear Kai's voice in my head, letting me know the odds were impossible.

Actually, the odds of all those events randomly occurring at once aren't impossible. Extremely unlikely, but not impossible.

I startled when I actually heard Kai speaking in my mind. I looked down and, sure enough, I noticed the tiny wiggle from a mirror gecko crawling into my boot.

Glint! I thought. *Kai, what's going on? Is there really a Drekai raid going on right now?*

Worse, Kai thought back. *It's not a raid. The Drekai are here because—*

Suddenly, Kai's thoughts got muffled, then disappeared altogether. In my mind, I heard some clanging like weapons clashing together. Then I heard some screams, followed by Kai yelling something. Then, all at once, the mindlink went out, and I heard nothing more.

Glint poked her head out from my boot, her gigantic, shiny eyes looking panicked. Kai was in trouble.

I had to get out of here.

I reached out to Thorn again to let him know we had to get to Kai, then returned my attention to the Mage Hunters.

The Mage Hunters still held me fast as they stared down the street at the battle between the Drekai and the people of Steel Rim. They were probably wondering whether or not to intervene.

They wouldn't have to wonder for long.

I breathed in, readying myself to access my ether. In a sharp movement, I caught both the enforcers by surprise as I yanked my arms free from their silver-gauntleted hands. They recovered quickly, reaching to restrain me once more, but I had the window I needed. Ether flowed through my arms and my eyes flashed gold as I formed my dragonhook spear. It sprouted hor-izontally between both my hands, extending outward so both enforcers had to jump back to avoid getting stabbed. In reality, their silver breastplates would've shattered the starglass spear on impact, but their instinct to dodge had gotten the better of them.

I whirled my weapon above my head, then took off down the street toward the battle.

"Get him!" the older Mage Hunter yelled.

I burned more ether, using levitation to launch myself into the air as I ran. Just in time, too, because Jaira's silver chain whip ripped through the air right where I'd been running. It barely missed catching my feet.

"Not today, Helga!" I called over my shoulder. I did a little flip in the air before touching back down.

"Asher!" I heard my dad's voice coming from back near our house. I didn't look back.

I dashed down a side street, the Mage Hunters hot on my tail, when Solrac appeared at my side, running with me toward the fight.

"Get the Psion, too!" I heard the older Mage Hunter call out. Soon, all three were chasing us down the street.

"How brilliant is this?" Solrac said, only a little out of breath. "If we're lucky, maybe we can get the three of them to join the fight. Then, perhaps the Drekai will do us the honor of slaying them."

"That's fine by me," I said as we got close enough to really see what was going on in the heart of Steel Rim.

The town square had become a bloodbath. Several guard members and a few Drekai lay dead. There were even a few of the Drekai's dragons and armored ridgerunners lying still. For a moment, my heart sank, but then a warm pulse through our bond let me know Thorn was okay. He was circling overhead, looking for Kai.

Drekai were swarming the wide, open square, the cobblestone circle at its center, and the dusty streets. These Drekai looked even fiercer than the illusory one Solrac had made during his meeting with the Knights of the Torch.

Some wore bronze chest plates or held shields, but many wore no armor at all over their wrap tunics and loose pants that tightened at the ankles. Patches of brightly-colored scales grew along their exposed shoulders and elbows, serving as a sort of natural armor. Many had spikes growing along their spines or tails lashing out behind them, and a few even bore large sets of wings. All of them had horns sprouting from their heads, but other than that, they looked completely human.

One Drekai with glowing Sentinel patterns flowing along his arms looked like he was commanding the pack of bronze-armored ridgerunners whose wolf-like jaws snapped at those defending the town. He must have been a Wildshaper.

One of the Drekai used her wide wings to fly into the center of town, landing on the back of Steel Rim's stone dragon buffalo statue. She took a menacing stance and held up her long-handled scimitars, then called out in a booming voice:

"*Miizka kan kun Riiska Zotuuri?*"

I didn't speak fluent Drekai, but my mom had taught me enough that I understood most of those words. She was looking for something.

No, not something. Some*one*.

Riiska Zotuuri.

Black Valkyrie.

Solrac and I looked at each other, and I could tell he understood, too.

Instantly, I was even more on the alert. Was the Black Valkyrie here? Now?

But why? Who could she be after? Honestly, I didn't care. This could be my chance.

The sounds of fighting rose in my ears until Solrac snapped me back to reality.

"Find your friends," he said. "I'll rally the Knights." He saluted me and darted off, firing another crossbow bolt back toward Jaira and her enforcers to slow their pursuit.

It bounced off the shoulder of the redheaded enforcer, not hurting him, but certainly freaking him out. Soot, Solrac was an excellent shot.

I wanted to find the Black Valkyrie here and now, but in my heart I knew I had to find Kai first.

I channeled ether and dashed into the town square, losing the Mage Hunters in the mayhem. Finally, I spotted my best friend by his clunky, excessive armor. He and Kari stood together in front of a group of townspeople, Baron Eidan himself whimpering among them. I recognized him instantly from his balding head and short frame, plus the thin, iron circlet he wore as a crown.

Thorn circled above, unable to dive into the fray without drawing too much fire from the Drekai. I told him to stay back unless I really needed him.

Kai and Kari each held one of Kari's custom-made, round shields, doing their best to protect the people from an attacking Drekai. The Drekai wore a fierce helmet, with holes in the top for his horns to come through. He slammed against their shields using a Drekai *raskalaata*, a heavy war boomerang that doubled as a kind of bludgeoning club.

I drained a little more of my ether as I used my levitation power to hover-run towards them as fast as I could. My chest felt just a little tight as I did—I'd have to be careful with how much ether I used. After all the etherarchy I'd done over the past twenty-four hours, my well wasn't exactly brimming.

I got to Kai and Kari just after the Drekai took another swing, yelling in accented Evgardian as he did so.

"Where is the Black Valkyrie?"

The frightened townspeople cowered while Kai and Kari held their ground.

"She's not here!" Kari yelled back.

The Drekai must've had orders not to take no for an answer, because he roared, swinging his *raskalaata* high above his head for another strike aimed directly at Baron Eidan.

The many times Baron Eidan had tried to get me into trouble with Mage Hunters or sneered at me for being a half-born flashed through my head. Part of me wanted to let the Drekai complete his swing.

But I dashed into the action, using my starglass spear to parry the Drekai's blow. The boomerang was heavy, but starglass was powerful, reinforced by ether. I used my leverage to redirect his strike into the ground, and he snarled at me for getting in his way.

The Drekai dropped his weapon and tried to grapple me with gauntleted hands. I levitated out of reach at the last second.

Out of nowhere, his tail came lashing toward me. There was some kind of blade strapped to its end, and it caught me, cutting a diagonal slash across the right side of my face. It wasn't deep, but red blood dripped down my chin.

Still better than a silvermark.

Before he could come at me again, I hover-darted behind him. I was fast, and with his armor on he didn't have time to turn around before I whacked my spear hard against the back of his helmet.

The Drekai's dragonfire green eyes rolled back in his head, and he crashed to the ground.

"Get out of here," I said to the townspeople, and they were more than happy to oblige.

I pointed to Baron Eidan as he looked up at me with wide eyes.

"You owe me one," I said, raising my eyebrows.

He whimpered, gave a little nod, then scurried away down a side street.

From the center of the town square, once again the winged Drekai woman's voice rose above the sounds of battle.

"Bring us the Black Valkyrie," she boomed in accented Evgardian. "I challenge her to single combat. She loses, she returns to the Dragon Isles with us."

More screams from the citizens of Steel Rim answered her, as did more clanging of scimitars and spears. Why did the Drekai think we were harboring the—

"You want the Black Valkyrie?" a silky, yet forceful voice commanded the town square.

I looked toward the mouth of main street, and so did everyone else. For a moment, the fighting came to a halt.

The cloud cover seemed to part just so the sunlight could shine down onto her and the two Mage Hunters who flanked her on either side. She was probably in her thirties, and steely, gray hair flowed over one shoulder, which indicated snowhead heritage somewhere in her family line. Where most Mage Hunters wore dusk blue cloaks, hers was a rich, velvety black. Even her metal pauldron was painted black, with a symbol of a starswan etched into it in silver. On her left cheekbone was the silvermark of a Psion—a double triangle shape.

The Black Valkyrie.

Her face was proud, with a light in her eyes tipping me off to the fact that she understood the effect she was having, and was enjoying it very much.

"Single combat would be entirely unfair," she declared, raising her black dragonhook spear and pointing it toward the winged Drekai. "I'll take you all."

She dramatically traced a rune in the air with her free hand, and one to match it appeared over her forehead, like a noble crown gracing her brow. Then she looked up and raised her hands. A handful of massive, mirrorlike raindrops fell from the sky, pulsing with violet light as they descended. I recognized it as dream energy, the same kind Kai had used to make his security arch in the den, and the same he drew from to make his illusions.

The drops hit the earth, expanding into mirrored pools filled with purple dream light. From each of the pools came forth the Black Valkyrie's signature ethereal familiars—black starswans.

Five swans rose out of the surrounding pools, glaring out at the crowd with starry, dark eyes as the mirrored puddles dissipated. Until this moment, I didn't realize a swan could look so menacing.

The Black Valkyrie didn't say anything more. Instead, she extended her hands wide on either side, as if to say 'Here I am. Come and get me if you dare.'

My eyes darkened as I gripped my starglass spear. I was ready.

I signaled Thorn through our bond. It was time.

Thorn's reply came back, burning through the bond like a forest fire. I stumbled as he warned me to stop.

The Drekai attacked. A group of them rushed the Black Valkyrie at once, and I saw her smile.

She ignited another golden rune. Then, with flicks from her delicate wrists, she used her telekinetic etherarchy to lift each of the Drekai raiders into the air by their armor or clothing.

They hung there, flailing uselessly as they protested. Then the Black Valkyrie made a pulling motion with her hands, wrenching the Drekai's weapons from them. She dropped each scimitar, boomerang, and warbow to the ground.

Suddenly, I was pretty glad I hadn't rushed in after her myself.

Barely trying to hide how much she was loving this, the Black Valkyrie cocked her head.

"Hmm," she said, and she had everyone nearby so captivated that her voice carried throughout the square. "Would you like to retreat now, or shall we destroy a few dozen of you first?"

More Drekai gave vicious war cries and stormed toward her.

"Fine," she said, raising an eyebrow. Then she lifted a hand high above her head, the Drekai's weapons floating up along with it. I stared in horror as each weapon turned on the Drekai who once wielded it.

The Black Valkyrie closed her fist.

Scimitars slashed the suspended Drekai. The boomerangs swung. The warbows fired. Each of the Drekai fell without another word.

That only riled up the rest of the Drekai. Ruthless vengeance filled their chests.

The Black Valkyrie took a step backward, letting the two Mage Hunters who flanked her have a turn. One was a burly man with a short beard. Angular, golden patterns lit up along his skin just as the first Drekai arrow flew toward his chest. The man gave a small smile, and the flying arrow bounced harmlessly away, breaking then falling to the dusty ground below.

Well, that was pretty impressive.

I took a closer look and noticed a Geomancer's silvermark on the man's cheek. I hadn't met a lot of Geomancers, but I knew they were a type of Sentinel magi that could take on aspects of rocks. I figured this man was using some kind of granite or quartz totem to become hard as stone, protecting him from attacks.

The other Mage Hunter already had a crown-like series of runes up and glowing over his forehead. It was hard to tell from where I stood, but at least one looked like the illusion rune Kai liked to use. He had a silvery snake with purple eyes draped along his shoulders. The light that reflected off of it was purple too. The Mage Hunter raised his silver sword and, together, he and the Geomancer took on the oncoming Drekai, flanking the Black Valkyrie as she fought expertly with her black dragonhook spear.

The Black Valkyrie's starswans flew in with them, stabbing with their beaks and launching shooting stars of purple dream energy at the Drekai.

More Drekai still attacked the town. They looted the nearest businesses and invaded the adobe homes facing the square.

I saw one run up to a humble family home and rip the wooden door off its hinges. Stars, she was strong. Inside, I saw a mother scream as she held her toddler close. Her preteen son stepped in front of them, wielding a kitchen knife. It was my father's friend Korhal's family. They needed help.

I ached to take a stab at the Black Valkyrie, but she was too well-protected right now. Might as well let the Drekai wear her down first.

"Kai!" I yelled out, already on my way to help the defenseless family. Kai followed close behind.

I caught the tail end of the Drekai's words as she yelled at the woman. *"...oliikus tykiia taaza?"*

The woman looked up at her with confused, terrified eyes. I didn't fully understand what she'd said, either. Something about there being emptiness here? Emptiness was the wrong word—it was more like the word 'void.' But what did that mean? I really needed to brush up on my Drekai language skills.

With a jab from my spear, I got the Drekai looking at me instead of Korhal's family.

But that meant the Drekai was looking at me instead of Korhal's family.

Maybe Valla was right—I did make a pretty good distraction.

More of the Drekai's companions had noticed me too. Thorn dove from the sky like a lightning bolt to protect me from behind as I faced off with the first Drekai woman.

The Drekai cried out in rage as red blood seeped into her tunic from where I'd stabbed her. Then she swung her two long-handled scimitars toward me. I swung back, blocking her blows with my spear.

Before she had the chance to make another strike, I burned more ether. I focused my energy, forming clunky, raw starglass all along her swords, throwing off the balance of the weapons. I made them too heavy for her to wield and the clubbed ends hit the ground as she held onto their handles.

I didn't stop. I grew more and more starglass all along the blades, then kept growing it up her arm. She protested and spat at me as she realized she was stuck. My chest felt even tighter than before. That had taken a lot of ether.

I spoke through heavy breaths: "*Akho ralaani kaisehva.*" I was pretty sure that was Drekai for 'sorry about that.'

She gave me an offended glare. Oops. Maybe I'd accidentally told her I was sorry she smelled bad.

I needed to brush up on my Drekai.

In the center of the square near the dragon buffalo statue, I kept tabs on the fight with the Black Valkyrie, watching for an opening. She and her Mage Hunters had taken out several more Drekai and ridgerunners. I noticed Jaira and the two enforcers fighting alongside them now. Lothar kept looking over at the Black Valkyrie every once in a while, an almost worshipful look on his face.

Gross.

Solrac and Valla were over there, too. Solrac had a psionic rune alight on his own forehead as he wielded his runemarked seaxe. He kept shooting blasts of dream energy from the end to knock out his opponents. Valla's swords were a blur. Gold Sentinel-patterned lines flowed from her forearms onto the blades, and she moved with an almost wolflike grace.

Four expert Mage Hunters and one slightly below average one surrounded the Black Valkyrie, not to mention the black starswans and that silver snake. If even Solrac and Valla hadn't landed a shot on her, there was no way I could get in there for a strike of my own.

But still, I had to try.

I was so busy looking for an opening to the Black Valkyrie that I didn't notice the ridgerunner, decked out in Drekai armor, diving toward me.

Barely dodging its charge, I stumbled backward, falling to the ground and dropping my spear. The draconic creature rounded on me, wolfish claws tearing toward my nose.

With a whizzing sound, a large net spread over the ridgerunner. The beast whimpered, then fell to the ground in a tangled heap.

I looked to my left, and there was Kari in a warrior's stance, holding her crazy new crossbow invention.

"Good timing!" I called out.

"It worked," she said, beaming at her weapon with pride.

I was about to tell Thorn to finish off the ridgerunner before it could free itself, but a mountain of red fur was already pouncing on it. His Majesty.

Stars, what a good dog.

Just then, the Drekai woman with the wings—she must've been their leader—yelled again in Drekai.

"*Vitaakya!*"

Retreat.

I guess she'd changed her mind about that whole single combat plan.

The Drekai who hadn't fallen withdrew. Within moments, they had all fled, running or flying toward the badlands to the east.

The dust settled, and suddenly everything was eerily quiet.

I had the distinct feeling of being watched, so I dismissed my spear, my eyes returning to their normal dragonfire green. It didn't seem like the Drekai were coming back. Kai used a hand motion to dissolve all of his dream barriers. People cautiously filtered into the square until at least half the population of Steel Rim had gathered together. They looked at the Black Valkyrie like she was a hero.

If they only knew...

Kai, Kari, and I slipped into the crowd. I didn't want Jaira to notice me, but it seemed she was caught up in the Black Valkyrie's victory as well.

Solrac and Valla had slipped away from the forefront. I scanned the crowd, and sure enough, I spotted Solrac trying to blend in a short distance away, Valla at his side. Solrac was looking intensely toward the Black Valkyrie. But that wasn't strange, since everyone was looking at her.

The strange part was that she was looking back at Solrac.

I couldn't read the emotion behind her midnight blue eyes. For a second, she looked angry. But the next moment, a mask of smug calm took over as she broke eye contact with him.

If I was a betting guy, I'd bet our entire hoard that those two had history.

The Black Valkyrie took a step toward the center of the square, runetracing as she did. It looked like an illusion rune—Kai would know which one specifically.

Then she spoke, her smooth voice amplified to ten times its natural volume.

"People of Steel Rim. You've seen today what comes of letting your magi remain here unchecked."

Kai looked fascinated. Despite what we'd just been through, he whipped out his black notebook and started writing.

"Auditory illusions for amplifying the voice..." he muttered.

Called it.

The Black Valkyrie continued. "You let your magi roam freely. To thrive and multiply. It's a wonder the wild dragons haven't laid waste to Steel Rim already. And now your magi have drawn the wrath of the Drekai upon themselves."

I didn't buy that. If anything, it was the Black Valkyrie who'd drawn the Drekai here. But then again, most here didn't speak Drekai and wouldn't know that as surely as I did.

"Then why are you here? Aren't you a magi yourself, Vidya?"

Solrac's voice rose from the crowd. He had a distinctly self-satisfied grin on his face as he stroked his goatee.

Was that her name? Vidya? So they did have a history. Called it again.

The Black Valkyrie's jaw tensed, and for a second, I saw murder flash in her eyes. But she quickly regained her calm and continued her speech.

"Luckily, I, the Black Valkyrie, and my Mage Hunters arrived in time to save your town from ruin by those barbarians."

"Let me guess, you want us all to bow down in gratitude?"

Solrac laughed loudly and took a mocking bow. The crowd looked uneasy, but I had to hand it to Solrac. It took guts to heckle the Black Valkyrie herself.

The rage boiling behind her eyes told me she wanted nothing more than to throttle the wisecracking noble, but she ignored him and went on.

"Those who surrender the names of Steel Rim's unregistered magi will be richly rewarded." With that, she runetraced, a psionic rune appearing over her forehead. She raised a hand, and a sack of coins jingled as she telekinetically lifted it into the air for all to see.

"Here!"

I jolted when I heard Baron Eidan's hoarse voice call out.

I made eye contact with him from across the square.

No way.

I had literally saved his life minutes ago. He wouldn't...

He pointed to me. "Asher, the half-born, son of Akayto, is a magi!"

Apparently, he would.

That did it. There was no such thing as a good noble.

Those standing nearest me stepped away as the Black Valkyrie followed the baron's pointing finger. When she saw me, she did a double take. Did she remember me from all those years ago? I doubted it.

"Bring Asher forward," the Black Valkyrie said in a hard voice, and one of her Mage Hunter lackeys was at my side in an instant. He wrapped his silver chain whip around my hands, then dragged me to the center of the town square.

The Black Valkyrie telekinetically floated a bag of coins to the greedy hands of Baron Eidan. I glared at him, but he wouldn't make eye contact with me again.

The townspeople watched on as I stood right between the Black Valkyrie and the dragon buffalo statue. Her Mage Hunters stood by so there was nowhere to run. I caught sight of Kai and Kari in the crowd, horrified looks upon their faces. Kai had his notebook out, and it looked like he was desperately trying to think up a plan, but one look told me he had nothing.

"Let the execution of this magi stand as an example for all of you," the Black Valkyrie said, scanning the crowd with narrowed eyes. It was almost like she was looking for someone.

Just then, Thorn dove out from behind a longhouse, intent on saving me. Lothar nodded to a large, deep green evren with a short horn on her nose. The evren sprang into action, intercepting Thorn by using the claws at the corners of each of her four wings to pin him to the ground. She was bigger than Thorn, and must have been on her second ascension. She didn't look happy as she obeyed Lothar's order, and if I had to guess, I'd say the redhead had forced a bond with her by taking her heartscale against her will.

The Black Valkyrie was so close. This was the chance I'd been waiting for. I tucked my thumbs into my palms and began quietly shimmying the silver chain over them. I could feel the cold of the silver through my fingerless climbing gloves.

Kai and Kari were powerless to save me. Solrac probably had the guts to stand up to the Black Valkyrie, but it looked like he and Valla might cut their losses with me. At least Thorn had tried.

No one was going to stop her.

Just like I hadn't stopped her when she'd taken my mother.

"Magi are a danger to Evgard," the Black Valkyrie announced, taking a step toward me and raising her black dragonhook spear. It had a silver swan symbol on it too. Couldn't have her enemies dying without being extra sure who had run them through.

At last, I got the chain over my thumbs. The Black Valkyrie glanced upward, as if searching the skies. Wasn't she after Solrac or Valla? She had seen them already in the crowd, so I wasn't sure who she was searching for.

The chain slid over my knuckles. The Black Valkyrie placed the blade of her spear at my throat, casting one last hopeful look out over the crowd.

Turned out, I didn't care.

The silver chain whip fell to the ground, and my eyes flashed gold. Burning enough ether to send my heart racing, I conjured a new, extra sharp dragonhook spear of my own from starglass.

I windmilled the spear, catching the Black Valkyrie off guard. I knocked her spear from her grasp and sent it clattering to the ground. The crowd gasped.

With a yell that held years of pain and resentment over the loss of my mother, I jumped into the air, spear poised to strike at the Black Valkyrie's blackened heart.

I was too focused to realize she must've runetraced. A casual flick of her wrist wrenched me upward by my turquoise scarf.

I gagged, dropping my weapon in order to grab at the scarf and keep my neck from snapping. My feet flailed stupidly beneath me as I struggled to breathe.

Below me, the Black Valkyrie stuck out her bottom lip in a pout reeking of superiority.

"Astromancer, I see." With one hand she kept me aloft, while with the other she picked up my spear and examined it. "Not a bad one either. And you have spirit. Perhaps we should send you to Evyndara for the magi cure instead."

"No!"

Another voice rose above the shocked murmuring of the crowd. Oh no. Dad.

The rune for the Sight glowed from his forehead, granting a form of vision to his blind eyes.

"I've got another magi for you, Black Valkyrie," Dad shouted. The crowd parted as my dad held up a crossbow and took aim. "Me."

With that, Dad pulled the trigger, firing a bolt straight at the Black Valkyrie.

Chapter 8: Bait

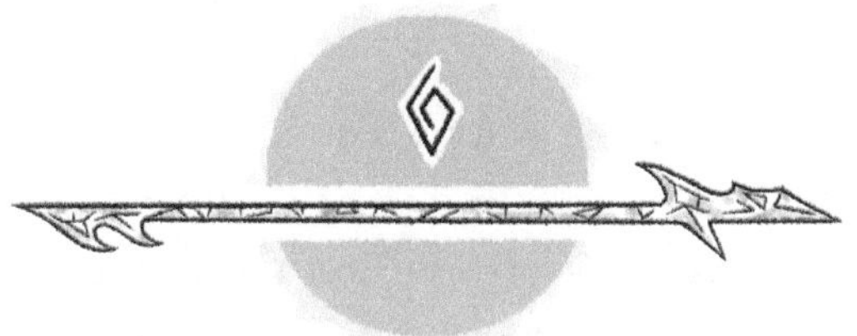

Dad's shot flew true. The Black Valkyrie quickly dropped my spear, thrusting her hand forward to psionically stop the bolt.

She succeeded, stopping dad's bolt mere inches from her chest.

But the bolt's tip didn't stop.

My dad must've been keeping a mageslayer bolt. The tip was silver, impervious to etherarchy, and loosely attached, for situations just like this.

The Black Valkyrie reeled backward as the tip embedded itself in her left shoulder.

She gasped in pain, and all the runes over her forehead vanished. That released her hold on me and I came crashing back to the ground, trying to catch my breath. I noticed one of the Mage Hunters was sweating, panic evident on his face as their leader stumbled backward.

He hurried to steady her, and I realized it was the Mage Hunter who'd had the illusion runes going during the fight with the Drekai. The runes were still glowing over his forehead, pulsing in and out as he tried to catch the Black Valkyrie. His dream snake watched his back.

I clambered to my feet. The Black Valkyrie was wounded—This was my chance.

Apparently, I wasn't the only one who thought so.

Swords raised, Valla was already rushing toward her. Solrac saw Valla rushing through the crowd and called out after her, but she didn't stop.

The Geomancer Mage Hunter leapt into action, blocking Valla.

Valla didn't waste a second. Glowing gold patterns appeared on her hands and face as she drew a throwing knife from her boot and hurled it at the Geomancer. The knife impaled his hand, and he cried out.

But Valla wasn't done. While he writhed over his injured hand, she stabbed him in the chest with her seaxe. He roared, but didn't go down, so she stabbed him twice more.

It was brutal, but finally the Mage Hunter fell. Valla stepped past his body toward the Black Valkyrie, and the illusionist Mage Hunter looked horrified as Valla approached with white, wolfish eyes. His silver snake spat starlike purple dream energy at her. She moved to block it with her blades, but it passed straight through them and hit her. It seemed to drain her energy, but not enough to stop her.

The crowd dispersed, the people of Steel Rim fleeing toward the safety of their homes, while the Knights of the Torch endeavored to regroup.

The Black Valkyrie's eyes still looked dazed, but at the same time surprisingly flat and emotionless.

The older enforcer who'd interrogated me raised a silver sword to cut off Valla's attack, slowing her down. Meanwhile, I picked up my spear from where the Black Valkyrie had dropped it. I was so low on ether. My heart felt tight and weak. Still, I dashed forward and swung at the Black Valkyrie, only to be blocked by Jaira, who'd stepped between us.

Her sword was silver, which made my spear shatter on contact.

Lothar swung at me next, and I tried to levitate out of the way. But with how little ether I had left, my hover jump ended up being more of a sad, little skip. His silver sword raked against my armored jacket, cold silver far too close for comfort.

I was so distracted, I barely felt Glint hop into my boot. But I heard Kai's voice clearly in my mind.

Double trouble, like with Karl, Kai said.

Surprisingly, I understood. Within a second, I saw Kai's illusion ether-archy flickering above me, then a second, illusory Asher stepped from where I stood to just off to the side.

Over my forehead, I saw a faint, golden light. The illusory me had a rune glowing over his head as well, and I realized Kai was tricking the Mage Hunters into thinking I was the one making the illusions.

Jaira and Lothar looked from me to the illusion, unsure of which one to attack. Jaira made a choice, swinging her blade at the fake me. Fake Asher's eyes glowed gold, and he levitated out of the way.

Lothar stood by, jaw hanging open as he watched fake me. He didn't even try to raise his sword.

I pulled out my father's skyseeker dagger and whirled into action. It didn't have as much reach as my spear, but at least it wouldn't shatter on contact with silver.

While fake me distracted Jaira, real me kicked her from behind, sending her sprawling. She dropped her silver sword and ran into Lothar, who dropped his silver chain whip in his attempt to catch her.

With Jaira disarmed, I wasted no time before rushing toward the Black Valkyrie. But Valla was faster. I saw the older enforcer lying dead at her feet as she made the last leap toward the Black Valkyrie, who lay in the arms of the worried-looking Mage Hunter, his dream snake hissing threateningly.

"Valla!" Solrac cried out, his strong reaction giving me pause. But Valla was too focused on her target to notice him. Nor did she notice when Jaira pulled a dagger from a sheath strapped to her thigh. She threw it at Valla at the same moment Solrac jumped between them—as if he'd known what Jaira had been about to do. A psionic rune was alight over his forehead, and he tried to stop the dagger with telekinesis. But the dagger was entirely made of silver, and it embedded itself in his gut.

Solrac doubled over in pain as Valla slashed toward the Black Valkyrie with her seaxes, her blades aimed straight for her neck.

As Valla's blades made contact, the Black Valkyrie exploded in a burst of a million black feathers.

Valla and I stumbled backward as feathers erupted from where the Black Valkyrie's body had just been. Then, one by one, the feathers disappeared in tiny blinks of purple light.

Even Jaira and Lothar looked dumbfounded. Jaira reached toward a feather as it vanished into violet nothingness.

"What in the void?" Valla said, frustrated and confused.

"Not the void. Astra, the dream realm..." Solrac muttered, clutching his stomach. "Drak. That wasn't Vidya. It was one of her starswans wearing an illusion."

"A powerful illusion," Valla said.

"Although," Solrac said, grunting in pain. "If I had to guess, I'd say she was still controlling the swan. But she's no illusionist. Someone else must've been working it..."

We all looked toward the Mage Hunter who'd been holding the Black Valkyrie—or rather her starswan illusion. Sure enough, the complex series of illusion runes over the Mage Hunter's forehead had winked out. The silvermark on his cheek was that of a Seer, which meant he was a Mystic—he was definitely the one responsible for the trick. He looked nervous and exhausted.

"Solrac," Valla said, finally realizing how badly he was wounded.

He grunted but managed a weak smile.

"Don't worry about me," he said. "This is actually the best thing that could've happened..."

"Why?"

"Because... I've been wanting a new... silver dagger..."

Then Solrac stumbled, eyes losing focus as he fell. Valla caught him.

Meanwhile, the illusionist Mage Hunter held out some kind of smooth, white gemstone. Golden runes glowed up from it.

Suddenly, the rock cracked. A golden beam of light shot upward from the stone, then split, forming a long rip in the air. Golden light rimmed the tear, but inside was pure white.

I recognized it instantly. It was a rift—a portal. This was the kind of etherarchy my dad could do.

That stone... it must be a Rifter's anchor.

The illusionist Mage Hunter grabbed his fallen partner's body—it was a miracle he could lift the Geomancer's heavy-looking form—then pulled both of them through the rift. His snake hissed one last time, the purple interior of its mouth visible. Jaira and Lothar followed close behind. The green evren flew through too, swift as a bat.

It hit me that this was my last chance. These Mage Hunters would know where the Black Valkyrie was—the real Black Valkyrie, not some starswan illusion.

Not thinking super clearly, I moved to follow them. If I could jump through after them, maybe I could still get to the Black Valkyrie...

Lothar's boot disappeared into the whiteness, and I reached out after him.

But before I could reach the rift, Thorn intercepted me. He narrowed his dragonfire green eyes as he stood firmly between me and the portal. Through the bond, I felt a warning flare as my wyvern urged me not to be stupid.

Behind him, the gold-rimmed portal closed in on itself and winked out.

There was no way to know where the exit rift was. The Mage Hunters were gone.

It was probably for the best. Thinking about it for half a second made me realize just how stupid following all those Mage Hunters would've been. I sent a flare of gratitude to Thorn, and he nuzzled me with his serpentine nose.

Now that the action was over, a wave of exhaustion flooded over me. My heart felt shaky and strained from how much ether I'd used in the past forty-eight hours. The Mage Hunters would've killed me without so much as a proper fight if I'd gotten through.

Valla held Solrac in her arms as his eyes fluttered. It looked as if he was trying to regain consciousness, but he just couldn't fully open his eyes.

Valla laid him down, then looked around. She spotted a tan-cloaked member of Baron Eidan's personal guard and grabbed him by the scruff of his cloak.

"Get a medical zone set up for the wounded. Don't just stand there! Go, now."

The guard nodded frantically, then scurried off, either to fulfill Valla's demand or else to run as far away from her as possible. His Majesty was already at Solrac's side, nuzzling him with his nose. Valla knelt near Solrac as well, golden patterns glowing across and around her hands as she used her Sentinel regeneration powers to tend to his wound. Her etherarchy wouldn't be able to do a lot since the wound had been made by a silver dagger.

She looked at me with something like respect, then nodded. She may not have liked me at first, but she and I shared something deeper now. A desire to rid the world of a brutal tyrant.

I sat on the ground, barely able to stand. I saw Kari with my dad, helping organize the Knights of the Torch to tend to the wounded. My dad seemed to be looking for me, the Sight rune still glowing above his forehead. I waved to him—I wondered what a wave looked like to a blind man using the Sight—and he looked relieved to see I was alright.

"Asher," Kai appeared at my side, dark eyes wide with worry.

"What is it?" Despite my fatigue, I prepared to burn the last dregs from my ether well. Thorn limped to my side, gold patterns tracing along his wings and neck, healing him from where the large, second ascension evren's wing-claws had held him down.

Kai swallowed.

"I just sent Glint to check on the hoard. Asher, it's gone. The money, the dragon eggs. Everything in the den—It's completely gone."

As exhausted as we were, we climbed on Thorn and flew to the sand-stone ridges of his den. He could barely lift Kai and me. We stumbled off his back and staggered into the den.

I almost tripped on the rocks at the mouth. Glint the mirror gecko stood on top of the boulder that normally guarded our hoard, jumping up and down.

Thorn joined us, and emotions from my wyvern flooded into me through the bond: Fiery rage at the thought of intruders entering our cave. Protective energy as he searched for the clutch of dragon eggs. Then, dim coals of disappointment.

Kai was right—The eggs were gone.

I looked around the den. Sure enough, someone had pushed the boulder aside, revealing the empty cache that had once held every valuable we owned.

The only thing left in the den was the scratchy prison shirt from Whitestone Hall I'd left there the night before. I cursed myself—had whoever robbed the den used it to track us?

A wave of emptiness hit me, too. Our savings were supposed to be enough to send my dad to Skygard. Kai and Kari, too. They were supposed to be going there. To safety.

On the ground at the cave entrance, something caught my eye. I'd been so focused on Thorn's emotions that I hadn't noticed it on the way in, but now I went over to the dusty rocks and picked up a small, folded piece of parchment.

I opened the sheet and found a note written in an elegant, curling script. It was a little hard for me to read, but I managed to decipher it.

Thank you for the coin and dragon eggs. The Mage Hunters will find great use for them.

At the bottom of the page was a black insignia in the shape of a swan.

I had no doubt who had left this letter.

The Black Valkyrie.

For the second time in my life, she'd taken everything from me.

I fell to my knees, letting the note flutter to the ground. I stared blankly ahead, unable to fully process what had just happened. This couldn't be real.

Thorn sent me a glow of sorrow and guilt. He felt responsible for failing to guard the eggs. I looked into his green eyes and tried to emote back to let him know it wasn't his fault. I didn't blame him.

I blamed *her.*

Kai stared at the empty den. He slowly stood and silently meandered around the cave, looking for anything the Black Valkyrie might have left behind. But there was nothing. She'd taken it all.

Angry fire like I'd never felt before rose from my very core. The Black Valkyrie couldn't be allowed to wander the realms unchecked, able to take whatever she wanted, kill whoever she wanted. Nobody was willing to stop her. Those who tried to got themselves killed.

I was ready to pay that price.

I got to my feet. My face determined, I headed for the entrance to the cave.

"Where are you going?" Kai's voice echoed in the emptiness behind me, but I didn't stop.

"I'm going to find Solrac," I answered. "The Knights of the Torch were keeping watch on her movements. He'll know where to find her."

Some of the Knights had turned the Drunken Drake's tavern room into an impromptu medical zone. A couple of medics tended to the wounded, who sat or lay wherever there was space. Some had their injuries wrapped at tables; others applied poultices while resting on woven blankets in corners or along the edges of the walls. Families and others gathered around their loved ones, so there was a general uproar inside the drake-skeleton bar.

A couple Knights of the Torch who'd been in the meeting were holding a ravenhelm and a set of gleaming, silver enforcer's armor. It was from the female Mage Hunter who'd interrogated me—the one Valla had killed. I couldn't blame the Knights for taking the valuable armor.

Kari was sitting near the bar, examining a long, silver chain whip. For a second, I wondered if she'd looted the fallen enforcer's body as well, but then I remembered the moment during the battle when the redheaded Mage Hunter had dropped his weapon. Kari must've picked it up.

Near where she sat, Kai and I found Solrac lying on a wide bench, Valla on a short stool by his side. A couple of other Knights hovered nearby.

To my surprise, my dad stood with them as well, leaning against the wall and talking to Valla in hushed tones.

I barged in.

"I need to talk to Solrac," I announced. Valla immediately shushed me.

"You wake him, you die," she said.

"But—"

She gave me a stern look, and I shut my mouth. I'd seen what she did to those Mage Hunters.

I whispered. "What are you doing here, Dad? Do you and Valla know each other?"

Valla cocked her head. "Akayto's your father?"

"That's right," Dad said with an audacious, over-the-top wink.

"That makes sense," Valla muttered almost inaudibly.

"You're in the Knights of the Torch, aren't you, Akayto?" Kai said, realization dawning on his face.

"Solrac would like that," Dad said, keeping his voice low. "I hear he's recruiting again."

"When isn't he recruiting?" Kari whispered, and Valla shrugged in agreement.

I was confused. "You knew about all this? About Kari going to meetings?"

Dad nodded. "Kaidan, Kalari, and I ran into Solrac when he was in Steel Rim a little over a decade ago now, if I'm remembering correctly."

Valla gave a single nod. Dad continued, speaking even more quietly so that nobody else would hear us.

"Kaidan and Kalari liked what he had to say. Told us about how the Knights of the Torch fought for a better Evgard for magi. Kai had just started manifesting his powers, so they joined up. Thought it'd give Kai his best chance at growing up safe."

Kai's brow furrowed. I wondered what he was thinking.

"Zerana didn't like it," Dad said, and I bristled a little at the mention of my mom's name. "She worried the Knights weren't as strong as they needed to be to make a difference. And she felt some members at the time were dealing in... dark etherarchy."

"Dark etherarchy?" Kai said.

"I'm not sure what she meant. But she had reservations, that's for sure. About one member in particular."

Valla's eyes darkened. "Vidya."

Vidya. Wasn't that the name Solrac had called the Black Valkyrie?

Wait... so that meant...

"The Black Valkyrie was in the Knights of the Torch?" I said, disgust filling my voice.

Dad nodded. "Yes. Turned out, Zerana's instincts were right. The Black Valkyrie returned to Steel Rim to bring in Zerana later. That's when..."

Dad's blank eyes filmed over, and he turned away to hide his tears.

"That's when the Black Valkyrie killed Mom," I finished, more anger rising in my chest.

Dad nodded. "Vidya and her Mage Hunters claimed your mom was plotting against Evgard with the Drekai. Zerana was a half-born, so it was easy to find an excuse to get rid of her."

I felt a hand on my shoulder. I turned and saw Kari, looking me in the eye and breathing deeply. She was trying to calm me down. I didn't want to calm down.

"So what was the Black Valkyrie doing in Steel Rim today?" Kai asked.

"Solrac has a theory," Valla said. "He thinks she's after the Farseer."

"The Farseer?" Kari repeated. "In Steel Rim?"

"We were with him at his hut three nights past near Naga Bay," Valla said. "An army of Mage Hunters led the chase, following us to get to the Farseer. She wants him dead."

I shuddered a little. Everyone had heard of the Farseer, the legendary soothsayer who could see all. According to local lore, the Farseer had been alive since our ancestors first came to Evgard on their skystone-powered skyboats. The myths all said he was a noble protector of magi.

Apparently, the Knights thought he was more than just a legendary figure. And so did the Black Valkyrie. I mean, Valla said that she and Solrac had even met him. I didn't realize the Farseer was someone you could just visit like that.

"Vidya thought that by executing a sad, wimpy little magi boy in front of a crowd, she'd draw out the Farseer himself," Valla said matter-of-factly.

"Excuse me?" I protested.

"Solrac's convinced she wasn't really going to kill you, Asher. He thinks it was all a plot to get the Farseer to intervene." She stared me dead in the eye. "I, on the other hand, think she was absolutely going to kill you."

"Same," I shrugged.

"What about the Drekai?" Kai asked. "What brought them to Steel Rim?"

"It's all about the egg," a croak came from the bench by the wall as Solrac struggled to sit up.

"I will kill all of you," Valla glared at each one of us in turn, as if any of us were responsible for waking Solrac.

Solrac winced as he clutched at his side. They'd washed and bandaged his wound, but it still looked like he was in a lot of pain. Valla's regeneration could only do so much for a wound inflicted by silver.

"The egg?" Kai prompted.

"The true dragon egg King Rodan stole from the Dragon Isles," Solrac said as Valla helped him sit up. "The Drekai are void-bent on keeping it out of Vidya's hands. And they're right. If she and the Mage Hunters get their hands on a true dragon, we're all doomed."

I didn't like thinking about it. The Black Valkyrie was already too powerful. The last thing I wanted was for her to have one of the most powerful creatures in all of Evgard at her beck and call.

Kai was scratching some notes now, and piped up. "So both the Drekai and the Knights of the Torch want the egg. Why don't we all just work together? We'd be stronger against the Black Valkyrie and increase our odds of success."

Solrac laughed, which made his wound bleed through the bandages. That made Valla swear at Kai.

When Solrac regained composure, he answered. "Clearly, you're a generation or two removed from those who fought in the Dragon Wars. Drekai and Evgardians don't really mix."

I flinched at that, and so did Dad. Nobody else seemed to bat an eye. I guess none of theirs were dragonfire green.

"No," Solrac said with a shake of his head. "That's why we need to steal the egg before Vidya can cook up a reason to take it, or the Drekai overwhelm the city. We need to cross the Scar and get to Keep Drakfell, where King Rodan has the egg under lock and key. We'll need to put together the right team to pull this off. Myself, Valla, and His Majesty, of course."

I jumped as the bloodhusky rose from under the bench where Solrac lay. His Majesty barked loudly. He caught sight of me and licked my hand. I scratched him behind the ears.

Solrac went on. "We'll need to send word to Boone and Jax—that is, the *real* Boone and Jax. We'll need their finesse and muscle to pull this off."

Kari stepped forward. "I want to come too. I can help with weapons and armor."

"You'll be a valuable asset on the team, Kari." Solrac nodded.

Kai cast a worried look at Kari before stepping forward himself.

"I want to come too."

Kari protested. "Kai, no. It's too dangerous."

"That's why I'm not letting you go alone."

"Excellent," Solrac smiled. "We could use an illusionist like Kai. Especially if Vidya has one on her team strong enough to pull off that starswan facade. We'll have to fight fire with fire. You're in, Kai."

Kai gulped, but nodded.

At last, Solrac's gaze settled on me.

"We could use a good distraction," he said with a wide smile.

"No," Dad spoke up. "Asher, please. I learned long ago I can't control you, but I'm begging you. For your mom's sake, don't go."

I looked into my dad's pleading, unseeing eyes. Sightless, because of the Black Valkyrie.

I thought of Thorn's den. The money and treasure that Kai and I had worked so hard for years to save. Gone, because of the Black Valkyrie.

Then I remembered that day three years ago. Mom had been tending the cactus garden out front. I'd been practicing with starglass on the porch.

The Black Valkyrie had come alone. Mom saw her approach and hurried to get me inside the house. I watched everything from the window.

The Black Valkyrie ordered Mom to come with her. As an unregistered magi, Mom was required to accompany the Black Valkyrie to Evyndara to receive the new so-called magi cure. She had Mom in silver manacles. Now I knew how she'd known Mom was a Shadowbinder in the first place.

Dad had fought back. He'd pulled out a crossbow and taken a shot at the Black Valkyrie, just like in the town square today. Only that bolt hadn't been silver-tipped.

The Black Valkyrie had used her psionic power to stop the bolt by simply raising her hand. She'd thrown the crossbow from Dad's hands with more telekinesis. Dad had reached up to runetrace. He was probably going to use his powerful rifting etherarchy to portal the Black Valkyrie far, far away from there.

But she'd seen it coming. With a burst of purple dream energy, the Black Valkyrie shot Dad, directly in the eyes. Rifters can't teleport to places they can't see.

The blow blinded my father and knocked him out. No doubt trying to protect me and my dad, Mom went with the Black Valkyrie peacefully that day. My dad would've followed, would've saved her, but he didn't know how to use the Sight so well back then. We received word of her death within two weeks.

I'd done nothing.

I'd watched my mom go to her death that day. My mom was dead because of the Black Valkyrie.

I looked up at my dad, then at Solrac.

"I'm in."

Dad looked down. I knew I was breaking his heart. But I had no choice. This mission would get me close enough to the Black Valkyrie to finally do something. I had to go.

Solrac nodded, looking around at his team.

"Take the day to rest and get some sleep. Top off your ether wells at the ether vent in the hideout if you can. We leave at dawn."

Vision 2

Solrac sat inside the secret planning room of the Knights of the Torch in the basement of Steel Rim's tavern, the Drunken Drake. Valla stood at his side.

Solrac pulled the slender bone hoop from the pocket of his tunic. The gold threads of the dreamweb shone with light, along with the runemarked crystal at its center.

"You don't have the strength," Valla warned. "Not with your wound."

"But I must find the strength," Solrac replied, holding up the dreamweb. "If we're to make a plan of our own to get that egg, we must ask the Farseer if he has any information on King Rodan's plans."

"We can call upon the Farseer later, when you're well."

"No," Solrac insisted. "I want to spend our travel time planning. We must contact him now."

He stubbornly held up the dreamweb between himself and Valla. He runetraced with his off hand, and a golden dreamweave rune appeared over his forehead.

Purple smoke began to swirl around the dreamweb, surrounding Solrac and Valla. It wasn't warm nor cool, but carried the faint scent of lavender.

As the smoke hit them, their eyes glazed over. From the outside, it looked as if the two of them were in a trance. Meanwhile, their spirits remained fully awake and active as their minds entered a dreamlike state.

The spirit of the Farseer was there, standing tall before them. His red robes flowed outward as he clutched his staff, his eyes white and glowing from within his hood, his skystone at his forehead. The mythraven ruffled its feathers as it perched atop his staff.

"Solrac, Duke of Glacia, and Valla of White Cliff," the Farseer nodded to each of them in turn. "What is it you seek?"

"We must know of King Rodan's plans for the egg," Solrac responded. Back inside his physical body, sweat formed at his temples from the effort of calling upon the Farseer. Valla's spirit cast his spirit a worried look.

"And fast," Valla put in. "If that's not too much trouble, oh Great Farseer."

"No trouble at all," the Farseer replied, gesturing grandly to the smoke at his feet.

From within the smoke, a vision gradually materialized.

A stately council chamber with a long table in the center appeared. Proud stone walls with tan tapestries bore the dragon fang crest of Drakfell.

The candles that provided light for the people sitting at council burned low. The meeting must have gone late into the night.

At the head of the room, a majestic white drake slept, tired from his daily labors to keep the keepdom safe. King Rodan's stormscale drake, Rex.

"The Drekai are moving in on Keep Drakfell," the Captain of the Guard said, the bags heavy under her eyes.

"Yet they don't attack," King Rodan replied, stroking his short, black beard. "Perhaps they don't know it was me who stole their egg?" White streaked his hair at his temples and hairline, not signs of aging, but remnants of snowhead heritage. A simple steel crown rested upon his brow.

At his side, Queen Liana, with flowing dark hair and a delicate crown, laughed. "That might've been a possibility, my love, if you hadn't insisted on donning your bright white ascension armor and holding up the egg for all to see on your way home."

Snickers came from around the table.

"I enjoy my ascension armor," King Rodan mumbled.

"And I'm not complaining," Queen Liana said, placing a hand on his chest. "You look good in white."

The queen gave her husband a somewhat provocative look, and the Captain of the Guard cleared her throat.

"Perhaps we can return to our strategy?"

"Of course," King Rodan said, straightening up.

"We'll need to draft more soldiers into the guard," the Captain of the Guard continued. "If we are to stand a chance against the increased skyfalls and the dragons they bring, and now the Drekai, should they choose to attack."

"The instances of shadow wasting are increasing as well. Soon our registered Lightwielders won't be able to make enough liquid light," another advisor added.

"Let's hope the egg convinces High King Magnus to come to our aid," Rodan added. "He's neglected to reply to our requests, though I can't understand why."

"I just received word from my family in Skygard of rumors on that score," Queen Liana said. "My cousins seem to think that the High King's son has been taken ill."

"That's no excuse for neglecting a keepdom in need," King Rodan countered.

"Even if the high prince is sick with the shadow wasting himself?"

A hush fell over the room. From their places watching the vision from the Drunken Drake basement, Solrac and Valla exchanged troubled looks. They remembered the strange scene the Farseer had shown them in the woods. The omenfire had depicted High Prince Mason, followed by a flash of bright blue lightning. But what did it mean?

"And what of the Farseer? Rumor says you've been meeting with him," the Captain of the Guard accused.

"And what if I have? I will do whatever it takes to save our keepdom," Rodan said, silencing the room.

There was a dark tension for a moment, broken by a younger advisor.

"What about a bond? With a true dragon fighting at our side, the Drekai would be more hesitant to attack. And Evgard would finally have to take us seriously."

"I've tried bonding the egg," King Rodan said somberly. "It will not choose me."

"Nor me," the Captain said in a rush. "Nor any of my commanders. We can always force the bond—"

"No," a new voice spoke up. With dark, white-streaked hair, a short beard, and bright, topaz eyes, he looked very much like the king, though his sword was a more reasonable size. He wore ascension armor of his own in red, purple, and black.

"Who's that?" Valla's voice overlaid the vision.

"Aradan," Solrac answered. "King Rodan's brother, and the head dragon keeper for Keep Drakfell."

"Hush," the Farseer complained, refocusing Solrac and Valla on the vision before them.

"I must strongly advise against a forced bond," Aradan said, bringing a hand down sharply onto the table. "Such a dragon is never happy."

"Who cares if the dragon is happy so long as it's obedient?" The Captain of the Guard crossed her arms.

"For one thing, the dragon cares. It *will* make it weaker."

"Enough," Queen Liana spoke up. "I have the solution to all of Drakfell's difficulties."

The room quieted, and everyone stared at the queen.

With a smile, she spread her hands. "We throw a party."

Everyone kept staring, and the sound of a spiny cricket could be heard faintly from the window.

"Excuse me, your highness," the Captain of the Guard said skeptically. "But... a party?"

Queen Liana nodded eagerly. "A grand gala to honor the egg. We'll send out invitations to all the nobility across Drakfell. First, those closest to us will try their hand at bonding the egg. Then, if a bond still hasn't been made, we'll send every member of our guard through in hopes of the true dragon choosing one of them. It will be great fun. I have just the dress for it—it matches your ascension armor, my king."

She winked, and King Rodan blushed. Solrac and Valla got the feeling he was excited about the dress.

The Captain of the Guard seemed to be mulling it over. "That's actually not a terrible plan. It will maximize our chances of bonding the egg naturally."

She nodded to Aradan.

"And hopefully give us time to increase the guard's numbers sufficiently before the Drekai can move more of their forces to the mainland," the Dragon Keeper approved.

"Then it's decided," King Rodan said firmly. "On the eve of the Summer Solstice, Drakfell will host a gala to honor the true dragon egg. This will gain us a bonded true dragon and the support we so desperately need from Evgard."

"No, that's too soon," the Captain of the Guard objected. "We need time for more nobility abroad to come."

"Fair enough," Queen Liana said. "We will host a gala for the true dragon egg in two months' time." She nodded curtly at the Captain of the Guard.

"And if the egg still doesn't bond anyone willingly? Do we force the bond then?" the Captain of the Guard asked, almost eagerly.

King Rodan looked down. "Perhaps."

Suddenly, a man at the far end of the table stood. He was very tall and thin, with knobby knuckles and sunken cheeks, one of which bore a Woodweaver's silvermark. He must've been Keep Drakfell's High Mage. His long, elegant staff, adorned with amber crystals, had begun flashing with etherlight.

"Your highnesses," he said, narrowing his eyes. He seemed to be looking directly at Solrac and Valla.

"I believe we are being watched," the man said. "Quickly, put on your silver circlets."

The man put on a pair of gloves, then passed out thin, silver crowns to everyone seated at the table. As King Rodan and the rest placed them on their heads, blotches of darkness appeared over the vision.

Soon, all went black, leaving the Farseer's smoke void of any visions. The Farseer looked down at Solrac and Valla.

"What excellent information," Solrac said with a grin.

"We'll need to be careful of their High Mage," Valla said, absently touching the handle of her seaxe. "He's too observant for his own good."

"We can handle him," Solrac assured her. "But at least now we know what we must do. Valla, dust off your ball gown. We've got two months before we sneak ourselves into that party and steal the true dragon egg."

Chapter 9: The Scar

Most of Drakfell was dry badlands, but the Scar took 'desert' to a whole new level.

The Scar lay between the cliffs of Steel Rim and the inland Dragonstorm Sea that separated the west from Keep Drakfell, the capital of the Badlands Keepdom. The wasteland was so vast that even when I'd looked at it from Thorn's back, high above Steel Rim's Smoky Peaks, I couldn't see the end of it. Only certain groups of nomads were crazy enough to travel through the Scar.

From what I'd seen, everything in the Scar was the same shade of drab light tan. Craggy, stony rock formations rose up every once in a while, but it was mostly dry, sandy, nothingness. I'd heard that whatever vegetation was resilient enough to grow amidst the stale earth was quickly eaten by oversized sand rats, which were in turn eaten by rattledrakes. Those creatures were quickly eaten by the Scar's real predators: wild dragons, sandsharks, and dreklings. And those were only the beasts I'd heard of.

Needless to say, most travelers went south through Rattledrake Pass and around the Smoky Peaks to avoid Drakfell's armpit. Only the truly desperate crossed the Scar.

Naturally, we were saddling up to go. We didn't have time for a leisurely journey—we had to get to that true dragon egg before the Black Valkyrie could find a way to steal it for her own nefarious purposes.

Outside the Drunken Drake, Kari sat hunched over a long piece of wood, vigorously rubbing some sort of long, yellowish stick against its flat surface. When I asked what she was doing, she barely looked up to let me know she was coating the wood with wax from scale bees. A little later, I saw her attach the smooth, waxy wood to the bottom of some kind of sand sled which she and Valla hooked onto the back of His Majesty. The bloodhusky barked, eager to begin the journey as we loaded up the sled with supplies—mostly water, though I was sure to pack some extra pieces of drakalope jerky for Thorn.

I was just as anxious as His Majesty to get started. A much needed night's sleep had refilled my ether well, and after throwing some spare socks into a satchel, I was ready. Judging by the numerous items still to go on Kai's packing list, not to mention the stacks of books he was meticulously trying to squeeze into his bag, I had some time to kill.

Thorn must've realized that too, because he began flying loops in the air as I held on tightly to his saddle. He sent me a feeling of warm longing through our bond, and I knew exactly where he wanted to go before we said goodbye to Steel Rim.

Together, we flew to the top of Steel Rim's highest cliff. Looking east, we saw the Scar. But my favorite view was to the north.

A secluded valley sat nestled between the cliffs, surrounded by high, rocky ridges. The valley itself was the greenest thing around for miles, with tall grasses waving beside a clear, blue lake. From up here, I could see a couple of dragon buffalo grazing on the array of colorful wildflowers below.

Mom and I used to hike up the rugged, dry cliffside in order to get a look at the verdant valley. It was hard to get into the valley without flying or using archonic levitation powers, which is how Mom and I had been able to find it in the first place. Sometimes we would bring a picnic and sit on the edge of the steep mountains to enjoy the view.

Once when I was about twelve, I'd wanted to move into the valley. I'd thought we could build a home right there among the lush grasses. Nobody would try to hurt us just because we were magi. We could hunt the buffalo and drink from the lake. It sounded pretty perfect to me then.

Mom said that sounded nice. But she preferred to look at the valley from above without going down into it. She loved how pristine and natural it was, untouched.

Thorn sent me a feeling like longing embers through our bond as I remembered my mom. I wished he'd had a chance to meet her, and I could tell he felt the same.

I inhaled deeply, looking over our valley. Sweet fragrances from the wildflowers rose up to meet me, and a cool breeze from the lake rustled my hair, pulling it loose from its knot.

A tiny figure drew my attention toward an outcropping partway up the cliffside. The jutting stone had been my mom's favorite spot to sit and think. She called it '*Kiivi Zariika*,' which was Drekai for 'Cozy Rock.' Some of her favorite cactus varieties grew just a short distance beyond that spot.

It was my dad's favorite place to go now and, of course, he was sitting there now, waiting for me to notice him.

He must've known I'd come to Mom's valley one last time before leaving. Part of me wanted to pretend I hadn't noticed him sitting there—it would be easy, since Dad couldn't see, and I didn't know how far out his ether sight went—but I knew he felt we needed to talk. Besides, I couldn't leave without saying goodbye.

"Might as well get this over with," I muttered to Thorn as we flew his way. Through our bond, I felt a sensation like sparking coals, and I could tell my dragon was reminding me to be more positive.

Thorn and I landed on an open patch of ground near *Kiivi Zariika*, and I climbed up to join my Dad. I could hear him quietly speaking, and I noticed the Mystic rune for the Sight glowing over his forehead. He must've thought he was communicating with Mom in Etheria now. I bit my tongue to avoid letting him know just how crazy I thought that was. Now wasn't the time to start a fight.

Dad must've heard me approaching, because he hurriedly said goodbye. He left the rune glowing over his forehead so that he could see my aura as I sat beside him on the outcropping.

We sat for a few moments in silence, me looking over the valley with physical eyes while Dad looked it over with ethereal ones.

Finally, Dad spoke. "You better watch yourself on your trip."

"Says the blind man," I replied with a jab from my elbow.

"Exactly. I can't, so you'd better do it yourself, eh?"

Dad turned toward me with the same lopsided smile I had. I knew it killed him that he couldn't come along with us. But I'd overheard Dad talking with Solrac last night. Solrac had convinced him he'd be better off helping the Knights of the Torch in Steel Rim until we'd succeeded in stealing the true dragon egg. Dad agreed that it was for the best; after all, he would only slow the team down. I'd been worried about Dad staying in Steel Rim now that he'd revealed his etherarchy during the fight with the Black Valkyrie. But Dad assured me that he could buy a few months of Baron Eidan's silence. Dad planned to give the Baron the bragging rights that came with mounting a certain giant craghopper's head on his royal wall.

"In all seriousness, though," Dad's smile faded. "I know I can't stop you from going with the Knights. I learned a long time ago that I can't control your choices."

I folded my arms, listening.

Dad continued. "Just... Don't let anyone else control your choices, either. Those are yours. You are as free as you choose to be."

"Okay," I said, not entirely sure what he was getting at. "Thanks, Dad."

"I have something for you," he added, tracing another rune in the air. The corresponding rune appeared over his forehead, and a tiny, golden crack appeared in the air before him.

Dad reached through the micro-portal and into his rift hold, an ethereal pocket he used to store things. When he pulled out his hand, he held six runemarked stones, three white and three black.

"Are those..." I started.

"Rift anchors," Dad confirmed. "Took me a while to get them right, but they should work in the hands of anyone who can channel ether, not just Rifters like me. They come in pairs."

Dad laid out the stones on the ground before me, shuffling them so that each white anchor corresponded to a black one. I noticed little marks scratched into the sides to mark the pairs.

"The white ones open an entrance portal. Keep those close to you," Dad explained. "The black ones are exit portals. Put those wherever you need to go. You never know when they'll come in handy."

Dad collected the stones and handed them to me. Before I could slip them into my satchel, Dad took one of the black ones back and held it close.

"This one stays with me. You have the entrance, but I want you to always have a way back home when you need it."

When I looked into Dad's eyes, they were glassy. Against my will, a film of tears formed over my own eyes too.

I scooted closer to Dad and wrapped my arms around him. He squeezed me back.

"Mom says she'll be keeping an eye on you," Dad said. I bristled a little, but didn't say anything.

Kai had probably completed his extensive packing list by now. I let Thorn know through the bond that it was time to go.

Dad and I said one last goodbye before Thorn and I took off.

I turned in my saddle, getting one last look over the valley. A pang of worry struck me, and I wondered if I'd ever see this place again.

It was hard to believe that just on the other side of this beautiful wonder was the bleak, desolate Scar.

Thorn and I glided along the cliffside back toward the group, landing next to Kai, who was busy adjusting the massive backpack he wore over his clunky armor. He was considering a final backup quill, then added it to his pack as we landed.

"Don't tell me you're going to wear all of that through the Scar," I said with a snort.

Kai glared. "You won't be laughing when I'm protected while the dreklings tear you limb from limb."

I shrugged. "I'll take my chances."

"You really shouldn't be flying right now. Thorn needs to save his energy. What were you doing up there, anyway?"

"Nothing," I said, grabbing some jerky from my satchel and taking a bite before transferring the satchel to Thorn's saddlebags. The rift anchors were hidden safely inside. Even Kai didn't know about the valley, and for whatever reason, I wanted it to stay that way.

He didn't press me further. Instead, he pulled out his black notebook and began writing.

I peeked over his shoulder, and saw that he'd written Solrac and Valla's names, along with the names 'Boone' and 'Jax' on the next page. When Kai saw me looking, he shut the book.

"What's this?" I asked with a grin.

"Shh," Kai put a finger to his lips. "I'm keeping a journal of observations about everyone Solrac put on the team."

"Why?"

"Just because, okay? I want to be sure of whom we're working for. Why they're all here. Who we can trust."

"True. Solrac is nobility, so we automatically have to assume he's a terrible person," I half-joked.

"Not only that, but in addition to my suspicions of him, we're going to want to know more about Boone and Jax when they join us. We also need to learn about Solrac's history with the Black Valkyrie."

Now that actually seemed like a pretty good idea. Maybe I could find out more about her weaknesses. I needed to learn everything I could—not to mention improve my fighting skills for when I got another chance to take her down.

"I've actually got a theory on Valla," Kai said, quietly so that he wouldn't alert the Wildshaper woman that we were talking about her.

"Oh? So, what motivates her? Thirst for blood? Extreme sketchiness?"

"Based on her determined attack pattern from yesterday's battle, I think she's here for the same reason as you are."

"And what's that?"

"She wants to see the Black Valkyrie dead."

I looked over toward Valla, who was securing supplies to His Majesty's nomad-style sled. Her array of silver scars caught the bright daylight. I wondered where she'd gotten them.

Maybe I wasn't the only one the Black Valkyrie had left her mark on.

Day one traveling in the Scar was awesome. Harsh sunlight beamed down on us as Thorn and I led the way east. Thorn wanted me to ride him the whole time as we journeyed, but Kai was right. Thorn really struggled to carry more than two riders at a time, and crossing the Scar would take time. He needed to save his strength, so we all walked.

Behind us came Kai and Kari, each carrying a small pack. Valla and His Majesty were next, the bloodhusky pulling the nomad sled Kari had modified for the sand. His Majesty was a big dog, but we'd still packed only the essentials. A lightweight tent in case of sandstorms and enough food and water to get us to the other side. Valla had traveled through the Scar several times, so she knew what we needed. Still, the biggest thing on the sled was Solrac himself.

Solrac had tried walking this morning, but despite Valla's attempts to heal him with her Sentinel's regeneration powers, his injury was still no better. Valla said that meant Jaira's blade had been made of pure silver rather than an alloy, which meant it would take longer for the silver's ether-blocking properties to work its way out of Solrac's system.

Still, he did his best to make the most of the situation, insisting that the injury was the 'best thing that could've possibly happened.' Not only did Solrac have a shiny new dagger sheathed at his side, but Solrac was certain that with his injury, the Black Valkyrie's team would think they had a huge advantage.

The way I saw it, they did.

But that didn't take the wind out of my sails as we embarked on our mission. Thorn and I often flew ahead of the group, trying to get a better view of the upcoming rock formations. I wondered when we were going to see some dreklings or maybe some of those sandsharks everyone was always talking about.

Eventually, as the sun began to set, I fell into step with Valla. Now might be a good time to do some digging.

"So," I began. "I can't help but notice you and the Black Valkyrie aren't exactly the best of friends."

Valla growled at me out of the corner of her mouth.

"Oh, come on," I said. "What'd she do? Burn your village? Kill your dog? Steal your boyfriend?"

"Stop!" Valla called out, loudly enough for the whole group to hear. Everyone turned to her, and Solrac stirred from where he was sleeping on the sled.

I pressed her. "What? Whatever it is, I approve."

"Shut your obnoxious mouth, or I'll slice it off your face," Valla threatened, then turned away from me and addressed the group. "We need to make camp for the night."

Without so much as another glance my way, Valla began unpacking the sled. I guessed that meant our conversation was over.

We set up camp in a sandy area beside a large, craggy rock. Once we got the tent set up, Valla directed Thorn to breathe a jet of lime green fire into a small circle of tan desert stones. Not a moment too soon, because once the sun set behind the distant cliffs of my hometown, the air got chilly.

We sat around the fire as Valla passed out rations of dry bread and jerky. It wasn't the fanciest of meals, but I was ravenous and didn't complain.

Kai looked absolutely exhausted. I was pretty sure his tunic was covered in sweat under all that armor. He pulled out a canteen of water and took a tiny sip from it.

Valla noticed. "Kai, have you been drinking enough?"

Kai tried to nod. "Been taking small drinks every now and then. To conserve it."

Valla exhaled deeply. "You need to drink more at a time so you don't get sun fever. Also, unless you want to lose every ounce of water in your body to sweat, you need to lose the armor."

"Can't. Protection. Dreklings. Wild dragons."

"For a smart kid, you're really stupid. Lose the armor."

"Can he at least put it on the sled for His Majesty to pull?" I chimed in, coming to Kai's defense.

His Majesty perked up at the sound of his name.

"No," Valla said. "His Majesty is pulling enough."

"Try this," Kari said, getting up and helping her brother slip out of his heavy pauldrons and chestplate. She stacked the armor on the inside of Kai's ridgeshield. Then she pulled out a length of rope from her own pack and tied it to the shield. She practiced pulling it along the sand a couple of times. It worked pretty well, the centerline of the shield helping the makeshift sled slide.

"It's not a perfect solution," Kari said. "But it'll keep you from dying out there, little bro."

Kai nodded, then took a medium sip of water. He didn't even stop her from patting his head. He must've been exhausted.

A huge yawn came from the sand sled. "What'd I miss?" Solrac stretched, then winced as he felt at his wound.

"Valla's just playing babysitter," I said with a chuckle.

"And hating every minute of it," Valla glared at me.

"I have just the solution to bring a more cheery spirit to the camp," Solrac said, rummaging through his pack. He pulled out a small wooden lute.

"No," Valla said. "You need to save your strength."

"What I need is to show you all the song I've been working on in my head as I rested."

With that, he runetraced, a golden psionic rune appearing over his forehead. With a gesture from his hand, Solrac telekinetically lifted the lute into the air and it began to play itself.

The sand seemed to dampen the sound of the plucked notes, which made them sound lonely. Somehow, that feeling fit, with the five of us plus His Majesty and Thorn, sitting small and alone in the bleak, moonlit wasteland of the Scar.

Solrac began singing, his voice rich and confident as it accompanied the lute.

The Scar is stretching on and on
But our Knights know no fear
In fact, we've faced a greater foe
Than any we have here
We've slain Drekai, Enforcers too
And though this desert's the hottest
We've fought far more and still prevailed

Against that dark, feathered goddess

Our team, though small, is strong and bright
And we know what to do
For fighting through the shadow's fear
Akayto's blind shot flew true
Swift Valla's blade did most of all
Kai and Kari quick reacting
Thorn and His Majesty kept guard
While Asher was distracting

And in the end, we won our fight
Though in all the confusion
We were distressed to find that we'd
Been fighting an illusion
Still, we will win, though we fight foes
Far greater than a Kraken,
And in the end, it's us who'll steal
The egg of the true dragon

His last note lingered in the stillness, punctuated by the howl of a distant ridgerunner. We shared a moment of pleasant silence before getting ready for bed.

We pulled tightly-wrapped bedrolls from our packs. We each found places all around the dying embers of the campfire.

Within moments, Kai, Kari, and Valla were sound asleep. Even Thorn snored softly as he lay curled up beside one wall of the large rock.

I was about to lay out my things and sleep as well, but I noticed Solrac still sitting up on the sled.

I made my way over to him and took a seat. One thing I'd learned from hunting craghoppers was how important it was to know my enemy.

I was about to casually strike up a conversation about Solrac's old pal, the Black Valkyrie, when he did it for me.

"Vidya's not as dark and evil as you think, you know," Solrac said, the last flickers of firelight catching in his brown eyes.

"My dead mother would argue otherwise," I answered, though I wasn't entirely sure if that was true. Part of me wondered if even after all the Black Valkyrie had done, Mom would've still tried to think the best of her.

"Fair," Solrac muttered with a sad half-smile.

"How do you know her? The Black Valkyrie?"

"Don't call her that," Solrac said, and for a moment, something sharp and serious replaced his usual lighthearted tone. "Using that title only gives her more power. Adds to this character she's created. But that's not the real her. Beneath it all, she's still Vidya, and using her name will weaken her."

I could get behind that.

"Vidya," I repeated, the name sounding strange on my tongue. "Tell me about her."

Solrac relaxed as he began, his eyes lighting up a little.

"We met when we were both still teenagers. I was the spoiled Heir Duke of Glacia, while she was a runaway from some noble family in Keep Evgard. They'd found out she was a Psion, and planned to have one of their servants join the guard to serve as Vidya's proxy. The proxy soldier would pay off Vidya's debt to society—the debt owed for being born a magi—while Vidya herself languished under lock and key for three years."

As Solrac spoke, he absently traced a simple illusion rune, employing the same etherarchy he'd used back in the Drunken Drake to make a small, illusory Drekai on the map. This time, his fingers formed the likeness of a girl. She had steely gray hair and looked about fourteen years old. She wasn't wearing black, and without an air of superiority in her dark blue eyes, I almost didn't recognize the Black Valkyrie.

Or rather, Vidya.

Solrac held the illusion in the palm of his hand. His Majesty, who'd been curled up by Solrac's feet, sat up when he saw the tiny illusory Vidya. He panted gleefully.

Huh. Maybe His Majesty wasn't as good a judge of character as I'd thought.

"Neither of us was happy with our lot," Solrac went on. "So when we met, we ran away together. The circus was in town, and we figured what better place for a couple of misfits like us. I sang and told stories, and she was an amazing acrobat."

The little Vidya illusion did a backflip in Solrac's palm, followed by a complicated tumbling routine up his forearm.

"Sometimes we'd perform together in plays the company put on. I was alright, but Vidya's acting was really something else."

He got a faraway look in his eye, and it hit me like a disgusting ton of bricks.

Solrac had been in love with her.

Maybe he still was.

I tried not to get sick to my stomach as Solrac longingly watched his illusion leap back onto his palm, then smile and wave to an invisible crowd.

"She loved creating new characters," Solrac said. "Sometimes she took it too far. Once, she got so into her role as a farmhand that the company almost left her behind. We couldn't find her for a day, but eventually discovered she'd been living in a pen of wyvernhogs on a ranch outside the city."

Solrac laughed, recalling the memory. Then his smile faded.

"That's what I worry about most: that this whole Black Valkyrie persona is just another character she's lost herself in. That woman giving overblown speeches in Steel Rim... that's not the Vidya I know."

Solrac closed his fist, and the illusory Vidya burst in a golden shower of etherdust.

"That doesn't excuse her from all the things she's done," I said. "She's killed hundreds of innocent magi, Solrac."

Solrac sighed, and for a split second something sinister flashed in his eyes. I subtly scooted a half-inch away, worried he was going to attack me or something.

But as quickly as the darkness had come, it was gone. Solrac gave one of his big, overdone grins.

"Best get yourself to sleep, Asher. My wound's acting up and I couldn't sleep if I tried, so I'll take first watch."

With that, he slapped me on the back just a little too hard.

I arranged my bedroll beside Thorn and closed my eyes. He shifted, covering me with his wing. Even with his added warmth shielding me from the cold desert night, sleep didn't come to me for a long time. I secretly wished my mother were here to sing me her old dragon's lullaby to help me relax.

When I finally drifted off, evil, black swans turned backflips in my dreams.

Day two in the Scar was a little monotonous. Turned out there wasn't much out here besides craggy, tan rocks and dry, tan sand.

Kai did better dragging his armor behind him than he did wearing it, but he still looked pretty exhausted.

Thorn was excited when we found a massive sandshark skeleton, which was by far the most interesting thing to happen all day. It was three times longer than Thorn from tail to jaw, with four rows of razor sharp teeth. Valla pulled one of the teeth out and put it in her pack. Probably to make into a Wildshaper's totem later. Although, the thought of Valla wildshaping into something as deadly as a sandshark with geomancy powers sent shivers up my spine.

Day three in the Scar convinced me that deserts are the most dull places in existence.

Day four in the desert, I discovered the darkest danger in the dunes. Boredom. If I had to stare at another tan colored rock or another stretch of endless sand dunes, I was going to throttle myself.

Thorn tried to help me pass the time as we slogged on. We played a game where I'd walk behind Kai. Every once in a while, I'd burn ether and shoot a tiny bit of starglass onto his right boot.

After a few hours of this, Kai started inexplicably veering to the right as he walked. He'd notice once he got far enough away from the group, then hurry back to correct his course.

Through our bond, Thorn laughed hysterically every time Kai veered off track. It was the most entertaining thing out here, so I kept adding more and more starglass to Kai's right boot.

Eventually, Kari noticed the chunk of white, solid ether coating her brother's shoe and alerted him to my crime. Kai didn't talk to me for the rest of the day.

Days five and six in the Scar blended together. But on the sixth night, a roaring sound cut through the dark sky above us. A fiery meteor fell over our heads, landing several miles to the east along our path with a soft, distant thud. Thorn gazed in its direction as an odd longing, almost like hunger, pulsed through our bond.

"That skyfall was close," Kai said.

"Too close," Valla grumbled. "We'll have to take a detour in order to avoid it."

"Should I fly over there and see if I can find us some skystone?" I asked. I'd never actually seen a skyfall up close before.

Valla gave me an annoyed glare. "Sure. That is, if you're interested in getting yourself killed. Dreklings are probably hatching and swarming the area as we speak."

She pointedly brushed past me as she adjusted our course southeast.

Day seven in the Scar began as mind-numbingly as any other. We passed by more rocks and sand, broken up by the occasional tumbleweed.

I fell into a pattern of shooting little bursts of starglass at the runners under His Majesty's sand sled. Kari had rubbed the wooden planks with beeswax, but when I hit them with extra smooth starglass, they slid along the sand even more effectively. Every time His Majesty went over a dune, he didn't even have to pull on the way down.

I was just about bored and reckless enough to see what would happen if I secretly added starglass to Valla's right boot, when Kari cried out.

Kari was at the front of the group, waist deep in sand and sinking fast. The sand that was swallowing her up looked exactly the same as the rest of the Scar's sands, but clearly this was some kind of quicksand.

"Kari, grab hold," Valla called out, falling onto her belly and reaching out a hand.

"Can't reach!" Kari said, panic rising in her voice. "We need some kind of—"

But the last half of Kari's sentence was muffled as the sand pulled her in. Only her hand stuck out over the top now.

I leapt toward Kari, eyes blazing gold. Using levitation, I skidded along the top of the quicksand, grabbing Kari's hand just as she was about to slip under.

Right away, the sand pulled my arm in up to my elbow, but I held fast to Kari. I yanked with all my might, channeling levitation etherarchy through my arm and focusing it on Kari.

I don't know why I did it, it just felt right. Ether flowed through my fingertips until all at once, Kari came flying out of the sand, propelled by my archonic levitation powers. Another breakthrough.

Together we rolled, dusty sand puffing up around us. I pulled Kari along as we scrambled back toward safer sands.

Kari coughed and gasped for air. Kai was at her side in a flash, a hand on her back. She seemed shaken up, but otherwise unharmed.

I couldn't say the same for our supplies.

The extra smooth starglass I'd added to the sled had done its job too well. His Majesty howled as the sled slid down a dune toward the quicksand. At least a couple of bedrolls and the tent slipped off along the way.

Solrac sprang into action, flinging himself off of the sled and onto the safe sand, slashing the ties to His Majesty to free him from the sled. Solrac cried out in pain as the jump reopened his wound.

The sled disappeared into the sand, a jet of sand shooting up where it sank out of sight. Solrac tried to runetrace, but by the time he got a telekinetic rune up and running, the sled was gone. The Scar had swallowed up all but a small bit of our supplies.

"Drak, Asher!" Valla cursed at me, her eyes storming. "Your sooty starglass is what made the sled slip into the jetsands."

"I was just trying to help," I said weakly.

"You were impulsive and foolish."

Thorn jumped between Valla and me and gave her a warning growl as he narrowed his green eyes. I tried to calm him down through our bond, but Valla was fuming and Thorn didn't back down.

"It's alright," Solrac said with a grunt as he held his side. "This is actually the best thing that could've happened."

"Not even you can spin this," Valla hissed.

"No, no," Solrac said. "Things are going to be just fine."

"How do you figure? We're in the dead middle of the drakking Scar, surrounded by jetsands, with only the water and supplies on our backs."

"At least we have backup," Solrac said, pointing upward to the east.

We followed his gaze, and there in the sky was a bright white burst of ether. It exploded in a star-like shower of white and gold light. Another bolt like a comet launched from the ground below the first one, bursting the same way as the first.

"That's Boone, alright," Solrac said. "He and Jax are close. And it looks like they're in trouble. That's Boone's distress signal."

Valla paled. "It looks like they're right where that skyfall landed. We'll never reach them in time."

"Maybe I can," I raised a hand. "Thorn and I."

"Brilliant," Solrac clapped his hands. "Go quickly. It would be quite distressing if my friends were to die a horrible death in the Scar because you didn't arrive fast enough. We'll find our way around the jetsands and meet you there."

He didn't have to tell me twice. Valla still looked like she wanted to gut me like a wingtrout.

I swung a leg over Thorn's back and prepared to take off.

"Asher," Kai called. "Take Glint."

The little dreambeast scurried up my foot and dove into my boot.

I nodded to Kai, then focused on the white and gold ether explosions occurring several dunes and rock formations eastward.

Finally, something exciting. I mean, people's lives were in danger, so I tried not to get too thrilled, but I couldn't hide my smile. I felt a warm glow from Thorn as well, and I couldn't tell if he was more excited about exploring the skyfall or the prospect of a fight. Maybe both.

"Come on, Thorn," I said, swinging my leg over his saddle. "Let's fly."

Chapter 10: Mud Pots

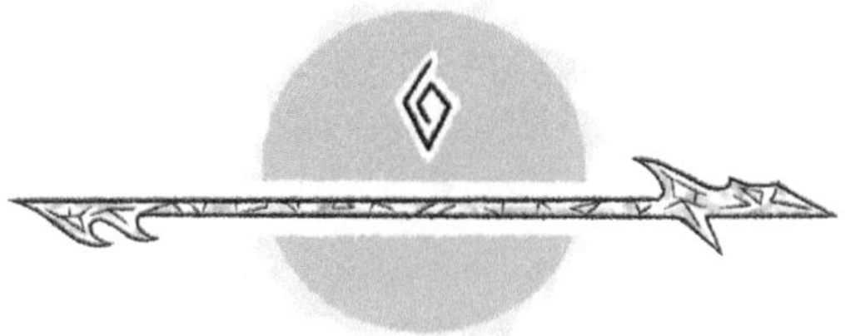

The smell hit me long before I got to Boone's signal. It was like a wyvernhog had snuck into a drakehen coop and broken all the eggs, then left them rotting for a week. I recognized the smell as sulphur and pulled my turquoise bandana up over my nose to try and soften it. It didn't help much.

We rushed over the barren Scar. Except for one particularly weird looking cactus, everything looked so similar. The only real landmark I could pinpoint was the tall, squarish mountain with a feature jutting out from it that reminded me of a drake horn, rising among the flatlands just to the north.

After about ten minutes, we came up on the source of the flare. A long, tapered skid mark ran beneath us across the land, and I realized we were flying over the path the skyfall had taken when it hit last night. Sure enough, the marred earth ended in an enormous crater.

The meteor had landed on the edge of the source of the sulphuric stink. A whitish gray bed of mud pots lay steaming next to the crater. Some of the earth here was cracked and dry, but there were at least a dozen large, circular pustules of boiling white mud. The largest one was the size of a pond, deep below a huge, caked pile of dried mud that rose over it like a cliff.

The liquid mud was slowly collapsing into the crater, burying the meteor. So much for trying to snag a skystone.

Backed against the gargantuan mud pot was a trio of desperate-looking people fighting for their lives. A horde of dreklings from the sky-fall—at least twenty—wielded crude weapons made of old dry desert wood or jagged pieces of their own eggshells.

I'd only seen a drekling up close once before. One had tried to break into our home when I was young. Dreklings were like wild dragons—they wanted to devour every drop of ether they could find. Mom and Dad had fought the thing off. There was still a coppery stain outside our window from where they'd spilt its blood.

These dreklings looked a lot like that one. Hunched creatures with draconic faces and arms long enough to almost drag along the ground when they ran. They had clawed feet and hands, and scaly bodies. Some grew spines along their backs, and they all had long, lashing tails.

As far as I knew, they couldn't speak. They communicated with each other using some kind of otherworldly gurgling that reminded me of metal grating against stone. Some said they were a kind of Drekai, but they were nothing alike—these things were completely inhuman.

As Thorn and I descended, we got our first look at the real Boone and Jax. They looked exactly like the illusions Kai had used when we'd infiltrated the Knights of the Torch's meeting at the Drunken Drake.

Boone was tough and wiry, with tan, leathery skin and short white, snowhead hair. He wielded a pair of curved-gripped daggers with forward pointing blades. As I watched, he shot jets of pure ether off the ends of each of them. Both blasts hit true, white ether burns spiraling onto the nearest drekling's chest. Wherever the ether darts hit overloaded the drekling's nerves. With Boone's precision, its heart stopped as it fell to the ground.

Now *that* was some astromancy. I made a mental note to ask Boone for some tips if we made it out of this alive.

Kai had nailed the details of Jax's appearance, too, right down to the maroon bandana wrapped around his head. Gray hair stuck out from the bandana at wild angles, and the guy's muscles were out of this world. He'd clearly ripped the sleeves off his buckskin tunic in order to better show off those shoulders. A psionic rune glowed over his forehead as he telekinetically pushed and pulled a pair of fanged battleaxes to fight off the dreklings.

The third person was completely unexpected.

Her long, dark red hair whipped behind her as she brandished her spear against the dreklings. Her face was fierce and her stance strong. A Soleian sun-shaped necklace flashed, standing out against her outlander's dragonleather armor. She stabbed at an oncoming drekling, catching it in the chest. She swung to redirect the beast's momentum, sending it to a scalding death in the boiling mud pot behind her.

She wiped sweat off her forehead with the back of her hand as she looked around for her next victim, and for a second I felt like the world had stopped moving.

She was awesome.

I didn't realize I'd slowed our descent until Thorn sent me a feeling like a poke from a hot needle. Right. Focus.

These people needed help.

We flew in fast, and I burned ether to form my starglass dragonhook spear. A hulking, manic drekling lunged toward Boone while his fight with another drekling distracted him. I leaped off of Thorn's back and used the hook of my spear to wrench the drekling away before it could take a bite out of Boone.

The drekling made a choking sound as it noticed its own copper blood flowing from the leg I'd snagged. It howled, turning its energy on me.

I windmilled my spear, hitting it in the chest and taking it down.

Boone gave a whoop when he saw what I'd done.

"Well, ain't this a critter-killin' time! Thank you kindly, stranger!"

His northern accent was even stronger than the one I'd used back at the tavern, but I realized I'd actually done a pretty good job of matching its gravelliness.

I gave him a smile and a salute. Then, almost unconsciously, I looked over my shoulder to see if the redheaded girl had seen me take down the drekling.

If she had, she was occupied now. She slashed with her spear, and for the first time I noticed a strip of curling, dark shadowfire that lined the edge of her blade.

My heart almost stopped.

The girl was a Shadowbinder.

Just like Mom had been.

Sure enough, the girl's eyes glowed gold as her spear arced through the air, keeping several dreklings at bay. The shadow-edge hit one drekling's arm, and I saw the etherarchy start eating away at the beast's scaly hide.

Yep, that was a shadowblade alright. Mom had used one all the time, her shadowbinding powers eating away at grime or other messes around the house. A couple times, like when that drekling had come for us, I'd seen her use a shadowblade just like this one.

This girl just kept getting cooler.

"Duck, Dragon-boy!" Jax yelled at me. I had just enough time to heed his warning before one of his telekinetically-charged axes went flying over my head, embedding itself in a drekling's shoulder.

That drekling had almost taken me out. I needed to focus.

Thorn was doing his part, swooping in like a falcondrake and grabbing a drekling by his clawed feet. The creature squirmed and chortled as Thorn flew up, dropping it into one of the boiling mud pots below.

I gripped my starglass spear while the others fought on. Together, we downed drekling after drekling, killing some and tossing others, wailing, into the mud. But the more we battled the dreklings, the more seemed to appear. Just our luck that this was a particularly massive skyfall—most only brought three or so dreklings.

I realized they were emerging from holes in the piles of cooler dried mud. They must've already burrowed here and started a hive after the skyfall.

To the side, Thorn swooped in to grab another drekling—but they were ready for him. When he flew low enough, three of them leaped and grabbed onto him, trying to hold him down.

Thorn roared, and I felt his rage through our bond as the dreklings dragged him toward one of the boiling mud pots. I raced toward him, my spear jabbing into the one holding Thorn by the neck.

The mud pot beside Thorn roiled, and an enormous, grayish bubble burst, sending white hot mud soaring into the thin skin of Thorn's wing. He bellowed in pain, as with a mighty thrash he freed himself from the dreklings. He swung his bladed tail, flinging the other two dreklings into the mud pot. We'd already killed so many, but more and more dreklings came creeping out of the hollow pockets in the caked piles of dried mud.

Glowing golden patterns traced themselves onto Thorn's wing, the skin there healing as more dreklings battered at his shoulders and tail.

"There are too many of them," the redheaded girl shouted as she dispatched another drekling.

Boone shouted as he shot off more ether bolts. "I'll be a drakpat before I go down to a scorchin' swarm of dreklings!"

But Boone looked like he was slowing down. Sweat beaded on his forehead, and the golden etherlight in his eyes flickered.

Jax looked like he was going to black out any minute from ether overuse. I watched as he used his Psion powers to heft a gigantic, muddy boulder the size of me into the air. With a grunt, he telekinetically hurled it toward four oncoming dreklings.

The dreklings got squashed, but Jax's eyes rolled back in his head as his rune went out and he fell to the ground, passed out. Blood started trickling from his nose.

"Scorch, Jax! Ain't that just a fine kettle of nagas," Boone growled. "Now we gotta haul your sorry hide outta here on top of it all. We should leave him behind for that, right, Shaya?"

"Not on your life," the redheaded girl answered with an angry slash from her shadowblade spear.

"Aww, you're no fun," Boone grumbled.

So that was her name. Shaya.

Thorn gave a pained whimper, which once again brought me back to reality. His wing looked fit for flying again, but more dreklings were coming at him. He'd taken too many hits to the tail and leg. The uncanny mutterings of the dreklings grew louder as more and more crawled out of the dried mud.

Shaya looked over at me, taking down another drekling with her shadow-bladed spear. "Well, stranger, thanks for helping, but it looks like we're still gonna die."

"Maybe not," I called back, trying to think like Kai.

I looked past the sea of dreklings to the towering mud piles and an idea crossed my mind.

A truly terrible idea.

"Get Jax onto my wyvern's back!" I shouted. "Then follow me!"

I dove to Thorn's side, driving the dreklings back with my spear.

Out of options, Shaya kept the dreklings at bay while Boone helped me heft Jax's limp body—stars, this guy was heavy—onto Thorn. I burned ether, and formed patches of starglass in key places around Jax's sides, legs, and shoulders, molding it to Thorn's saddle.

"No pressure," Shaya called out as yet more dreklings came for us. "But... *pressure.*"

"Ready," I said once Jax was somewhat secure. "Now, come on!"

Though almost a dozen dreklings lay dead on the cracked surface along the mud bank, there had to be at least thirty live ones preparing to rush us. A swarm stood between us and the largest boiling mud pot.

And more were still coming.

Naturally, I charged forward, rushing right into the middle of the pack.

That caught the dreklings off guard, especially when my vicious wyvern came darting through along with me. The dreklings cleared a space for just long enough for us to get through.

Their surprise didn't last long. Within seconds, Thorn, Boone, Shaya, and I had a snarling mob of dreklings in hot pursuit.

"Where in the void are we going?" Shaya said as we ran side by side. "We can't outrun them."

"Don't have to," I answered, steering us up the side of the tallest dried mud pile. The chalky mud broke underfoot as we climbed.

It didn't take long to reach the top. We halted, the brittle, dried mud breaking up beneath our feet as we looked out over the largest and deadliest boiling mud pot of all. Thick, white hot sludge splashed up all around.

The dreklings arrived behind us. I brandished my spear, driving them back, then threw it into the mass of them. They stopped, then looked at us, ready to charge. Shaya gave me a perplexed look.

I gave her a wide, lopsided grin.

"Jump!" I yelled, grabbing her hand on one side and Boone's on the other before leaping off the top of the fast-eroding pile.

Shaya screamed. Boone laughed. Thorn leaped as well.

To my pleasure, the dreklings had been following us closely enough that they didn't have time to stop. They skidded off the edge right along with us.

The boiling mud fast approached below, the heat rising up to greet us.

Then, I burned ether.

My eyes blazed gold as I levitated. Just like I'd done in the quicksand with Kari, I let the ether flow through me and into the others so they levitated alongside me.

The levitation gave us just enough of a boost to skim over top of the boiling bubbles of deadly mud.

I couldn't say the same for the dreklings.

They fell and disappeared into the mudpots, splashing at our heels. I could feel the mud burning my boots, and I hoped Glint was safe in there.

Thorn was still recovering from his injuries, so he spread his wings to catch the heat from the mud pot, gliding well enough to keep himself and Jax from falling in. Shaya and Boone caught on to my levitation strategy, and burned ether of their own to aid in it.

Every Archon could levitate, but not all of them were good at it. Boone hovered strongly by my side, but Shaya seemed to be struggling. I held more tightly to her hand.

We made it to the other side of the boiling, muddy pond. Almost all the dreklings had fallen in, thanks to the dried mud cliff crumbling under their weight and dumping them all into the mud pot. The few who were left hollered and squealed in anger from the other side.

We'd made it out.

Breathing heavily, Boone clapped a hand onto my shoulder.

"That," he said, dark eyebrows lowering over his serious face, "was stupider than a draccoon drunk on draquila. But I'll be scorched if it ain't worked."

I smiled, then looked to Shaya, wondering what she'd thought of my stunt.

Instead of gazing upon me with admiration, she was at Thorn's side, checking on Jax. She placed a hand gently over his forehead.

"How's our reckless Psion?" Boone growled.

"He'll live," Shaya said, sounding more annoyed than relieved.

"Good. Now..." Boone said, turning to me. He casually placed a hand on one of the daggers now sheathed at his hip.

"What's yer name, stranger? And more importantly, who sent you?"

I held up my hands to show I wasn't an enemy. "Asher of Steel Rim. Solrac sent me. He and Valla are just over those dunes, ten minutes as the wyvern flies."

Boone almost looked convinced, but he narrowed his already squinting eyes.

"The Hunter's Torch is lit again?" I added with a shrug.

Boone relaxed and nodded. He thrust out a hand and I took it, clasping at the forearm.

"Thanks for your service, fellow Knight."

It surprised me how good it felt when he said that. Like I belonged to something.

Just then, a couple of dreklings let out loud, otherworldly wails from the other side of the pond. It looked like they were starting to wonder if they could make their way around to get another bite at us.

Boone set his jaw. "Best make like a drakalope and dart. Where'd ya say Solrac and Valla were at?"

With Thorn unable to carry us all, I led the group southwest back the way I'd thought we'd flown. But before long, a rustling in my boot made me stop.

Glint popped out, looking a little shaken up after that fight with the dreklings. She crawled her way up to my hand with her little, webbed feet. I was glad to see she was okay.

Asher, you alright? Kai's voice spoke in my mind.

Fine. Found Boone and Jax. And a girl traveling with them...

I tried to keep my mind from latching onto Shaya. How skilled she was with a spear, and the way her eyes stormed as she used shadowfire. The way her hair whipped out behind her like a deep red extension of the wind. The way it felt when I'd held her hand as we'd jumped off the mud cliff...

Oops.

Well, okay then, Kai thought, intrigued by my interest.

Found that Jax guy though, I thought, deflecting. *We'll have to mess with Kari about the sleeves he lost on his tunic.*

Ugh. Anyway, Kai continued. *Valla says to find a safe place to make camp, then have Boone send up another flare. Kari found a way around the jetsands. We're on our way to you.*

I agreed, then Glint cut off the connection. I relayed the message to Boone and the others.

Boone chose a place beside a large cluster of cacti to make camp. The cacti grew in patches, with a flat sandy area in the middle. The tallest clump of the spiny plant made a patch of shade just large enough for Boone. He lay down with his head against a rock, wrapped his dragonscale cloak around him like a loose blanket, then pulled the tan bandana around his neck up over his eyes.

He was out within seconds, snoring softly. Impressive. I guess after our fight with the dreklings, he'd earned some rest.

But adrenaline was still coursing through me.

Jax was just starting to come to. I dissolved the starglass that secured him to Thorn's back and he slid to the ground, rubbing at his temples. He half-heartedly listened as I brought him up to speed.

"Whatever, Dragon-boy," he muttered, sitting down beside a cactus of his own and massaging the sides of his head with two fingers.

Thorn curled up as well, closing his eyes. Through our bond, a feeling like a bed of coals let me know he was going to try to rest and let his Sentinel etherarchy get to work on regenerating his wounds. He'd really taken the brunt of the hits for us. Glowing, angular golden lines traced their way around his injuries.

Glint hopped out of my boot and found a nice spot to lie down in Thorn's shade.

That left me and Shaya.

My heart skipped a little at the thought, and Thorn must've caught on to my quick surge of emotion. He sent me a fiery chuckle through our bond and melodramatically averted his gaze to give us privacy.

I did my best to smooth the longer hair on the top of my head, pulling it back into its knot. Then I stepped into place beside her.

"So, Shaya the Shadowbinder?"

She chuckled a little. "What gave it away? Could it have been the shadowfire on the edge of my spear?"

"That helped a little, yeah," I laughed.

She smiled widely, and the corners of her eyes crinkled. She looked like she smiled a lot.

Shaya stuck out her chin as she stared off into the distance, almost as if she were evaluating something. She cocked her head, and I followed her gaze toward that towering, square-shaped mountain with a horn formation.

Shaya was so transfixed by the mountain, I couldn't help but smile as I stepped directly between it and her.

"Excuse me," Shaya said. She had a light eastern accent.

"You're excused." I crossed my arms.

Shaya tapped a finger on her chin. "The other Knights that are going to meet us—it'll probably take the rest of the afternoon for them to get here."

"Probably, yeah."

Shaya grinned widely. "See Kaliiko Mountain over there?"

I nodded, translating the Drekai word for 'chief' in my head. Her excited energy was contagious.

Shaya put a hand on her hip. "I'm gonna go climb it."

I glanced back at the mountain, its flat top reaching high into the air above the Scar. From where we stood, it wasn't too far off. Maybe a few hours.

I looked back at Shaya's eager face. Her bright eyes were light brown, with tiny flecks of blue in them. They reminded me of earth and sky.

"I'm in," I said.

Shaya raised an eyebrow. "Sure you can keep up?"

"Of course."

"I'm coming too," a voice said from behind me. When I looked, Jax stood a couple of feet away. His eyes were still half closed. His nose had stopped bleeding, but it was pretty obvious his ether overuse headache was still taking a lot out of him.

"Oh, no you don't," Shaya said, grabbing Jax by the shoulders and turning him around. "You're going to lie down in the cactus shade and rest like Boone."

"But—"

"No buts. Drink from your canteen and try to sleep off that headache. I'll be back to check on you soon."

Jax grumbled something unintelligible, but Shaya had given the order with such authority that he obeyed. But just before going back to his shade patch, he looked from Shaya to me and gave me a not-so-subtle glare.

I didn't know their history, but if I had to guess, I'd say Jax had a little bit of a crush on Shaya. He probably wasn't thrilled about the idea of Shaya spending the afternoon with me.

But I was.

"Come on," Shaya smiled up at me as she hurried toward the mountain. Thorn reassured me he could watch over the group as they recovered, egging me on with a suggestive tilt of his head. I laughed and took off after Shaya.

We couldn't find a trail when we got to the base of the mountain. We had no gear and no plan—just my style, and I had a feeling it was hers as well.

The mountainside was slightly less dry than the majority of the desert. Scrubby bushes, creeping cacti, and gray oak trees with pale green, spiny leaves sprang up all throughout the dirt and stone.

We both felt a sense of urgency as we hiked. Something inside us was driving us to reach the highest point on the boxy mountain.

While we traversed the craggy inclines, searching for the fastest way up and hovering-climbing where necessary, Shaya told me about how she'd met

Boone and Jax. Mage Hunters had captured her, and were taking her to a cell in Ghost Lake's prison. They'd been about to silvermark her when Boone and Jax broke in and got her out. From there, she'd used her shadowbinding to assist them on their mission to retrieve information on the magi cure, which had resulted in their needing to fight some kind of abnormally powerful drake.

"I grew up hearing tales of the Knights of the Torch," Shaya said as we hiked. "Although the way my family talked about them wasn't exactly positive. With them, everything was always by the book, which meant buying into Evgard's anti-magi propaganda. My older sisters… well, they're Mage Hunters."

I must've made a face, because Shaya chuckled sadly before continuing.

"You can imagine my family's reaction when I first manifested powers."

"I can't imagine," I said, casting her a sympathetic look. "My mom was the opposite. Always telling me I should be proud of my scaly ears and astromancy."

"She sounds wonderful." Shaya gave a sincere smile, and I felt my chest grow warm.

"So what happened then?" I asked, hover-jumping to avoid a cluster of sharp rocks. "Once your family knew you were a magi?"

"I ran away." Shaya tried to say it casually, as if leaving home had been no big deal. But I could tell that her decision had left her with unseen scars.

"My sisters tried to find me," Shaya continued, speaking carefully. "But I'm a Shadowbinder—hiding in the darkness is kind of my thing. When Boone invited me to join the Knights, I jumped at the chance."

I'd lost myself in Shaya's story, and before I knew it, we'd reached the top of the mountain.

The top of the peak was pretty narrow, especially toward the hornlike formation at the far corner of the square. I could practically hear my dad's voice in my head warning me about going out too far and falling.

He always seemed to forget that I was an Archon who specialized in levitation. I was a lot of things, but 'afraid of heights' was not one of them.

Apparently, neither was Shaya. With a grin, she scooted her way along the narrowest part of the rock, inching her way toward the high ledge of the cliff.

With a spring in my step and a racing heart, I followed.

We reached the farthest, highest point of the cliff, sitting side by side and swinging our legs out so they dangled over the edge. Part of me wanted to jump off, and see if I really could levitate to the bottom. Looking at the steep drop hundreds of feet below was exhilarating.

And then there was the view.

From here, we could see the Scar stretch on for miles ahead. The usual craggy rock formations broke up the sandy scape, but from up here, we could see so much more. The whitish gray mud pots where we'd fought the dreklings looked tiny, and the crater from the skyfall had filled completely with mud. There was definitely no retrieving that skystone now. In the distance, a golden yellow cloud swirled through the air—a sandstorm. The silhouettes of some cliff-dwelling wild evren flew across the cloudy sky.

I looked toward the girl at my side. Her eyes were alight with excitement as she took in the scene, feet swinging carelessly off the edge of the mountain.

I laughed out loud. Suddenly, the Scar didn't seem so dull after all.

"So," Shaya began. "What about you? How'd you get roped into the Knights of the Torch?"

I told her about Kai and I following Kari to her meeting. She laughed heartily when I told her about impersonating Boone and Jax.

"This here view's better'na slice of dragonfruit pie after a long day huntin' drakalope," I growled in my gravelly Boone voice, barely able to keep a straight face.

Shaya cracked up. "Not bad. I'm pretty sure I've heard him use nearly that exact phrase."

"Where does he come up with them?"

We laughed again, then I went on to tell her about the battle at Steel Rim. When I got to the part about Vidya, a shadow crossed over her face.

"Vidya?" she asked. "You know the Black Valkyrie's real name?"

I nodded, recalling Solrac's words. "Calling her Vidya makes her less of a threat. She's not this impossible, unbeatable entity. She's just another regular person who can be beaten."

"I disagree," Shaya said.

"Oh?"

"She's not just another regular person." Shaya nonchalantly gathered a group of pebbles into her hand. "Calling her by a human name... It makes her seem too normal. What she does is anything but normal. Bringing in all those magi—She doesn't deserve to be called something so mundane."

I understood her take. To me, Vidya wasn't normal either. I wondered what Shaya's history with the Black Valkyrie was like. Had she ever met her? With two older sisters in the Mage Hunters, it was possible.

"Who told you her name?" Shaya asked, tossing her pebbles one-by-one over the edge of the cliff. "Solrac?"

"Yeah. You've met him?"

"No," Shaya said quickly. "Boone talks about him a lot. Jax too. They say this Solrac guy is very... aware of the Black Valkyrie."

"You could say that," I said. "Personally, I think they had a thing way back when."

Shaya's eyes went wide. "You're kidding."

"Wish I was," I laughed. "Can you imagine getting romantically involved with someone who turned out to be a psycho magi killer?"

Shaya laughed back, then playfully shoved me.

In order to not lose my balance and freefall off the cliffside, I reached out to steady myself on the thing closest to me.

Shaya.

I grabbed onto her upper arm, and in response she grabbed my other hand to keep me grounded.

I found myself staring directly into those light brown eyes, the flecks of blue dancing. The air was getting windy and a little chilly, but the way her thin fingers laced through mine made me feel like my whole body was on fire.

She didn't let go.

"So," I said with what I hoped was a charmingly crooked smile. "You and Jax aren't..."

I trailed off, and her eyes went as round as evren eggs.

"No," she said. "No, no, no."

I shrugged. "Just had to ask. You were taking awfully close care of him earlier."

"Jax isn't my type. All muscle, no finesse."

"And what is your type?"

"Wouldn't you like to know."

Shaya went to give me another playful shove against the chest, but I held my position by gripping her hand more tightly.

Her eyes brightened as she raised one eyebrow.

Suddenly, a piercing rumble echoed across the sky. We looked up as lightning flashed and the clouds burst, drenching us almost instantly.

"It never rains in the Scar," she said, raising her voice to be heard over the downpour.

"We'd better get back to camp," I said and Shaya nodded in agreement.

We scrambled to our feet, and I was sad to let go of her hand. Once we were a safe distance from the ledge, Shaya let out a whoop, spinning around in the rain with both hands outstretched.

"Don't you just love it?" Shaya sang. Her dark red hair was plastered against her face and down her back, but she didn't care.

I laughed again, watching her dance.

"Yeah. I really do."

Chapter II: The Inventor

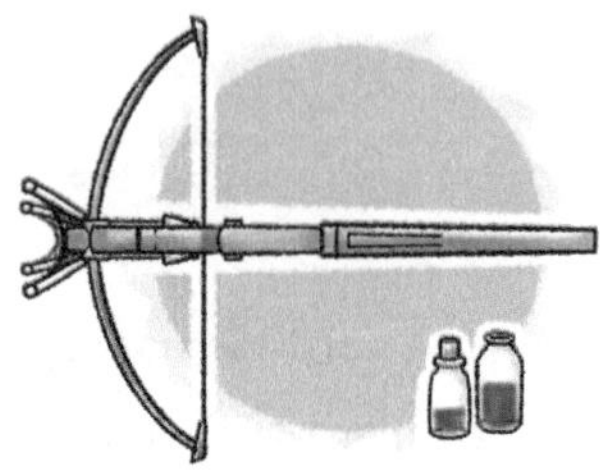

KARI

Kari couldn't help but roll her eyes when Asher and the new girl returned to camp dripping wet and splattered in mud. No matter where he went, Asher always found a way to get messy. It was a wonder he and Kari's neat freak little brother got along so well.

Kari watched as the group reacted to their return from the mountainside. Most seemed happy to see them. Kai was relieved that Asher was alive, but a little miffed that Asher hadn't taken Glint with him so they could stay in communication in case anything had gone wrong. Valla was still upset with Asher over his starglass stunt with the lost supplies, but Kari could tell she was secretly glad he was alright. Boone didn't even look up from where he lay, eyes closed, against the rock.

Solrac woke up from resting for long enough to say hello and introduce himself to Shaya. Solrac had her stand in front of him while he traced the rune for dissolving illusions—the same one he'd used on Kai and Asher back at the Drunken Drake. He waved his hand over her, but nothing happened. He'd done the same thing to Boone and Jax when they'd arrived at the camp, stating that he wasn't interested in being fooled by another illusion-clad starswan.

True to form, Solrac declared Shaya's joining the team to be the greatest thing that's ever happened. He took the opportunity to remind everyone that the Knight's of the Torch were, in fact, recruiting.

Even His Majesty was excited about the new girl. Solrac cocked his head as the bloodhusky leaped from his place under Jax's arm and bounded over to Shaya, licking her hand.

"If His Majesty approves, so do I," Solrac shouted over the rain.

Jax's reaction to Shaya's return made Kari squirm just a little. He wrapped his long, strong arms around her in a hug and let her know how worried he'd been.

That was fine. Kari knew it was only natural to worry whenever anyone went anywhere in the Scar. It was a dangerous place.

Kari recalled the first time she'd met Jax. It was only briefly during a Knights of the Torch meeting in an outlander town near Steel Rim.

After the meeting, Jax had approached and shamelessly flirted with her. The way he'd hit on her was braggy, a little clunky, and anything but subtle.

Kari had loved it.

Kari spent most of her time either over a workbench or looking after Kai and Asher to make sure they didn't kill themselves. She knew Asher had never seen her as anything more than an older sister. Kari occasionally worked with other blacksmiths or woodworking types in town, but they only ever saw her as a peer.

Jax was the first guy who truly saw her as a girl.

But with the way he looked over Shaya to make sure she was okay... Kari guessed he saw all girls that way. Kari wasn't special.

That was fine.

Kari had much better things to occupy her mind than thoughts about a guy. Before they'd left Steel Rim, Solrac had given her a special mission.

Kari needed to figure out a way for etherarchy to beat silver.

No matter which of the nine magi types someone was, they would always be vulnerable to silver. It served as a block, stopping a magi's flow of ether. Kari had seen that firsthand when the Black Valkyrie and her Mage Hunters had taken on the Knights of the Torch in Steel Rim. Their blades and chain whips had left the magi powerless. Solrac still hadn't completely recovered from the wound he'd taken from the silver dagger.

Kari was sure that even the unmatched etherarchy of the Farseer himself would fall to a single silver blade. Countering a law of nature like that was an impossible task.

Those were Kari's favorite kinds of tasks.

While the back of her mind tinkered with ideas for beating silver, Kari returned her main focus to her latest invention. They'd lost most of their supplies back in the quicksand, and while she'd been sad to lose the nomad sled, Kari loved the challenge of needing to think up something new. Bonus points if the group's survival depended on it.

She was grateful the dragonhide nomad's tent had survived the quicksand. She'd noticed Kai getting thirsty again, which gave her an idea. She'd used four tall, well-placed cacti plants as posts and then inverted the tent's dragonwing-bone supports to form it into an inverted dome when she saw the storm clouds coming. The outside of the tent was mostly waterproof. Then, using the sturdy needle and thread she always kept on hand in her pack, she'd sewn up any holes in the tent, including what was once the doorway. Then she'd used the last of her stick of wax from scalebees to complete the waterproofing in the more vulnerable places in the hide.

The rain was a blessing from the goddesses. Already Kari's makeshift rain collector was halfway full. Once the storm ended, she planned to fold over part of the old tent bottom, then, with a little more creative sewing, they'd have plenty of water to keep them going until they made it to the nearest town, a place called Ghost Lake. That was where Jax and Boone had just come from, on their way back to report in Steel Rim.

Where Jax had apparently helped Boone save the new girl, Shaya.

Kari was determined not to think about it. She wasn't one of those girls who got hung up on the first guy to give her the time of day. Even if that guy had muscles the size of sledgehammers and a jawline sharper than the end of a chisel.

Valla and Kai helped Kari put together an improvised nomadic sled using a couple of weathered juniper logs. Kari couldn't get them sanded down and polished nearly as well as the original, plus she was out of wax for the runners. Luckily, with only a little persuading and one threatening look from Valla, Asher agreed to keep the runners slick with smooth starglass. They'd just have to make sure not to run into any more jetsand.

His Majesty pulled the new sled, topped with the carefully sealed-off water tent and occasionally Solrac. He was walking better these days, but had to rest often. Valla looked worried about him, and Kari could tell she'd love nothing more than to get him to an experienced healer. The nearest one they knew of was in Ghost Lake. All the more reason to hurry through the last bit of the Scar.

The days passed with sun and sand, and the evenings passed with the group gathered around a campfire. Solrac sang and psionically played his lute while Valla watched for approaching danger, eyes outlined in glowing gold patterns to enhance her vision with the senses of a polar wolf. Valla also spent some time meditating to attune the sandshark's tooth she'd taken to turn it into a Wildshaper's totem.

Asher and Shaya took more adventurous—if less efficient—paths around craggy rocks, Asher using his levitation every once in a while to keep them from slipping too far when they got up high. Shaya wasn't nearly as good with levitation as Asher was, but then again, Asher had spent years climbing up sheer cliffs as a cragchaser.

Kai took notes in his black leather book while Boone practiced sharpshooting by sending off ether blasts at stacks of rocks. Boone attempted to teach Asher to do the same, positing that it was 'easier than scaring the wings off a dragon buffalo,' but that style of archonic power didn't seem to come as naturally to Asher. Interesting.

And Jax... well, Jax's favorite activity seemed to be weightlifting. Every chance he got, Jax would light up a rune over his forehead, then grab a couple of large, tan rocks. Biceps bulging, he'd use his telekinetic powers to press down on the rocks while using his arms to lift up against the force. If that wasn't enough, he'd telekinetically hold his axes in the air and use the handles to do pull-ups. It made it more of a challenge, he said. Kari could understand that.

Most nights Valla led the team in sparring. She and Solrac hoped things wouldn't come to a fight, but they felt it was best to be prepared just in case they encountered the Black Valkyrie and her Mage Hunters again. Valla had them dueling in pairs, which was fine until Jax and Asher went up against each other. Kari wasn't sure why the boys felt the need to try to prove themselves superior to one another. But after Asher lost a lock of hair to a psionic axe shot and Jax took a levitation-powered boot to the face, Valla stopped letting them spar against each other.

Long after everyone else was asleep, Kari would brainstorm ways to get past the silver problem.

Before they'd left Steel Rim, Solrac had given Kari a small silver coin he'd picked up off of the fallen Mage Hunter. The coin had the Hunters' symbol on one side—a triangle with a sword cutting through the center. On the other side was the crest of Evgard, a true dragon surrounded by an ornate woven pattern.

Each night, Kari would stare at the coin, turning it over and over in her hands. If Kari had been a magi, she knew the silver would've felt like touching ice, and pain would've shot through her fingertips and cut off her ether. As it was, she felt only a cold, hard coin as her thoughts raced.

She knew that silver was extremely malleable. Perhaps she could fashion some kind of heat-producing weapon? But that would only end up bending or melting the Mage Hunters' silver, not eliminating it.

Silver was reflective. But turning the Mage Hunters' weapons into mirrors wouldn't do much to help the team.

Kari had claimed that Mage Hunter's silver whip after the battle in Steel Rim. She was toying with a few ideas of what to do with it, but none that would solve the silver-neutralizing problem.

Finally, they were within a day's travel from Ghost Lake. The landscape was beginning to shift from sand to something slightly sturdier. Kari was growing tired of eating the gamey lizard meat Thorn hunted for the group. And even with careful rationing, they were nearly out of water, so the idea of getting to a place with 'lake' in the name sounded marvelous. Even if Boone said it actually had tons of ghosts in it too.

"Oh no," Valla muttered, coming to a stop in front of Kari.

Kari looked up toward the northeastern horizon, following Valla's line of sight.

There, fast approaching and growing steadily, was an enormous, billowing cloud. It was a dark brown, made from trillions of particles of tan dust and sand whipping around and around at high speeds.

"Dust storm," Valla announced to the group. "We need to take cover."

"Can we outrun it?" Jax asked.

"Let me rephrase," Valla said. "We need to take cover *now*."

She directed them to a grouping of sandstone ridges that were standing out from the dunes. Each ridge grew at an angle, so they would provide some shelter from the oncoming storm.

"Hug the leeward side," Valla instructed. "The storm's almost on us. If sand starts to fall off of the ridge and onto you, move to another one."

Each ridge was only big enough to shelter one to three people, or in Thorn and His Majesty's cases, one wyvern or bloodhusky.

Valla had them all dampen their bandanas and cover their mouths with it, then she took shelter with Solrac. Boone made sure to pick a ridge only big enough for one, so that nobody would bother him. Kai, Asher, and Shaya found a place to huddle together, which left Kari alone with...

Jax.

The storm's winds filled Kari's ears. They only had about a minute left.

"I guess we'd better get cozy then," Jax said, raising his eyebrows twice in quick succession.

"I would've said 'sheltered,' but cozy works too," Kari coyly replied.

Jax let out a single grunt of a laugh, then grabbed Kari by the hand and pulled her down with him under the ridge.

Not a moment too soon, either. The moment they were safe, the dust-ridden winds hit in full force. Tan clouds raced by on either side of the ridge, with the curve of the rock and the howling wind giving them a strange sort of privacy.

The abruptness of it made Kari jump, scooting closer to the center of the rock and, by extension, closer to Jax. Then the dust settled somewhat, and Jax pulled down his bandana from over his nose and mouth. Kari did the same.

"Hello there," he grinned, leaning into it by putting an arm behind Kari's back.

"Hello yourself," Kari said, not mad at all about the way this sandstorm was going.

"I was actually hoping to catch you without six other pairs of eyes hanging around," Jax said.

Kari laughed. "Eight if you count Thorn and His Majesty."

"Good point."

Jax tilted his face toward Kari's. He was a fast mover, that was for sure. But Kari liked fast.

Then, all at once, Jax's eyes went from magnetic and alluring to freaked out.

"Soot!" He jumped back a little, one arm leaving the safety of the ridge for a second. He yelped when the dust storm grazed his elbow.

"What?" Kari looked around for the source of Jax's sudden anxiety.

"Spydra. We must've found the entrance to their den."

Jax pointed to a small hole at the base of the sandstone ridge. Sure enough, creeping out of it was a spydra—a multi-headed dragon spider.

It was about the size of Kari's thumbnail.

She laughed loudly, much to Jax's frustration.

"What's so funny?" He folded his arms, and Kari wasn't blind to the way he tucked his hands under his biceps to make them pop more.

"It's just... that's probably the smallest spydra I've ever seen," Kari said between laughs.

"Hey, not all spydra are puny. They can grow as big as dogs. Void, Boone's seen a queen spydra as big as a drakking house."

"But this one's so cute and widdle," Kari said, her voice slipping into baby talk.

"For now."

"Come on, Jaxy, wanna meet the widdle baby spydwa?" Kari went to pick it up with her finger.

"Hey!" Jax grabbed her hand at the wrist. "Okay, number one, never call me 'Jaxy.' And number two, be careful. It may be small, but all spydra have Shadowbinder venom. It can burn away your skin."

Kari chuckled, but stopped reaching for the spydra. Then she rifled through her pack for something to block the little entrance to the miniature spydra den so that Jax could relax. She pulled out her little silver coin, and after scooching the spydra back inside, lodged it into place against the sandstone.

"Alright," she said. "If it'll make you feel better, I won't pet the venomous beastie. But it's still up in the air on whether or not I'll call you Jaxy again."

"I'd like to see you try," Jax shrugged, his toned shoulders perfectly visible with his sleeves ripped off the way they were. Kari thought Jax tearing his sleeves off was ridiculous, of course, but she wasn't mad about the result.

Kari raised one eyebrow defiantly.

"Jaxy."

With a playful look on his face, Jax grabbed Kari by the shoulders, pinning her in place. He pulled her close, his mouth just inches from hers.

Kari closed the distance herself.

She liked the way his lips felt—just a little bit dry from all the walking and water conservation in the desert. She liked the way his rough hands moved from her shoulders to the middle of her back. She liked the way he smelled. Like rich earth, with a hint of something almost metallic—perhaps because of the battle axes he kept strapped to his back. The scent reminded her of her shop back home.

As she kissed him, Kari opened her eyes. On the edge of her vision, she noticed the silver Mage Hunter's coin she'd used to block the spydra den.

One tiny spydra had crawled its way atop the coin, and Kari watched as one of its two heads spat a little jet of venom onto it.

Where the venom met the silver, it started slowly corroding away, leaving a minuscule trail along one side of the coin.

Kari gasped, pulling away from Jax to reach past him for the silver coin.

Jax startled, then subconsciously brought a hand to the handle of one of the axes on his back. "What? What's going on?"

"The spydra venom!" Kari squealed, brushing the little spydra off the coin and examining it more closely. "It dissolved the silver!"

It wasn't a lot, but somehow the spydra's ether-powered venom had left a mark.

"Okay?" Jax said, a little confused.

"What element, I wonder, allows the venom to penetrate the anti-ether in the silver?" Kari mused. "Perhaps because the acidity is tied not just to the etherarchical, but also to an organic component?"

She examined the coin closely, then bent down to inspect the hole of the spydra den. Then she continued muttering to herself.

"Obviously the silver is canceling out some of the effects, since the venom more strongly affects the sandstone than it does the silver. But that's okay, that's okay. It's a start. I just need to find a way to amplify the venom's power against it."

"Uhh... " Jax cautiously reached out a hand toward Kari. "Are you okay?"

"Better than okay!" Kari grinned, unable to contain her excitement. "Jax, I'm going to need your help."

Jax looked skeptical. "Sure."

Kari laughed again. "You ever milked a spydra for its venom?"

Chapter 12: Sandy

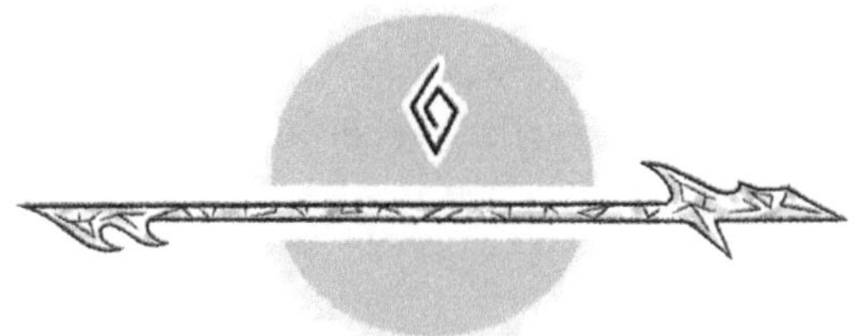

I would've thought the dust storm was fine if it weren't for the sharks.

As Kai, Shaya, and I hid on the leeward side of our sandstone ridge, Shaya noticed them first.

"Asher..." she said, tugging on the corner of my sleeve and pointing into the storm.

At first it was impossible to see much through the wall of high-speed sand and dust. But as the storm blew on and things got clearer, I could just make out the fins rushing along the edge of the sand. The sandsharks swam—or whatever it was these Geomancer land sharks did—beneath the surface into the group of sandstone ridges we were hiding in. These shark fins had a strange glow to them. Bright blue light sparked in the wake of the gray fins that looked like they were trailing wispy gray clouds.

No, more like they were *made* from wispy gray clouds.

It looked strikingly different from shadowbinding etherarchy, which had a much more flame-like quality. These umbral creatures emitted an inky, smoky grayness that seemed to sink into the earth.

"Soot," Shaya swore. "Those are umbral sharks."

The rushing wind of the storm was too loud for us to yell and warn the rest of the group. Maybe if we were quiet, they'd just swim by?

"I've read about umbral creatures," Kai whispered. "Any animal can go umbral, but it's not known how or why. They're the carriers of the shadow wasting. One bite or scratch and you're infected as the disease slowly numbs and grays out more and more of your skin until you're an empty shell of the person you once were."

"Thanks for that," I whispered back, scooting closer to the sandstone and away from the sharks.

"He's right," Shaya said. "I've seen firsthand what umbrals can do."

"Let's not get bitten or scratched, then," I suggested.

Unfortunately, I guess the sharks weren't on board with my plan. This sandstone refuge must have been a hunting ground for them during sandstorms.

With a mighty leap, one of the sharks launched out of the sand right toward us.

Kai, Shaya, and I screamed as it snapped its jaws. The three of us scrambled away from the safety of our ridge and into the storm.

I was grateful Valla had made us put damp scarves over our mouths, because a blast of dust whipped into my face right away. It felt like an army of tiny rocks was cutting at my cheeks. If not for my scarf, I wouldn't have been able to breathe.

Time to warn the others... or at least draw more of the sharks our way.

"*Sandsharks!*" I yelled out over the din of the storm.

I wasn't sure if anyone heard me.

They could have been surrounded too for all I knew, though it looked like more umbral fins were headed our way.

Kai had put on his heavy armor after the storm had started, and it looked like it was serving him well, his massive ridgeshield effectively blocking the brunt of the dust heading his way. I tried to mimic the design, my eyes flashing gold as I conjured two starglass shields, one for Shaya and one for me. Starglass was lighter than Kai's steel, so I added a few holes to our shields to allow some airflow and keep us from getting swept away like kites.

While I was at it, I summoned my starglass spear and signaled Thorn to stay low and not make a sound. The storm would throw him around if he got involved. I just hoped the umbral sharks wouldn't notice him.

The first umbral sandshark was hot on our tail, followed closely by more.

"Come on!" I yelled to my friends, the wind ripping my voice away. Luckily, Kai and Shaya seemed to understand as we banded together and ran for our lives, shields up to stop the wind, but mostly to protect us from umbral shark bites.

We needed to get to the other ridges. Solrac and Valla's was closest.

We pressed through the storm toward their sandstone hideout, jabbing at any shark that got close, but it looked like they were just testing us for now. I could see them more easily as the storm began to clear, and from the pissed off look on Valla's face, she'd just noticed the sharks too. Although honestly, Valla's face rarely *didn't* look pissed off, so there was a chance she was just over there being herself. His Majesty was with them already. He must've felt the sharks coming and warned them.

Solrac leaped into action, runetracing fast. His long seaxe flew from its sheath and into the dust storm. It hovered there for a second, then Solrac made a twisting motion with his hand. The sword began to spin, faster and faster until it became a blur. As the rushing wind came at the long blade, the seaxe's circular motion produced a counterwind of its own, making a safe, sand-free pocket for Solrac, Valla, and His Majesty to run in.

A sandshark leaped toward Valla and His Majesty. Sweat beading at his temples, Solrac redirected his psionically-spinning sword to slice the thing to ribbons.

Rather than keel over dead, the umbral sandshark dispersed into wispy, gray smoke. For a second, a pair of lightning blue eyes hovered alone mid-air, then they vanished too.

Soot. That was ominous.

Solrac and Valla kept running, their trajectory merging with ours. It looked like Solrac understood we still needed to get to Kari and Jax. Valla slashed at the closest umbral sandshark with the warsword from her back, the long blade cleaving the beast into two inky halves that dispersed into the wind.

More sharks were approaching fast. It looked like they hadn't appreciated some of their own getting killed. Solrac really didn't look like he had the energy to be on his feet for long. Already bits of sand were starting to break through his sword-fan... thing.

"As enjoyable... as... this is..." Solrac said. "Perhaps... we should get to... the others... as quickly as possible?"

Thorn sent me a feeling like warm, reluctant relief as he emerged from his ridge. The storm was slowing down enough that he dared come out. Within moments, Thorn came hurrying toward us from across the sands. A swell of concern rose through our bond as he realized Kari wasn't with us.

I was glad to have Thorn close by again, and His Majesty too. Boone was close behind, grumbling something about the drakking sandsharks disturbing the peace. He deftly shot one with ether when it got too close to him, making it puff into smoke as well.

That left only Kari and Jax. Where could they be?

Suddenly, the tooth around Valla's neck lit up with gold Sentinel patterns. I remembered the nights she'd spent meditating while holding the sand-shark tooth she'd taken, and my eyes popped as I got to see it all come to a head now.

Two tan sharkfins sprouted along the sides of Valla's forearms, accompanied by more Sentinel markings. Her eyes went completely black, like a shark's. She leaped, then dove back down, but when she hit the sandy earth below, it didn't stop her. The geomantic aspect she'd taken on from wildshaping allowed her to sink beneath the sand, disappearing from view.

A second of stillness passed as two sandsharks raced toward us beneath the surface. We braced ourselves.

Before the sharks had the chance to take a bite at us, their misty fins burst into shadowy clouds that blew away in the wind. Between the two columns of vanishing smoke, Valla shot upward out of the sand, her warsword poised.

We all just stared at her in awe for a second.

"Valla," Solrac gawked. "Has anyone ever told you you're quite skilled?" Valla harrumphed, but I could tell she enjoyed the compliment.

Now that the dust was settling, I saw that more smoky, gray sharks were circling us, their fins showing above sand level. It looked like they were slowly closing in using some kind of hunting pattern.

I heard a scream and then saw Kari and Jax running out from behind one of the ridges. I guess they'd finally noticed the sharks. About time.

Both Kari's and Jax's cheeks looked flushed. My eyes narrowed at Jax. I wondered what had been going on behind that rock.

Finally, the wind let up enough so that Solrac could shut off his rune. The spinning seaxe slowed, returning to his hand as Solrac stumbled from the exertion.

"Everything's just wonderful," he assured us.

Looking at the ring of shadow-wasting-inducing umbral sandsharks surrounding us, I wasn't so sure.

His Majesty and Thorn gave mighty roars and bared their teeth. Valla wielded her warsword while Jax reached for one of the axes strapped to his back. Shaya gripped her spear, Boone unsheathed his twin daggers, and Kai and Kari readied their crossbows.

The lingering dust storm whipped at my hair as our group stood with our backs to each other, bearing arms against the circling sharks.

"We have to charge them," Valla said, her eyes still black like the sharks.

"But won't that leave us unprotected?" Kai asked.

"No, they're about to turn the ground below us to jetsand," Shark-Valla said.

I glanced down, and sure enough, the ground beneath us was starting to quiver.

Soot.

We charged.

I dove toward the nearest misty gray fin, stabbing my starglass spear as hard as I could right at the sand near the fin's base.

The sand rose around my feet as the freshly stabbed shark dove upward in rage.

As it arced out of the sand, I found myself riding on its back, losing hold of my starglass ridgeshield in the process. I grabbed the nearest thing I could for balance.

That thing just so happened to be the shark's misty fin.

I gripped my spear in one hand and the fin with the other as I rode the sandshark.

The shark reared up then thrashed, trying to shake me off. It made me think of the thrill of riding Karl the craghopper.

That reminded me. This shark was epic enough that it deserved a name. "Steady, Sandy!" I yelled into the wind.

Sandy twisted her body in on itself, trying to snap at me with wide, toothy jaws. I took cover on the other side of the fin. I didn't want to take any chances. One bite from an umbral creature out here would give me the shadow wasting for real. Was this a curse from the goddesses to get back at me for pretending to have the shadow wasting back in the Drunken Drake?

I raised my spear, preparing to stab Sandy in the back—sorry Sandy—when suddenly she dove beneath the sand's surface.

Within half a second, I was eating dirt. Or, sand.

I rolled a few feet, then sat up, coughing. For a second, everything was still.

Then Sandy popped out of the ground directly underneath me, launching me up into the sky along with her.

I may or may not have screamed as those shadowy gray jaws went for my torso.

Just in time to not become shark bait, I tapped into my ether well and levitated myself out of reach.

But Sandy was determined. We both fell back toward the earth, and I saw an opening.

Her teeth were inches away from my thigh. With a grunt, I swung my starglass spear as we fell, stabbing upward through the roof of Sandy's mouth.

She instantly turned to mist as we hit the dune below. Gray clouds swirled around me, vanishing into the wind, followed last by Sandy's vibrant, lightning blue eyes. As they winked out, I noticed a thumb-sized chunk of glowing blue crystal hovering around where her heart had once been.

The raw crystal dropped to the ground with a soft thud, fading from blue to white before my eyes. At first I thought it was a skystone, but it lacked that sort of otherworldly shimmer. It was just a chunk of quartz, filled with what looked like a few residual drops of ether, but not enough to channel. I left it in the sand as a grave marker for the mighty fallen sandshark.

I looked around as I got to my feet and saw that the team had eliminated several sharks of their own. The rest of the shiver of sandsharks retreated southwest, following the dying dust storm. Boone spun a starglass dagger out from under his dragonscale cloak, taking out one final shark with an expert ether shot. It burst into wispy gray clouds.

Stars, I had a lot to learn from him.

I did a quick head count and was relieved when I discovered everyone was safe. A shark had taken a bite out of Kai's ridgeshield and Kari had lost quite a few crossbow bolts, but my friends were alive and well. Thorn hurried to my side, and while my dragon hadn't sustained a bite, I noticed his right wing had taken quite the beating. That would make it hard for him to fly until his regeneration powers finished healing him. Still, he proudly sent me burning feelings of accomplishment for his brave fight against the sharks.

We regrouped, gathering around the dune where I'd dispatched Sandy. Everyone looked exhausted, like they could use a big drink of water and a long nap.

The only problem was, Kari's water-tent was lying limp and empty beside the sandstone ridge where we'd secured it before the storm hit. A shark must've shredded it with its sharp teeth.

All we had now were our own packs.

"Ghost Lake is less than a day's travel east," Valla said, gesturing with her warsword. "If we start now, we can make it by sunset."

Nobody wanted to travel right then, especially with no food or water. But there wasn't really another option.

I let my starglass spear and ridgeshields shatter and vanish into stardust as the group prepared to set out toward Ghost Lake.

Suddenly, a pile of sand rose up. One last umbral sandshark dove from under the surface, heading straight for Kai as he finished taking off his armor and piling it onto the remains of his shield for travel.

Kai stumbled back, fumbling for anything to defend himself. I darted toward him, but there was no way I could re-summon my spear and make it in time.

But Valla could.

The shark leaped from the sand, jaws eager to close on Kai's head. Valla lunged between Kai and the umbral shark, warsword slashing. The shark disappeared in a wispy, gray cloud, leaving behind a chunk of quartz the same way Sandy had. But right before vanishing, it clamped its sharp teeth onto Valla's left leg.

She fell to the sand, clutching at her leg. Even through her tight brown leggings, I could see the shark had bitten her. Already, jagged grayness surrounded the bleeding wound.

"Valla!" Solrac shouted, falling to his knees beside her leg.

"I'm sorry," Kai stuttered. "Valla, I'm so sorry."

"It's alright," Valla's face contorted as she held her leg. "Your... ah... your father once saved my life. Now that debt is repaid."

Solrac untied the deep crimson bandana from around his neck and carefully wrapped it around Valla's leg. Blood soaked it immediately.

"Well, at least it's red to match, eh?" Solrac said, a halfhearted smile falling into place on his face. But even his optimism faltered as he looked at Valla. As a Sentinel, Valla could do some degree of regenerative etherarchy. I watched as angular, gold Sentinel marks appeared on the backs of her hands. She pressed them to her leg, where other angular golden marks beneath Solrac's scarf must've been looping around the wounds. Solrac's bandana stopped filling with new blood, and some relief crossed Valla's face.

But her etherarchy couldn't stop the shadow wasting. Even now, I could see the blotchy, jagged grayness creeping out from the edges of the scarf.

"How long before the shadow wasting takes over everything and she..." Jax trailed off.

"Don't be stupid," Solrac snapped. "The shadow wasting is treatable."

"Sure," Boone put in, a serious look on his leathery face. "If you can get some liquid light on it 'fore it spreads."

"Liquid light?" I asked.

"Lightwielding etherarchy," Shaya said, eyes fixated on Valla's leg. "It should heal the shadow wasting—if we get it soon enough. Otherwise, only Lightwielders can keep it under control."

"Which is why I can't fathom why all of you are still standing around," Solrac got to his feet. "We need to get to Ghost Lake immediately."

"And if we can't find no Lightwielder in Ghost Lake?" Boone asked.

"We will find one!" Solrac spat the words, and everyone but Boone jumped backward a little.

Solrac traced a rune, then scooped Valla up in his arms. He didn't seem to struggle too much, and I could tell that he was telekinetically lifting her upward by her clothes to assist him.

Valla squirmed a little. "Solrac, I can still walk on it—"

"No."

"But—"

"*No.*"

Solrac led the way east, cradling Valla in his arms. If his dagger wound from Steel Rim was bothering him now, he didn't show it.

I couldn't help but notice Shaya walking off to the side, far away from Solrac and Valla, a troubled expression on her face. I jogged over and fell into step beside her.

"You know someone who has the shadow wasting?" I asked.

"What?" Shaya looked up, eyes flashing ahead to where Solrac carried Valla. "Oh. Yeah, my um... my sister's got a friend with it. It's really hard to watch. I'd rather not talk about it if that's okay."

I nodded, leaving Shaya and catching up to Thorn. Through the bond, he sent me a spark of concern.

"I know, buddy," I said, patting him on the back of the neck. "I'm worried about Valla too, but I'm sure she'll make it."

Thorn gave a low grumble, wishing he could fly Valla to safety. But with his wing the way it was, he needed more time to regenerate.

I could hear Solrac's determined footsteps trekking across the sand, and had to hurry in order to keep pace with him. I squinted at the horizon, hoping that he was right, and that the town of Ghost Lake would be our salvation from this void that was the Scar.

The town of Ghost Lake sat half on the edge of the lake, and half *on* the lake.

I knew it wasn't a big city, but it was way larger than Steel Rim. Dozens of homes surrounded the town wall, most with some kind of wooden corral holding lazy wyvernhogs or aldrakas. Kirin-riding ranchers tended long-horn cattledrakes, and I even saw one guy riding a dragon buffalo as he swung a lasso to rope one around the horns.

A rundown sign, capped with the skull of a torradon bull, stood near the road leading into town. The locals had clearly shot it with crossbow bolts or throwing knives more times than I could count. Someone must've used it to practice their axe-throwing, then left the rusty axe lodged between the wooden slats.

I thought Solrac would extinguish the psionic rune he was using to carry Valla as soon as we started seeing people, but he didn't. I guess since he was already silvermarked, he didn't care who saw him. The rest of us had to rid ourselves of any signs of etherarchy or we'd get reported to the Mage Hunters.

There were more homes built on stilts in the lake itself. Old men sat on their front porches, sleeping in rocking chairs with fishing rods in their hands, the end of their lines bobbing in the water. Somewhat unstable-looking wooden bridges connected the homes to the rest of the town. The further out over the water the homes and bridges went, the higher they got, probably so any passing boats could flow easily beneath them.

The whole town had an eerie calmness about it. Barely any wind blew here, and the surface of the water was disturbingly still. It felt almost like there was some kind of otherworldly presence here. When I asked, Boone let me know they didn't call it 'Ghost' Lake for nothing.

One big street ran through the center of Ghost Lake, starting at the edge of town and going right over the lakeshore, and ending with an enormous building standing about a half mile into the water. Thick stilts supported it, and a tall tower jutted out from the building's square base.

"That there's the Mirror Sanctum," Boone said, shielding his eyes from the sun as he looked out toward the building. "Drakked Ghost Lake people say it's a holy church for worshippin' the goddesses, but I ain't never seen a soul prayin' in there. Just undercover Mage Hunters practicin' all manner of shadiness."

Boone pointed out a few more buildings in Ghost Lake. They had a large library built on the docks right over the shoreline and a big general store. I also found out that the water Ghost Lake sat on wasn't really a lake at all, but was part of an inland body of water called the Dragonstorm Sea.

"So named for the stormin' pods of naga that traverse 'neath the waves," Boone said. "That's why them stilts lift the whole town higher the further out over the depths it goes."

Right on the edge of town stood a tavern with a big, wooden sign over it reading 'The Drowsy Drekling.' I recalled the ferocious dreklings we'd fought at the mud pots in the Scar. They'd been anything but drowsy.

Solrac barged into the tavern, still holding Valla tightly against his chest and demanding to know if there was a Lightwielder nearby.

At first, nobody in the grimy saloon wanted to answer. I couldn't blame them—unless they were among a keep's nine registered magi, any Lightwielder they knew would be an outlaw.

Solrac looked like he was about to pull out his seaxe and start threatening patrons when a voice called out from behind the bar.

"I think I can help you find what you're lookin' for, Solrac."

An incredibly curvy girl in a form-fitting dress with sleeves that fell off her shoulders stood leaning over the bar. She had dark eyes lined with some kind of charcoal to make them stand out, and she wore a draccoon-hide hat, the beast's scaly tail hanging off the back of her head.

Solrac hurried over to her while the rest of our team limped tiredly after him.

The girl casually scrubbed the inside of a glass with a dishrag of questionable cleanliness.

"Boone, Jax, Shaya," she smirked. "Back so soon?"

Boone folded his arms. "You bet, little lassie."

The girl chuckled a little, then looked up. Her eyes passed right over me and landed on Kai.

The girl let out a low whistle. "Y'all didn't tell me you were bringin' me back a real man. Well, ain't you just my type."

"Um..." Kai said, shifting awkwardly as the girl checked him out from head to toe.

"Enya," Solrac said sternly. "I need a Lightwielder. I need one now."

"Alright, alright. Hold your kirin. I don't have a Lightwielder, but I've got the next best thing below if you can tell me a certain phrase," she whispered.

"The Hunter's Torch is lit again," Solrac said in a rush under his breath.

The bartender girl, Enya, nodded. She gave Kai a wink that made him deepen in color all the way to the tips of his ears before gesturing toward a door behind the bar.

"Lucky you got here when you did. We're almost out of liquid light, what with all the new skyfalls and umbrals runnin' amok," Enya said as Solrac rushed through the door with Valla, His Majesty following close behind.

"As for the rest of you..." Enya turned back to us and put a hand on her hip, accentuating her hourglass shape. "...how's about a couple of rounds on Solrac's tab?"

Enya got Solrac and Valla to the Drowsy Drekling's waning supply of liquid light in some back room while we got ourselves set up at a table. Thorn contacted me from outside through the bond, and let me know he was going to take a dive in the sea once his wing finished regenerating. I let him know that we'd catch up later, and promised to keep him in the loop on how Valla was doing. I warned him of the naga, but he didn't seem worried.

Enya also informed the group of some news. According to Enya, rumors were flying across the realm that High King Magnus' son was gravely ill with the shadow wasting. Everyone knew of the High Prince, Mason Drakeslayer, who famously did what his moniker implied—slew the mighty frostdrake who'd long terrorized the northern keepdoms.

The others seemed troubled by this news, and Boone muttered something about needing to inform Solrac and Valla the moment they were finished. I felt sorry for the high prince, although I doubted the high king spent much time thinking about any of the common folk stricken with the shadow wasting, so I wondered why the people of Evgard cared so much about one sick noble.

The setting sun filled the tavern with deep reddish light as Enya brought over several bottles filled with some kind of orange liquid, probably some kind of whiskey, as well as a few pitchers of plain water.

"For the weak," Enya said with a sly grin as she placed the water at the center of our table.

Enya laughed as Kai and Jax immediately went for the water. According to Kai, alcohol really messed with Mystics to the point that they couldn't runetrace if they drank too much. Archons and Sentinels had to be careful, too, but Mystics got hit the hardest.

Boone poured himself a tall glass from the orange whiskey and downed it in half a second. Apparently, he wasn't worried about his ability to channel etherarchy while intoxicated.

I reached for one of the orange bottles, but Kari slapped my hand.

"Oh no," she said, shaking a finger at me. "The last thing you need is to get tipsy."

With that, she poured me a glass of water. I shrugged and chugged it.

Enya brought out a few platters of wyvernhog ham, cornbread, and some kind of potato hash. It was the first meal we'd had since losing our supplies that wasn't lizard meat, and stars, did it taste amazing.

After a while. Enya plopped herself down at our table, right between Jax and Kai.

"Alright, handsome." She rested an elbow on Kai's shoulder. "I'm off duty. How's about we go around back and I find out if those perfect lips of yours are any good at kissin'?"

Kai choked on his bread, and Boone cracked up, slapping his knee. Kai looked so startled, I had to choke down a laugh myself.

"Uh, no thank you," Kai managed once he'd swallowed his bite.

"Later then," Enya winked, then turned to face the rest of the table. "So how's about a little wager? Who here thinks they can guess which of us has kissed the most people? My money's on the tall, dark, and handsome half-born."

Boone laughed heartily again, and about half the group couldn't help but break into grins, including me.

"Asher?" Kari said. "Nah. He plays the charmer, but he's too much of a goody-goody underneath it all."

"Hey!" I said. "Goody-goody?"

"It's not a bad thing," Kari laughed. "How many girls have you kissed then?"

I hesitated, trying to gauge the group, but knowing I couldn't lie. Kai knew me too well. "Three," I said hesitantly, not sure whether to be proud or embarrassed.

Technically, Kari was the first girl I'd ever kissed. I'd been five, and she was seven. One of her friends had wanted to throw a pretend wedding ceremony, so she'd paired us up and made us exchange marriage bracelets woven from grass. She'd insisted Kari and I kiss as part of the ceremony. Kari had needed to squat down to reach my lips back then.

My next kiss had been last year. I'd been seeing a girl from the other side of town. I'd been really into her, and one evening I'd finally gotten up the courage to kiss her.

Unfortunately, the next night I'd seen her with one of Baron Eidan's younger brothers. I'd spotted them wearing marriage bracelets just last month.

Another good reason to mistrust nobility.

My final kiss had been with Valla when I was disguised as Boone. But I wasn't about to bring that up now.

"Three?" Jax smiled from ear to ear, an air of superiority on his face as he looked down at me. I shrank a little inside, and I had a sudden desire to sock him in the gut.

"Nothing wrong with that," Kari smiled. "I've only kissed two people."

I felt a little better hearing that. That meant, besides me, Kari had only kissed one other person.

"The first was a couple years ago when this gorgeous traveling bard came through Steel Rim."

Oh.

I guess that meant Kari didn't count our kiss from when we were kids. I tried not to let anyone see me blush when I realized I probably should've said I'd kissed only one person.

Kari went on. "We met after one of his shows, but he left town the next night. That's why I decided never to go for a bard again."

"Here here," Shaya piped up, holding up her orange glass. I wondered what Shaya had against bards. I'd have to ask her later.

"That's one," Enya said, taking a swig directly from one of the bottles. "Who's your latest?"

Kari's cheeks flushed, and she and Jax exchanged a look.

Soot. Kari and *him*? He wasn't good enough for her. My urge to pick a fight with Jax grew.

Kai seemed to think the same thing as he watched his big sister bat her eyelashes at Jax.

Enya reined our attention back to her. "Well, I've kissed eleven, and counting. That means so far I'm winning. Boone?"

Boone laughed and leaned back in his chair. "Nah. This is a conversation for you youngun's. But I'm as entertained as a rattledrake watchin' a drownin' ridgerat. Carry on."

"Shaya?" Enya grinned.

Shaya's face was stone as she sipped her whiskey.

"Four."

We all waited for her to expand on that, but she just kept sipping.

"I'm still in the lead then," Enya said. "Jax?"

Jax smiled, looking down and shaking his head.

"What?" Enya said.

"Amateurs." He looked up and took a gulp from his glass of water.

He waited until he had everyone's full attention. Even Shaya looked interested to hear how many girls Jax had kissed.

With an arrogant smirk, Jax finally answered.

"Seventy."

There was a general uproar at that.

"Seventy?" Enya whistled, thoroughly impressed.

Shaya looked disappointed, while Kai looked like he was doing math in his head, trying to divide the number of kisses by the number of years in Jax's life or something.

Kari's expression was unreadable, but she didn't look too bothered. Why wasn't she upset about this revelation? Jax had just shown himself to be the loser I'd always suspected he was, and Kari didn't even care.

I couldn't help but protest. "How can you kiss seventy different girls? There's no way you really cared about that many people."

"Who said anything about caring about them all? I never learned half their names," Jax replied, and I could feel my anger rising.

"I think if you kiss someone, you should at least give them the respect of knowing their name. How about the girl sitting next to you?" I said as I gestured to Kari. "Can you tell me her name?"

Jax got to his feet.

"You got a problem with me, Dragon-boy?"

I stood too. Jax was more muscular than me, but I was taller.

"Guys, guys," Enya stood up too, motioning for us to sit down. "I'm not in the mood to deal with a bar fight tonight. You don't even have the excuse of being drunk. Relax."

Neither Jax nor I wanted to break first, so we slowly sat down at the same time, following Enya's hands.

"There we go," she said. "Now, the moment we've all been waiting for. Kai, how many?"

Kai traced the rim of his glass with a finger. "Well, I'd only ever kiss a girl with whom I had a high likelihood of a successful future relationship. At least an eighty-seven percent chance of estimated success. Maybe eighty-five, depending on the girl."

"Yah-dee yah-dah," Enya said. "How many kisses?"

"Zero," Kai replied.

"Zero?" half the group replied in unison.

"Well," Enya said as she adjusted her draccoon skin cap. "I'll fix that."

Then she leaned over and planted a kiss right on Kai's mouth.

Kari, Jax, and I couldn't help but burst out laughing at the totally stunned look on Kai's face. Boone let out a whoop. Enya pulled back and winked.

"Uh..." was all Kai could manage, but he couldn't hide the small smile playing at his lips.

"Don't worry," Enya added. "You got more than an eighty-seven percent chance with me. At least, you've got a one-hundred percent chance of havin' some fun."

We laughed again.

"As fun as this is," Shaya said, not amused, "we'd all better find Solrac and get to bed. We'll need our rest for tomorrow."

"That's right," Boone said, standing as well. "Tomorrow's the big day."

"What's happening tomorrow?" I asked.

"Why, the reason Solrac put all y'all and me on the team," Boone leaned in. We all leaned toward him as well, so that the rest of the tavern's patrons couldn't overhear.

Boone smiled.

"Tomorrow we run our first heist."

Chapter 13: Don't Mess With the Owl

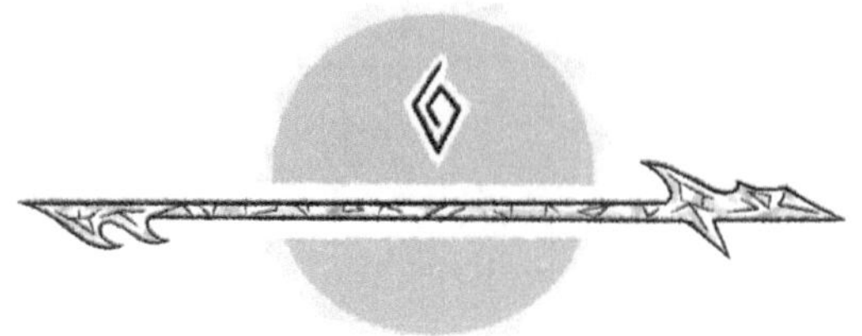

"I can't believe this. Literally everyone has an important job but me."

I kicked the thick, wooden beam that held the boardwalk aloft above me. The wooden raft I stood on wobbled just a little with the waves, despite being anchored to the shallow sea floor and tied to the beam.

"You don't think being my bodyguard is important?" Kai said, half o-ffended and half distracted as he scribbled down runes in his black leather notebook. He sat on the raft next to me, the fading daylight streaming onto his pages from between the slats of the boards above us.

"Nobody will ever find us down here." I folded my arms.

"That's what you said about Thorn's den."

"Fair point. But come on, that jerk Jax gets to run point while I hide out down here?"

"Jax has more experience than us."

"What about Thorn? He has no experience, but still gets to be the getaway dragon for the point team."

As I mentioned his name, Thorn sent an excited feeling through the bond like a torch blazing to life. He reminded me of how he'd saved me at Whitestone Hall. Okay, so maybe he *did* have some getaway dragon experience.

"And what about Valla?" I added. "She got injured fighting the umbral sandshark just yesterday, but even she gets to do something that matters."

"Solrac got her some liquid light from the tavern's stores in time. She's probably going to be fine. Besides, Solrac's plan would never work without Valla turning into a weasel."

I sighed. The group had spent all day going over the plan for tonight's heist. Kari had sewed disguises while Kai had practiced runes. Valla had been resting, regaining her strength. And Boone, Jax, and Shaya had been studying the layout of Ghost Lake's Arcanum.

The Arcanum was a huge edifice built on the boardwalk above where Kai and I now hid. It had a tall tower on each of its four corners with one rising above the rest in the center, and was home to thousands of dusty, old books.

Apparently, one of those books was important enough to risk all of our lives to get.

"What's so great about this tome of illusions anyway?" I mused aloud.

"Il Toma Ilusor," Kai corrected, barely looking up from his notes. "It contains some of the most powerful runes in Evgardian history. Runes used by the ancient Guardians."

"Sure, sure."

"We need those runes in order to build a convincing replica of the true dragon egg. We'll need to employ illusions far beyond my current abilities. According to Solrac, these runes go beyond what even the Farseer can do."

The jittery inflection in Kai's voice betrayed just how thrilled he was about this old book. For his sake, I hoped our heist went well.

Even if I had the lamest job.

"I mean, even His Majesty gets to be a lookout on the docks instead of hiding out under them."

"Shush," Kai held up a finger. "I'm about to mindlink the team."

I felt a little wiggle from the inside of my boot, where Glint clung to my ankle. Or rather, as Kai had called her, 'Glint Eight.'

She was one of nine little copies of Kai's mirror gecko. I didn't fully understand how, but Solrac and Kai had been practicing combinations of runes since we left Steel Rim in order to split Glint into nine different versions of herself. Solrac called them 'dream mirrors.' I'd overheard him explaining to Kai that it was the same etherarchy that Vidya had used to make her starswans. There was really only one swan, split six different ways.

The process fascinated Kai, and he'd picked up on how to split his dream-beast quickly. Apparently it was easier with smaller ethereal familiars. Now, each member of the team had their own little mirror gecko clinging to them, allowing Kai to mindlink all of us at once.

Kai had assured us that only thoughts and images we wanted to share could be broadcast over the mindlink. He also instructed us only to transmit relevant information so as to keep the mindlink from getting muddled.

Suddenly, I could feel the mindlink blooming to life inside my head. It felt like a small pinprick in my consciousness, a lot like the way Kai used Glint to communicate with just me, only broader somehow.

Can everyone hear me? Kai asked in my mind.

A chorus of affirmative responses reverberated inside my head, as if they were bouncing off the sides of my skull. This was going to be hard to get used to.

This is fantastic, Solrac's thought rose above the rest. *Excellent work, Kai. And Glints One through Nine, of course.*

The Glint copy in my boot squirmed with appreciation.

Now, Solrac continued. *Is everyone in position?*

Boone's thoughts answered back first. *Valla, Jax, and I are hidin' outside the Arcanum's entrance, ready as a ridgerat in a cornfield.*

What does that even mean? I mused, not realizing I'd sent the thought through the mindlink. Oops.

Never question the ridgerats, Boone thought.

"Focus, please, Asher," Kai said out loud as he sat next to me on the deck.

"Sorry."

Solrac thought to us again. *Ridgerats aside. Everyone else?*

Shaya's voice appeared in my head, and my heart started to race just a little.

I'm with Boone's group, invisible. At least, I think so.

I sure as void can't see you, darlin', Boone thought.

Shaya had been hesitant at first when she'd learned that Solrac's plan for stealing the tome involved using her Shadowbinder's invisibility power. She claimed it wasn't a power she'd practiced with much, but in the end, Solrac convinced her to give it a try.

Kari and I are on the bridge, Enya's thought came through. *Just set the first charge. Only eight more to go.*

I'd been highly concerned this morning when I'd learned that Enya was the Knight's of the Torch's go-to explosives specialist. It hadn't eased my mind at all when she'd said, "I just have a natural talent for getting things to explode."

Excellent, Solrac thought. *I'm in position as well.*

He sent us an image of his view from the window of one of the upper rooms in the Drowsy Drekling. It was the perfect vantage point for watching both the entrance to the Arcanum, as well as three of the Arcanum's four watchtowers. Behind the large library, Ghost Lake's Mirror Sanctum loomed, a high bridge connecting it to the Arcanum's deck.

Two guards kept watch from each of the Arcanum's towers, except for the one nearest the Arcanum's back door. That one was guarded closely by a gigantic, man-sized ethereal owl.

I'd seen the owl myself earlier that day. She was moonlight white with dark starry runic markings on her. She had huge, sharp violet eyes that seemed to glow, and was extremely fluffy.

She was also extremely dangerous.

The owl was the beloved ethereal beast of the High Mage of Ghost Lake. According to Boone, the High Mage was a cruel man who used his Seer powers to dominate his fellow archivists at the Arcanum.

Now remember, Solrac thought to everyone. *What's the number one rule of this operation?*

In mental chorus, we gave the answer Solrac had drilled into our heads all day.

Don't mess with the owl.

That's right. Don't mess with the owl. Whatever we do tonight, that's the one thing we must avoid in order to keep the High Mage from discovering us. If we alert him, the Mage Hunters in the sanctum will be on us within minutes. Don't mess with the owl, got it?

We mentally agreed.

Excellent, Solrac thought, and I could easily picture him clapping his hands together with delight. *It's time for the one-night-only performance of 'The Night the Knights Took a Tome.' Ladies and gentlemen, prepare to be amazed.*

I made a miniature Thorn out of starglass while I used the mindlink to keep up with the real action. The wings were extra hard to get just right, especially in such tiny proportions.

Meanwhile, in my head, Solrac sent the group images of what he was doing.

He traced a dreamweaving rune in the air, its golden copy appearing over his forehead. From his perspective, the soft glow shone down from just above his line of sight. Then, Solrac focused in on one of the guards on the tower nearest his vantage point. Through Kai's group mindlink, I could see Solrac point two fingers at the guard, locking in his shot.

Then, he fired a focused dart of dream energy at the guard.

It was a direct hit, right to the guard's forehead. She sunk to the ground in an instant, asleep from the dream energy.

Her squadmate didn't have time to react before Solrac nailed him in the head with a dream dart of his own. Both guards on the first tower went down without a sound.

Solrac took care of the two guards on the opposite tower with equal ease. The other two towers—including the one with the ethereal owl—guarded the back door, which meant we didn't need to worry about them if all went according to plan. Now, there was nobody watching the Arcanum's front entrance.

Guards are down, Solrac said in our heads. *Go!*

Suddenly, the mental picture switched from Solrac's point of view to Boone's. He and Jax hurried toward the grand, intricately carved double doors. I saw Boone's arm reach out toward the handle, and that's when I caught my first glance of Valla in frostweasel form as she perched on Boone's leather gauntleted forearm.

She was about eight inches long with a thin tail. Her fur was snow white, her eyes their usual shade of dark brown. Tiny gray Sentinel patterns marked her little weasel body. She was absolutely adorable.

Aww! Kari's reaction burst onto the mindlink. *Valla, look how cute you are!*

Valla's grumbling thought answered back. *I'll have you know, frostweasels are one of the Northern keeps' most vicious predators.*

But just look at that sweet, itty bitty nose, Kari gushed.

I felt Valla's eye roll as she snuck into her hiding place inside Boone's large sleeve.

Quiet down, y'all, Boone thought. *We're goin' in.*

Through Boone's eyes, I got a look at the inside of the Arcanum. A short hallway opened up into a vast rotunda. The center of the room showed off a big, bronze mirror, decorated with stars to honor the Arcanum's patron goddess, Streya. Basically every inch of wall in the circular room was packed with books. Most looked like they hadn't been opened in years, which made sense to me in a last chance town like this. The rugged people I'd met so far didn't exactly seem like reading types.

"Amazing..." I heard Kai mutter next to me as he took in the inside of the Arcanum. I chuckled under my breath. Our library in Steel Rim was a joke next to this.

There was a small door at the end of the room, with a staircase that led to the upper floors and the restricted tower. That was where we needed to go.

Well, not me. Just the people with important jobs.

Boone and Jax, with Valla the frostweasel in tow, made their way deeper into the library. As they walked, I caught sight of their reflections in the central mirror.

Valla obviously looked the most different from her usual self, but Boone and Jax's likenesses startled me. Both of them wore long, loose, black robes, tied at the waist with a black cord. Hoods hung over their backs, and both wore a black circlet around their heads. Boone's had a white crystal in the center of his forehead, where Jax's had a flat, black space and no crystal.

That was because Boone was playing a full Son of Streya, whereas Jax was playing his apprentice. Apprentices still had to earn their crystals.

I tried not to smile as I watched them through the mindlink. Not only was this the first time I'd seen Jax without his maroon bandana tied across his forehead, but it was also the first time I'd seen *him*, but not his shoulders. His obnoxiously huge muscles were lost in a sea of black fabric.

I hoped he would survive.

Boone's line of sight was focused on a large, wooden desk near a back door at the far end of the room. Or rather, on the twenty-something-year-old arcanist behind the desk.

She too wore the black robes of a follower of Streya as she read from a stack of books and papers. She didn't look up as Boone and Jax approached.

"Excuse me, Sister," Boone said without a trace of his usual northern accent, as my brain did the mental equivalent of a double take.

"My apprentice and I were wondering if you could settle a debate. You see, he thinks Streya is the eldest of the goddesses, but I'm quite certain the mind goddess came after the spirit goddess, Solei. What say you?"

The Sister of Streya finally looked up from her book. The mindlink switched from Boone's point of view to Jax's.

Time to watch a master at work, Jax thought arrogantly. It was hard, but I managed to block my disgusted retort from entering the mindlink.

I watched Jax lean on the arcanist's desk, and I got a very strong 'suave eyebrow raise' vibe. The woman checked Jax out, her eyes lingering for a second on his jawline as she considered him. It felt really strange watching it from Jax's own eyes.

She stared at him for a second longer before turning her focus to Boone. Where her reaction to Jax had been neutral at best, she really seemed to like what she was seeing with Boone.

"I haven't seen a sophisticated gentleman like you around these parts," she said, tucking a lock of hair behind her ear as her eyes shone up at Boone.

Jax accidentally sent a string of surprised and somewhat offended emotions through the mindlink. I chuckled out loud.

"Uh..." Boone said, and the mindlink switched back to his point of view. "Thank you very much, Sister. We're just passing through on our way north to the Bramblewilds, but we had to stop and get a look at Ghost Lake's fabled Arcanum."

"Naturally," the arcanist said. Then she glanced at Jax, a disappointed look on her face. "And obviously Streya is the middle born of the three goddesses, hence mind is the bridge between body and spirit. That's something you should've learned before entering your first sanctuary."

Through Boone's eyes, I saw Jax's crestfallen face. Guess he wasn't used to rejection.

Change of plan, Solrac thought to the group. *Switch roles. Boone, you flirt to distract the arcanist, and Jax, you go with Valla and Shaya into the restricted tower.*

Boone mentally agreed while Jax thought a grumbling reply.

"I have noticed he's ill-prepared for the life of a true follower of Streya," Boone shrugged. "I do what I can, but with some pupils it's all in one ear and out the other."

"I know," the Sister said. "I won't even tell you about one of the girls I apprenticed with."

"But please, tell me."

Boone sidled closer to the arcanist as she chatted on. Meanwhile, the mindlink jumped to Valla's perspective.

Valla the frost weasel slunk from her hiding place in Boone's sleeve. She lithely leapt to the floor, then scurried under the desk.

From there, she wrapped her tiny paws around the leg of the desk and shimmied her way up to the top. The arcanist was fully engrossed in her conversation with Boone, so she didn't notice as Valla used her hind paws to shove the top drawer open and sneak inside, her extra sharp weasel vision allowing her to see inside the near darkness of the drawer.

She pawed her way through papers, scrolls, and inkwells. The back of the drawer was coated in a layer of dust, and Valla let out a tiny weasel sneeze.

Aww, commented Kari. *That was the cutest thing I've ever heard.*

Shut up, Valla mentally replied.

Finally, in the back corner of the drawer, Weasel-Valla found a shiny, gold key.

She clutched the key close, then scampered out of the drawer and down the leg of the desk. Instead of returning to the folds of Boone's sleeve, she jumped into Jax's.

Well done, everyone, Solrac thought. *Jax, Valla, leave Boone with the arcanist and move on. Shaya, where are you?*

Shaya's point of view burst on to the mindlink. She must've dropped focus from her etherarchy, because as I watched her hands, her invisibility flickered, then went out so that she was visible again. Now that she'd snuck past the arcanist and made it to the alcove with the forbidden tower, it didn't matter as much. Better to conserve her ether.

She stood at the roped-off end of a long hallway. At the other end was an intricately carved wooden door.

Use the Lightwielder's torch, Solrac thought.

Shaya reached into a pouch at her hip. She pulled out a bronze torch about the size of her hand.

The torch wasn't lit—instead, a white crystal was embedded in the top. Through the mindlink, I felt Shaya concentrating on activating the torch, lending it some ether.

Suddenly, it blazed to life, shooting a wide, white beam of light through the prisms of the crystal.

As the light poured into the hallway, it revealed about fifty thin, violet beams of concentrated dream energy that had been cloaked using an illusion. Each beam bridged the width of the hallway at a different angle, making a sort of maze to keep out intruders. One touch would knock you out and set off an alarm.

Shaya set the Lightwielder's torch down on the ground so that its light kept the dream beams visible. Then, she sprang into action.

I almost got dizzy as I watched her navigate the beams from her own perspective. She squoze under some, tumbled around others, and even threw in a backbend or two to get past more. My jaw fell open as I watched her acrobatic prowess in my mind. She didn't touch a single dream beam.

Shaya finished with a probably-unnecessary front flip over the final beam, then twisted a violet crystal set in the doorway at the end of the hall.

When she twisted the relic, every dream beam sputtered, then went out.

Stars, Shaya, I thought through the mindlink. *That was the most amazing thing I've ever seen.* She hadn't even used any levitation to do it.

I told y'all Shaya'd be better for the team than a drakapple for a scaly mule, Boone put in.

Impressive, Solrac said, and I sensed something deeply sincere behind his voice.

It's nothing! Shaya thought back to all of us, but I could feel her bright smile though the mindlink. *What are you guys waiting for? We have a tome to steal.*

The mindlink switched to Jax's point of view. He and Valla, still in frost weasel form, ducked under the forbidden section's warning rope and ran down the dream beam-free hallway toward Shaya. When they arrived, Jax's gaze looked Shaya up and down. She wore a tight, black outfit, probably to ensure she didn't hit any beams on her trip down the hallway. Though, the way Jax's eyes ran over her, he was clearly enjoying the way it hugged her body.

Admittedly, I did too.

Jax, you have three seconds to keep your mind to yourself, Shaya said through the mindlink, her tone stern and disapproving. I briefly wondered what Kari thought of this, but then again, she seemed unfazed by Jax having kissed seventy girls.

Jax looked away, grabbing the little gold key from his robes. He shoved it into the lock on the door and turned.

Jax, Shaya, and Valla the weasel entered the Arcanum's restricted tower.

The inside was paradise for Kai. The tower held at least as many books as the main floor. Rows of shelves covered the walls from the floor to the high ceilings. Tall ladders on wheels leaned against the walls so that patrons could get at the higher books. Apricot-sized glowing spheres floated all around the room, each filled with some kind of liquid. Some were yellow, some deep magenta, and others blue like moonlight. The liquid inside moved, little bubbles rising and sliding along the insides of the spheres. The spheres almost looked like they were alive, slowly lighting up the ancient books as they went.

Drak, Jax thought. *How're we supposed to find the tome in all these books?*

Il Toma Ilusor is deep blue, Solrac thought. *With silver lettering along the spine.*

Wonderful, Valla thought. *You just described half the books here.*

That's why we sent three of you! Get started!

A gold cloud surrounded Valla as she wildshaped back into human form. The cloud dissipated, then Valla, Shaya, and Jax began scouring the bookshelves. The mindlink still displayed Jax's perspective as he pulled out blue book after blue book.

This here book search is takin' forever, Enya commented through the mindlink.

Look at the bright side, I thought. *At least we now have evidence that Jax knows how to read.*

Mental chuckles echoed through my brain, along with a splash of frustration from Jax.

Watch yourself, Dragon-boy, he thought.

Soot, Solrac swore over the mindlink.

What is it? Valla responded.

The High Mage, Solrac said, his thought betraying slight panic. *I've spotted him heading into the Arcanum. Boone, intercept him!*

The mindlink switched back to Boone's point of view just as the arcanist desk girl was in the middle of a story about her days studying with the Sisters in Keep Drakfell proper.

"...and that's when I knew the path of Streya was superior to the path of Selene—hey!"

Boone darted away from the arcanist, leaping in front of the High Mage, who was making a beeline toward the back door that led up to the restricted tower.

"Excuse me, kind sir," Boone said, his northern accent slipping slightly into his words. "I wonder if you could settle a debate I was having with this here young lady. See, she thinks the path of Streya is—"

"Step aside," the High Mage said with a wave from his long, wooden staff. The staff was carved with a whole row of Mystic runes, and held a large, white crystal stuck to its top.

Wait, not just a crystal—A skystone.

Stars. This was a foe we really didn't want to have to face.

The High Mage sidestepped Boone.

"Beggin' your pardon, High Mage, sir—" Boone tried again, desperately reaching for the High Mage's shoulder.

The High Mage jerked away. "Enough. My seership has granted me a vision wherein our Arcanum was beset by rebels tonight. Now, step aside."

The High Mage walked even more briskly, quickly closing in on the staircase.

Enya, we need a distraction, Solrac thought. *Blow the bridge, now.*

Can't, Enya thought back. *Kari and I aren't clear. We're in the middle of settin' the last explosive.*

From Boone's eyes, we watched the High Mage disappear up the staircase leading to the alcove of the forbidden tower. Pretty soon, he'd see that his dream beams had been deactivated in the hallway.

Drak, Solrac cursed again. We all felt his uncertainty and rising panic. *We need a better distraction.*

I took a step toward the edge of the raft where Kai and I hid.

"What are you doing?" Kai said, brows furrowing.

"I can't just sit here. I'm gonna do it."

Kai and I locked eyes, and he didn't need a mindlink to know what I was thinking.

"No," he said, brown eyes widening.

"I'm going to."

"Asher, *no*."

"Yes," I said as I burned ether, my eyes flashing gold. "I'm gonna mess with the owl."

Chapter 14: The Bridge

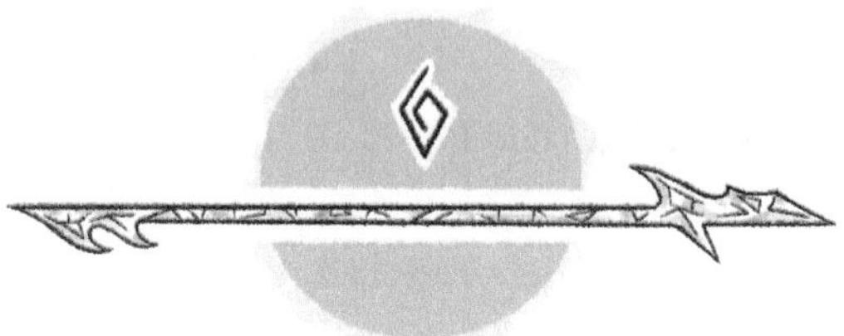

Thorn abandoned his position and met me on the dock. At least *he* liked my idea. Within moments, we'd flown up to the watchtower where the man-sized ethereal owl stared out into the night.

I didn't waste any time. From Thorn's back, I burned ether to form a ball of starglass.

Then I chucked it at the back of the owl's head.

The owl's body didn't move, but his head rotated one-hundred-eighty degrees so that those gigantic purple eyes bored into me.

We had a quick staring contest, neither of us moving for a moment.

Then, the owl let out a single, angry hoot.

That did it. The sound alerted the guards on the other watchtowers, and the clanking of weapons and armor sounded in my ears.

But that was nothing compared to the chaos that erupted in my head. The mindlink switched to my perspective, and everyone had an opinion about the angry owl that was now slowly spreading its wide wings in front of me.

Boone's thought came first. *Why's the High Mage rushing back toward the south tower faster'na hunted fanged shrew? Oh...*

What in the void is going on? Kari thought.

Drakked if that isn't... Solrac thought as he registered what I was seeing over the mindlink.

Who messed with the owl? Shaya thought.

Asher, you didn't. Valla's anger was clear.

Asher messed with the owl? Enya thought.

Asher messed with the owl, Kai confirmed, his thought sounding grave.

There was a quick moment of tense silence as the owl hovered above Thorn and me. Then she dropped her wings, revealing the High Mage himself standing behind them. Soot, he was faster than I'd expected.

His face was the perfect blend of smug arrogance and bitter rage. His long, black robes caught the twilight breeze, and the white crystal at his forehead glinted against the light coming from the chunk of skystone in his runemarked staff.

Soot, Dragon-boy, Jax swore over the mindlink. *Try not to die.*

Yes, it would be nice if our valiant distraction were to avoid death, Solrac agreed. *Asher's bought us some time, but the High Mage has undoubtedly alerted the Mage Hunters by now. Everyone, move quickly.*

A few guards arrived from inside the tower, pulling out crossbows and taking aim at me. Thorn roared. The High Mage put up a hand to stop the guards' firing.

"Once I teach this thief his place, the wyvern is yours to muzzle," he said.

Fiery anger filled my heart at that thought. Thorn's too. Oh, this High Mage was going down. I burned ether, summoning my starglass dragonhook spear.

The High Mage laughed. "I'm a Seer. You cannot hope to defeat me in combat. I can see every move you plan to make."

Without thinking, I leapt down from Thorn's back and onto the tower in front of the High Mage and his owl.

"Lucky for me," I said, aware of my entire team watching me through the mindlink, "I've never been good with plans."

With that, I sent an ether blast at the owl from my spear.

It was a sad effort, and it dissipated before reaching him, which made the Seer laugh at me. That gave me a chance to throw a one-handed spear jab at his throat, which he blocked with his staff. Luckily, his focus on that made him miss my last-minute sucker punch to his gut.

The punch knocked the wind out of him. Clearly this guy had never taken a hit. Thorn flew in to distract the owl and guards while I fought the High Mage.

Fighting the High Mage was like tricking Kai's memory reading. I just needed to imagine doing something different than what I was actually doing.

It wasn't easy. The Seer sent out a pulse of purple dream energy along the ground toward my feet. I jumped it easily, but he must've known I would, as he sent out a second pulse just as my feet touched the ground. At once, I felt a wave of tiredness wash over me. A few more hits like that would knock me out.

I was vaguely aware of Solrac's movements over the mindlink. He'd left his post, coming around near the base of the southern tower to get a shot at the guards here. Sure enough, two dream darts sent both guards to the ground.

Over the mindlink, I saw Solrac taking aim at the High Mage next, but before he could fire, Kari's thoughts interrupted.

Mage Hunters on the bridge!

Drak again, Solrac thought. *On my way. Valla, Jax, Shaya, find that tome and get down here!*

I jabbed again at the High Mage, whirling my spear at the last second to swipe at his legs with the smaller blade on the other side. I didn't see that coming, so neither did the High Mage. He grit his teeth and jumped back as I sliced his shin.

Next, I imagined shooting another ether dart at him. That caused him to put up a violet dream energy barrier to block. But the shot never came as I hover charged straight at his chest.

This was kind of fun.

The High Mage foresaw my move just in time to dodge the tip of my spear, but couldn't avoid me tackling him.

Boone's voice came through inside my head. *Just left that little desk darlin' after tellin' her our star signs weren't compatible. Ain't no way an assertive, dynamic little ridgerunner born at the first of the year can be with a hardheaded craghopper like me... woulda been too fiery. She'll sleep tonight with brokenhearted dreams of this snowheaded Son of Streya. Anyway, on my way to the bridge.*

The High Mage traced a new rune, then threw out his fist toward me. A translucent, violet blade sprouted from his knuckles like an extension of his arm.

Soot. Kai certainly didn't know how to do that with his dreamweave powers.

The High Mage slashed his new dream blade toward me, and I instinctively blocked it with my starglass spear. The High Mage growled when my spear stopped his blade—He was probably used to fighting regular weapons, which his dreamblade would pass right through. But my spear was archonic, made from pure ether.

Enya's voice came through the mindlink. *I just got the final explosive set. Kari's tryna hold off the Mage Hunters, but—*

The rest of her thought cut off. I shuddered to think why.

I'm almost there, came Solrac's reply.

I've got the tome! Shaya shouted in our minds as I blocked another slash from the High Mage's dreamblade.

Solrac answered. *Good. Now get out of there!*

I imagined stabbing the High Mage's arm, but instead rushed in and grabbed hold of his beard. He looked completely caught off guard as I stared right into his wide eyes. My gaze flashed to the skystone on his staff.

I quickly added starglass to the hook on my spear, turning it into a chisel like the one on my skyseeker dagger. I used it to pry the stone right off the top of his staff. As the stone loosened, I grew more starglass onto the end of my spear to catch and encase it on my blade.

The High Mage was still trying to figure out what in the void was going on when I yanked hard on his beard. I hover-dashed away with his skystone, just dodging a stab in the back from his dreamblade.

"Asher! Thorn!"

I looked up and saw Shaya waving her arm from one of the windows in the central restricted tower.

Right. Thorn was supposed to be the getaway dragon.

Just like the High Mage, the owl must've been able to anticipate Thorn's strikes, too. Thorn still hadn't been able to land a hit on the arrogant bird. I watched as they circled each other in the air, the owl swooping to avoid strikes from Thorn's tail.

I sent a burn of urgency to Thorn, directing him toward Shaya in the window. He gave a growl, then disengaged from the fight, soaring upward.

I leaped onto the tower wall, readying my spear for the High Mage's next strike. But he had a strange, faraway look on his face, as if his eyes were seeing something beyond what was in front of him. Then he cast his gaze toward the bridge.

"Fools!" he shouted. "You will not destroy the Mirror Sanctum!"

With one flap of her wings, the owl was at the High Mage's side. He leaped onto her back, and together they took off toward the bridge.

"Soot," I muttered, then sent my warning thought through the mindlink. *The High Mage is heading for the bridge.*

And so was I.

Thorn was already swooping toward the bridge, struggling under the weight of both Jax and Shaya, although it looked like Shaya was using a little levitation etherarchy to make it easier on him. Valla was back in frostweasel form, which made her weigh next to nothing as well.

From the outer wall of the tower, I could see the action on the high bridge that connected the Arcanum to the Mirror Sanctum.

I removed the skystone from my spearblade and caught my breath for a second. A warm energy pulsed through me as I touched the stone, and I could feel another reserve of ether, like my own ether well. It glowed more dimly than the skystone I'd stolen at Whitestone Hall, so I knew the High Mage had drawn a lot from it while fighting me.

Instinctually, I breathed in. The skystone's glow went out completely as I felt my own internal ether well refill. My well wasn't even close to full—stars, it hadn't even been enough to get me back up to halfway—but it was something. I pocketed the drained stone.

From my vantage point on the tower of the Arcanum, I surveyed the scene.

Solrac, His Majesty, and Boone fought the same four Mage Hunters we'd seen back in Steel Rim. It dawned on me that when the Mage Hunters rifted away from the town square, they must've gone to an anchor here in Ghost Lake—probably in the Mirror Sanctum.

The young, redheaded Mage Hunter, Lothar, fought alongside his green evren against His Majesty. The bloodhusky bared his teeth as he swiped at the four-winged dragon.

Solrac's seaxe and Boone's ether blasts went up against the silver weapons of the other three Mage Hunters. The dark-haired jailer's daughter, as well as the illusionist—though I didn't see a rune up over his forehead now—blocked every blow. His snake spat purple stars of energy that passed through Solrac and Boone's armor.

I did a double take when I saw the fourth Mage Hunter. It was the hulking Geomancer. He was alive and well, standing menacingly over Kari, while Enya already lay still off to the side.

Hold up, I thought over the mindlink, sending the group a mental picture of what I was seeing. *Valla, didn't you kill this guy back in Steel Rim?*

I heard Valla growl back in our heads as she caught sight of the Mage Hunter. *Drakking Geomancers... too resilient.*

The Geomancer's skin erupted in gold Sentinel patterns as Kari fired her crossbow. She aimed at his vulnerable underarm, where his chest plate ended. The gold patterns glowed bright and Kari's bolt—which should have done a lot of damage at such a close distance—bounced off of him as if it had hit a solid block of granite.

The Geomancer smiled, then reached toward Kari.

I had to get over there. Without hesitation, I jumped off the edge of the tower, burning ether to ease my fall. Then I hover-charged onto the high bridge, the gently-lapping water far below. Above me, Thorn raced toward the action, still carrying Valla, Jax, and Shaya.

Kari's terrified perspective played over the mindlink, but I saw from my own angle as the Geomancer raised his silver sword above Kari's head.

My eyes blazed as I put on an extra burst of speed, but the bridge was too long. I wouldn't make it in time. None of us would.

But that didn't stop Jax.

A psionically-powered ship's anchor shot through the air. Jax must've telekinetically pulled it from a boat below the bridge. The anchor rammed into the Geomancer, knocking him sideways. Kari thanked Jax through the mindlink and darted away, joining Solrac.

The Geomancer slid, his broad frame slamming into the rails along one side of the bridge. His momentum splintered the wood, and the Geomancer almost fell into the water below. He flailed for a moment, but steadied himself.

Figuring I could finish the job myself, I hover-dashed toward him, throwing my shoulder into his chest to knock him off the bridge.

Thump.

Gold Sentinel patterns swam in my vision as I reeled back from the impact. It was like I'd just hit a stone wall.

In my head, I heard Kai trying to direct the fight. *Boone, can you get to Asher before that Geomancer rips his head off?*

The mindlink showed Boone's right starglass dagger shattering against Jaira's silver sword, and his reply was strained. *Little busy with this sootling.*

Ah, Kai's frustration came through. *If these Mage Hunters would just come at you guys one at a time, I'd have the perfect plans to take them down.*

Wonderful, Valla's thought was sarcastic. *Maybe if we ask nicely, they'll hold still while we slit their throats.*

We could use a little help over here, too, Kari put in, showing us an image of Solrac psionically controlling a dagger to get around the illusionist's lashing whip. The floating dagger dropped to the ground when the silver chain hit it.

Soot, Kai swore. *There's silver everywhere.*

It's almost like they're trained to hunt magi, Valla said.

On my way, Kari, Jax said, jumping off of Thorn's back as he landed on the bridge. Thorn roared as Shaya slid off his saddle and hurried over to Enya, making sure she was alright. Thorn took to the skies again, watching for the owl and the High Mage. Valla wasted no time either, launching her furry, frostweasel body toward me.

Duck, she thought, and I did, just in time.

Her tiny claws poised, she latched onto the Geomancer's cloak. Then she scurried under the collar of his tunic and went for his throat.

The Mage Hunter yelped, squirming as Valla zipped around under his clothes, biting and clawing at his chest and back.

Having recovered from my run-in with the Geomancer, I hurried to where Boone faced off against Jaira. She swung her sword with a vengeance, effectively using the silver to block Boone's ether blasts.

"We meet again, darling Helga." I gave a lopsided grin as I readied my dragonhook spear.

Jaira sneered as she struck my blade. My starglass weapon shattered into a million gold specks of spent ether.

"Like I said before," Jaira smirked. "You're really not my type, ether-cursed."

Stars, if we were going to keep running into Mage Hunters, I should start carrying a non-ether powered weapon. I had my dad's skyseeker dagger, but that wasn't exactly the best weapon for fighting a sword. Still, it was better than nothing.

I drew the long dagger and burned more ether, levitating to dodge her next strikes. She drove me back, separating me from the rest of the group.

A long hoot resounded from above us and I looked up to see the High Mage flying in on his owl, dodging around Thorn, a ripple of violet energy blasting toward the bridge. He made a twisting motion with his hand, and the energy matched the movement to come rushing across the bridge like an ocean wave.

Block it, Kai ordered over the mindlink.

How? came a few replies.

The Mage Hunters were ready, their silver armor and swords stopping the low pulse from downing them. Solrac runetraced just fast enough to put up a dream barrier for himself. Boone jumped just in time, levitating above the wave. I tried to do the same, but with a well-placed strike, Jaira made me miss the timing.

The blast hit the rest of the team as well.

A wave of exhaustion hit us, and I got the sudden urge to lie down and take a nap. The dream pulse hadn't been enough to knock any of us out—probably because the High Mage no longer had the extra ether boost from his skystone—but stars, everyone had lost a lot of energy.

We need to do something about him, Kai ordered through the mindlink. His thoughts felt strained. Running this many Glints for the mindlink must've been taxing.

Boone, go, Solrac thought. *He's a Seer. He'll read your next move, so be careful.*

On it, Boone replied. He used his levitation to take off then, hovering high in the air, he fired off multiple ether blasts at once toward the High Mage and his owl. Boone hollered as he fired wildly, driving the ether-depleted High Mage back toward the Arcanum.

Kari just took a hit, Jax thought tiredly.

Thorn, I thought through both the bond and the mindlink. *Get her out of here.*

I heard a roar from my wyvern, and out of the corner of my eye I saw him struggling to carry Kari away from the bridge. Some dream energy had hit him too. Enya was gone. Shaya must've already gotten her out as well.

Just then, I heard a pained squeak and realized the Geomancer had finally grabbed hold of Valla's frostweasel tail. He held her up in the air, a triumphant grin on his face.

Solrac must've heard the squeak too because he recklessly disengaged from his fight with the illusionist. The anchor Jax had pulled from the ship earlier still lay nearby on the bridge. Solrac raised a hand, psionically lifting the anchor and sending it rushing toward the Geomancer.

The anchor caught the Mage Hunter off guard, and one of the pointed ends speared him right through the gut. I winced. The Mage Hunter fell limply onto the wooden slats of the bridge, releasing Valla.

Solrac's distraction left him wide open for an attack from the illusionist. Jax tried to get between Solrac and the illusionist's whip, barely grabbing the Mage Hunter's wrist in time to stop the strike. The illusionist's snake hissed, spitting a purple dream star in Jax's face. A wave of fatigue seemed to hit him.

The redheaded Mage Hunter saw his opening, lashing out his own chain whip and tying Jax's hands up in it. Jax cried out as the icy silver restrained him. Meanwhile, the illusionist bounced back, grappling Solrac with his own silver chain. His Majesty whined as the Mage Hunter captured Solrac, giving the green evren the chance she needed to pin him to the bridge with the claws on her forewings.

"You're next," Jaira warned, the relentless swipes from her silver sword keeping me from rushing toward my friends. I could barely block them with my dagger.

The Mage Hunters harshly wrapped Solrac and Jax's wrists with their silver chain whips so they couldn't free themselves, much less channel ether. Lothar raised his blade to deliver a killing blow.

Suddenly, six pools of shiny water spilled into existence all around them. The Mage Hunters froze as purple, energy-filled water rose out of the pools and took shape. Six black ethereal starswans spread their wings, bursting from the pools and flying circles around Solrac, Jax, and the Mage Hunters.

Soot, Kai's thought matched my feelings exactly.

That isn't... Jax thought through the mind link. Then I heard him speak one word out loud.

"Mom?"

I stopped in my tracks, almost allowing Jaira to land a hit. I hover-leaped her blade just in time.

Had Jax just said 'mom?'

Wait, I thought over the mindlink, disbelief coloring my tone. *Jax... Jax is...*

The Black Valkyrie's son, Jax confirmed as he scowled at the circling starswans.

But... I tried to collect my thoughts. *Vidya and Solrac...?*

Jax isn't Solrac's, Valla clarified.

I fought the urge to vomit. It turned out my instinct to dislike the arrogant hotshot had a good basis.

The swans flew into the Mage Hunters' faces, flapping their wings angrily. Three starswans dove toward the green dragon, stopping her from further harming His Majesty.

What was going on?

Solrac frowned at the swans, looking just as concerned. Then he set his jaw.

Enya? he thought through the mindlink.

I'm here, came her groggy response.

Blow the bridge, Solrac commanded.

What? thought Valla.

Kai was confused. *But all of you are still on it.*

Valla can wildshape into a dragonhawk. Asher can levitate to safety. Thorn will come for His Majesty and Jax, Solrac replied with determination. *Blow the bridge.*

But— Valla protested.

Blow it, Enya!

This time, Enya didn't hesitate to activate her ether-powered detonator.

The first explosion thundered from the direction of the Mirror Sanctum, accompanied by an eruption of emerald green dragonfire. Then, with three more earth shaking booms, the entire Mirror Sanctum went up in flames.

Jaira's eyes went wide as the fire leapt high into the air. Admittedly, mine did too. I hadn't realized just how thoroughly Enya had done her job.

The explosives at the Mirror Sanctum triggered the one that Enya and Kari had placed at the far end of the bridge. That triggered the next explosive along the bridge, this one even closer to us.

The Mage Hunters caught on.

The green evren sprang into action, Lothar gracelessly leaping onto her back. She was on her second ascension, so she was big enough to carry the illusionist as well. Jaira, not about to get left behind, gave a perfect lash of her whip, wrapping the end of it onto the green dragon's saddlehorn. She held on tight to her end of the chain as the dragon, struggling under the weight, flew to safety.

The third explosive went off. I felt the pulse of heat across my face.

Thorn swooped in, just like Solrac knew he would, and gently grabbed His Majesty in his talons. But as Jax tried to jump onto his back, the end of the silver chain around his wrists caught in the slats of the bridge.

The fourth explosive went off, the smoke spilling toward us from across the bridge. The supports beneath us wobbled. A black dragonhawk streaked across the sky—Valla's escape.

Jax couldn't free himself. He waved for Thorn to go, and Thorn did, a pang of worry sparking through our bond. Solrac stood strong, the starswans still circling him.

I knew I had just enough ether in me to levitate myself to safety if I jumped now. But the tight, fluttering sensation in my chest told me I didn't have enough to do more.

The fifth explosive went off, and I felt the bridge supports collapse.

At the last second, a flash of red hair appeared amidst the smoke and splintering wood. Shaya had been on the bridge as well, invisible. She must've been trying to sneak up on the Mage Hunters.

My heart caught in my throat.

Shaya sprinted toward Solrac, grabbing him around the waist as the bridge gave out.

Asher, I heard Shaya's voice over the mindlink. *Jax.*

I knew what she wanted me to do. She wanted me to save the Black Valkyrie's son.

I hover-dashed toward Jax, white ether trailing behind me like a comet as the sixth explosive went off beneath my feet.

My ears rang as the rest of the world went silent all around me. It was only black smoke, green flame, and splintering wood as my feet stumbled through empty air.

I felt the cold rush of silver chains as I reached out for Jax's hand. I bit back the pain, holding onto him and doing all I could to keep us levitating above the wreckage.

I saw Shaya and Solrac shakily reach a dock-supporting column far enough from the bridge to be safe. Good.

Jax and I wouldn't make it that far. Thorn reached out to me with a panicked flare through our bond—He'd saved His Majesty but couldn't make it to us in time.

Just as I felt like my chest was about to explode from ether overuse, and I was sure the seventh bomb would finish us off, one thought took hold of my mind:

Dad's rift anchors.

I pulled a pair of runemarked stones from my satchel as we fell. I threw the black one as far as I could, funneling some ether into the stone and praying it was enough to levitate it to the safety of the dock beside the Arcanum.

With the final fumes from my ether well, I activated the white rift anchor. Beneath me, a gold-rimmed portal ripped to life.

My eyes rolled back in my head as Jax and I disappeared into the whiteness of Etheria.

Fragment - Jaira

Jaira stared into the reflection of the green flames dancing across the dark surface of Ghost Lake. The locals around these parts said spirits liked to float along the still water at night. But from where Jaira stood on the shore, all she could see were the sorry remains of the Mirror Sanctum burning bright.

Jaira exhaled bitterly. She and the other Mage Hunters had worked tirelessly with the town guard to put out the fires before they reached the arcanum, but they'd been unable to save the Sanctum. Lothar and his evren were out flying amongst the ruins, searching for anything worth salvaging. But Jaira feared the secrets the building once held now rested at the bottom of the eerily still lake.

Jaira's upper lip twisted in frustration. Even worse, they'd lost track of Asher and the other Knights of the Torch in the process.

If Jaira had known the thieving little half-born had been with the Knights, she would've ended him herself back at Whitestone Hall. But she'd only just come back from the Mage Hunter Academy, still unsure of how to properly fulfill her duties. Only a month or so had passed since then, but to Jaira, it felt like a lifetime.

The sound of beating wings drew Jaira's attention. A single black swan glided toward her, landing at her feet. Before Jaira's eyes, the swan's form went watery, shining with gold light as it splashed upward into the air.

Then the swan was gone, the likeness of the Black Valkyrie taking its place. The Mage Hunter, Illyan, must've been nearby, allowing the Black Valkyrie to communicate through his illusion projected onto her ethereal swan familiar.

"Hello, Jaira," the black-clad illusion gave a pleasant smile.

Jaira reverently inclined her head. "Forgive us for our failure today, great Black Valkyrie." Jaira looked up boldly. "Though, I believe you have some explaining to do."

The Black Valkyrie laughed through her illusion. "Not one to mince words, I see. I like that. You're almost too good at your job, you know."

Jaira scowled. "We were about to capture the Knights when you…"

"Interfered?" the Black Valkyrie offered.

Jaira nodded.

The Black Valkyrie gave a small, smug smile. "Do you know why those fools were here in the first place?"

"To destroy the Mirror Sanctum." Jaira gestured toward the still-burning building atop its platform over the lake.

"That's what they wanted us to believe. But were you aware that prior to obliterating the Mirror Sanctum, the Knights of the Torch robbed the arcanum?"

"No," Jaira admitted. "The High Mage did mention a premonition about some danger there, but he said it must've been about the Mirror Sanctum."

"One day you'll learn that premonitions can be wrong."

"Perhaps," Jaira frowned. "But that doesn't explain why you stopped us from capturing them. Then we could've retrieved the stolen items as well as brought the magi in for execution."

"And in doing so, lost our much greater prize," the Black Valkyrie spoke harshly, and Jaira bit her tongue. "The Farseer. He's the true mastermind behind the Knights of the Torch. We catch *him*, we stop hundreds of rogue magi across the realm."

Jaira stood up straighter. She couldn't believe she'd overlooked that. Although Jaira still got the feeling there was more to the Black Valkyrie's interference on the bridge—something she wasn't telling Jaira and the others.

"Besides," the Black Valkyrie continued, "now we know about the Knights' safehouse here in Ghost Lake. In the morning, we'll make an example of the Drowsy Drekling tavern. Tie up a few more loose ends here while Shaw recovers from that unfortunate incident with the anchor, and we'll move on to Keep Drakfell. There, we'll draw out the Farseer once and for all. Doesn't that sound better than capturing a few magi on a bridge?"

Jaira nodded, her fingers absently tracing along the silver whip at her belt. "The Knights will rue the day they crossed the Black Valkyrie."

The illusion smiled. "I knew I was right to keep you around, Jaira. Your loyalty will not go unrewarded."

With that, the illusion went translucent before splashing onto the sandy shore. The black swan spread its wings, taking off into the dark sky.

A cold feeling rushed over Jaira, as if a brisk wind were cutting across her face. But her hair and clothing remained completely still, unmoving.

Jaira, she heard someone say her name. Jaira turned around, expecting to see the Black Valkyrie, back to give some last minute instruction. But Jaira saw nobody.

"Ilyan?" she called into the darkness. "Lothar?"

But the other Mage Hunters didn't answer. Jaira was alone—she was sure of it. Jaira turned back to the fiery reflections in the water. As she stared into Ghost Lake's inky, still surface, she could've sworn she saw a pair of glowing, blue eyes staring back at her.

Jaira cocked her head, taking a closer look at the water. Suddenly, something replaced the cold emptiness she'd been feeling before, something strong and powerful. Perhaps Jaira didn't feel so alone after all.

Chapter 15: The Dragonstorm Sea

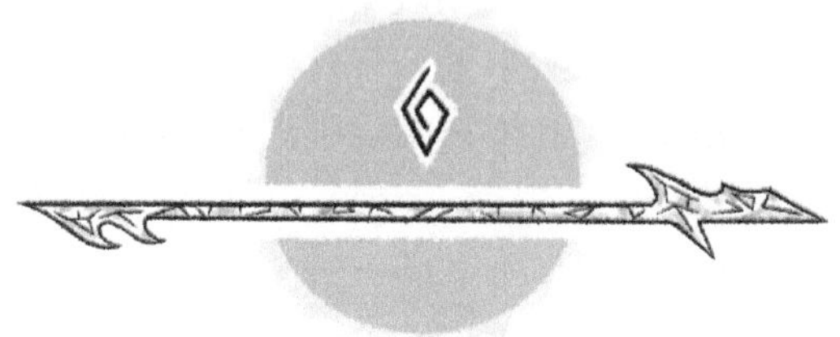

When I finally opened my eyes, all I could see was blue sky. The sound of waves crashing against the hull of a ship rushed in my ears, along with Valla's annoyed voice.

"You just had to mess with the owl."

I sat up with a grin. "Did you expect anything less?"

Valla rolled her eyes. She sat on a pile of boxes near the front of the ship's deck. A large, carved figurehead of a naga, a deadly water dragon, rose proudly off the bow behind her.

A low growl from behind me made me jump. Thorn pressed his black and bronze nose against my cheek, sending a fiery feeling of relief through our bond.

"Don't worry," I reassured him as I rubbed his nose. "I'm just fine."

"You'd better be," Valla said. "I've spent the past twelve hours healing you and Jax after you decided to blow yourselves up."

"Technically, it was Enya who blew us up," I said. Valla shook her head, but I think she was hiding a smile.

I looked around. I sat on a bedroll near the central mast. When I glanced upward to my side, I saw a wide, rectangular sail. It was Drakfell tan, and proudly bore another depiction of a naga, its long, scaly body winding around itself in the sail's center.

My hand went automatically to my chest. My heart still felt a little jittery, but I could already tell my ether well was refilling.

"Pretty stupid of you," Valla commented, her eyes fixed on the sea ahead of us. "You're lucky your ether overuse only knocked you out. I've seen magi die trying stunts like that."

"I do specialize in stupid," I said. But inside, I heard Dad's voice urging me to be more careful.

"Solei be praised," Boone called out as he wandered over from the back of the longship. "You must have someone in Etheria lookin' out for you."

I remembered what Dad said about Mom keeping an eye on me. I wished I could believe stuff like that. Thorn nudged me again, and I felt another surge of happiness.

"Shaya," I said, suddenly. "And Solrac and the rest. What happened? How did we—"

"Hold yer kirin," Boone casually crossed his arms and leaned against the mast. "Everyone's fine. Shaya's up ridin' higher than an adolescent evren last I checked." Boone pointed a finger upward, and sure enough, I saw red hair streaming from behind the sail as Shaya clung to the top of the mast. A laugh escaped my lips as Boone went on.

"Enya's back in Ghost Lake gettin' stitched up. Should be back workin' at the tavern by nightfall. Solrac's below tryna contact the Farseer, and Kari's—"

"Asher!" Kari appeared in a doorway toward the back of the ship that must've led to the area below deck. Kai was close behind her. They ran toward me, nearly knocking me back down with the force of their embrace.

I laughed and hugged them back.

"I hear you saved my... Jax's life," Kari said, pulling out of the hug and ruffling my hair. "I owe you one."

My Jax? I was about to make fun of Kari for that, but the joke died on my lips. Jax was the son of the woman who killed my mother.

I shrugged. "It was nothing."

"It was crazy," Kai put in, pulling out his black leather notebook. "You had a very low likelihood of success. And the odds of you waking up after overextending your ether like that..."

He shook his head. I shrugged again.

Thud.

We almost lost our balance as the ship jolted.

"What in the void was that?" Boone drew his starglass daggers from their sheaths at his hips faster than the eye could see. He must've formed another to replace the one he'd lost.

Thud. Thud.

The ship rattled again. Jax and Solrac appeared in the doorway from below.

"What's going on?" Jax asked, bracing himself against the doorframe as another *thud* bumped the ship.

"Naga," Valla said, eyebrows lowering. "Not many—maybe one or two."

"Thank the goddesses it's not the dragonstorm," Solrac said.

"They want something," Valla said, peering over the edge. She gripped the side as the naga rocked the ship again.

"Of course," Boone said. "Any of yous tryna sneak a skystone aboard? No naga can resist a nugget of skystone."

Suddenly, my pocket felt heavy. I pulled the chunk of skystone from the High Mage's staff out of my jacket. It glowed brightly in my palm. I'd drained it during the fight yesterday, but now it was brimming with fresh ether, having refilled while I was unconscious.

THUD. THUD THUD.

"That'll do it." Boone eyed my stolen treasure.

Thorn sniffed at the skystone, an excited light in his eyes. Solrac laughed and walked toward me.

"This is the greatest thing that could possibly have happened," he said with a wide grin.

"Right. Drawing every naga in the Dragonstorm Sea is wonderful." Valla's sarcasm was as strong as Solrac's optimism.

Solrac held out a hand. "May I?"

I narrowed my eyes, unsure. He probably just assumed all plunder from our missions belonged to him. Baron Eidan always assumed every nice thing in Steel Rim was his.

I cautiously passed him the skystone.

The skystone's light reflected onto Solrac's dark eyes, bringing out flecks of emerald green toward the center. I remembered what Solrac had said back in the Drunken Drake—something about having half-born blood a few generations back?

Solrac strode over to Thorn and tossed the skystone to him.

"What're you—" I started.

Thorn opened his jaws wide, catching the skystone in his mouth. He swallowed hungrily, and I felt a sensation like beams of light through our bond.

Kai was indignant. "You just wasted a perfectly good skystone."

Solrac grinned as he hurried to undo the buckles of Thorn's saddle, letting it slip to the ground. "Wait for it."

The naga stopped bumping the boat as Thorn contentedly smacked his lips. Then, my wyvern went perfectly still.

Suddenly, his draconic, fiery green eyes flashed bright gold.

I stumbled backward. Thorn was a Sentinel, not an Archon. Next, an elaborate golden rune I didn't recognize appeared over his scaly forehead like a Mystic. Finally, angular Sentinel markings glowed up from all over his skin, and a cloud of golden ether encompassed him entirely.

Everyone backed away, giving Thorn a wide berth as the golden cloud expanded. Thorn's black and copper scales fell in chunks like shattered crystal from within the cloud.

Nerves gripped my heart, as did a little excitement. I could feel Thorn's elation through our bond more powerfully than ever. Whatever was going on, he liked it.

The cloud finally dissipated, followed by the Mystic rune and the archonic glow. Thorn dropped back onto the deck, but he was different now.

He was larger, his hide thicker and his musculature stronger. He had more ridges along his neck, and his stag-like antlers were more grand, with twice the number of sharp points. The copper markings along his black hide were more intricate and a shade or two closer to gold.

As he spread his wider wings, I heard a woody cracking noise. The scales along his flanks, neck, and back erupted into thick, gleaming, diamond-shaped bark, as if they were some kind of built-in Woodweaver's armor. Thorn roared gleefully, then the armored scales retreated back to normal.

That was a power I'd never seen from him before. I realized what the skystone had done.

Thorn had just ascended!

So that was the secret to dragon ascension, so closely guarded by nobility. Skystone.

"I'd wondered what power he'd gain when ascending," Kai said, eyes wide with wonder. "I thought maybe making ether berries or folians, but it looks like he got diamondoak armor. I'll bet he can regrow his tailblades faster too." He started taking notes.

"We'll want to gather the shed scales and hide to make you some proper ascension armor now," Solrac told me. Thorn bowed to Solrac, then playfully nudged him with gratitude.

Thorn sent me a powerful feeling like a crackling bonfire, and I laughed out loud. Our bond seemed to have doubled in strength and intensity. I ran toward him, rushing to refasten his saddle. As I leaped onto his back, I realized it barely fit him now.

"What are you doing?" Kai asked.

"Taking my new dragon out for a whirl!" I yelled as Thorn smiled and used his muscular hind legs to launch us off the deck and into the sky.

I filled my days at sea by riding Thorn above the stormdeck longship. I was grateful Solrac had access to a ship just big enough to land a dragon on board. Maybe traveling with a noble wasn't all bad.

When we weren't flying, Thorn practiced fishing for various types of small naga with his tailblade while I worked on my astromancy with Boone. I was still having trouble getting my ether to take the form of energy blasts, the way Boone did to shoot with his daggers. He'd helped me learn how to charge starglass with ether, but I still couldn't get it to blast out.

Jax and I sparred on the deck on long afternoons. We were still so evenly matched, and the duels rarely ended in a victory so much as they ended in Kari or Shaya stopping us from doing any real damage—either to ourselves or the longship. Now, every time I saw his steely hair or cold, dark blue eyes, I saw those of his murderous mother.

I channeled that into my fighting. When I swung my starglass spear toward Jax, an extra boost of ether-power filled every strike. One time, I'd hit him in the ribs with the flat of my blade, and a jet of white ether had pulsed from the end of it. Jax had yelped as a sharp, painful sensation hit his nerves, and when he'd taken off his shirt afterward, jagged white marks spiraled from where I'd struck. Valla said the blast had been mild enough that the mark would fade, but that I needed to be more careful when I had breakthroughs in my etherarchy.

But I couldn't help but be excited. Every breakthrough I had prepared me for the day when I'd finally face Vidya.

Jax refused to spar with me for a couple of days after the whole ether-burning incident, but Shaya was willing to help me get the practice in. She was quick and agile as she dodged my strikes, only offensively swinging her shadowspear toward me when she really wanted to hit hard. Her calm fighting style contrasted harshly with the way Jax fought—as if he was actually trying to kill me. The way I fought with Shaya was more like a dance.

The rest of the team kept themselves busy as well. Kari spent a lot of time below deck experimenting. She'd only burned one hole in the boat so far, but she swore she was making progress. She seemed even more distracted than usual lately, and had at least two or three different projects spread over her worktable. It held vials of spydra venom, a pilfered Mage Hunter's whip, not to mention some of the scales and hide Thorn had shed during his ascension. Jax tried to get her to slow down for a second, but Kari enjoyed being busy.

Shaya liked watching the waves from her new favorite perch—between the horns on top of the naga figurehead. She fearlessly sat on the point of the ship, feet dangling dangerously over the water. The wind tossed her long, red draketail hairstyle like a flag. She said she loved feeling like she was part of the boat itself. That made me smile.

Kai, on the other hand, was no fan of our time sailing across the Dragonstorm Sea. He was chronically seasick, and spent most of his time curled up below deck. When he wasn't nauseous to the point of passing out, he was reading through our stolen rune book, *Il Toma Ilusor*, or taking notes in his black journal.

I found him on his bedroll below doing just that. I sat next to him and looked over his shoulder at the page he was working on. He scrawled notes in tiny handwriting underneath a one-word heading.

'Shaya.'

"Still working on your journal of observations about the team?" I asked, trying to get a better look at his notes on Shaya.

He nodded, still writing.

"What are your top secret conclusions about Shaya then? Think she likes me?"

Kai finished up his tiny notes with a period. "Do you really want to know?"

Suddenly, I felt nervous. I checked the doorway to make sure nobody was listening in. Then I turned to Kai.

"Shoot."

Kai scanned his notes. "Yeah, I'd say there's a ninety-two percent chance she likes you."

I jumped, burning just a tiny bit of ether to levitate. "Yes!"

"But," Kai said, running a finger over his notebook. "I can't figure out why."

That took the levitation out of my step. "Whoa, harsh."

"Not that. I'm mean, of course you two like each other—you're both daredevils who egg each other on. What I can't figure out is why Shaya is working with the Knights of the Torch."

"What do you mean? It's because she wants a better world for magi."

"Right, but that's too obvious."

I raised an eyebrow.

"I mean, everyone here has a complex motive for being here. Take Solrac. Sure, he believes in the cause and all..." Kai trailed off, then lowered his voice to a whisper. "But despite the Knights of the Torch's financial straits, I think he's really in it because he wants to bond the true dragon egg himself."

I almost laughed, then thought about it for half a second. Solrac may be an okay guy, and he'd just helped Thorn ascend, but I had to remember he was nobility. Nobles were always after more power and prestige. Maybe Kai's theory had some merit.

"And Boone's in it because he hates the Mage Hunters. I haven't asked for sure, but my guess is that they took someone from him."

I thought about how Boone wore a short, bristly beard and a marriage bracelet on his left wrist. But I'd never heard him talk about a wife.

"Jax is simple," Kai went on. "He wants to earn Solrac's approval."

"Really?" I smiled, not totally sure why I liked the idea of Jax desperately trying to impress someone.

Kai nodded. "Kari pretends all she wants is to throw all her skills into a just fight for magi freedom."

Kai went so quiet I could barely hear him, and suddenly he couldn't make eye contact.

"But I think she's really here because she hopes we'll find Mom and Dad."

"I thought we knew they were..."

"But what if they're not?" Kai looked up at me with knit brows and round, brown eyes. I realized that it wasn't just Kari who was here because she still had hope of finding their parents.

"Then there's me," I said with a smirk, trying to lighten the mood. "Everyone knows exactly why I'm here."

Kai tilted his head. "Except you, maybe."

"What are you talking about? I'm here to kill the Black Valkyrie. Isn't that why you all chose not to tell me Jax was Vidya's son? I've been practicing astromancy with Boone—I think I'm nearly ready to take her down."

Kai shrugged, then took a few notes in his journal.

"What?" I said, reaching for the black leather book. "You don't have a list of observations about me, do you?"

Kai held the notebook out of my reach, then tried to change the subject.

"So you want to hear why Valla's in it?"

I grabbed him by the arm and started wrestling him to the ground to get that notebook.

Of course, that's when Kari appeared in the doorway.

"Charming, boys." She rolled her eyes. "Just when I was starting to think you'd grown up a little."

I let Kai go, and he clutched the notebook securely to his chest.

Kari took a few more steps into the cabin. "What's this about Valla?"

"Kai thinks he knows her true motivations for being in the Knights," I said.

"I do," Kai insisted, flipping his book open and scanning his notes. "Valla, like Asher, despises the Black Valkyrie and wants to kill her herself. The Black Valkyrie must've apprehended someone she loved, too, and she's out for revenge."

I crossed my arms. "I guess we'll have to see who gets there first."

Kari shook her head, looking down. She was laughing.

"What?" Kai and I said in unison.

"You guys." Kari looked out into the hallway to make sure we were alone. "That's not why Valla's here."

Kari laughed again. Kai and I looked at each other and shrugged.

"You're so blind," Kari said. "Yeah, she hates the Black Valkyrie. But it's not for the reasons you think. Valla's in the Knights because she's in love with Solrac."

Pieces clicked into place in my mind as I realized Kari was right. The way she cared for Solrac in the Scar, the way she watched him sing. The way she rolled her eyes at the ridiculous, overly-positive things he said.

"Huh," Kai said, taking furious notes in his journal. "Why didn't I think of that?"

"'Cause you're a guy," Kari chuckled. Behind her, I saw Jax cross the doorframe on his way to the deck above.

Kari instantly stood up, subconsciously smoothing her hair.

Now it was Kai's and my turn to laugh.

Kari whirled on us, challenge storming in her eyes. "What?"

I gently elbowed her. "Looks like Valla's not the only one with a boy on her mind."

"I don't have a boy on my mind," Kari held her nose in the air, then slyly looked back at us. "At eighteen, I consider Jax a man."

Kai rolled his eyes so hard he ended up throwing himself onto the cabin's cot, while I pretended to vomit in the corner.

"Honestly, I don't know what you see in that arrogant jerk," I said.

"It's true," Kai agreed. "I'd estimate at least a ninety-one percent chance of him breaking your heart."

Kari muttered something about how juvenile we were as she checked her hair one more time in a small silver coin from her pocket before nonchalantly adding, "Anyway, I was just stopping by to tell you I've finished the design for your ascension armor. I should have some of it finished pretty soon." Then she gave us a smug little wave before disappearing through the door after Jax.

Kai and I laughed as she left. I was excited about the ascension armor, but I couldn't help but worry for her. Jax wasn't the kind of guy I trusted with my best friend's big sister.

I was just dozing off later that afternoon when shouting from the deck startled me. That, combined with the sudden, violent rocking of the boat, knocked me off the cot and onto the cabin floor.

Voices above yelled, and I couldn't make out exactly what they were saying, but I heard one word over and over.

Storm.

I scrambled to my feet, rushing out of the cabin and up the stairs to the deck.

I fully expected to see a thundering, tumultuous sky. But there wasn't a cloud in sight.

Still, the boat swayed more fiercely than if we'd been caught in a hurricane. Flashes of lightning crackled below the waves, lighting up their surface. That brought to mind the name of the waters we sailed.

Dragonstorm.

"I knew things were going too smoothly," Valla muttered from beside me at the below deck entrance. "Goddesses just had to throw some more soot our way."

"What's going on?" I called.

"Drakked naga are stormin' the boat!" Boone yelled over the chaos. "We must've gotten caught in the ol' Dragonstorm herself!"

Kai appeared behind me, wearing his full set of armor. He was clearly taking precautions in case we ended up in a fight with some bloodthirsty naga.

"Everybody get below!" Kari ran up to us, grasping Jax's hand. I wasn't sure if they were holding hands for stability in the storm or for other reasons. Probably both.

"No!" Valla stopped Kari from heading through the doorway. "They'll just break through the hull. We have to show them we won't go down without a fight. Hurry them along so their storm will pass."

Valla instructed us as we took places around the deck of the longship. As a boat that regularly crossed the Dragonstorm Sea, it came equipped with enough mounted heavy crossbows for us and the rest of the crew. First we tethered ourselves to our crossbow stations, so we wouldn't get swept away into the roiling sea. Then we each took aim down into the wild waters. Apparently, not all the water dragons shot lightning from their mouths with Lightwielder etherarchy. If we could take down enough of those mythic ones, the storm would calm and the naga would move on.

But getting a good shot was nearly impossible. The naga's storm shook the boat violently and pushed us far off course. I tried to hit one of the naga as they leapt out of the water all around us, making larger and larger waves. But I only got off one shot, and missed so badly that when one naga hissed at me, it seemed like it was laughing.

Valla was doing alright, though. Already she'd hit two of the water dragons, and she was fairly certain one was one of the Lightwielders. Thorn was faring better too, flying over the turbulent water, launching his tail-blades at the naga as quickly as he could regrow them.

Then, with a huge flash of underwater lightning, the ship lurched. I gripped the side, the force almost throwing me overboard.

Kai wasn't so lucky.

Kari screamed as her brother tipped over the side of the ship, his tether snapping from the weight of his clunky armor. It had made it too hard for him to hold on.

It would also make him sink. Not to mention be extra-likely to get lightning fried.

I immediately cut my tether and ran to help Kai.

I'd be way more useful levitating over the water than stuck with some crossbow I could barely aim.

But Thorn signaled me through the bond, activating his new wood-woven armor. He'd handle saving Kai. My newly ascended wyvern friend dove toward the water, shrugging off naga attacks as he went for Kai. Then suddenly, the world lurched.

Or at least the ship did.

I turned, coming face to face with the biggest wave I'd ever seen in my life. I definitely should *not* have cut my tether.

The wave crashed into us, and swept me right off the boat. All at once, I was under the sea.

Everything seemed to be moving in slow motion. The water had knocked me far, to the edge of the dragonstorm. Naga darted around our ship, pushing it further and further from me as their whip-like bodies flitted past.

The distant underwater lightning was strangely beautiful, like fire seen through curling smoke.

I floundered for a moment, trying to get to the surface, when one naga snaked back toward me, its long, scaly body shining in the dappled sunlight. It opened its jaws and started jetting my way.

My eyes flared gold and I surged upward, levitating to the surface and away from the naga. I'd thought I'd shoot into the air as I broke the surface, but the pull of the water sucked me back down.

I looked back toward our ship and saw nothing but waves. Frantically, I spun around in the water, searching for some kind of direction.

But the naga was back again, leaping out of the water and coming at me, ready to take a bite.

I burned more ether, trying to use levitation to propel myself out of the way and hopefully above the water. I managed to dodge the naga's mouth, but its tail lashed around, striking me in the back.

I cried out and water filled my mouth.

That's when another naga, then another joined the first. The water around me roiled.

Soot.

At least I'd drawn three naga away from the boat. Though, I had no idea how far away the longship was now.

I reached for the pouch at my belt—the one that held my father's rift anchors. Maybe if I could throw the exit one high enough I could rift myself to safety above the water.

I fumbled the stones as I tried to get at them before the naga got to me. My heart sank just as fast as the black exit rift anchor. It was long gone before I could do anything to stop it from disappearing into the sea.

The dragonstorm's waves tossed me, and no matter how much ether I burned, I couldn't control my levitation enough to get out of it.

And I was getting tired.

My muscles cramped as I struggled. Through all the fear, I felt the fire of Thorn's panic through our bond. He'd saved Kai, but he could only feel a vague direction from me.

I tried to show him where I was so he could come find me. But everything was just generic water now. Waves, scales, and water. He'd never find me.

A naga leaped from the water, it's long, toothy, maw wide as it came for me.

I braced myself the best my exhausted body could.

Then, just before the naga could snap at me, something snapped up the naga.

At first, I thought Thorn had somehow found me out here. But this dragon wasn't a black and copper wyvern.

In shock, I watched as a huge, deep burgundy wyvern cracked the naga between his powerful jaws. He was majestic, and had such intense horns and ridges along his neck and tail that I was sure he was on his third ascension. He had what looked like a crown of long starglass spines sprouting from his head.

The wyvern circled in the air above me, coming back my way. That's when I heard a voice.

"Grab my hand!"

I didn't think. I shut my eyes tight, kicked, and used a burst of levitation to get myself out of the water just enough to grab the hand that reached out.

The dragon rider clasped my wrist, pulling me up and out of the water, then swung me onto the wyvern's back behind them.

Naga chomped at us from the water below. But the wyvern shot upward into the sky, leaving the naga behind us.

I caught my breath as I held the rider around the waist. Finally, I was coherent enough to realize that I had my arms wrapped around a girl with long, dark hair.

She turned her upper body toward me, a dimpled smile on her startlingly pretty face. She had these intense, bright, amber-colored eyes, and the thickest set of eyelashes I'd ever seen.

"You're lucky Glass and I were fishing nearby and saw you in the storm," she called over the wind in a smooth voice that felt like music.

"Hi," I said lamely.

She laughed with a tiny snort, and even that somehow sounded lyrical. "Hi."

We flew over the Dragonstorm Sea. Looking eastward, I could see the shoreline and the mountainous skyline of Keep Drakfell beyond. I sent the image to Thorn, and he relaxed, knowing I was safe. He sent me a sunny warmth through our newly strengthened bond. Our team was safe from the dragonstorm now. He'd head back to the ship to meet me there.

"I'm Asher," I said, basking in the breathtaking view.

"Nice to meet you, Asher. Are you always in mortal danger when you meet new people, or is this just one of those days?"

"Oh, I'm definitely always in mortal danger."

"Hold on tight," she laughed into the wind, then threw her head back as the wyvern dove at high speed.

I held her tighter around the waist to avoid getting thrown into the open sky. I wasn't used to riding a dragon with someone else in control, but I had to admit, this was pretty awesome.

The girl's hair streamed behind her and into my face. I laughed, brushing it away.

The wyvern showed off a little more, rising and falling with the wind, and even throwing in a loop at the end. I held fast to the girl and enjoyed the ride.

"Where's your dropoff?" she shouted behind her after a moment of some of the most fun I'd ever had.

I scanned the sea below. From this high up, it was easy to spot the Knights' ship. As we dove toward it, I didn't see anyone on deck—they must all be below.

I dropped from the wyvern's back, landing on the deck and looking back up at the girl.

"Wait," I shouted up at her. "I didn't catch your name!"

"That's true," she said, tapping a finger to her chin like it had just occurred to her.

"So, you're going to tell me, right?"

She smiled down at me mischievously. "If you want that, you'll have to find me again to earn it." She winked at me, knowing exactly how much she was driving me crazy.

Then the nameless girl and her glorious wyvern flew eastward over the sea toward Keep Drakfell.

Chapter 16: Keep Drakfell

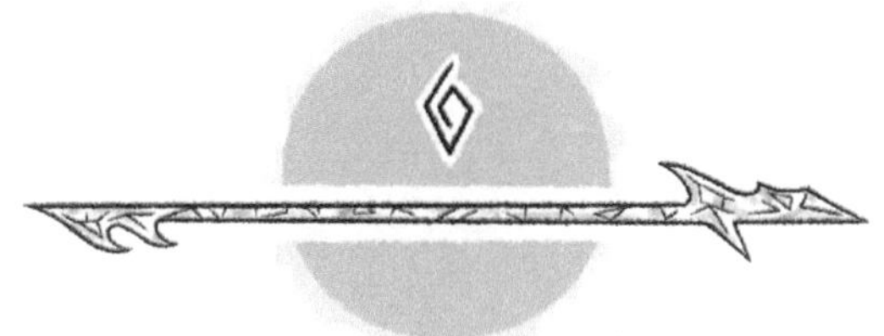

Thorn landed on the deck shortly after I did. He was thrilled to see I was okay, and let me know through our bond that the rest of the team was belowdecks.

I found them in the captain's cabin. They stood in a wide circle, everyone intensely watching Solrac. Solrac held a carved hoop with gold threads pulled tight within. The threads were shaped like a nine-pointed star, and a little, runemarked quartz crystal hung suspended along the center threads. Solrac looked like he was about to use it to perform some kind of ritual.

He caught sight of me as I peeked around the door. I raised an eyebrow at him, and he raised one back.

"Why are we stopping?" Shaya said, frustration evident on her face. "Every second we waste is another second we leave Asher in danger."

My heart glowed at that. Shaya was worried about me?

Solrac broke into a wide grin. "I don't think we need to summon the Farseer to find Asher after all."

I stood a little straighter, pointing to my chest and mouthing to Solrac. *For me?*

He chuckled.

"What?" Shaya practically shouted, her cheeks flushing red. "Yes, we do. We have to do whatever it takes—"

"Shaya," Solrac said, grandly gesturing to the doorway. "I give you... Asher of Steel Rim."

Everyone on the team turned to me, and I held out both hands and gave an over-the-top bow, paired with my best and most charming grin.

"Asher!" Kai and Kari rushed over, throwing their arms around me.

"You've got to stop nearly dying on us," Kari said, burying her face into my shoulder.

"I'll consider it," I laughed.

Looking between Kari and Kai's heads, I saw Shaya staring at me with... shock? Frustration? Relief?

"Hey," I said, pushing past my friends toward her.

She was still looking at me like I was one of the naga. She shook her head a couple of times, then threw her arms around me.

I hugged her back tightly. Behind me, I heard Kai and Kari ushering the rest of the team out of the cabin to give Shaya and me some space.

She held me long and close as she whispered in my ear.

"Never scare me like that ever again, okay?"

A thousand tingles ran up my arms, and my heart beat faster.

As I held her, I realized Shaya smelled like something between fresh air and the bark of a tree. I liked it. A lot.

Finally, she pulled back, but I kept holding her around the waist as she looked up at me. Her eyes looked so much older than seventeen, as if she'd already lived a whole lifetime of hardship, but was still here, standing strong.

"It's not fair," she said.

"What?" I said, my voice coming out lower than usual.

She searched my dragonfire green eyes as she reached up a hand, her finger tracing the back of my ear up to the scaly, teal, pointed tip. A shiver ran down my spine.

"You deserve better, Asher," she said as she pulled away, casting her eyes toward the ground. She started walking away.

I grabbed her by the hand, pulling her back toward me.

"How about this," I said with a crooked half-smile. "I'll never scare you like that again, and you never say something that ridiculous ever again."

Shaya laughed, and it was like birds singing.

"I mean it." I put a hand on her shoulder. "You have no idea how incredible you are. Please don't forget that."

Shaya covered my deep tan hand with her fair one. She seemed lost in thought. Then she squeezed my hand once before placing it on my chest.

"I'm glad you're alright."

She gave me one last pained smile before leaving the cabin and heading down the hall. My heart melted just a little as I watched her go.

Keep Drakfell was by far the largest city I'd ever seen.

I'd thought Ghost Lake was big, but Drakfell's chief city blew it away by comparison.

A grouping of small mountains rose up some distance from the eastern edge of the Dragonstorm Sea. The capital of the Badlands Keepdom spread from the shore all the way to the base of the mountains.

Misty smoke billowed from various points along the mountains, the city, and especially from a large field to the north. It gave the whole place a powerful, dangerous vibe. Boone explained that the central and tallest mountain was actually an inactive volcano. The magma flowed beneath the earth, causing hot springs and geysers to dot the keep. It wasn't smoke I was seeing, but steam.

According to Solrac, it made for some fantastic baths.

The streets of Drakfell were an odd mix of wood slats, cobblestone, and naturally packed dirt. The buildings, too, were made of either cut stone or wooden planks. Many of the longhouses had the classic Evgardian rooftops, shaped like upside-down boats. They were reminiscent of the skyboats our ancestors supposedly rode in on when they first settled the continent.

Everything here was fifty times grander and a hundred times busier than in Steel Rim. We passed by the high, black and white stone wall of Keep Drakfell's citadel. It encircled the castle's grounds, and I could see more steam rising from somewhere within the courtyard. The angular towers of the castle itself soared above the rest of the city, and its sharp stonework looked distinctly different from the humbler homes surrounding it—somehow more... perfect. As if the goddesses themselves had constructed it. Valla agreed, letting me know that, like the rest of the Capital Keeps, it had been made in Evgard's earliest age by what history called the ancient Guardians.

All of this splendor was so clearly built with etherarchy, yet housed one of the noble families who would see magi executed.

Drakking hypocrites... For good measure, I kicked a clump of loose dirt at the wall.

Squads of guards wearing Drakfell's signature, tan cloaks milled about the keepdom. The soldiers seemed on edge as we passed them. I soon realized they were staring uncomfortably at Solrac—or rather, at the Psion's silvermark on his left cheek. Some looked fearful, while others regarded him with contempt.

One guard finally got up the courage to approach Solrac, asking if he could please provide proof of registration.

As I watched Solrac pull out a scroll and hand it to the guard, my palms started sweating. I felt hot and a little lightheaded.

It was completely irrational—I'd been living as an unregistered magi in Steel Rim all my life. I'd passed the silver rod test innumerable times. But this wasn't some backwater outlander town. This was Keep Drakfell. If they discovered I was a magi here, they wouldn't botch the execution.

Gulping, I looked around at the tightly-clustered, ramshackle buildings of the city. They seemed to close in on me little-by-little.

The guard finished looking over Solrac's registration scroll, then handed it back with a little bow.

"Carry on, Duke of Glacia. Enjoy your visit to Drakfell."

"Why, thank you," Solrac replied jovially.

We asked him if he was worried about people knowing he was here in the city, particularly a certain black swan-themed leader of the Mage Hunters. But Solrac reminded us that she hadn't let the Hunters kill them back in Ghost Lake. It was almost like he wanted the Black Valkyrie to find him.

Not that he'd be easy to find in a place so crowded and with such a wide variety of people. I saw every shade of hair, skin, and eye color here. Some people rode the finest kirin I'd ever seen, while others had saddled up lowly scrub kirin. Every once in a while, I overheard voices with accents, from northerners like Boone to easterners with accents twice as strong as Solrac or Shaya's. I even saw a few half-borns like me, and one full Drekai leaning against the side of a barrel as he chewed the end of a piece of straw.

I relaxed as we traveled deeper into the heart of the city. Gradually, I actually began to enjoy the exotic sights and smells. The way the wooden trellises towered dangerously up the sides of buildings; the barking dragonmutts who chased ridgerats down dark, labyrinthine alleyways. We passed several street vendors with carts selling naga bowls and the most savory-looking dragon buffalo wings I'd ever smelled.

"Please?" a ragged voice rose from the ground near one of the alleys. I jumped a little when a beggar man with blotchy gray patches covering his skin reached out toward Solrac. The man's eyes were glassy, the parts that should have been white tinged bright blue.

Behind the man in the shadows of the alley I saw several others. A few of them had similarly gray skin, while others just looked tired and hungry.

"Victims of the shadow wasting," Kai whispered as we passed by.

"Some yes. Others are refugees from towns destroyed by the rising number of skyfalls," Valla grumbled.

Solrac tossed the man several large coins. He gratefully collected the bounty and hurried back to the alleyway to show the others as we continued down the city path.

Nobody seemed too fazed by the fact that we traveled with a bloodhusky and a second ascension wyvern. Many guards looked like they had bonded dragons of their own as they kept watch over the city.

Finally, we arrived at our destination. This tavern was far and away the nicest I'd ever seen.

Misty steam rose from several vents spread across the roof of the tavern. It had elegant, smooth stone walls on all sides, and a sign over the door in curly script read 'The Dreamy Drakalope.' A panel beside the lettering bore an insignia of a large dragon jackrabbit with antlers like a deer.

Solrac led us inside, and I immediately understood the tavern's need for rooftop ventilation. About half of the round tables in the bar stood not on the tavern floor, but in the center of steaming, round hot springs scattered throughout the room. Patrons sipped draquila and whiskey from the comfort of the warm water.

Each pool was perfectly formed, with smaller stones lining the sides to help it hold its circular shape. I couldn't be sure, but the perfect arrangements made me wonder if Geomancers had helped build the tavern.

Beyond the amazing bath works, this was also the tavern I felt least likely to get stabbed in.

Solrac chatted with the bartender for a short while before giving her the Knights of the Torch's passphrase. I was beginning to wonder if the Knights exclusively worked out of taverns. We headed down a long set of stairs to the Knights' secret base as Kai muttered something about the Knights needing better security measures.

It was the most luxurious place I'd ever set foot in.

Thick, rich, red rugs carpeted the floors, and exquisite tapestries lined the walls. The threads of the tapestries wove together into fine depictions of Evgardian history, all told from the perspective of the Knights of the Torch through the ages. They showed the Knights defending the Keeps against the arrival of the Drekai. Battles between magi and non-magi. Knights closely protecting skystone and fending off dreklings and other dragonkind.

Ornate doors lined the common room, each leading to private quarters. There were enough for each of us to have our own room, with more to spare. I wished for a second that Thorn could come inside with us, but there was no way he'd fit down the staircase. He sent me a warm feeling through the bond, and I felt better knowing he was perfectly happy to stay in the tavern's dragon stables. Besides, he'd already caught a tasty drakalope as he explored the natural hot springs outside the tavern.

The central feature of the hideout was the extra large, steaming, private pool in the center of the common room.

"Ah," Solrac sighed, closing his eyes and breathing in the humid air. "My favorite hideout. Furnished it myself."

He didn't waste any time. He flung off his outer clothing so that he wore only a light tunic and a pair of short underpants, then slipped into the steaming water.

He propped his arms up on the side as he sat down. "Anyone care to join before we get started on our first strategy meeting?"

After stripping down to their underclothes, Valla, Jax, Kari, and Boone all took their places inside the spring with Solrac. I followed, too excited to try out the spring to resist.

Shaya and Kai hung back, pulling up fancy, high-backed chairs near the pool instead. Shaya said she wasn't in the mood to get wet, and Kai insisted that everyone getting into the spring would leave the group too vulnerable.

"Fine by me," Solrac smiled, leaning his head back against the stone. "You can head upstairs and fetch us all drinks, then."

Kai grumbled but obeyed. Soon he returned, balancing a serving tray bearing eight tall, bubbling glasses.

I'd never tried a drink with bubbles like that in it before. Kai said the bar had a carbonated spring out back, and so fizzy drinks were the Dreamy Drakalope's specialty.

"It's called golden boltbrew," Kai said.

"Alcoholic?" Jax asked before taking one.

"Nope," Kai said. "We've got too many Mystics on the team."

"You're no fun," Valla muttered. But Jax looked relieved as he took his glass.

"Indeed," Solrac said, taking a drink of his own. "Dull, but wise. That's why we like you, Kai."

Kai looked unsure whether Solrac had just complimented or insulted him as the rest of us grabbed drinks from his tray.

I took a swig, and the carbonation hit me like tiny sparks of lightning in my mouth. That, paired with the flavors of salted caramel and cream, made me break into a grin as I relaxed into the water. So far, Keep Drakfell was pretty great.

Once we'd all settled down, Solrac cleared his throat.

"Now, down to business. I talked with the barkeep upstairs before coming down, and Keep Drakfell is nervous. Drekai spies have been spotted near the geyser fields outside the Keep, and a group of them have set up a small base just to the north. They want the egg back."

"So, the Drekai have declared war on Drakfell then?" Valla asked.

"Not yet. But King Rodan is worried that war with the Dragon Isles is on the horizon."

"King Rodan's a drakked fool," Boone said. "Shouldn't'a taken the egg if he weren't ready to pay the price."

"Isn't war what King Rodan's trying to avoid?" Kari added.

"It is a bit ironic," Solrac mused. "In trying to get help from High King Magus to save Drakfell from the skyfalls, he took the true dragon's egg. Yet doing so might be what brings his keepdom to ruin."

"So why doesn't the High King help?" Kai asked.

Jax scoffed, and not subtly, either. Kari gave him a look and a small shove. I noticed her hand reach for his under the water. I resisted the urge to flick spring water into his smug face. What did she see in him?

"An excellent question," Solrac said with gusto. "The thing is, the rumors about High Prince Mason becoming sick with the shadow wasting are true. Because of this, the High King hasn't been easy to reach. Not only that, but Drakfell in particular has fallen out of favor with High King Magnus. See, Evgard's eight keepdoms are always in competition with one another. A few key factors determine which of the eight is the top keepdom. Military strength, political prowess, and wealth. And by wealth, I'm talking about skystone."

Solrac traced an illusion rune, then thrust his hand toward the center of the pool. Across the pool's surface, an illusory map of Evgard appeared between all of us. The map started off flat, but when Solrac pulled upward with his hand, it became three dimensional.

Kai's eyes widened, and he pulled out his black leather journal and began taking notes.

"Now," Solrac continued. "Evgard Capital's darlings have always been the Twin River Keepdoms, Evyndara and Evyndale."

Solrac pointed to the eastern border of the map, and the River Keepdoms grew to fill the space. Kai took more notes.

"These keepdoms have excellent guards, political charm coming out of their ears, and they collect scads of skystone from skyfalls when they come. With a bigger population and a guard as strong as they have, they're easily able to fend off the dreklings the skyfalls bring, leaving the skystone theirs for the taking."

Solrac's illusory map depicted a tiny skyfall, a dragonfire-green meteor shower, within Evyndara's border. Then the map shifted again, focusing on the Keepdom of Drakfell. I could see the large, Dragonstorm Sea dominating the center, with the Scar to the west. When I saw the cliffs of Steel Rim, I got a little lump in my throat.

"Drakfell was never going to be as high on High King Magnus' list as Evyndara or Evyndale," Solrac went on. "But in recent years, the Badlands Keepdom has dropped to the bottom. Drakfell's guard is severely lacking in both numbers and organization, with too much ground to cover. They used to bring in plenty of skystone, but with the recent increase in skyfalls, they haven't had the soldiers necessary to fight off the dragons. This makes the dragons more powerful, since they're getting the skystone, making Drakfell's task even more impossible. Hence, they've turned to desperate measures."

Jax scoffed. "Yeah, like flexing for the High King by snagging a true dragon egg."

"Exactly," Solrac said. "And it might have worked, if not for the Mage Hunters."

"What do them scorchin' sons of dragonmutts have to do with it?" Boone glared at the mention of the Hunters.

"I think they're feeding the Great Uniter reports that Rodan is secretly disloyal to Evgard."

"Why would the Mage Hunters do that?" Kai asked.

Solrac stared into the illusion over the still water. "I don't know. But I think it plays into why Vidya's after the egg as well."

That gave me an idea.

"Hey," I said, standing halfway up and splashing water at Kari and Jax. That earned me a giggle from Kari and a dirty look from Jax.

I went on. "Rodan would probably roll over and hand Vidya the egg on a silver platter if she asked, right?"

"Actually," Kai spoke up. "All true dragons are mythic by nature, so the egg wouldn't do well on a platter made of silver..."

"So," I said with a grin, ignoring Kai, "why doesn't Valla just use her wildshaping to shapeshift into Vidya, waltz up to King Rodan, and take the egg?"

Silence met me for a moment before Valla rolled her eyes.

"Wildshaping doesn't work that way, genius," she explained as if she were talking to a child. "When I shift into a frostweasel, I can't just look however I imagine like it's some kind of Mystic illusion. I become what I, Valla, would look like if I really was a frostweasel. So if I tried to wildshape into another human…"

"You'd just be wildshaping into yourself," Kai finished, taking notes.

"Anyway," Solrac added. "Vidya can't just ask Rodan for the egg. She doesn't have that kind of authority, and if she tried, it would anger the other keepdoms. Despite what Vidya may wish, the Mage Hunters don't run the realm."

"She'll just take it and run after Drakfell's weakened by war with the Dragon Isles," Valla said bitterly. She gave an annoyed look to her empty glass, then reached across Boone to take Kari's right out of her hand. Kari looked startled as Valla took a casual sip of the golden boltbrew.

"That's why we have to take the egg first," Kai said.

"Splendid, Kai," Solrac said, nodding with respect.

"So what is the Mage Hunter's game?" I asked. "What do they plan to do with the egg?"

Nobody answered. Probably, nobody wanted to think about it.

Finally, Boone piped up, his eyes remaining closed as he relaxed in the water. As he spoke, a sort of dark stillness settled over the pool.

"Don't reckon I can answer that, but Jax'n I uncovered some kinda skystone experiments going on in Ghost Lake's mirror sanctum. I ain't sure what, but it sure as the void were somethin' sinister."

"That's why we blew up the bridge at the Mirror Santcum," Kai said, realization dawning in his eyes. "That's where they were running the experiments?"

"Sure as a ridgerat is nasty," said Boone. "Whatever they was doin' in there weren't natural. Was like they was hurtin' the skystone from the inside out. Reminded me of my time fightin' in the Dragon Wars in Kohlbor—an' they was dealin' in darkness for sure. I blame the Gray Ones."

"Gray Ones?" Kari asked.

Jax spoke up. "Torsten follows the Gray Ones. He says they're these Spirit creatures that try to influence people here in the physical plane."

"Who's Torsten?" Kari said.

Jax looked down, suddenly embarrassed. "My father. I haven't seen him in years, but last I heard, Torsten's involved in some kind of Gray Ones-worshipping cult. He really believes the Gray Ones are ethereal beings, inspired by the goddesses."

"Misled as a draccoon after dairy," Boone muttered. "You'da thought ol' Torsten would've learned his lesson after what happened to Misthaven."

"Regardless," Solrac said, "the citizens of Drakfell are almost out of time, and desperate to protect themselves. They only have two options left for assistance."

Solrac redirected the map once more, this time focusing on the large keepdom to the south. Where the land in Drakfell was mostly tan, this keepdom was almost all a shade of reddish orange. An enormous, redrock canyon cut through the keepdom.

"Rengard," Solrac said. "Outside of the Twin River Keepdoms, Rengard has the strongest army. Our King Rodan has been trying to secure an alliance with them for years. Even promised his daughter to one of Rengard's mid-tier noble families. But he can't wait for that to pan out."

"What's the other option?" I asked, leaning forward.

"The Farseer," Shaya surprised us all by answering before Solrac. "But it depends on who King Rodan fears more, the Farseer or the Black Valkyrie."

Shaya's face darkened as she spoke.

"Exactly," Solrac said slowly, eyeing Shaya, puzzled. "Anyway, that's why we must get that egg. We don't want the choice to be Rodan's. Once we have the egg, I plan to sell it back to the Drekai."

"What?" Jax sat up straighter.

"Of course," Solrac said. "It's an all-around win. The Drekai will pay handsomely for it, which will save the Knights from financial ruin. The Drekai get their egg back, and we'll even throw some of the profit Rodan's way to get Keep Drakfell out of hot water. On the condition he stops the crackdowns on magi in the cities, of course."

I had to admit, that wasn't a bad plan.

"Have you spoken to the Farseer since we arrived in Drakfell? Is he here?" Shaya asked, and I noticed a sort of tiredness in her eyes.

"Not yet," Solrac said.

We sat in the steaming spring in silence for a moment. A dripping sound came from somewhere above.

"I don't know about all of you, but I sure could use another drink," Shaya stood up and began heading for the door.

"I'll take one!" Valla raised her empty glass and Kari's too. A couple of others echoed the sentiment.

"Wait up," I called after Shaya as I hopped out of the pool and reached for my dry overclothes and boots. She gave me a little smile.

We never got around to bringing those drinks down to the group. Once we were out of earshot, Shaya admitted she could use a break, so we told the barkeep the orders and ran off to explore the city.

First, we walked to the foot of the nearest mountain. The Dreamy Draka-lope was decently close to the slopes. We considered climbing it, but didn't want to deal with the city's wall guard.

Instead we took a walk through the city streets of Keep Drakfell, passing by citizens, carts, and stray dragonmutts as we went.

We walked in comfortable silence until we reached a small market. I found a couple of barrels for us to sit on. Shaya leaned back against a stone wall, and I did the same.

"Can I ask you something?" she said.

I rolled my head against the wall to look at her, then raised an eyebrow. "Anything."

She laughed, and the tiredness in her eyes vanished for a moment. "I..."

She trailed off, her eyes focusing on something behind me. I tensed.

"What is it?" I asked.

"Don't look now," Shaya mumbled, "but Jax is on the street behind us."

"Why? What's he doing here?"

"I think I have an idea," Shaya sighed, sounding annoyed. "He's here for me."

"No way."

"Way," she said. Then she looked me square in the eyes. "Will you help me get him to stop thinking about me once and for all?"

"Uh, sure?"

Then Shaya kissed me.

Before I could fully register what was happening, I was kissing her back. I got lost in the moment, my hands reaching around the back of her head. Adrenaline coursed through my veins, and my heart beat so loudly I was sure Shaya could hear it.

Unfortunately, Jax wasn't deterred.

"What in the void is going on here?" He stood directly in front of us, folding his arms against his chest and using his fists to push out his stupid biceps even further.

Shaya and I pulled back from each other.

"Jax of Blackfjord, go back to the hideout this instant," Shaya said sternly.

"I just wanted to make sure you were okay," he said, frustration evident on his smug face. "And from the looks of things, you're not. You just got kissed by an amateur. Why don't you let a pro show you how it's done?"

Shaya looked at Jax with disappointment.

"Hey," I said, my anger rising as I got to my feet. "She said back off. So back off."

"I think you need to back off, Dragon-boy."

"What's your problem? One minute you're all over Kari, the next you're coming onto Shaya? This isn't some game."

"If it was, I'd be winning."

"Boys," Shaya stood as well, trying to calm the situation. But I was way past calm.

"You can't just mess with people's hearts like that," I said, clenching my fists. "Kari's feelings aren't a joke."

"No, they're not," Jax agreed. "But you are."

His midnight blue eyes stormed in a way that reminded me too much of his mother's. It only made me more angry.

"You want to go, Dragon-boy?"

"Anytime, Swan-spawn."

Based on the murderous look on Jax's face, that hit hard.

But not as hard as Jax's fist.

My jaw bloomed with pain. I fell to the ground. I scrambled for only a second before I was back on my feet and taking a swing of my own.

Jax caught my fist before it could hit his face. But he didn't see my other fist going for his gut.

He doubled over, and my next instinct was to burn ether and form my dragonhook spear. But somewhere in the back of my mind, I knew if anyone saw me using etherarchy, we were done for.

So, it was just me and my fists against super buff, workout-obsessed, muscle-maniac Jax.

I was vaguely aware of Shaya protesting in the background as I reached for Jax's head. In what might've been the stupidest move of my life, I grabbed the corner of the maroon bandana he always wore and yanked it off.

When Jax looked up at me, his eyes were bright with fury and a vein bulged on his forehead.

Oh stars.

Survival instincts kicked in, and I ran.

I darted down the street with Jax in hot pursuit. I had to fight the urge to speed up my running with levitation. It wasn't long before I reached a place where several street carts blocked my way.

Out of options, I turned to face Jax. In another idiotic move, I raised the maroon bandana, egging Jax on like I was some kind of rodeo performer. I guess that made Jax the torradon, which made sense since he was so full of dragon bull—

Soot. It worked. Jax charged, tackling me into the nearest street cart.

The merchant protested as we smashed his cart, his wares of tiny bottles of herbs crashing all around us. The scents of wildflowers mixed with those of tar and pine as Jax wrestled me to the ground.

He pinned both my arms with one hand and reeled back for another punch to my face with the other. Before he could strike, I bucked like a craghopper, throwing him off of me and onto the ground.

I raised my legs then thrust them forward, launching myself off my back and onto my feet.

I heard a lot of yelling and chaos from the people all around us, but I was too focused on the fight to pay it any heed. Jax was just getting up when I jumped at him from behind, wrapping my arm around his neck.

He stood and swung, trying to grab me. But I held fast, doing my best to choke him out just enough to stop him.

But even his neck muscles were too solid for me to have much success. He tucked his chin and reeled back, then suddenly thrust forward, throwing my entire body over his hulking shoulder.

I flew through the air then rolled on the dusty Keep Drakfell street. Jax was above me in an instant, his fist poised for a jaw-breaking punch.

But before he could land the blow, his eyes rolled back in his head and his whole body went slack.

For a second, I wondered if I'd somehow managed to knock him out and win this impossible fistfight.

Then Jax's huge, muscular frame fell sideways away from me, revealing a pair of guards behind him. One guard held out the butt end of a spear, which he'd clearly just used to knock out Jax.

In my heart, I knew it was my turn next, and there was no time to try and get away.

"Thanks, gents, we did it together," I said, throwing the guards a quick salute.

The last thing I remember was the spear conking me on the head.

At least it wasn't my nose.

Chapter 17: The Dragon Dens

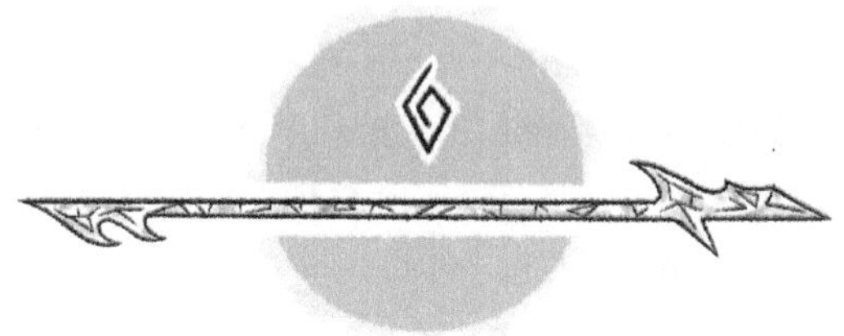

I'd only just opened my eyes when a pile of tan cloth flew toward my face.

"Oof," I mumbled as I gathered the jumble of fabric into my hands.

"About time you woke up. Now put that on and report outside, double pace."

I blinked up at the stranger. He was probably about twenty-five, with a neat haircut and the crisp uniform of the Keep Drakfell guard. I didn't figure him to be the guard who had knocked me out. This guy looked too mild for that.

He didn't wait for me to respond before turning on his heel and marching out the door.

I groaned, rubbing my head and jaw as I sat up and took a good look around. I was on a rickety cot in some ramshackle barracks. It wasn't much, just four walls, a few more broken-down cots, and some very battered spare weapons lying in a pile in the corner.

That surprised me. Solrac had mentioned that Drakfell's guard was struggling, but this was worse than I thought.

I looked down at the clothing in my hands. A black tunic, some light dragonleather armor, and a guard's cloak in Drakfell tan.

Not sure what else to do, I started changing. They probably wanted me to take off my turquoise scarf, but I left it proudly around my neck. Judging by the state of these barracks, the guard had bigger problems.

Outside the sad little building, I found the clean-cut guard and a few others in uniform standing in a line. Among them was Jax, his own maroon bandana tied back around his head. Guess I wasn't the only one with a defiant streak. He didn't make eye contact with me as I joined the line.

"Hey half-born," the guard on my left said brusquely. "This yours?"

She tossed me a leather cord with a small, black and copper scale tied to it. My heart jumped into my throat as I caught Thorn's heartscale. I hadn't thought to put it in the secret slot at my belt before getting into the street brawl with Jax. I felt stupid for not realizing it was missing earlier.

"Thanks," I said, hesitating before slipping the cord back around my neck. As the scale rested over my heart, I felt the bond bloom back to life like a roaring fire.

"We'd just gotten you back to the barracks when this big, ticked off wyvern showed up looking for you," the soldier said. "Tipped us off to check for a heartscale. The thing's in the dens with the rest of the guard's dragons now."

Before I could respond, the clean-cut guard stepped out of line and faced us.

"New recruits," he nodded first to Jax then me. "Welcome to the Keep Drakfell guard. I'm Captain Sven, the leader of your squad. After causing a public ruckus, it has been determined that the two of you must serve the community through three months' service."

"Wait, what?" I said. "I'm a soldier now, just like that? I thought recruits had to train for, like, three years or something before being allowed into the guard."

"Normally, that's the case," Sven said. "But not in Drakfell. Not lately," he grimaced, sounding genuinely forlorn.

Sven went on. "With Drekai spies on every side and an army marching west, the city guard is in dire need of every soldier we can get our hands on. But Squad Nimble never gives an excuse for a poor performance."

A couple of the guards next to me snickered.

"Something funny, Friga?" Sven said, his nose turned up.

"Nah, I'm good," the soldier next to me bit back her smile.

"Excellent. Because today, the commanders have assigned us a very important duty."

"Scout patrol?" another guard asked hopefully.

I felt my hopes rising as well. Sure, Jax and I had accidentally gotten ourselves conscripted into the city guard. But I pictured myself soaring above Keep Drakfell on Thorn's back as a scout. I'd get a good view of everything in the city—and maybe even catch a glimpse of the Black Valkyrie or the dusk blue cloaks of her Mage Hunters.

"Better than scout patrol," Sven said seriously, then stiffened up and barked the order. "Squad Nimble! Report to Dragon Keeper Aradan at the dragon dens for stable duty!"

He said it as if he'd just told us we'd been assigned to be the personal high guard to the king himself. But the groans of my new squadmates tipped me off that stable duty was about as lame as it sounded.

"For Evgard, unite," Sven added, trying to inject his enthusiasm into our squad. We weakly responded with Evgard's salute, pounding our right fists to our left shoulders.

To get to the dens, we had to cross a large field within the castle walls. It was full of the guards' dragons out for exercise. Wyverns and evren stretched their wings in the sky above while drakes ran around the field below. The occasional dragon would either swoop down or pounce at holes in the ground, and I saw one evren come back up with a drakalope in its jaws. Keep Drakfell must've kept the field stocked with prey.

Across the field stood the southern wall of the citadel. A massive gate stood proudly at its base. The entrance to the dens.

I'd heard the dragon dens here were extremely majestic.

A series of interconnected caverns lay underneath the Keep Drakfell citadel. The caverns varied in size, some only large enough to hold two or three dragons, while others held as many as fifteen or twenty in one place. Scattered amongst the more natural cavern shapes, some of the cave walls had been cut at perfect angles. Those had definitely been carved out using some kind of geomantic etherarchy. Based on the thick layers of cave moss, they must've been built ages ago.

Drakes stayed on the ground level, with wyverns in dugout clefts in the rock partway up the wall, and evren hanging from the ceiling or cavern sides. Each dragon had been awarded a personal wooden stall, but the dragons only mildly heeded the barriers. Most wandered freely throughout the dens, snacking from the scattered troughs filled with meat and grain. Torches hung along the walls, saturating the air with an orangish tint.

We stood in one of the larger caverns, drakes dozing behind us in their stalls as we waited before the head dragon keeper.

He was a stately man with dark hair, a short beard, and bright topaz eyes. His hair was streaked with white, a remnant of his snowhead heritage. A long black ascension blade hung in a fine Brookborne scabbard on his back, specially designed to make it easy to draw and stow, but also to show off part of the sword's black blade. Nobles always had their priorities in line. I didn't think much of it when he walked into the cavern from one of the tunnels, but Jax let out a small gasp.

"King Rodan?" Jax said with wide eyes.

The keeper laughed. "I get that a lot. But no, the king wouldn't be caught dead in public without his pristine ascension armor and fancy crown."

The keeper laughed again. Jax still looked confused. One of our squadmates leaned over and whispered to him: "King Rodan's brother." Jax mouthed the word 'oh,' and nodded in understanding.

Captain Sven stepped forward from our line. "Dragon Keeper Aradan. We're ready to receive our afternoon duties."

"Please, Sven, just call me Aradan."

"Thank you for the offer, Dragon Keeper Aradan."

Aradan rolled his eyes as if he'd had this conversation with the straight-laced squad captain a thousand times.

"I see you've got a couple of new soldiers."

"Of course," Sven said, gesturing to each of us in turn. "Jax and Asher."

"Pleasure," Aradan nodded to us, and I nodded back.Then Aradan cleared his throat as he addressed the group.

"Alrighty then. Sven and Friga, I'm going to need you to see that all the troughs are stocked. Korvald and Jax, muck out the northwest quadrant."

Jax audibly groaned, and I did my best to hide my laughter. I kind of loved the idea of Jax having to scoop dragon dung all afternoon.

"Dan, Aili, and Asher, you'll be mucking out the southeast quadrant."

My laughter quickly sputtered out. Jax still didn't look me in the eye, but he let out a satisfied harrumph. I made a face in his direction.

"Ah, there's my favorite assistant," Aradan said as heavy footsteps entered the cavern.

When I turned toward the newcomer, I almost had the wind knocked out of me.

Sitting astride a sleek drake was the girl who'd rescued me from the Dragonstorm Sea. Her dark hair had been long and flowing when I'd last seen her, but now she wore it piled in a bun on top of her head. Her unforgettable amber eyes widened a little when she saw me. Did she recognize me in my new Drakfell guard's uniform?

She gracefully dismounted the drake and placed a hand on Aradan's arm.

"Actually, I could use some help today. What if I borrowed... I don't know... that soldier for the afternoon?"

She casually pointed to me, and my heartbeat doubled in speed.

"Asher?" Aradan said. "Sure thing. Alright, squad, let's get to it!"

With that, Aradan and my new squadmates dispersed, leaving me alone with the girl.

I gave her a lopsided smile. "So, seeing as I found you again, I guess you owe me a name now."

She lifted her chin as she playfully looked me over. "I don't know what you're talking about."

"Oh, come on. Don't mess with me like that."

She took a few steps closer, then touched a finger to my chest as she looked me dead in the eye.

"I reserve the right to mess with you in whatever way I choose."

The way she looked at me gave me a not-so-small adrenaline rush.

"Now come on," she said, waving me down one of the tunnels. "We have work to do." The drake followed her, and so did I, an unstoppable grin on my face.

The tunnels were wide enough that the drake could walk next to her, with room for me on her other side. I fell into step beside her as we traversed the tunnels.

"Guess I owe you one for getting me off of mucking duty," I said as we walked.

"Oh, we're definitely still on mucking duty. Just not the southeast quadrant."

My face fell. "Oh."

She gave me a sly look. "No, we're mucking out the elite den where the highest nobility keep their dragons."

"Pretty sure noble dragon dung is even more vile."

"How'd you know?"

"Because... nobles are the worst?"

"No," she said with a laugh. "Some of the nobility feed their dragons a richer diet. That's what makes their feces worse."

A slight skip in her step, she sped ahead of me along the tunnel as I gave a melodramatic groan.

The cavern that housed the elite dragons was basically identical to all the rest. Except, of course, that the wooden pens for each dragon were made from oak instead of pine. I hoped the nobility felt really good about that.

Thorn met up with us there, following our bond. I worried for a moment that the girl would kick him out of the elite dragon cavern, since his bond was pretty much the opposite of a noble. But after giving me a warm greeting, Thorn bounded right over to her.

"Hello again, you great hunk of scales and antlers," she laughed, rubbing Thorn under the chin. He gave a low growl of contentment.

"How do you know Thorn?" I said, cocking my head.

"Thorn," she repeated while rifling through her pack. "That's a perfect name for you, huh, big guy? Thorn." She pulled out a scrap of jerky and tossed it into the air in front of my wyvern. Thorn snapped it up in his serpentine jaws. "I was on duty when they brought him in. Got him all set up with his own stall. Had no idea he was yours, of all people."

Thorn nuzzled the girl's arm, sending me a fiery wave of approval through our bond. Stars, she'd sure gotten my wyvern to like her fast.

"Now," she said, opening a wooden closet near the cavern entrance and withdrawing two wide, rectangular shovels. "We work."

It didn't take long for me to learn more than I ever wanted to know about the different varieties of dragon dung.

The evren stalls were by far my favorites. Their tenants dropped stone-sized, basically odorless pellets. I'd never paid attention before, since Thorn always did his business alone in the forests near Steel Rim, but wyvern feces was a lot like dragon buffalo chips. Fast-drying, brownish-gray piles.

But if I never saw—or smelled—another drake dropping again, it would be too soon. They got my shovel dark and sticky with every scoop, and every time we got to another drake stall, I had to pull my turquoise scarf over my mouth and nose just to survive.

We scooped and scooped, hauling load after load to a large furnace in the center of the cavern. Another fun fact about dragon dung was how flammable it is. Apparently, this furnace and others like it throughout the dragon dens provided heat to the entire citadel. I made a mental note to tell Kari about how it worked, since it really was a pretty ingenious system.

Nasty, but ingenious.

We chatted as we worked. I tried once more to get her to tell me her name, but she insisted it was much more fun watching me struggle.

"Why don't you try and guess?" she said as she shoveled.

"Hm," I said, pausing my work to look her over. "You look like a... Hildegarde?"

"Eew! There should be a law against naming your children Hildegarde."

"So, that's a no. How about Olga?"

"Ugh. You're dangerously close to getting a shovelful of dragon dung flung at you."

"Okay, okay," I laughed. "Give me a hint."

"It comes after K and before M."

I gave her a puzzled look. "L?"

She smiled, her round lips quirking to reveal a dimple in her right cheek. "Exactly. I'm Elle."

"Elle," I repeated, enjoying the way it felt on my tongue.

"Asher," she said back.

We passed the time in silence for only a little while before Elle began to sing. Her voice had a rich, ethereal quality to it, almost like it came from another world. There was a slight echo in the cavern, which only added to the enchanting beauty of it all.

Her brilliant voice stood in stark contrast to the words she sang. She was clearly making them up as she went along, her beautiful song featuring absurd lyrics about scooping dragon dung.

Shovelful by shovelful,
Our noses get destroyed
Still better to scoop dragon dung
Than be stuck in the void
In the dung heaps deep as nether
We'll muck out these stalls together

Every scoop so fresh and nasty
Pellets, pies, and dragon's blast we
Shovel 'til the day is done
But with a friend, it's much more fun
A little cocky, but cute and sweet
Bet you're glad we got to meet
So I could save you, on a whim
I'm still not sure if you can swim...

And though the work is hard to do

I was in hysterics by the end of her song. It shocked me how much fun I was having mucking out dragon stalls.

We'd just started on the last row of stalls when I brought up how many of the nobility were bonded to dragons on their second or even third ascensions. I almost told her about the nobility's secret—using skystone to get their dragons to ascend—but stopped myself. I didn't want to break Solrac's confidence, even if he was technically an uppity noble himself.

"I love seeing what changes they go through after ascending," Elle said, leaning her shovel against a stall. She stroked a curled-up drake along her spiny, dark blue back, and the drake purred contentedly.

"Me too," I replied, thinking of Thorn. He'd gone back to his own stall for some well deserved rest.

"I remember the first time I saw a third ascension dragon," Elle said. "I thought it was the most incredible thing in all of Evgard."

"Well, I guess you've never seen an ether vent," I teased, recalling the ether geysers found in the caves near Steel Rim.

"Well, have you ever seen a dragon moose?" She put her hands on her hips, challenge in her eyes.

I fired back. "No, but I bet you've never seen a sandshark."

"No, but I bet you've never seen the Dragon Mists."

That took me aback. "You've been to the Dragon Mists?"

Everyone in Evgard knew about the Dragon Mists, a wall of white fog that cut off the Keepdom of Rengard's southern border. Meteor showers fell constantly in the Dragon Mists, bringing all kinds of dreklings and etherarchy to the wild dragons that lived there. The Mists themselves were deadly, rumored to be infused with wild ether. Nobody went into the Dragon Mists without a death wish.

"Saw them from a distance," she replied. "I traveled to Rengard a few years back, and you can just make them out from their capital city."

"Wow," I said. "Impressive. You almost got me there. But have you ever seen a craghopper the size of a wyvern?"

"Craghoppers don't get that big."

"Karl did." I grinned, and animatedly told her about taking down Karl the craghopper. She laughed when I told her about riding him like a dragonbull.

"Well," Elle said. "I may not have seen a craghopper like Karl, but I have seen the most impressive thing of all."

"Oh yeah?" I folded my arms.

She gave that mischievous grin I was really starting to like.

"You ever seen a true dragon egg?"

My heart dropped into my stomach.

I slowly shook my head.

"They have one," she said. "Here in the dens."

She looked around to make sure we were truly alone, then leaned in closer.

"Want to see it?"

All I could manage was a stunned nod.

Vision 3

Solrac and Valla stood together in the common room of the hideout. Kai stood behind them.

Everyone else was out. Kari was purchasing supplies for one of her experiments. Boone was searching for Jax, Asher, and Shaya, who'd disappeared after this morning's briefing. Solrac had assumed they'd gone exploring, but they'd been gone so long Boone volunteered to try and find them.

Even though they were quite certain they wouldn't be disturbed, His Majesty stood guard at the hideout entrance. He seemed anxious. He probably wouldn't fully relax until Jax made it back to the hideout safe and sound. He'd always shared a special bond with the young Psion.

Once again, it was time to call upon the Farseer. Kai was humbled to be invited to join Solrac and Valla. Solrac had thought it was about time for Kai, a Seer himself, to meet the legendary Farseer.

Solrac used the Farseer's dreamweb to perform the summoning. The web pulsed with golden light, and he placed it carefully on the edge of the room's central hot spring.

Almost at once, eerie, purple smoke began to fill the room, flowing out from the dreamweb and spilling across the surface of the hot spring and over the edge. It smelled faintly of lavender. When the smoke touched the trio's feet, their eyes glazed over and their minds entered a dreamlike state, their spirits separating from their bodies.

Almost as if he was rising out of the pool itself, the Farseer appeared before Solrac, Valla, and Kai. He stood tall and proud, his staff in his hand, and his large, rune-covered mythraven perched upon his shoulder.

"You were right to summon me, Solrac, Duke of Glacia, and Valla of White Cliff." The Farseer's voice echoed throughout the hideout as he looked down on Kai. "And welcome, Kai of Steel Rim. It has been many years since I have seen you. How you've grown."

Kai cocked his head. "I didn't know we'd met."

The Farseer nodded. "Your parents sought me out when they discovered your gifts. I am glad to see you well." Kai nodded, still looking a little stunned as the Farseer continued. "I bring dark tidings. First, the Mage Hunters have destroyed the safehouse at Ghost Lake."

"Drak," Solrac swore. Kai and Valla's faces looked grim.

"Most of the Knights' operatives fled. They are on their way to Skygard now," the Farseer assured them. "Now, the reason for my coming. I have been keeping careful watch over the decisions of the Drekai Empress, Khaisa. Waiting for her to make up her mind about what action to take against King Rodan's theft."

The Farseer opened his arms wide, gesturing toward the pool at his feet. Solrac, Valla, and Kai's spirits came closer, leaving their bodies behind as they peered into the spring.

"Her decision has been made," the Farseer said, and the vision opened.

Lush, green forests. Foliage so thick an axe couldn't cut through it. A delicate layer of fog blanketed the wet earth. Mossy pines reached toward the endlessly raining sky. Tall, intricately carved buildings with peaked roofs made to mimic the spines along a dragon's back dotted the landscape. Many of the grand structures were overgrown with the tangling roots of temperate rainforest trees, molded so that the roots left room for doors and windows to swing open. There were winding bridges spanning pools of water, as well as ornate, wooden spires adorned with depictions of dragons and animals.

The Dragon Isles.

Clang!

The sound of *raskalaata*, heavy Drekai war-boomerangs, banging against each other resounded throughout the clearing in the trees. A wide circle marked the combat field.

Two Drekai dueled in the field. Solrac and Valla knew how the Drekai valued one-on-one combat. This was an honor duel—a real fight, often to the death. The Drekai used them to settle scores, solve conflicts, or even sometimes just to prove themselves.

The royal company stood outside the circle, cheering the fighters on. The empress herself sat atop the moss-covered chair in the center of her palanquin, which her servants had set down just outside the clearing. Her own bright green true dragon crouched regally behind her.

The empress was the emblem of Drekai power, with her flowing emerald clothing that perfectly matched the dragonfire green of her eyes. Her dress wrapped across her torso, leaving the patch of green scales on one shoulder exposed. Her horns were long and spiraled, and draped with dazzling green gemstones. An ornate crown adorned her brow, and a smooth, rich green dragon heartscale hung from a fine gold chain around her neck.

"She sure knows how to stick to a theme, eh?" Solrac's voice overlayed the vision.

"Shut up and watch," came Valla's reply.

To the empress' left and right sat a pair of generals, each wearing thick, battleworn bronze armor.

One was a tall, muscular woman with the face of a killer. She had a long, lashing, violet tail that flicked dangerously as she sat.

The other was a younger man, no older than twenty. He had tousled black hair streaked with red, and black and red scales grew along his shoulders, cheekbones, and hairline. With his broad chest and strong arms, he gave off an air of authority, despite being so young. A pair of wings were tucked behind him.

"*Toviian ka olaat arkiiti...*" the violent-looking general began, speaking in the Drekai language.

The surface of the Farseer's spring rippled, and the translation to Evgardian overlaid the Drekai's words.

"I hope you have taken the time to consider my plan, Empress Khaisa," the general said.

The empress shared a look with her true dragon. "We have considered both of your proposals."

"And?" the violet-tailed general asked. Both generals looked to the empress with anticipation.

"And while I trust that your armies would be more than sufficient, General Zora, I believe that the retrieval of our true dragon egg requires more finesse. We will enact General Kheradok's plan."

"What?" the first general hissed. The empress's bond narrowed his dragonfire green eyes. The general turned her gaze onto the other general.

"Weak pacifist," she muttered to him under her breath. The red-and-black-scaled general ignored her remark as he inclined his head deferentially toward the empress.

"Thank you, Empress Khaisa."

"To attack Drakfell would be to declare war on all of Evgard, an outcome I believe the Mage Hunters are all too eager for," the empress said. "We must avoid this at all costs. The war we wage with Etheria has left too many Drekai infected with the shadow wasting already. A division of our attention—fighting two different wars on two separate fronts—would come at too great a cost to bear."

General Kheradok nodded, while General Zora made a low, grumbling noise.

The empress went on. "Your rogue force was unsuccessful in capturing the Black Valkyrie in Steel Rim. Her place in our plans is not yet fully understood. Leave her be for now."

General Zora glared. "But we suspect she's dealing with the Gray Ones. Besides, they're saying Evgard's high prince is sick with the shadow wasting. I suspect something more sinister, and I believe the Black Valkyrie may have answers—"

"Leave her be, General," the empress's eyes flashed, and her true dragon let out a low warning growl. General Zora stood down as the Drekai leader continued. "We have enough forces on the mainland already, poised to strike should the need arise. Already Drakfell's king is afraid. I wish to retrieve the egg swiftly and quietly." The empress turned to General Kheradok, and he straightened.

"You will leave tonight, General Kheradok," she said, placing a tender hand on the nose of her true dragon. "Travel to Keep Drakfell, and challenge the king to single combat for the egg. His pride will drive him to accept. Do not fail your people."

The general took a knee and bowed his head before Empress Khaisa. Then he stood, spreading his wide, black and red wings before taking to the sky.

Behind him on the battlefield, one Drekai fighter finished her opponent with a blow to the head.

Chapter 18: The True Dragon Egg

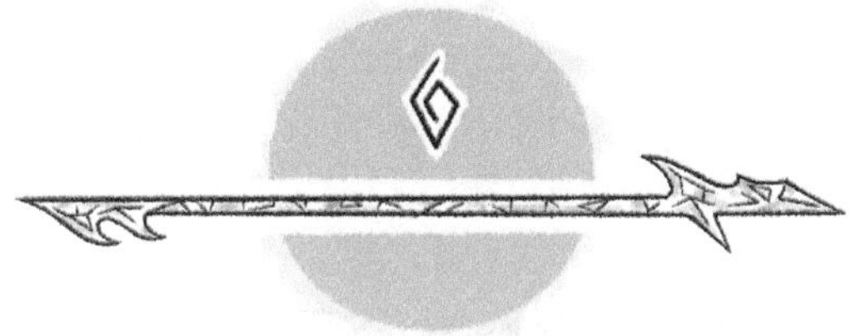

The hatchery dropped my jaw.

The cavern was large enough that a third ascension wyvern was flying around the stalactite-covered ceiling. I recognized him as Glass, the dragon that had helped Elle save me in the Dragonstorm Sea. Through the hatchery's ceiling came a small rush of water, which flowed into a tiered spring with a series of trickling waterfalls spilling into one another. The base level spring was the largest, and a black drake on his third ascension drank from it.

Beneath the pool was an enormous bed of sand. Even from where I stood at the cavern entrance, I could tell that the sand radiated heat.

In the nest of sand sat upwards of fifty dragon eggs.

And I'd thought the haul of eggs we'd stolen from Whitestone Hall was impressive. That paled in comparison to this.

The scaly drake eggs seemed to carpet the ground, each buried about halfway in the sand. Leathery wyvern eggs lay on the sand's surface, while the shiny evren eggs—I assumed—lay buried completely in the round little lumps of sand scattered throughout the nest.

In the center of the nest lay a glorious, third ascension evren. Her scales were a pale shade of violet, and she had a pair of long, twisting horns sprouting from the back of her head.

"Hello, Lyra," Elle said, carefully stepping around the eggs to make her way to the evren.

It's good to see you, Elle.

It jarred me as the silky, smooth words appeared in my mind. I looked around for just a second before realizing it was the pale violet evren who'd spoken to our minds.

Elle put a hand on the evren's right forewing, and I felt an aura of relaxation settle over the room. The dragon must've been projecting her contentment. Stars, I had yet to meet a dragon here that Elle hadn't already won over.

"May we see the egg?" Elle asked.

The dragon obliged.

She lifted her wing to reveal the most mythical dragon egg I'd ever seen.

Nestled in the sand near her body sat a fist-sized, elongated sphere in gleaming, pearlescent white. Hundreds of delicate scales covered its surface. But the most fascinating thing about the egg was the way it pulsed with a sort of living, white energy.

It was beautiful—No, it was beauty itself.

Almost without thinking, I began walking toward it, drawn by the life inside.

The violet evren stiffened, protectively drawing her wing back over the egg.

"It's okay, Lyra," Elle assured the dragon. "He's a friend."

Perhaps, Lyra's thoughts reverberated in my mind. *But I should like to read him first.*

"Read me?" I asked skeptically.

"Relax," Elle said. "Lyra's a dreamwatcher evren. A Seer. She'll see if you're trustworthy, and if you're lucky, she might even check to see if you have any negative omens hanging over your future."

"Yeah, just checking for omens," I said with a shrug. "No big deal."

Elle chuckled and waved me forward. I was careful to avoid stepping on any eggs as I approached the third ascension evren.

As I did, I noticed all three dragons in the cavern had turned their gazes on me. The evren may've been the one directly guarding the egg, but all three constantly had their eyes on it.

Keeping one forewing over the true dragon egg, Lyra used the other to reach toward me. Using a talon on the corner of her wing, she gently touched the center of my forehead. A rune glowed to life over Lyra's forehead, and a warm feeling washed over me.

Interesting, Lyra said in our minds.

"What's interesting?" I said, eager to know what she saw in my future.

A piece of advice, Elle, my friend. Do not trust this one with your heart unless you wish for a fight.

Elle raised an eyebrow at me.

"Wait, what? What does that mean?" I asked. A fight between Elle and who? Was the dragon talking about Shaya? Things were still so new with her, and I wasn't even sure where we stood. And things with Elle were even newer. I felt blood rush to my cheeks.

A dark choice lies before him, Lyra continued.

"What choice?" I asked, though I was getting the feeling Lyra wasn't going to expand on any of her ominous one-liners.

Then an intense vibe settled over the cavern as Lyra narrowed her draconic eyes. Suddenly, she started trembling a little, then all at once, she pulled back her talon and let the rune at her forehead dissolve.

"What is it, Lyra?" Elle said, rushing to the dragon and putting a hand on her forehead with concern.

Strange, Lyra's voice came through. *The convergence of the mythic stars... No Seer has foreseen a divination tied to it in centuries. I cannot see his role, but it is key.*

"Was any of that supposed to make sense?" I said, glancing at Elle. But she was still looking at Lyra with worry.

"Elle? Lyra? Anybody want to explain what that meant?" I said, waving to them.

Lyra shook her head, her long, twisting horns reaching upward behind her.

Time will reveal the meaning behind this, Asher of Steel Rim. For now, I will allow you to approach the true dragon egg.

With that, she pulled back her wing so I could get a better look at the egg.

From this close, within the pulse of white life I saw tiny, extra-bright flashes. They reminded me of a fluttering cluster of fireflies, only a thousand times brighter.

Again, I felt drawn in by the egg. I reached toward it, but Elle grabbed my hand first.

"Wait," she said. "Not that I think the egg would necessarily choose you, but to touch the egg with a bare hand would risk allowing it to bond you."

"Would that be a bad thing?"

"It would be a complicated thing," she said, her gaze falling on the egg. "Whoever bonds this egg will be subject to King Rodan. Trapped into doing whatever he orders her or him to do. Bonding it would mean losing your freedom."

Elle looked at me, sincerity gleaming in her bright amber eyes. I pulled my hand back.

"Don't want any nobles influencing my decisions," I said with a laugh.

We sat together in silence for a moment, staring at the egg. The pulsing shine reflected in our irises.

Then, Elle began to sing again. Only this time, instead of tears of laughter, my eyes just filled with tears, plain and simple.

Stars above
Stars within
Shining on as you dream

I recognized the song instantly. It was a lullaby—the one my mother used to sing to me as a child.

The one she sang to help me fall asleep the night before she was taken.

Guarding you
Guiding you
So much more than they seem

Weave your way
Through the thrill
Reaching out to know why

Know that we
all are one
United under the—

The song wasn't finished yet, but Elle stopped when the sound of footsteps filled the cavern. I looked down, really not wanting the newcomer to realize I was practically sobbing.

"There you are, Elle," Aradan's voice called out. "Asher, I just sent the rest of your squad home. You're free to go."

Beside me, Elle stood and turned to the head dragon keeper.

"I need your help, Elle," Aradan continued. "The king is hosting some special guests whose dragons need accommodations."

"Of course," Elle replied. "Who are these guests, if I may ask?"

"The Black Valkyrie and her Mage Hunters."

My heart stopped beating.

The Black Valkyrie—Vidya. She was here in the citadel. Right now.

Maybe it was because I was feeling vulnerable after hearing Elle sing my mother's lullaby. Or maybe it was because I was just plain tired of waiting for the right opportunity.

My hands balled into fists, and I looked up at Aradan with storming, dragonfire eyes.

"Where are they now?" I asked. Aradan and Elle both seemed a little taken aback by my intensity. When they didn't answer, I asked again. "The Black Valkyrie and her Mage Hunters. Where are they now?"

"Uh, I believe they're preparing for dinner with the king and his family. Which is why, as I was telling Elle, we need to hurry and get these dragons settled."

I wasn't quite sure where I was going, but I knew some of these tunnels had to lead to the castle above. I picked one at random, and started making a beeline toward it.

"Asher, where are you—" Elle started. Before she could finish, Thorn came flying into the cavern.

My heightened emotions must've alerted him that I was about to try something really stupid. He zoomed to my side, giving a little roar as he blocked the tunnel.

Out of my way, Thorn, I thought to him through our bond. He sent back a fiery feeling of strength, along with impressions of Kai and Kari. What would they say if they were here?

He sent another impression, this one of my father. The pleading that would be in his eyes, begging me to be rational.

Thorn sent me one more impression. I wasn't sure if it was because he was on his second ascension now or what, but it was the first time Thorn's thoughts had ever come across to me in the form of words.

Breathe.

It jarred me, and I stopped dead in my tracks. Thorn looked at me with such seriousness in his draconic eyes, I was compelled to listen.

I inhaled deeply.

Enough calm settled over me that I was able to think rationally. The last thing I wanted was to squander my opportunity to fight the Black Valkyrie. Even if by some miracle I was able to navigate the citadel and find her, I didn't stand a chance when she was surrounded by her entourage. Between Jaira the jailer's daughter, her redheaded partner, the illusionist, and the Geomancer who just kept coming back, I didn't stand a chance.

Vidya was here in the castle. We knew where she was now. I needed a strong plan before going in. Blind rage wouldn't avenge my mother.

Thorn relaxed as I realized this. Elle and Aradan were still looking at me with concern.

I let out a somewhat forced laugh. "I've never been great with directions. Which tunnel leads out?"

Aradan pointed the way, and I said goodbye to Elle. Then together, Thorn and I left the hatchery.

Jax and I arrived back at the hideout at almost the same time. He still wouldn't look me in the eye as we went through the Dreamy Drakalope and gave the passphrase to the barkeep. We walked down to the secret underground base in silence as well.

The team was relieved to see us back safely. Apparently Boone had been out searching for us all day, and had only gotten back just before we did. Shaya had been searching for us too. She'd lost track of us during our fight, then hadn't wanted to get arrested herself once she'd realized what had happened.

Solrac was thrilled when he saw our cloaks and heard that the guard had conscripted us. He declared it 'the greatest thing that could have happened' as he mused over the possibilities of having the two of us working undercover in the guard.

He asked what information we'd been able to gather during our work today. I told the group about Elle taking me to see the true dragon egg in the hatchery. I left out Lyra the dreamwatcher evren's odd reading of me, but told them about the Black Valkyrie and her entourage staying at the citadel.

"This is all fantastic intel," Solrac clapped his hands together. "I'll need Kai to read your mind and pull your memory of the egg itself. It will be enormously helpful in building our replica."

Kai nodded to me, and I sensed a twinge of jealousy. I knew how much he loved dragons, and yet I was the one who got the chance to see the hatchery. It didn't seem fair. At least he'd get to see it secondhand.

"What about you, Jax?" Solrac turned to my new undercover squadmate. "What valuable information were you able to glean throughout your day?"

"While Dragon-boy was busy flirting his way to a peek at the true dragon egg," he shot me a sideways glare, "I swiped us one of these."

He proudly pulled a scrunched-up piece of paper from his tunic pocket. It had probably once been cream colored, but now it was so badly covered in dragon dung from Jax's time mucking out stables that it was now a strong-smelling shade of brown.

"Uh... what is that?" Valla said, unimpressed.

"You're s'posed to throw that away when you're done, son." Boone wrinkled his nose.

Jax looked indignantly at the sheet. "It's an invitation to King Rodan's gala next month. You know, the one we're trying to break into to run the biggest heist of our lives?"

We all stared at Jax's nasty, dilapidated, unrecognizable sheet of paper.

Solrac clapped a hand on Jax's back. "Good thinking, Jax. Filching a gala invitation was definitely on our to do list."

"Still is," Valla muttered under her breath, and Kari laughed. Jax shot Kari a glare, and she blew him a kiss.

The group broke up, most of us making our way to one of the many rooms in the hideout to prepare for bed. I was beat after my day working in the stables, and was about to head to bed myself when Kari tapped me on the shoulder.

I turned around to see her beaming at me, her hands hidden behind her back.

I couldn't help but smile, too. "You have that classic 'Kari-just-invented-something-awesome' face."

She nodded vigorously. "I just invented something awesome."

"Well then. Show me!"

From behind her back she pulled out a pair of slick, black dragonleather bracers. She'd added some coppery trim to the seams of the arm guards, but the parts that stood out to me most were the black and copper wyvern scales running along the sides.

I grabbed for the bracers. "No way. These aren't—"

"Your very own ascension armor," Kari squealed excitedly. "From the scales Thorn dropped when he ascended. I'll finish the rest of it once I've perfected beating silver."

I handed them back to Kari immediately, holding out my arms so she could help me buckle them on. She eagerly did so, explaining that since

Thorn was a Sentinel dragon, the bracers should come with some regenerative powers.

"Similar to the way Thorn regenerates his tail spike after launching it," she explained.

"Guess I'll have to get hurt sometime and see what happens," I said, admiring the bracers.

"I'm sure it's only a matter of time," Kari assured me.

I thanked her again before she headed off to bed, promising her I'd take careful notes on how they worked once I got to see them in action.

The next few weeks were full of resting up, preparing for the heist, and working in the dragon dens with Elle. That was by far my favorite part of the day.

Sure, we did a lot of mucking out of stables. But sometimes we got to restock feeding troughs, mend and polish saddles or dragon armor, which apparently was called barding, and even take the dragons out to the field for exercise. With her, every activity was ten times more fun.

When I wasn't infiltrating the guard, I was back at the hideout. Knowing the Black Valkyrie was at the citadel renewed my desire to practice my astromancy with Boone, and likewise, Boone wanted to learn a little from me.

My skills were improving every day, and Boone was progressing well with making keys and smaller items out of starglass. I was kind of jealous of how fast he was learning. According to Boone, "Apparently you *can* teach an old dragonmutt new tricks."

I'd learned how to consistently charge my spear with ether, and even how to force that charged ether directly into a target on a strike. But, unfortunately, no matter how much Boone worked with me, I still couldn't master shooting my ether in energy blasts.

We'd set up a couple of the tavern's empty bottles on a decorative oak table in the hideout's common room. Boone practiced his quick draw, expertly whipping out one of his holstered starglass daggers. Then, with a white flash, he blasted the first bottle to bits with a comet-like shot of ether.

At that exact moment, Kari walked into the room, yelping at the sound of shattering glass.

"Yee diggety!" Boone whooped. "We gotta get ourselves some clay dragonbats to practice with. This ain't drak near hard enough."

"Drakes alive," Kari said, a hand on her heart. "Do you have to do this in the hideout?"

"Sure do!" Boone resheathed his dagger. "Asher, yer up."

I closed one eye, focusing on the next bottle the way Boone had done. Then, in a quick motion like he always did, I pointed my spear toward the bottle, feeling the ether rush through the starglass. Boone said the starglass helped focus the ether.

But before the ether became energy and blasted toward the bottle, it slowed down considerably. At the pace of a scalesnail, it squeezed itself out from the end of my spearpoint.

Rather than forming into a comet of ethereal energy, it dripped off the edge of my spearblade as a strange, whitish gold substance.

"Well that's more pitiful th'na dragon shrew with its tail cut off," Boone said, doing nothing to boost my confidence.

"Gee, thanks," I said.

"What is it?" Kari said, staring at the whitish liquid that now formed a small puddle at my feet.

"I know, Kari; I failed. You don't have to rub it in."

"No, no," she said, hurrying over and squatting down next to the puddle. She dipped a finger into it, examining the substance.

"Do you mind if I take some of this to run some experiments on?"

I shrugged. "Be my guest."

She grinned, then called out in a thunderous voice. "*Jax!*"

Within moments Jax threw open the door to one of the rooms. He looked disheveled and extremely on edge.

"I'm almost done extracting the venom from the last spydra," he said raggedly. I wondered what voidish kind of experiment Kari had him working on. From the looks of things, Jax had no love for spydra. Yet he was sucking it up and helping Kari out. Hmm. Maybe he did actually care about her more than I gave him credit for.

I still couldn't forget his comments about Shaya though.

"Bring me an empty vial, would you?" Kari asked, eyes still fixated on the white-gold liquid.

Within moments, Jax returned with a tiny glass bottle. Kari carefully scooped the substance, finishing by collecting the last drop from my spear-blade.

She was giddy, barely looking up as she rushed back to the room with her new sample.

Boone, Jax, and I looked at each other and shrugged.

"Let's try having you shoot it from a starglass dagger. Maybe something shorter'll help." Boone said, giving me a pat on the shoulder.

When I wasn't practicing with Boone, I was sparring with Shaya. She was still looking pretty tired these days, but she was always up for a round with a spear.

We fought, shadowspear on starglass spear, for hours at a time. About half the time she won, while the other half I did. We got to know each others' fighting style pretty well. I mostly gained the upper hand whenever she opted for an unnecessary flourish or showy swing that I could take advantage of.

I told Shaya once that I worried I'd never get a fair fight with Vidya, since she always had some lackey around or her Mage Hunter silver. Plus, there was the fact that she could have any number of psionic tricks up her sleeve.

"I almost wish she was a Shadowbinder, because then I'd really have a shot at her," I said with a smile.

Shaya laughed. "Don't underestimate Shadowbinders. You only win when I'm going easy on you."

I watched the way Shaya's eyes crinkled up at the corners when she laughed, and couldn't help but smile back.

Finally, there were only two more weeks until King Rodan's big gala. Kai and I were alone in the hideout's common room. I practiced with my spear while he worked at a table, eyes bouncing between his black leather journal and some rune-covered chunk of stone.

At Solrac's insistence, I'd shown Kai my memories of the true dragon egg. Now, it was Kai's job to come up with a way to build a convincing replica. Kai had poured hours into the task over the past two weeks, and from the looks of the dark circles under his eyes, he'd already lost more than a little sleep over it.

"Asher, could you come over here?" Kai said with a yawn.

I joined him at the table. He was just putting the finishing touches on a rune that he was carving into the surface of a smooth, gray stone.

"I need you to try bonding this," Kai said, handing me the rock. It was a little larger than my fist, and decorated with illusion runes.

"Bond... the rock?" I asked.

"Yes."

"But it's a rock."

"I know it's a rock," Kai sighed. "I'm working on replicating the feeling of failing a dragon bond, trying to put it into the true dragon egg replica. That way, when we swap eggs at the gala, nobody will be the wiser. But I'm struggling to get the egg to *feel* like there's something living inside it."

"You mean, you're struggling to get the *rock* to feel like there's something living inside it."

Kai glared at me. "Just try to bond it."

I grinned, then turned my attention to the stone. I placed my palm over it, then breathed in deeply, focusing on forming a connection.

Whoosh.

A wave of purple dream energy blasted me from the rock, dropping me on my back. I gasped as the fall knocked the wind out of me, and a wave of exhaustion flooded my head. Then I realized, I was looking at my body laying there on the ground. My spirit was floating over it. What the…

A flame of alarm pulsed through my bond with Thorn. Then I felt warmth glow up from my forearms.

I looked down and saw that triangular Sentinel patterns had begun to light up along the ascension armor bracers Kari had made for me. The markings reminded me of the ones Thorn used when he was regenerating himself.

The tiredness began to lift from my mind as the regenerative etherarchy took effect, and suddenly I was back in my own body. I made a mental note to tell Kari.

"What in the void was that?" I asked, holding my head as I sat up. "I thought you were trying to build an egg replica, not a bomb."

"I was," Kai said, frowning as he plucked the egg from my hand.

"Enya's the team's explosive specialist. You trying to impress her or something?"

"No," Kai rushed to assure me, but his ears seemed to redden a little. "No, no, no. Definitely not."

"Next time you experiment," I got to my feet. "I volunteer Jax as the subject."

Kai looked dejected as he examined the rock. "I don't know what went wrong. I just want this heist to go perfectly."

"You'll figure it out. We still have a couple of weeks. Soon, we'll both get what we want."

With that, I burned ether and formed my starglass spear. I gave it a couple of practice twirls.

"You aren't really planning on trying to kill the Black Valkyrie at the gala, are you?" Kai asked.

"I mean, if she's there, it's like I've got approval from the goddesses."

"What about the heist? If you go off script and try to take her out, that could mess things up for the rest of the team."

"So what? The team can handle it without me."

"Don't be so selfish."

"Selfish?" I said angrily, thrusting with my spear. "So now I'm selfish to want to avenge my mother's death?"

"That's not what I mean."

"Think about it, Kai. What if you had the chance to end whoever took your parents away from you?"

"I would hope I had the restraint to not lose myself to some futile revenge mission."

I stopped practicing to stare at him. "Is that all you think I'm doing? Some futile revenge mission?"

"From where I stand, I see my best friend throwing his life away day after day, in hopes that he can throw it away once and for all in two weeks."

"You don't understand," I said, feeling my blood beginning to boil.

"No. It's you who doesn't understand," Kai spat back. "You think that by killing the Black Valkyrie, you'll finally find peace. You won't."

"Thanks for the insight. Did you get that from the Farseer?" I asked sarcastically. "You really think you know what'll bring peace? You freak out and blame yourself every time you mess up a rune. You shouldn't be lecturing me about peace."

"You want to talk about blaming oneself?" Kai was practically yelling now. "How about how you blame yourself for your mom's death? That's why you're here, isn't it? It's not for revenge, Asher. It's regret."

Any retort died on my lips. My mind flashed back to that day, when I'd watched Vidya take my mother away in chains. As she led her to be killed.

My dad lost his sight trying to save her.

And I'd done nothing.

A huge, angry lump rose in my throat and tears burned at the backs of my eyes. I wished I'd been blinded trying to stop the Black Valkyrie from taking my mother. I wish I'd lost a limb, or even my life.

I wished I'd done anything.

I looked away from Kai. My hands began to tremble.

When I looked up, my eyes were burning gold with ether. Without turning back, I hover-ran as quickly as I could out the door.

Barely restraining myself, I stopped using ether before I got anywhere public. Couldn't go getting myself arrested right now, not again.

I just had to get away from Kai for a minute. Anywhere but here.

I may not have done anything to stop the Black Valkyrie that day. But I sure as the void wasn't going to sit idly now.

I didn't care what stupid heist I might throw off. When I went to that gala in two weeks, I'd be ready.

The Black Valkyrie... no, *Vidya* didn't stand a chance.

Chapter 19: Stone

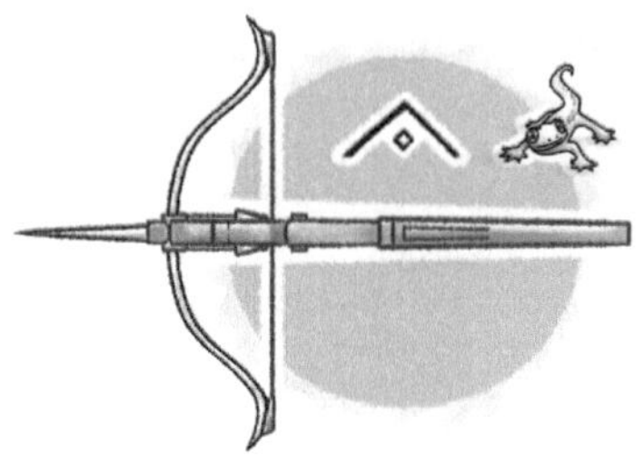

Kai

K ai left the Dreamy Drakalope shortly after Asher did, steamier than the hot springs within.

After their argument, Kai needed some air. He'd been cooped up inside the humid hideout for weeks, working on building a replica of the true dragon egg. He hadn't seen the sun in days, and he'd even lost sleep over it—all for what? So he could build a ridiculous, dysfunctional, dream-energy bomb.

Kai had no idea where he was going. He stormed down the streets of Drakfell, heading vaguely north as he tried to sort out his thoughts.

If Kai was honest with himself, what Asher said about his parents had gotten to him. The words echoed back in Kai's head.

What if you had the chance to end whoever took your parents away from you?

Kai was doing the opposite of ending the people who took his parents away. Rather, he was doing everything he could to help the Knights of the Torch.

What was the point?

As he walked, Kai pulled out his black leather notebook and turned to the pages with notes on each member of the team. He'd narrowed down the motivation of almost everyone by now, whether it was altruistic like Shaya, needy like Jax, or even romantic like Valla.

But the one person in the group whose reason for being here Kai couldn't decide on...

Was Kai himself.

Glint crawled out from Kai's shirt sleeve and onto the notebook. She blinked her large, mirrored eyes up at Kai.

She didn't do structured thought quite the same way a human did, but Kai didn't need a mindlink to his ethereal familiar to know what she was thinking.

She knew Kai hoped that by working with the Knights, he'd find his lost parents.

Kai looked away from Glint. It was a stupid thought. After all, there was about a one-point-three percent chance his parents were even still alive after all this time. Besides, Solrac and Valla had told Kai all the information they had about his parents. Kai believed they truly didn't know what happened to them, or where they were.

Mostly.

Glint let out a tiny, croaking grumble as she pawed at the notebook.

Right. Good idea. Taking notes and brainstorming always helped Kai feel better.

Kai barely registered that he'd walked past the city wall and all the way to the edge of town. He was practically at the geyser field north of the city now. He found a nice, shady spot under a small copse of juniper trees and sat down to write.

He opened to a fresh page, titling it 'Illusion Runes for Replica.'

He was about to scribble down his usual illusion runes plus a few from *Il Toma Ilusor*. But he'd already tried those. They'd almost gotten Asher blown up.

Deciphering the meanings of these ancient runes was complicated at best. He must've gotten the combination of runes wrong or something.

Kai bit at his lower lip, deep in thought. He pulled out *Il Toma Ilusor* from his satchel and began flipping through the old text.

What am I missing? he thought.

He absently traced his favorite illusion rune, adding some extra lines here and there to more closely match some of the archaic Mystic runes in the book. He placed the illusion over a nearby stone.

Suddenly, the stone no longer looked like a stone. It was a shiny white egg, covered in miniature scales like the true dragon egg. The extra lines Kai had drawn made it so it even felt like it weighed the same, and seemed to have the right texture and shape.

To the eye and touch, it was nearly identical to the one from Asher's memory.

But the light inside... the way it felt to be in the egg's presence...

It felt all wrong.

Exasperated, Kai looked back at the page in *Il Toma Ilusor*, carefully studying the runes. Two crossed lines beneath, two above. Ellipses in the center of the squares formed by the crosses.

Kai frowned. Where had he seen that rune before?

A memory from when Solrac and Valla had let Kai meet the Farseer flashed across his mind. A mythraven had sat perched on the great Farseer's shoulder. Kai drew a rune to access his own memories anew and replayed the memory in his head, trying to focus on details he hadn't paid much attention to when he'd lived it.

Yes. There it was. On one of the mythraven's rune-covered wings was the rune from the tome.

Kai reread the rune's description.

Capable of producing a complex emotional illusion. Can be overlaid upon a person or object, though if the casting Mystic wishes, this illusion may be projected through a separate person, object, or creature.

Ever since sharing a vision from the Farseer with Solrac and Valla, Kai had had some doubts. He suspected the Farseer himself of being a complex illusion. The mythraven could be serving as a projector. A dream creature that provided the illusion, both the visual and the feeling, of the man in the hooded robes. The Farseer... the actual Mystic casting him... could be anyone.

It could be Dad or Mom.

Kai quickly banished the thought. Dad and Mom were gone. To think it could be one of them using a legacy of Seer relics to project this generation's iteration of the Farseer was crazy.

Kai gripped the illusory true dragon egg in his hand. Asher was right. It was cold, empty—just a rock.

Kai let the illusion fade, then gave a yell as he threw the rock away from him.

He heard the rock bounce against one of the nearby trees before dropping onto the crusty earth below.

A low growl came from the tree.

Kai froze.

He turned to the tree, and his blood ran cold.

A pair of narrow, dragonfire green eyes stared back at him.

A large, mottled gray evren hung upside down in the tree, his wings wrapped tightly around his body. From the looks of things, Kai had just woken the dragon up from a nap.

Kai slowly reached for his black leather journal. He was sure he'd written down a plan for what to do if he ever encountered a wild dragon. Soot, why hadn't he thought to put on his heavy armor before storming out of the hideout?

Kai didn't take his eyes off of the evren as he flipped pages at a scalesnail's pace to avoid provoking it. He prayed to the goddesses that the evren would close its eyes and resume its slumber.

Kai broke eye contact to glance down at his notes.

Big mistake.

The evren dropped from the tree, catching itself with the wingclaws at the corners of each wing.

What a fascinating creature, Kai thought despite his rising panic. The dragon licked its lips.

Soot. It must've sensed that Kai was a magi, and was hungry for the ether well inside him. The evren crept closer.

Kai fumbled to grab the crossbow strapped to his back. At least he'd had the foresight to bring that along. No one in Drakfell walked around without being armed in some way.

Kai's fingers felt numb and clumsy as he struggled to load the crossbow and take aim. From this distance, he had a good chance of taking the evren down if he hit the throat. Even if he missed and hit a wing, it might distract the beast long enough for him to throw up some illusion runes. Kai could confuse the evren, then give himself a chance to reload. Then, he could try using dream energy to make the dragon lethargic...

As Kai hastily put some semblance of a plan together in his mind, the wild dragon inched closer. It showed no fear as Kai pointed the freshly-loaded crossbow at its neck. Perhaps it had never seen a weapon before?

Kai let the bolt fly.

Despite his shaky hands, the bolt zoomed straight at the evren's throat. A perfect shot. But a split second before the bolt hit the evren's hide, angular, golden patterns flashed across its scales. Sentinel markings.

Before Kai's eyes, the dragon's hide thickened, changing from scales to something that reminded Kai of solid stone. Granite, maybe? Its texture and density changed, and as the bolt made contact, it glanced harmlessly off its surface in a shower of sparks.

Kai inhaled sharply as he realized what had just happened. The evren's skin had taken on an aspect of rock—just like the Black Valkyrie's strong Mage Hunter, the one who should've died back in Steel Rim. And again on the bridge at Ghost Lake.

Geomancy.

This was a stonescale evren.

While the bolt hadn't harmed the evren, it had made it angry. The evren snarled, then leaped at Kai with bared fangs.

Kai barely had time to roll out of the way as he drew his illusion runes. Three copies of himself appeared, surrounding the evren. It reared back, confused.

So much for Kai's plan. Another crossbow shot would be useless against a stonescale.

What to do, what to do? Kai thought, desperately trying to form a new plan in his head.

Then he got an idea.

A crazy, foolish, Asher-quality idea.

Instead of fleeing from the dragon, Kai ran toward it.

The motion made the evren spin toward the real Kai. It roared, and as it spread its forewings, a row of razor-sharp stone blades appeared along its wingbones.

Soot, this dragon was remarkable. If he hadn't been fighting for his life, Kai would be scribbling down all sorts of notes in his journal.

The dragon swished its wings forward, taking out two of the illusory Kai's as it dove toward the real one.

Kai focused so hard on reaching out to the evren's mind that huge beads of sweat flowed along his temples.

Connect... Kai thought. *I have to form a connection.*

But the back of his mind was already hard at work, trying to piece together backup plans in case this crazy idea failed.

For a second, it looked like the evren was feeling some sort of link. Hope rose in Kai's mind.

Then the evren's eyes darted to the crossbow in Kai's hands. The dragon's pupils narrowed, and the fire in its eyes burned brighter.

It pounced, knocking the crossbow to the ground, snapping the string and crushing the neck.

So much for backup plans two and three.

Kai dashed a short distance away, making the last remaining illusory Kai cross the evren's path and run the opposite way.

It worked, the evren's gaze following the illusion.

Now would be the perfect time to run. Kai was ninety percent sure he could distract the evren long enough to get to safety.

It was the smart choice.

The safe choice.

Just like Kai always made.

Maybe it was anger from the fight earlier. Maybe it was Kai's frustration over the Farseer and his parents. But today, Kai wouldn't run.

Kai planted his feet firmly on the ground, determined.

The evren snapped at the last illusory Kai, dissolving it into starry ether dust. Then, it turned its gaze onto the final Kai. The real Kai.

Fear bloomed in Kai's heart as the evren leaped at him.

Suddenly, Glint came flying out of nowhere, flinging her tiny body at the evren's face.

She landed on its nose, clinging on for dear life. The evren went cross-eyed for a second, then began furiously shaking its head, trying to throw Glint off.

It bought Kai some time.

I need a new plan, Kai thought as he tried to catch his breath.

Breath.

Flashes of Asher breathing deeply before accessing ether surfaced in Kai's mind. Asher was an Archon—a spirit magi. Dragon bonds started as a spiritual connection, not a mental one.

If Kai wanted to have a real shot at bonding the evren, he needed to stop thinking like a Mystic and start thinking like an Archon.

No.

He needed to start *feeling* like an Archon.

As the evren clawed at its own face, trying to get rid of the dreambeast, Kai focused on breathing.

As much as it pained him to do so, Kai let go of his plans. He inhaled deeply, swallowing the crippling fear and replacing it with raw vulnerability.

The evren finally tossed Glint to the ground. Out of the corner of his eye, Kai saw the mirror gecko scuttle to safety.

The evren's full attention was back on Kai now. Kai exhaled, rooting himself in place. The evren might kill him now, but Kai didn't think about that. He didn't think about anything—he just felt.

He locked eyes with the evren, and for what felt like an eternity, nothing happened.

Kai breathed in. The evren breathed in, too, its chest rising and falling in sync with his own.

Then, all at once, a feeling like the strength of a mountain rushed into Kai's heart. Power like he'd never felt before solidified in his very bones.

He felt the connection from the evren. Something like respect and love and might all rolled into one.

Then, using the claw at the corner of a forewing, the evren scratched once at its chest. The motion sent the dragon's stony gray heartscale to the ground at Kai's feet.

Kai dropped to his knees before the dragon and picked up the heartscale. It felt cold and rough.

And right.

As Kai held the scale, he felt the bond solidify. Through the new bond, the dragon sent an image to Kai's heart. An image of Kai kneeling, paired with the feeling of strength and power radiating from Kai himself. It was how the evren saw him, Kai realized.

Kai took a few fearless steps toward his evren, reaching out a hand. The evren closed the distance, and Kai gently stroked the dragon's rock hard, gray scales.

The evren crouched low so that Kai could get a better look at his face. Kai hadn't been sure before, but now he felt strongly that the evren was male. He was bigger than most evren, but was still on his first ascension.

His face was long, his ears erect like a canine's. He reminded Kai of a dragon coyote. Kai admired his mottled gray scales—each one seemed to be a different, stony shade. Some were dark gray, and upon closer inspection, Kai realized that the darker scales actually formed patterns. It reminded Kai of the bronze marks on Thorn's black hide.

"Your name..." Kai said to the evren, thinking of his stone-like skin. "You're Flint, aren't you?"

He looked into the evren's eyes, and he seemed to smile.

Kai smiled back.

Then, Flint's markings burned with gold light, the Sentinel patterns glowing, and his scales became hard as stone.

CHAPTER 20: THE CHALLENGE

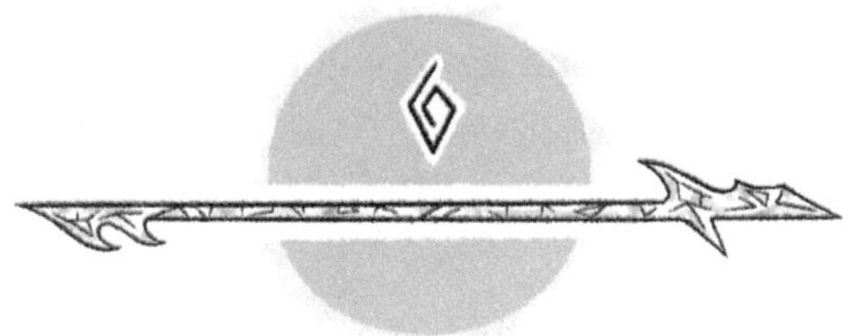

I knew Kai would return to the hideout eventually, but I never expected him to come back with a dragon.

Thorn and I liked Kai's new stonescale evren, Flint, right away. He was lively and tough, and exactly what Kai needed. Solrac declared Flint was the best dragon Kai could've possibly bonded, not just because he fit Kai so well, but also because he matched the stone of the surrounding mountains. It would be easy for him to find a hiding place near the Dreamy Drakalope. I immediately made fun of Kai for having an ethereal familiar named Glint and a bonded dragon named Flint.

Kai and I didn't talk about our argument earlier. But amidst all the excitement around the group meeting Flint, we nodded to each other, and I knew we were okay.

Jax and I got the day off from guard duties—apparently, it was our squad's turn on leave.

"Some leave," Jax said over breakfast. "They give us a single day off and call it leave?"

"But it's a whole day we get to spend together," Kari said, passing Jax another slice of bread.

"That's true," he smiled. "Let me guess. We're going to spend it extracting more spydra venom?"

"You sure know how to make a girl swoon."

They laughed, and I couldn't help but hand it to Jax. He'd really seemed genuine about his interest in Kari over the past few weeks. After our brawl in the streets, he'd seemed to take the hint, and was staying away from Shaya.

Shaya was making it easy, too. She spent most of her time cooped up in her room in the hideout. I'd tried to pull her aside to talk several times, but she almost always excused herself, saying she was tired. Maybe she just didn't like being cooped up in the city. Whatever the cause, I just missed spending time with her.

But I had to admit, I was enjoying working in the dragon dens. Or rather, I was enjoying working with Elle.

I stopped with a bite of breakfast halfway to my mouth. What if Shaya had picked up on how close I was getting to Elle? Was her tiredness just an excuse to avoid me because of her?

Don't trust this one with your heart unless you wish for a fight. Lyra the dreamwatcher evren's words replayed in my mind.

I shook my head. I didn't want to get anyone into a fight. Hopefully, things would sort themselves out on their own before they got too complicated.

Suddenly, the door that led from the tavern to our hideout swung open. Solrac strode in, reading a note and carrying a small package.

"Morning, everyone. How's my favorite heist team?"

Grumbles and 'good mornings' sounded from all corners of the common room.

"Anyone seen Valla?" Solrac asked, and Valla poked her head out from behind a large armchair.

"Here," she waved.

Solrac beamed, holding up the package. He unwrapped it to reveal a tiny crystal vial of golden liquid.

"Just got a fresh supply of liquid light," he said, making his way to where she sat.

I watched as he carefully rolled up the right leg of her pants. The place where Valla had been bitten by the sandshark showed the blotchy, gray imprint of a toothy semicircle. Every day, Solrac diligently applied a drop of the lightwielding ether product to Valla's leg, keeping the shadow wasting from spreading. I had no idea how long it would take to fully heal.

"Now," Solrac spoke loudly enough for all to hear. "They've sent word upstairs that our shipment of supplies is arriving today."

"The material I need for our gala disguises?" Kari asked eagerly.

"Indeed. Some of our fellow Knights from Skygard will be dropping it off today. Unfortunately, they're marked magi without noble titles, so they can't risk bringing it into the city. Too many questions. Someone will have to meet them at a pickup location in the mountains to the south."

"I'll go." I jumped to my feet. I was tired of the bustle and cramped feeling of Keep Drakfell. What better place to spend my day off from the dens than out in the mountains?

"I'll go too," Shaya appeared in the doorway of her room. I hadn't seen her all morning, but now she seemed to be staring intensely at the liquid light Solrac was applying to Valla's leg. When I looked over, she gave me an enthusiastic smile.

"Excellent," Solrac said, his focus on tending to Valla's wound. "I have the location written down on this note. You should probably leave soon in order to be on time for the meeting."

"And please be careful with the deliverables," Kari said.

"We will be," Shaya and I said at the same time. We looked at each other and broke into grins. I knew she was just as excited to get some fresh air as I was.

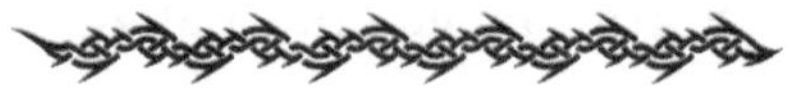

With Thorn on his second ascension, it was easy for him to fly both Shaya and me to the drop-off location. It was at the base of a low mountain, near an ancient-looking pine tree. Crudely carved into the bark of the tree beneath one of the lower boughs was the stylized symbol of the Knights of the Torch.

We hung around the tree for several minutes, but we'd made such great time that we were at least an hour early. The Knights from Skygard wouldn't be there for a while.

My gaze wandered to the peak of the nearby mountain. With a glint in my eye, I stepped in front of Shaya and pointed to the peak.

"So, we're obviously going to climb that while we wait, right?"

Shaya's eyes sparkled right back. "Obviously."

Thorn was content to hunt some drakalope while Shaya and I hiked on foot.

Before he left, he'd looked between Shaya and me, then taunted me with a mental image of Elle through our bond. That had made my heart involuntarily skip a beat.

Thorn, I'd scolded him through our bond. He'd responded with teasing sparks, then let out a little wyvern chuckle before flying off.

The land here was more lush than it was in the keep, and brightly colored wildflowers sprang up at our feet while towering pines lined the mountain ridges. We found no path to follow, but that was the way we liked it.

"I've missed you," Shaya said as we hiked side by side. "You've been in the dens every day for weeks since joining the guard."

"And when I get back to the hideout each night smelling like dragon dung, that keeps you from wanting to hang out with me," I gave her a lopsided grin.

She laughed, reminding me of the day we'd met. We'd hiked Kaliiko mountain together, laughing as we got caught in the rain.

"Really though," she said. "You're gone all day, then when you get back, you're training with Boone."

"You and I have sparred together a lot too," I reminded her. "You've helped me get good enough that by the time I finally get my shot at Vidya, I'll be able to take her down once and for all. I owe you for that."

Shaya sighed. "You and your undying quest for revenge."

"You sound like Kai."

"I just don't understand why you hate her so much."

I stopped walking, and Shaya did, too. Her rich, brown and blue-flecked eyes stared so deeply into mine.

I took a long breath in and held it for a second. Then I told her about losing my mom.

We kept walking as I told her my tale. I did a pretty good job of keeping my emotions in check, but when I got to the part about receiving word from the Mage Hunters that my mom had died, a lump rose in my throat.

When I looked over at Shaya, I noticed a tiny tear cascading down her cheek. She wiped it away quickly, probably hoping I wouldn't notice.

"Sometimes," I said, "you remind me of her."

Shaya went bright red from her nose to the tips of her ears. "Uh..."

"Not in a weird way," I rushed to dig myself out of an embarrassing moment. "I just mean she was a Shadowbinder, too. She used shadowfire the same way you do."

"I'm sure she was very talented," Shaya said, looking straight ahead. "Like her son."

"If I was so talented, you'd think I'd be able to do ether blasts like Boone can."

"You're better than you realize. In fact..." Shaya trailed off.

"What?" I prompted.

She hesitated before answering. "Do you ever just feel like running away from it all? Drakfell, the Knights. Everything."

"I guess I never thought about it. The Knights are my ticket to the Black Valkyrie."

"But surely you have plans for after all that."

I frowned. Shaya went on before I had the chance to answer.

"My sisters came to visit me last week. They met me just outside the city."

"Your sisters?" I asked, trying to remember what Shaya had said about her sisters that first day we'd talked. "The ones who joined the Mage Hunters?"

"Yes. They... they want me to join too."

"What?" I was taken aback. "You told them no, right?"

"They're family. I... I told them I'd think about it."

"How could you even consider becoming a Mage Hunter? They kill people like us."

"Some do, yeah. Like the Black Valkyrie and her entourage. But Asher, the Mage Hunters have access to etherarchy like we've never seen before. I saw some of what they can do in Ghost Lake when I first met Boone and Jax. If we had access to power like that, think of what we could do to change Evgard. The magi we could protect. It could change everything."

"And you think the Mage Hunters are the place to start when it comes to protecting magi?"

Shaya sighed. "We could change them. From the inside. I don't know; I just want to make things better—for all of us."

I didn't say anything. I wasn't sure what to say. Shaya was clearly distressed and conflicted after her visit from her sisters.

"You're special, Asher," Shaya said, reaching out to take my hand. "Once this quest is over, I just can't help but hope that you and I can continue working together."

I looked down at our clasped hands. My eyes ran along her arm, up her shoulder and neck, then finally came to rest on her face. She looked so sincere, so trusting. I remembered the way her lips had felt against mine, and my heart started thumping. Hope rose in my chest as I realized that maybe that kiss hadn't just been to get Jax off of her back.

I squeezed her hand. "I hope so too, Shaya." And I meant it. I felt so connected with her now that the thought of her leaving after all this was over made my heart ache.

She smiled up at me. "Come on. If we want to make it to the top before the Knights arrive, we'd better hurry."

She got a sneaky look on her face right before she dropped my hand. Then her eyes flashed gold and she took off with a short hover-dash up the side of the mountain. A faint trail of warped golden light followed her as she sped on. She was getting better at that.

"Race you!" she called behind her.

I laughed heartily before burning ether of my own. I accessed my levitation powers and hover-ran after her.

We barely made it back down the mountain in time to meet up with Solrac's contacts from Skygard. They handed over an enormous bundle, a burlap sack about half my height, and tied with string.

They also handed over a small, tightly-wound scroll: A note for Solrac and Valla with some important information from another of their contacts. After the messengers left, Shaya started unrolling the scroll.

"What're you doing?" I asked, trying to tie the burlap bundle onto Thorn's back.

"Aren't you curious?" she glanced through the writing on the scroll. I peeked over her shoulder, but it was all boring Knights of the Torch mumbo jumbo. Something about someone in Rengard named Cenrik securing the location of a Coven, and needing Solrac to send a spy to infiltrate it.

Shaya and I yawned a little before rolling the scroll back up. Then we mounted Thorn and began the flight back toward Keep Drakfell proper.

"Please tell me we're going to be outside getting all the dragons exercised today," Jax pleaded. "Or at least on feeding duty?"

The rest of Squad Nimble looked to Aradan, optimism apparent on their faces.

"Afraid it's another day of mucking out stalls," Aradan chuckled.

The squad groaned. From Aradan's side, Elle tilted her chin up at me.

I didn't mind mucking out stalls. It meant another day with Elle.

"You know where to go," Aradan said. "Report back at the end of the—"

Aradan never finished his sentence. Suddenly, a palm-sized black gem—an onyx—came flying from behind us, through the cave that led to the dens' gated entrance.

The onyx whizzed by, right between Jax and Sven's heads, and landed at Aradan's feet.

"What in the void is that?" asked our squadmate, Korvald, as he knelt beside the stone.

"Are those magi runes carved on it?" Sven said, eyes widening in horror, as if the very idea of a magi nearby filled him with fear. If only he knew.

"Soot," Jax swore as he looked more closely at the rock. "That's not just any stone. Those marks... that's a rift anchor. That means—"

Suddenly, the onyx burst to life. Korvald and the rest of us jumped backward as a jet of irregular gold light burst from the gemstone, forming a line from the ground to just above our heads.

The line of gold energy pulsed twice before it ripped itself open. Before us, a gold-rimmed, black portal floated in the air. The black interior meant this was definitely the exit portal.

Sure enough, within a second, someone came rushing out of the rift. Then another someone, followed by two more.

Not just anyone.

Drekai.

A fierce-looking young man led the raiding party. He wore regal, battle-worn bronze armor, and wielded a long-handled scimitar in one hand, while his gauntleted off hand held some kind of condensed dragonfire sphere. His windswept jet black hair was short, with streaks of red in it that matched the black and ruby scales that grew in patches along his shoulders, hairline, and cheekbones. His eyes burned with the same dragonfire green as mine, and I was surprised to see that he wasn't much older than I was.

The other Drekai clearly respected their young leader as they flanked him, glaring at us. One stepped forward, her eyes burning gold as she pointed to each one of us in rapid succession, starting with Aradan.

I yelped as a thick, black substance splattered onto my turquoise scarf over my collarbone. What was this stuff?

"To arms!" Squad Captain Sven shouted.

For a squad called 'Nimble,' it sure took us a minute to get our weapons at the ready. I'd nearly forgotten all about the standard-issue long seaxe they'd given me along with my uniform.

Luckily, Aradan didn't hesitate to leap into action. Drawing his black ascension blade from the Brookborne scabbard on his back, he leapt between the Drekai leader and Sven.

Not a moment too soon. Sven was still fumbling with his sword when the Drekai swung his scimitar toward his head. Aradan blocked it just in time.

"You," the Drekai shouted in heavily-accented Evgardian, "the brother of King Rodan."

Aradan grunted as he swung his warsword again.

The rest of us finally got our act together enough to take on the rest of the Drekai. It became clear very quickly that while Sven and maybe Friga had actual training, the rest of the squad barely knew how to hold their seaxes and spears. They must've been pulled off the streets like Jax and me.

Sven had stumbled initially, but he fought well, calling out orders as he blocked another Drekai scimitar. Friga twirled her spear with such agility that I finally realized why the guard had named this squad 'Nimble.'

A Drekai lunged toward one of my less experienced squadmates and I jumped in, throwing up my sword to block the Drekai's blow.

It worked for about a half-second, then the Drekai roared and twisted her scimitars, sending my blade skittering across the floor.

Soot, I wished I could summon my starglass dragonhook spear right now. But I had to hide that I was a magi.

I dove after my sword, barely bringing it up in time to block the Drekai's next swing. Friga joined me, she and her spear sliding right in the way of the Drekai.

Meanwhile, Jax was using the twin axes he always kept strapped to his back. While he couldn't use psionics to telekinetically push and pull on them, it looked like his excessive workouts hadn't been for nothing. He fought well against another Drekai.

A yell from the black-and-red-scaled Drekai leader made me turn my head. I saw him chuck the ball of green dragonfire at Aradan's chest.

It bounced off his breastplate, then fell to the ground at Aradan's feet. When it hit the ground, it exploded, sending Aradan flying backward into the cave wall.

"Aradan!" Elle shouted. Then, I saw her whip back a fold in her skirt and draw a gleaming sword of her own. It was a unique style, and I thought I recognized the thin blade from some of the books Kari always had open in her workshop back home. Elle wielded a menacing Skygardian saber, complete with an elegant handguard.

Wait, what?

With a graceful spin, Elle swung her clip pointed blade over her head, bringing it down toward the black-and-red-scaled Drekai leader. She nicked him through a gap in his armor with a reverse cut and he yelped in pain.

He swung back, engaging Elle in combat, sword on scimitar. I had to keep from gaping as I watched Elle expertly duel the Drekai.

"Scorch," I heard Aradan swear as he beat back two advancing Drekai soldiers with his great, black ascension blade. "This black stuff must be some kind of shadowsilk—it's blocking communication through our bonds; I can't reach Lyra to send for help."

I checked in on my own bond with Thorn. I could still feel its place in my heart, but I couldn't reach him while the strange shadowsilk substance covered my heartscale. Scorch was right.

"Korvald," Squad Captain Sven called out. "Get to a commander and call for backup!"

"Yes, Captain!" Korvald yelled, scrambling away from the fight and running down the tunnel to the entrance gate. One of the fiercer-looking Drekai, a woman with both a *raskalaata* and a lashing, bladed tail, pursued him.

"Somebody cover him!" Sven shouted, fully preoccupied with a fight of his own.

Looking around, I realized that everyone had their hands full. Korvald wasn't experienced enough to stand a chance against that Drekai alone.

I bolted after them, my hand sweaty as I gripped my unfamiliar weapon.

"Asher!" I heard Elle shout as she disengaged from her fight with the young Drekai leader. She darted away from him and ran after me.

Despite the skirmish raging around me, I felt my heart beat faster.

She was worried about me.

Behind us, the Drekai leader held out his gauntleted hand. A crystal on the gauntlet began to glow. An emerald ball of green dragonfire formed in his palm, twisting in on itself with concentrated power.

He hurled it after Elle and me.

We ran, but the fireball rolled to the ground just behind our feet.

Then it exploded.

It launched us forward as it took out part of the cavern wall. Rocks and dirt slid, forming a tall pile behind us and cutting us off from the rest of the group.

"Stars," Elle breathed. "Aradan!"

"Korvald," I reminded her, and we scrambled to our feet and dashed down the cavern.

We found him doing his best to hold off the Drekai. The Drekai soldier was pummeling my squadmate with her heavy war boomerang as he fearfully blocked her flurry of blows with the haft of his spear.

We needed a few more seconds to get to him. I held my sword at the ready.

The Drekai's eyes flashed gold, while along the edge of her tail, white, translucent spikes formed out of starglass.

Soot. She was an Astromancer like me.

She lashed her tail forward, and all of the razor-sharp starglass spikes went flying straight at Korvald.

"No!" I cried.

Astromancy or not, I wasn't close enough to save him. Three thick spikes thudded into his chest, and he fell to the cavern floor.

Elle and I rushed the Drekai, swords swinging. I went low, trying to get to the Drekai's leg, while Elle stabbed toward her torso.

The Drekai must've anticipated my move, because she lifted her foot and stomped down hard on my sword with her boot. I struggled, but couldn't get it free. The Drekai swung her *raskalaata* at me, and I had to crawl backward on my hands, leaving my sword behind.

If it weren't for the Drekai's chestplate, Elle's strike would've ended our foe. At least the Drekai grunted as Elle's swing bruised her ribs. Once again, I couldn't help but be impressed. Elle's fighting style was both feminine and powerful, her skirts flying as she defended herself against the Drekai.

I was about to make another grab for my sword when the Drekai's eyes burned gold with ether again. The Drekai thrust her off-hand toward Elle, and Elle's sword began growing thick and clunky with excess starglass.

It became too heavy and imbalanced, and Elle dropped the sword. The Drekai smiled, raising her *raskalaata* and preparing to finish her off.

I couldn't let that happen.

"Elle!" I shouted as I rushed toward her, my own eyes glowing gold as I accessed my ether.

I hover-dashed to get there faster and slid between Elle and the Drekai's blow. I threw up my hands and starglass spread between them to form a dense shield.

The Drekai's weapon came down hard, but my starglass shield held strong. I braced myself against the thud of the heavy war boomerang, wishing I could turn and look at Elle.

What could she possibly be thinking now? Part of me worried she'd turn on me too, seeing me use etherarchy and deciding I was an enemy.

Well, it was too late to worry about hiding my etherarchy now. Half-relieved, I burned more ether and used starglass to create my dragonhook spear, as well as form starglass armor across my chest.

I stabbed toward the surprised Drekai. She dodged, burning more ether of her own as she grew more starglass spikes from her tail.

She lashed them toward me, and I windmilled my spear, blocking the spikes, then hover-dashed up the side of the cave.

I ran, flipping upside-down as I came at the Drekai from above. I slashed at her, cutting her arm as I levitated myself back to the ground.

She gave a guttural growl as she raised her war boomerang, adding starglass to it to sharpen it.

I was just landing when she wildly threw the boomerang, clipping me in the side. The starglass-enhanced blow was enough to crack my starglass-powered chestplate, and I went down.

I landed on the ground hard, getting the wind knocked out of me. The Drekai snarled as her boomerang returned to her and she stood over me, raising her tail and preparing to skewer me like she had Korvald.

Then suddenly, my fallen squadmate's spear sprouted through the Drekai's chest. The Drekai choked, then fell lifeless to the ground.

Behind her stood Elle, her face streaked with dirt and her hair flying out behind her.

She'd just saved my life.

And scorch if it wasn't hot.

My mouth was hanging wide open when Elle turned her glare on me.

"Quit it," she said, breathing heavily.

I closed my mouth.

"Not that," she hissed. "Your etherarchy. Before someone sees."

Right.

My eyes stopped glowing gold as I let my starglass armor and spear dissolve into ether dust and fade into the air.

I hastily got up from the ground and hurried over to her. "You're not going to... you know. Tell anyone?"

"Tell anyone what?"

"That I'm a—"

"Tell. Anyone. What?" Elle repeated, giving me an intense, meaning-ful look.

"Oh," I said. "Right."

I checked on Korvald, but he was definitely gone. A pang washed over me.

"He was supposed to warn the commanders," Elle said, taking charge. Without hesitation, she reached over and untied the turquoise dust scarf from around my neck. Despite the heaviness of the situation, I felt a slight rush as her fingers brushed against my skin, and didn't even bother to question her actions.

"There," she said, passing me the scarf. "Now you can reach out to Thorn. He's on the exercise field now—Signal him through your bond and have him fly down to the commanders in Guard Square. He's on his second ascension, so he'll be able to properly warn them."

I tried reaching out to my dragon, and Elle was right. Without the black shadowsilk substance blocking my heartscale, I could feel the connection as strong as ever.

First, I assured Thorn that we were safe, then relayed Elle's order. He sent back a flare of worry for us.

I go, Thorn confirmed.

Looking at my scarf, I could already see the shadowbinding substance was beginning to dissolve. Good. I didn't want it gumming up my mother's old scarf forever.

"Hurry," Elle said, pulling me by the hand. "Aradan and the others."

We got back to where the black-and-red-scaled Drekai's explosive drag-onfire had caused the rockslide. It didn't take much to shift enough rocks that we could squeeze back through.

I was relieved when we got back to the fight to find Aradan and the rest of Squad Nimble still alive. Scorched, but alive. The Drekai had beaten them, leaving them tied up on the ground while the Drekai themselves stood over them like conquerors.

They didn't see Elle and me slip in beside the rocks. Aradan caught our eyes and subtly shook his head to let us know we should stay hidden.

The young Drekai leader was speaking again in his accented Evgardian.

"We do not wish to spill any more blood. You are the brother of the king, are you not?" He pointed his scimitar toward Aradan, who nodded. "Tell him that I, General Kheradok of the Dragon Isles, challenge him to single combat in three days' time, on the day that follows the summer solstice. We will meet at the geyser fields north of Keep Drakfell. The victor shall claim the true dragon egg for himself."

I couldn't just sit here. If I moved closer, maybe I could do something to free the squad. But Elle placed a firm hand on my shoulder to hold me back.

"If your brother, the king, refuses," the young Drekai general went on, "Khaisa, the Empress, will send the armies of the Drekai here to Drakfell. See that this message is delivered to Rodan, the King."

With that, he traced a rune in the air with his finger. Another gold-rimmed portal appeared in front of him, this one white—an entrance portal. The general and his remaining Drekai soldiers stepped through.

As soon as the last Drekai soldier's tail disappeared through the rift, it winked out in a spark of gold ether.

FRAGMENT: KHERADOK

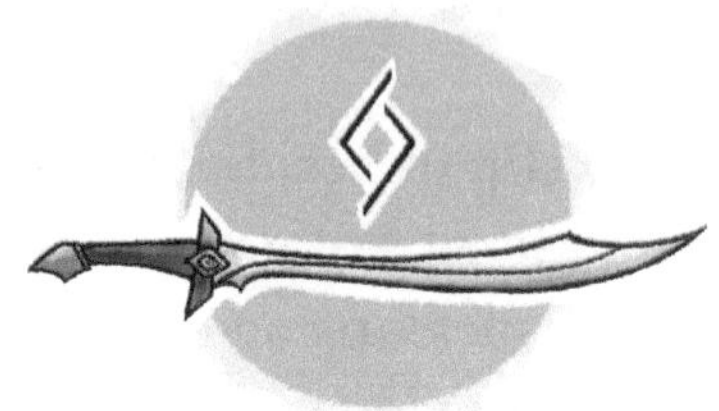

General Kheradok led the rest of his raiding party through his portal. They came out in a once-deserted glade of skyspruce just north of the geyser fields outside Keep Drakfell. He counted his soldiers as they stepped through the black-tinged exit.

"Raaku, Kirviio, Tarmohka..." Kheradok muttered under his breath as they followed him into the concealed Drekai war camp. "All but Verina. *Zaavu,*" Kheradok swore.

He nodded to his sentries as he entered the mass of peaked dragonhide tents. His raiding party marched toward the center of camp for immediate healing. Though his soldiers had all been injured, they had suffered only one loss.

They shouldn't have suffered any.

Verina had been a skilled soldier, but in Kheradok's opinion, she was too prone to violence. In fact, Verina's ruthless drive was one of the reasons his co-leader over the armies, General Zora, had insisted Verina accompany Kheradok on this mission. General Zora had long felt that Kheradok was too much of a pacifist to lead soldiers into battle. Empress Khaisa, on the other hand, valued the balance between Kheradok and Zora's distinct approaches to war.

They reached the war camp's central command, and Kheradok's raiders hurried to surround the tall wooden spire they'd set up there. The spire featured a carved true dragon, its long body winding up the post. Forming the creature's eyes were two pale stones infused with Sentinel regeneration etherarchy. Sentinel markings flowed outward from the carving's eyes, and simply standing within range of the healing rod would restore his soldiers' health within minutes.

Kheradok hung back as a proud woman in a regal wrap tunic approached him, her horned head held high. Keskit was his second-in-command for the mission, and for a moment, Kheradok wished he'd brought her to the dragon dens in place of Verina. Keskit valued discipline above all else, and wouldn't have gotten herself killed by failing to obey orders.

Keskit addressed Kheradok in their native Drekai tongue. "General Kheradok, we've been anxiously awaiting your return. I trust your mission was successful?"

"*Jhi*," Kheradok nodded.

Yes, the mission had been successful. But Kheradok's chest ached as he thought of Verina. He'd seen her pursue the young Evgardian soldier into the cavern. He'd tried to call out to her to stop—they weren't there to slaughter an ill-prepared squad of soldiers. They'd needed to impress upon the king's brother the serious nature of their message, which is why they'd come out with weapons at the ready. But Kheradok hadn't meant for anyone to get killed. It was like his mother always taught him:

Always know what side you choose, Kheradok, she had often said. *If you choose nothing, darkness will choose you. So, my* laaksi-rakaai, *always choose light, for light breeds more light. While violence breeds only more violence.*

Kheradok knew other soldiers still secretly mocked him for his outlook. They called him *Kaliiko Raaia*, which roughly meant 'Chief of Peace.' But Kheradok was firm and immovable in his convictions. And he *would* kill—only when it was the right thing to do for the greater good.

It was for this reason he was grateful Empress Khaisa had selected his plan to retrieve the egg rather than General Zora's. Her way would have ended the lives of thousands of soldiers, both Drekai and Evgardian. But Kheradok's plan required the loss of only one life.

That of King Rodan of Drakfell.

Kheradok was certain the king's brother would deliver the message, and that King Rodan would accept. His pride and honor would demand it.

"I will inform the empress that all is going according to plan." Keskit inclined her head gracefully, then nodded toward the cut on Kheradok's bicep. "Was that from the king's brother?"

Kheradok smiled to himself, and shook his head. "From a servant."

Keskit raised her eyebrows, surprised. "Better get to the healing rod. I won't keep you any longer." She gestured to the wooden spire, where many of Kheradok's raiders had already finished having their wounds re-generated. Then Keskit turned on her heel and returned to the dragon fang-ornamented command tent, presumably to inform the empress of their progress.

Kheradok looked at his right arm to examine the cut. It would almost certainly scar if he didn't heal it right away.

Although, that had truly been an extraordinary hit. Kheradok thought of the beautiful servant who'd pulled a sword from her skirts to defend her dragon keeper. She'd shown great bravery, and it impressed Kheradok that the mere servants of Evgard were so well-trained with a blade. Of course, she'd probably only landed the hit because Kheradok hadn't been expecting much from her.

Ah, there was the lesson from this skirmish. Never underestimate an opponent.

Kheradok turned away from the healing rod. He would keep this scar, both out of determination to remember that lesson and respect for the woman who taught it to him. It would join his other treasured battle scars, each one a lesson or a memory he'd collected.

Kheradok returned to his own tent at the head of the war camp, closest to the geyser fields. His tent was no bigger or grander than any of the others—in fact, one corner was dripping wet from the nearest geyser's latest spray.

Before going in, Kheradok looked southwest over the treetops. He could see the spires of the Keep Drakfell citadel. It was beautiful, even if it was the home of his enemies. But Kneradok knew the people of Evgard weren't his true enemies. Despite the warm air, Kheradok shivered. He just hoped he could defeat King Rodan swiftly so the Drekai could return their full attention to their war with the Gray Ones.

Chapter 21: Stars

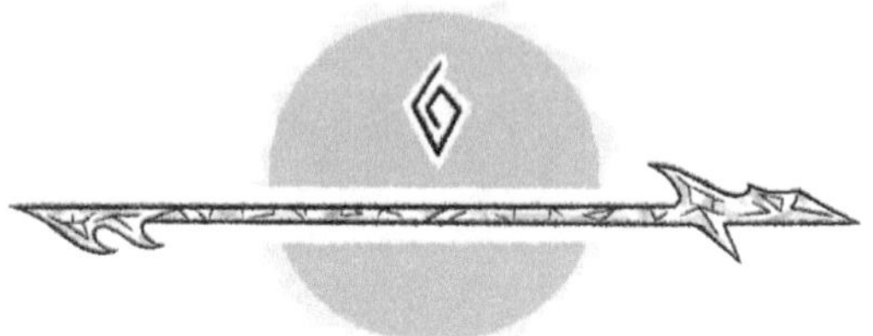

With the Drekai gone, Elle and I rushed over to untie Aradan and the rest of Squad Nimble.

"Will the king accept the Drekai's challenge?" Sven asked as Elle used her sword to cut through the bindings around his wrists.

"He will," Aradan said gravely. "And if I know my brother, he'll try to pull a fast one on the Drekai. He'll agree to fight, but I'll be drakked if he doesn't do everything in his power to get that egg bonded first."

"You think he'll move up the gala?" Elle said.

"I think he'll change the date of the gala to before the duel, yes."

Jax and I made eye contact. What would this mean for the heist?

Aradan went on. "A lot of further out nobles won't be able to make it in time, but it's Rodan's best chance to guarantee that the true dragon stays his."

"The dragon will belong to whomever bonds it," Elle said, setting her jaw.

"Right," Aradan gave her a look. I was sure he knew as well as she did that if anyone bonded the egg at that gala, King Rodan would keep them both closely guarded in his royal pocket.

Nobility. They made me sick.

"Asher?" Sven said. "Where's Korvald?"

I looked down at my feet and shook my head.

For a second, Sven looked like he was swallowing an enormous lump in his throat. Then he squared his shoulders and nodded. The rest of the squad looked devastated too, but it seemed to solidify their resolve. I was about to go with them down the cavern to retrieve Korvald's body when Elle pulled me aside.

"We have to talk," she said.

Right.

Elle knew I was a magi now. I guessed she wanted to talk about my status as an illegal, wild dragon-drawing, threat to society.

"Not now," she said. "Meet me tonight at dusk. At the gardens outside the citadel. There's a fountain with a statue of the three goddesses near the entrance."

I barely had time to agree before Elle was hurrying down one of the other tunnels that led deeper into the dens.

Later that afternoon, Jax and I were finally able to get back to the hideout. We told them about the Drekai and the honor duel, as well as Aradan's prediction that King Rodan would move up the date of the gala.

"If the duel's three days from now," Valla said, "that means the gala is in two."

"What excellent news!" Solrac exclaimed. "This is honestly the best thing that could've happened. I like the gala happening on the summer solstice. It just feels right."

"No, it doesn't." Valla folded her arms. "We thought we had two more weeks to prepare. We can't possibly be ready in two days."

"And yet, by Streya, we must," Solrac said cheerfully. "We'll just have to power pack the next two days, starting right now."

Solrac rose from his armchair and began barking orders.

"Kai, I want that egg replica finished and self-sustaining by tonight. Valla, forget doing recon on the local nobility before making a decision. Go turn into a weasel or dragonhawk or something, and swipe an invitation from the first estate you can find. Kari, where are you at with the disguises?"

"I'll head into town and get the last odds and ends I need right now," Kari said, gathering her satchel.

"I'll go with you," Jax put in, gingerly laying a hand on Kari's shoulder.

"Boone can go with me." Kari didn't look up from her bag, and I thought I noticed her subtly shrug Jax's hand away. "It's gonna cost a lot, and he has the group's marks."

Jax backed off, and I frowned. What was going on there?

"Perfect," Solrac plowed on. "Jax, I'll need yours and His Majesty's help to reopen an old servant's entrance to the citadel. It's been run over with rocks and debris, and we need your strength."

Jax nodded.

"Shaya, can you run into town as well?" Solrac pulled out a scrap of paper and scribbled something on it. "I have an underground contact who can get us astralock. We'll need it."

"Astralock? Doesn't that cause hallucinations?" Kai commented.

"Yep. Highly illegal, too." Solrac passed the scrap to Shaya. "Drakfell's black market is hard to get to unless you know the right people, or you're an invisible Shadowbinder. Can you handle that, Shaya?"

Shaya grabbed the paper and nodded eagerly.

"I can go with her," I said, a little worried about her picking up illegal drugs alone.

"That's alright, Asher," Solrac said. "I have a special task for you and me."

Everyone went their separate ways, leaving me alone with Solrac. He grinned at me, flashing his bright white teeth.

"Asher of Steel Rim," Solrac said. "It's time for a show."

Solrac and I brazenly walked right up to the front door of the citadel. We wore fine jackets and cuffs from Solrac's disguise pack, and for the first time in a while, every hair on my head was smoothed into a neat warrior's knot. It would probably all fall out in a matter of minutes, but still. Solrac had aged me up by sticking a smooth, fake goatee onto my face to match his real one, only mine was black like my own hair. This was without a doubt the fanciest I'd ever looked.

The squad on duty at the castle gate stopped us on our way in.

"State your business," the squad captain said, a hand on the hilt of her battleaxe.

"Why, the king and queen themselves are expecting us," Solrac said in a ridiculously chipper voice, even for him. There was no trace of his eastern accent.

"For?"

"Oh stars," Solrac said, putting a hand to his chest as he turned to me. "Alrik, please tell me you sent word that we'd be coming today."

"Stars yourself, Javrik," I responded in a voice just as overblown as Solrac's. "You were supposed to send word."

"By the goddesses." Solrac shook his head, then clapped his hand on the squad captain's shoulder. "I swear, never work with family, am I right?"

"Uhh..." she said, eyeing the two of us with suspicion. "Sure. But who are you?"

"Alrik of Naga Bay," I said with what I hoped was a charming eyebrow raise. "And this is my condescending half-brother, Javrik."

"Who are you calling condescending, scale-ears? At least my mother wasn't a half-born from the Dragon Isles." Solrac said.

I shrugged to the guard. "We've come to help prepare for the king and queen's gala."

Solrac gave a casual salute. "The new royal florists, at your service."

Solrac and I stood back to back, grinning grandly at the captain and her squad. They looked at each other as if making sure they weren't alone in thinking we were crazy.

Technically, they were right.

"These two *would* be florists," a guard muttered under his breath.

"Where are your flowers, then?" the squad captain asked.

"You must not be in the gardening industry," Solrac scoffed, and we shook our heads at each other with knowing looks. "Anyone who knows anything about flora knows flowers must be picked and brought last minute lest they wilt. We're here to look over the ballroom."

"Obviously," I added. It was shocking to me how smoothly this was going. Solrac and I were both dangerously good at bending the truth.

Luckily for us, the guards stepped aside and opened the gates. Solrac had been right in guessing that they'd probably been dealing with actual merchants and designers rushing around last-minute to prepare for the gala, so we blended right in. Aradan must've been quick about getting word of the duel to his brother, the king, because the citadel was already bustling with activity.

Some servants scrubbed floors while others rushed down the castle hallways carrying crates of ingredients for the kitchens. We made our way through the halls, only stopping twice to ask various servants for directions to the castle ballroom where the gala would be taking place.

When Solrac had told the squad at the gate we were here to inspect the ballroom, he hadn't been lying. In order for our heist to go smoothly, we'd need to know everything we could about the place the egg would be on display.

The ballroom doubled as the throne room and was by far the largest chamber in the entire castle. High, tan adobe brick rose up on four walls. Stone pillars supported the vaulted ceiling, and several wide windows and various doors lined the walls on every side.

Solrac took a more serious look at the ballroom as we pretended to be busy going about our floral duties. Servants hurried around the ballroom, setting up stands and tables. Solrac paid extra attention to the area just in front of the king and queens' thrones. They'd placed an ornate pedestal there, topped with a lush, silky pillow.

"That's where they'll put the true dragon egg," Solrac said under his breath.

Once Solrac was satisfied, we headed back into the hallway and I started walking back toward the castle gate.

"Hold on," Solrac stepped in front of me. "We have one more job to do."

He beckoned for me to follow him down a back hallway and up a set of stairs.

"Where are we going?" I whispered.

Solrac didn't answer. He walked with stealthy determination down another hallway. This one was lined with windows, leaving it bright from the sunlight outside.

Doors stood at intervals along the other side. Solrac counted the doors, finally stopping at one.

He looked around to make sure nobody else was near, then tried the handle. Locked.

He turned to me with a wide grin. "I knew it would be beneficial to have you along. Open it."

"Me?"

"No, Alrick of Naga Bay," Solrac chuckled. "Yes, Asher. Don't you remember what skill you showed me when we first met in the Drunken Drake?"

I remembered that day, and realized what Solrac was asking.

A sly look on my face, I burned ether and my eyes went from dragonfire green to gold. White, crystalline starglass began to form a long, thin shape in my hand.

Within seconds, I was holding a key.

I stuck it into the lock, and as expected, it didn't fit on the first try. What I didn't expect though, was the key shattering.

"Silver in the lock." I whispered.

"I was afraid of that," Solrac said, then pulled a shining stone from his pocket and handed it to me. "But I believe in you."

I looked at the stone in my hand, my eyes widening as I realized what it was. A skystone.

I took it and felt its warm power flow through me. This was going to take focus. I breathed in, and used the same technique I'd used to almost break out of my jail cell in Whitestone Hall, jiggling the key around in the lock. I felt the silver shatter my key again, but this time I surged more ether into it to reform it just as quickly as it dissolved.

My ether well started draining fast, and my chest tightened just a little. So that was why Solrac had offered me the skystone. I pulled some of its power into me as I poured more ether into the key, trying to keep it solid for long enough to tell how it should fit in the lock. This was draining. Straining, I carefully added more starglass here and there until I felt the key slide into place. With a final push of ether from the skystone, I solidified the key and gave it a quick turn before the silver could destabilize it once again.

Click.

I stopped the torrent of ether, and the silver shattered the key. But I'd done it.

Solrac clapped his hands together silently, overjoyed at my success. I grinned, happy to prove my usefulness to him. I handed the skystone back to Solrac.

Solrac's grin faded as he slipped through the door. It dawned on me that I had no idea what he was doing in this room, or what I'd just helped him do.

Kai's doubts about Solrac came rushing to the front of my mind, as well as some doubts of my own. Solrac was definitely hiding something. Kai was concerned he wanted the true dragon egg for himself. I just hoped I wasn't being tricked. After all, Solrac was a nobleman from the north. And if there was one thing I knew about nobility, it was that they were the absolute worst.

But it was too late to rethink my services now. Casting one last look down the hallway, I slipped in after Solrac and through the door.

My breath caught when I realized what room we were in.

The bed was neatly made, and several stacks of books sat handily on a desk in the corner. But it was the clothing that hung on the rack near the bed that made my blood run cold.

Black armor and boots. A black cloak with pitch-colored swan feathers lining the collar. And an unmistakable black pauldron with the insignia of a starswan in flight burned onto its surface.

This was where the Black Valkyrie was staying.

"Wha... what are we doing here?" I stammered.

Solrac paused for a second, taking in every detail of the room. Then he began to rummage through every bag, cupboard, and drawer in the guest chamber. He dumped the contents of a bag onto the bed.

"I need to know if Vidya and hers are here for the egg as well, and whether King Rodan knows it or not. I have to know what her plans are—what she wants with the egg."

"Um..." I began. "Maybe—and I'm just spitballing here—but maybe she wants to bond a true dragon, the most powerful creature in all of Evgard?"

"But why?" Solrac mused as he started rifling through a stack of papers on the desk.

"Oh, I don't know, for a sinister, evil power grab?" I offered.

"Vidya's more complex than that," Solrac assured me. In his hand, he held a small, diamond-shaped hand mirror. It wasn't ornately carved or jewel encrusted or anything, but he looked at it, transfixed, like he was staring at some priceless artifact.

"What's that?"

"Nothing," Solrac murmured. He may've been a good liar when it came to getting past the guards at the gate, but only an idiot would think that this little wooden mirror meant nothing to him.

"Right," I said, folding my arms.

"I haven't seen this in almost nineteen years. We traveled together for a private show, just the two of us, in Evgard's capital keepdom."

He spoke as if I wasn't even there, a faraway look in his eyes. I cringed, trying not to think about Solrac and Vidya in love on some trip together. It seemed impossible.

Suddenly, a black dragonhawk with green-tipped feathers scratched loudly at the window, causing both Solrac and me to turn. Solrac did a double take when he saw the bird.

It chirped quietly, as if in warning, then alighted from the sill.

Right on cue, the sound of footsteps echoed in the hallway.

For a second, my heart stopped. Vidya might be just outside.

My palms started sweating. If it was her, what would I do? Was I ready to face her, here and now?

Solrac set down the mirror and we hurried to hide beside the door of the chamber. I held my breath as the footsteps got closer and closer...

Then further and further.

I exhaled. It wasn't the Black Valkyrie.

"We should get out of here," I whispered.

"You're not wrong," Solrac said, frowning as he slunk back over to the desk. He cocked his head as he withdrew one of the books from Vidya's stack.

Solrac opened the book and scanned the first few pages, a look of deep concern etched on his face.

"Oh Vidya," he sighed. "Tell me you're not dealing in voidarchy."

Solrac closed the book and returned to the door, looking back and forth down the hallway.

"We should go," he said.

"What's voidarchy?"

Solrac ignored me again, rolling up the long sleeves of his florist disguise. Despite the warm day, he still wore his ornate bracers underneath. I guess I would've worn my ascension bracers myself if I'd known we were paying a visit to the Black Valkyrie's chambers.

Solrac looked over the room once more, then drew a complex rune and waved his hand. I jumped as strewn papers, and everything else Solrac had messed with rose into the air. The items zipped past each other as they psionically returned to their original places. It was like we were never there.

"Nice," I said. I'd gotten so used to Jax's brute use of psionics that I couldn't help but feel a little impressed.

He waved me into the hall.

We retraced our steps through the castle and back to the gate. I tried a few more times, but Solrac refused to talk about whatever he'd seen in that book. Kai was the biggest bookwyrm I knew, so I made a mental note to ask him about it later.

The sun was just setting when we returned to the hideout. Everyone was pretty exhausted from all the work we had to do to be ready for the gala. All anyone wanted to do was get some sleep.

Everyone except me.

I had a garden meeting to get to.

I went to my room, then counted to one hundred before sneaking back out again. The common room was deserted, so I hurried toward the door.

I'd just turned the handle when a voice from behind me made me jump.

"I know where you're going."

I spun around just in time to see Kai step out of the shadows.

"Soot, Kai," I said. "Why the lurking?"

"I just got back from saying goodnight to Flint when I saw you doing your sneak walk."

"I don't have a sneak walk."

"You totally do," Kai said, crouching low and making a big show of sliding stealthily across the room to where I stood.

I folded my arms. "Please tell me I don't look that lame."

"Hey. The point is, I know why you're sneaking out."

I felt my cheeks getting warm. "Uh..."

"It's okay," Kai reassured me. "You're meeting that girl from the dragon dens—the head dragon keeper's assistant."

"How in the void did you know that?"

Kai shrugged, then held up his black leather notebook. "Been keeping tabs on everyone, remember? You like her a lot."

"So what if I do?"

Kai laughed. "She's good for you—keeps you from forgetting what's really important."

I grunted quietly. I hadn't really thought of Elle as a distraction from my real mission to get revenge on the Black Valkyrie. To me, they felt like two totally distinct things. But if it made Kai feel better, he could think what he wanted.

"Go," Kai said, waving me toward the door. "Don't want to keep her waiting."

I smiled, and was about to slip out when I remembered what I'd wanted to ask Kai the next chance I got.

"Hey," I started, lowering my voice even more. "Have you read about something called 'voidarchy?'"

"Voidarchy?" Kai repeated, his brows knitting. "No. Why?"

I shrugged. "Just something Solrac said. Nevermind." I slapped Kai lightly on the back as I headed for the door. I didn't want to be late.

"Wait," he said, reaching into his pocket. "Take Glint Four."

The little mirror gecko leaped from Kai's hand onto the floor. She scrambled up my foot and crawled into her place inside my boot.

"Good idea," I said. "I could use a snack."

Glint Four poked her head out and stared at me with shiny, unamused eyes. I chuckled.

"Don't be out too late," Kai said with a wink.

I shoved him, then headed out the door.

I arrived at the gardens just as the first stars were beginning to light up the sky.

I walked a short distance along the garden path to the fountain. When I got there, my breath caught.

Elle stood silhouetted in the moonlight with her back to me as she looked over the pooling water. Her wavy, dark hair looked pitch black in the low light, and her tall, elegant figure was highlighted by the long, swooping skirt of her dress.

She usually wore simple, brown work dresses. This one, while still simple, was a rich shade of dark violet, and was made of something silkier.

I strode up to her, pushing my hair out of my eyes.

"Where does the assistant to the head dragon keeper get off wearing a dress like that?"

Elle whirled on me, a mischievous smile on her moonlit face. "Hey, a girl can like dragons and still look nice when she's off duty, you know."

"You look more than nice."

Elle put a hand on her hip. "I hope so. I'm meeting this guy I like, and I want to impress him."

My heart practically flew out of my chest when she said that. I swallowed, trying to play it cool.

"I thought you invited me here to discuss my uh... *display* in the dens earlier."

"You mean when you used astromancy to save me?"

"Look who knows her magi types."

"I know a thing or two. Everyone who works at the castle knows the citadel's High Mage is a registered Woodweaver, and I work with plenty of mythic dragons in the dens."

"Good point."

"I don't mind that you're a magi," Elle spoke softly and sincerely. "I still think you're an alright guy."

That should have elated me, but a sinking feeling hit my heart like an anchor hitting the sea. Elle trusted me, and I was probably the last person in the world whom she should trust.

"I'm trying to steal the true dragon egg," I blurted, then immediately covered my mouth with my hand.

Elle was taken aback. "What?"

I removed my hand to speak. "A group of us are. I don't know if it'll work, and it's for a good cause, but yeah. Thought you should know." I clapped my hand back over my mouth again.

"Huh," Elle said, taking the news surprisingly well. "Good luck getting past Lyra and the others."

"You're not upset?"

"No," Elle said with a smile. "Just promise me that if you succeed, you won't force a bond with it."

I nodded, breathing a sigh of relief to know that I wasn't deceiving her at all. No more secrets.

"Lyra," I said. "She's the dreamwatcher evren from the hatchery. She seemed to have... mixed feelings about me."

Elle laughed. "She doesn't dislike you. I've talked with her about you a few more times, actually."

I raised an eyebrow. "About me?"

Elle took a few more steps toward the fountain. In its center stood a life-sized statue of the three goddesses, Selene, Streya, and Solei. They stood on a pedestal within a large, circular pool. A natural spring powered the fountain, but right now the water was so still we could see the night sky above us reflected in the pool.

Elle looked down into the water's surface.

"Do you know the stars?" she asked, gazing at the reflection of the tiny celestial lights.

I joined her at the water's edge. "Not personally, no."

She laughed, a light, rich sound that made my heart glow. Through our bond, I felt Thorn get excited in response to my emotion. He sent back a warm pulse of approval. He really liked Elle.

"Lyra mentioned the alignment of three constellations," Elle said. "The Dragon, the Phoenix, and the Dire Wolf. They're the ancient symbols of mythic power. The convergence of these stars is coming."

"How do you know all this?" I asked.

"Anyone who's studied Evgardian history knows about the convergence. One happened almost a thousand years ago—the date of the last convergence of mythic stars corresponds to when our ancestors first arrived in Evgard."

"Sure." I shrugged. "I'm still not sure what any of that has to do with me."

"Neither is Lyra," Elle said, dipping the tips of her fingers into the water and sending ripples racing across the reflected night sky. "But I do know this: Asher, you're destined for greater things than you know."

That gave me pause. The image of me finally taking down the Black Valkyrie played in my mind. Part of me wanted to ask Elle what she thought—see if she would validate my quest for revenge like Valla, or question it like Kai.

But I kept my mouth shut. I still didn't know enough about Elle to know how she'd respond to the full truth. I couldn't risk it, especially if telling her could possibly put the Knights of the Torch in jeopardy, too. More than I already had, at least.

I stepped closer to Elle so that my chest was just centimeters away from her back. I could feel her warmth spanning the space between us as the night grew cooler.

"Didn't Lyra also mention something about you getting into a fight for my heart?" I said boldly. "You worried about that?"

Elle slowly turned around, a confident light in her vibrant, amber eyes as she looked up at me.

"Not worried at all," she said, raising an eyebrow. "As I'm sure you noticed in the dens this morning, I can handle myself in a fight."

"Oh," I said with a lopsided grin. "That's true. You do get a couple of points for holding your own against the Drekai in there."

"And I guess you get a few for that trick with the starglass."

"So what's the score then?" I asked as she leaned in even closer. Our mouths were so close I could feel her breath on my chin. She smelled sweet and woody, like fresh ember fern.

"I'd say that's two for Asher and three for me. Plus an extra one for me being the one to actually finish the Drekai off."

"Well, that's too much of a deficit for me," I said, my eyes flickering to the water just a couple inches away. I got the sudden urge to push Elle into the water, but I stopped myself.

Apparently, she'd gotten the same urge, but didn't show as much restraint. With a beautifully wicked grin, she grabbed me by the jacket and tossed me toward the water.

As I fell, I grabbed her hand to pull her down right along with me. At the last second before we hit the water, my eyes flashed gold, and I levitated us just above the surface.

Then, in what I hoped was an impressively smooth motion, I took Elle around the waist and rotated her with me. I held her just above the pool, the ends of her hair barely dipping into the water.

She looked up at me with surprise in her intelligent, dazzling eyes.

Without thinking, I closed the distance between our lips.

For a second, a jolt of panic ran through my heart. What if I was reading the whole situation wrong, and she didn't want this?

Then suddenly she was kissing me back.

Her hand cupped around my jaw as her warm lips moved against mine. I burned more ether to keep us aloft above the fountain, already wishing the moment would never end.

Eventually, she pulled back and looked up at me.

"I guess being an Archon comes with some perks."

"So, is that another point for me?"

Elle winked. "For that, I'll give you two."

I grinned as I levitated us back to our feet at the edge of the fountain.

"I guess that makes us even." I steadied her as she regained her bearings.

"Hmm," Elle said, tapping her chin. Then she put her hands on my shoulders and pressed her lips against mine once more. My heart thudded wildly in my chest.

"Almost even," she said, pulling back and giving my new favorite mischievous look.

"Wow. I guess you like me or something."

"Hold your kirin. A kiss isn't a proposal."

"I'll take what I can get." I couldn't stop smiling.

Elle took me by the hand and led me to the base of an enormous cinder-elm tree with thick leaves and twisting branches.

We sat together, leaning against the tree's trunk while breathing in the clean night air. Just when I thought the night couldn't get any better, Elle rested her head on my shoulder and began to sing.

It was a sweet, happy ballad about dragons dancing into Etheria. I'd never heard it before, but I immediately liked it almost as much as the singer herself.

Elle's song hadn't quite ended when we heard voices approaching us from along the garden path.

"Oh no," Elle said, sitting up straight. "I forgot about those two."

"Who?" I asked, squinting toward the strangers. They were still pretty far away, and there was no way they'd seen us yet. But even in the dark moonlight, I thought I made out the gleam of silver pauldrons and dusky blue cloaks.

"Mage Hunters," Elle confirmed.

"Soot," I said, my eyes widening at the approaching figures. By now, I could tell that one had bright red hair, and the other's voice was unmistakably snobbish.

Lothar and Jaira.

"If you'll excuse me," I whispered to Elle, trying to melt into the tree. I looked up into the dense branches.

I burned a quick flash of ether, then Elle watched as I hover-climbed into the tree.

"Where are you going? They don't know you're a... you know."

"Trust me," I whispered down. "These two aren't ones I want to mess with. Also, don't mention my name."

"Hey," Jaira called, waving at Elle.

"Shh," Elle subtly signaled for me to climb further into the tree, then hurried out to greet the Mage Hunters.

I slunk higher up into the branches, finally taking a seat on a strong, well-concealed perch.

Once I settled into place, I focused enough to catch the tail end of what Elle was saying to Jaira and Lothar.

"...already told you I'm not interested."

Jaira sounded annoyed as she replied. "But the good you could do is insurmountable. What can I say to get you to change your mind?"

Soot. Were Jaira and Lothar trying to recruit Elle into the Mage Hunters? I mean, after seeing her handle a sword, I couldn't blame them for wanting her.

I remembered Shaya mentioning her sisters asking her to join the Mage Hunters as well. They must've been recruiting like crazy—just like the Knights of the Torch were. I wondered what all that meant.

Shaya had been conflicted about how to respond to her sisters. But Elle seemed pretty confident in her answer.

"You can say whatever you wish, but it won't sway me."

My heart swelled to hear that.

"You may want to reconsider," Jaira's voice lowered so that I could barely hear. "Perhaps I could talk to you for a moment, woman to woman."

Elle and Jaira looked at Lothar, who was startled by the sudden attention.

"Uh," he stuttered.

Then Jaira lifted her chin at Elle, gesturing for her to follow. They walked along the garden path and out of earshot, leaving Lothar alone beneath the tree.

He fiddled with the hilt of his silver sword for a moment, accidentally unclipping it and letting it slide to the ground. He straightened, looking around to make sure nobody had seen. I rolled my eyes.

As Lothar bent down to grab the sword, I felt my leg begin to cramp up. Quietly, I adjusted my position.

Snap.

I froze as my heel broke a twig. Lothar jumped, assuming a fighting stance and looking to his left and right in quick succession.

Please don't look up, please don't look up... I thought, not daring to move.

Lothar looked up.

Soot.

His eyes widened to the size of dragon eggs as he saw me.

Not sure what else to do, I slowly raised a finger to my lips.

To my surprise, Lothar brought his own finger to his lips and nodded vigorously.

Okay.

Then he made a series of semi-readable hand gestures, first pointing to me, then to himself. He made a talking motion with his hand and mouth, then pointed simultaneously to Jaira and Elle with one hand while motioning to a tall nearby hedge with the other. He gestured with an arc as if to say 'meet me on the other side of the hedge after Jaira's done talking with Elle.'

I couldn't believe I'd understood that.

Thorn signaled me with a flare through our bond. *Want help?* he asked.

No, I've got this, I responded, only about half-sure that it was true. Thorn sent back grumbling sparks, but accepted it. Still, I could feel he was ready to swoop in the second anything went wrong.

Jaira and Elle returned.

"We thank you for your time," Jaira said, inclining her head.

"Yes, thank you," Lothar added with some kind of deeply awkward, overly polite bow. He must've been Evyndaran or something.

Elle looked at him like he was a total oddball, but nodded.

"Come on, Lothar," Jaira said, heading back toward the citadel.

"Actually," Lothar said. "You go ahead and tell the Black Valkyrie I'll be there soon. I've got to, ahem, relieve myself."

He shot a quick glance up toward me. I cringed, praying that he wouldn't get me killed purely by accident.

Jaira wrinkled her nose at her Mage Hunter partner, then told him to make it quick. With that, Jaira headed back toward the castle while Lothar hurried behind the hedge, casting one last over-the-top look my way.

Once Jaira was out of sight, I accessed my ether to float gently down from the tree. Elle put a hand on my arm.

"What was that all about? You know Jaira and Lothar?"

"I'll explain later," I whispered. "He wants to meet with me on the other side of that hedge."

Elle frowned. "Is that safe for you?"

"I can handle Lothar," I assured her.

We stared at each other for just a second. I had the urge to kiss her goodbye, but I wasn't sure if I should. Would that be rushing things too much?

Elle decided for me, giving me a quick kiss on the lips. I smiled.

"Be careful," she said, more like an order than a suggestion. Then, without looking back, she hurried off.

I took a deep breath and turned toward the hedge. I reached into my boot and gently pulled out the tiny mirror gecko within.

Glint blinked her large, knowing eyes at me, then placed her little foot deliberately on my palm.

I felt the mindlink bloom to life, Kai's voice echoing inside my head.

Asher? What's going on?

Kai, I thought through the link. *I'm about to do something stupid and I thought you ought to know.*

Oh stars, Kai thought back. *What are you doing?*

I slipped Glint into my boot as I walked toward the edge of the hedge.

Lothar, that redheaded Mage Hunter, invited me to a secret meeting. I'm heading in now.

It's probably a trap.

I squared my shoulders and rounded the corner of the hedge.

Probably.

Chapter 22: Oh Great Skymage

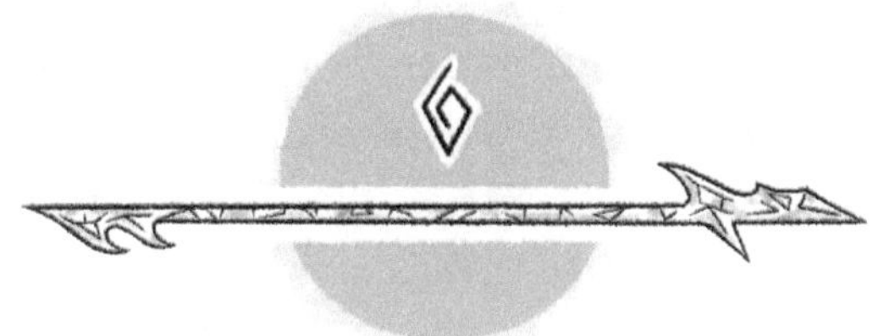

I did my best to walk calmly and casually, as if meeting with someone who'd trained to capture people like me was no big deal.

Lothar stood with his feet apart, hands clasped behind his back. He looked almost intimidating, his red eyebrows furrowed as he stared at me.

Asher, have I ever mentioned you're insane? Kai thought through the mindlink.

Once or twice, I responded. *Let's do this.*

Kai's reply was a muffle of mental groans. I focused on the Mage Hunter in front of me.

"I know what you are," Lothar said.

What in the void is he talking about? Kai's voice echoed in my head.

I crossed my arms, playing it cool. "What tipped you off?"

"You're not careful enough. I've seen you display your powers twice now, skymage."

Skymage? I asked in my head. *Kai, what's a skymage?*

I've never heard of it.

Soot, what do I do?

Hang on, I'm getting Solrac on the link—he might know. Just keep talking.

I felt Kai's focus leave my mind for a second.

Just keep talking, he'd said.

My specialty.

"Ah, yes. You've found me out," I improvised as I began to pace around him in a circle. "When did you see my great power?"

"The first time was in Steel Rim," Lothar said, and I detected a slight tremble in his voice. "I witnessed your astromancy as you fought the Drekai."

"That is true. You did witness my astromancy," I said, drawing things out as long as I could to buy Kai time to get more information.

Lothar continued. "But there was more. That day during the fight, there were three of you—illusion etherarchy. Only Mystics can access the Dreamweave, where illusion etherarchy comes from. I saw the rune over your forehead."

"Hmm, yes. Your knowledge of etherarchy is astounding," I continued stalling. "But what else?"

"Then in Ghost Lake," Lothar said. "You performed more astromancy, using your starglass and levitation. But I saw what you did to escape the bridge. The portal—you're a Rifter, too."

"Ah," I said. "What an astute observation." I wasn't even sure what 'astute' meant. It just sounded right.

Kai, where are you? I thought.

"That means," Lothar went on. "You're both an Archon *and* a Mystic. An Astromancer and a Rifter. To be born with dual types of etherarchy is impossible, which is how I know you're a skymage."

Asher? Kai's voice reappeared in my head.

Thank the goddesses, I replied. *What in the void is he talking about?*

Asher, Solrac here, Solrac came onto the mindlink. Kai must either be touching him or else he'd duplicated Glint again.

Hi, I said in my head.

Lothar thinks you're a skymage? Solrac asked.

Apparently, I responded. *Something about me being able to do two kinds of etherarchy. But that's only because Kai tricked him back in Steel Rim, and because he saw me use my dad's rift anchors.*

Interesting, Kai thought.

Drak, Solrac cursed. *Get Lothar talking. We have to find out what the Mage Hunters know about skymages.*

But what are *skymages?* I thought, growing irritated.

"Your silence confirms to me that my assumptions are correct," Lothar said, subtly placing a hand on the hilt of his silver sword.

I swallowed, then thought. *Guys?*

Repeat after me, Solrac thought. *Who has revealed to you the secrets of the skymages of old?*

"Who has revealed to you the secrets of the skymages of old?" I said, an air of superiority in my tone as I continued circling Lothar like a sandshark on the hunt.

"My own studies," Lothar said. "I've tried to convince the Black Valkyrie to let me in on the secret, but to no avail. She says I am not ready."

Double drak, Solrac said in my head. *Vidya's still after the old ways.*

What? Kai asked, also through the mindlink. *The Black Valkyrie's interested in people with multiple kinds of etherarchy?*

What do I say? I asked.

Solrac fed me another line. *She is wise to keep this from you.*

"She is wise to keep this from you." I almost choked as I called the woman I loathed 'wise.'

Solrac continued. *Such a rich secret is a heavy burden...*

"Such a rich secret is a heavy burden...."

...Especially for one who cannot yet command ether himself.

"...Especially for someone who cannot command even himself."

Wait, what? Kai thought as I flubbed the line.

"Excuse me, great skymage?" Lothar cocked his head.

He thinks I'm great, I thought, trying to keep a grin off my face. This was kind of fun.

I cleared my throat. "By which I mean, only one who has command over himself can handle such ancient secrets."

Nice save, Solrac thought.

I thought so.

"But my research has led me to some clues," Lothar said. "To obtain more than one ether well is costly to the soul. But no books have led me to discover how it's done. Is it linked to skystone? Heartscales? Many texts reference the Gray Ones."

The air turned just a little bit colder when Lothar said that last part.

The Gray Ones... Solrac thought. *Kai, hurry and get Boone. He knows more about the Gray Ones than anyone.*

On it, Kai thought. *But did he just say you can obtain more than one ether well? Meaning, it's an acquired ability, not innate?*

Yep, I thought back.

Keep talking, Solrac ordered.

"Were I to impart such a dangerous secret to you," I said aloofly, stepping right in front of Lothar's face. "What would you do with this knowledge? Become a skymage yourself?"

Lothar bowed his head with respect and what looked like a little fear. "One day, yes. But I would use my power only to serve Evgard."

Alright, you lousy drakpats, Boone's voice appeared on the mindlink. *What drakked fool's bringin' up the Gray Ones?*

The Mage Hunter thinks they have something to do with people called skymages, Kai brought Boone up to speed.

What'n the void's a skymage?

An ancient myth about magi who can access multiple types of etherarchy, Solrac thought. *Vidya and I used to read the old legends together.*

An' the redhead's been dabblin' with the likes of the Gray Ones?

Yeah, yeah. But what do I say? I thought, getting the urge to cover my ears with my hands to block out all the voices. But little good that would do, since the voices were coming from inside my head.

Boone's mind spun for a second before he sent his next thought. *Tell him if he knows what's good for him, he won't mess with them soulless murder spirits, the Gray Ones.*

"A word of caution," I said ominously, darkening my gaze. "The Gray Ones will only lead you down a path of darkness."

Lothar's eyes widened, and I saw the beginnings of sweat forming along his forehead.

Ask him what Vidya wants with the true dragon egg, Solrac thought, while at the same time Kai chimed in with a thought of his own.

Are the Gray Ones a real thing or just legendary? Or allegorical?

Boone's thought came storming back over the mindlink. *Drakkin' voids alive, they're real, and Solei help the soul who gets caught up in 'em!*

Ask about Vidya's plans, Solrac repeated.

Have you seen a Gray One, Boone? Kai asked.

I seen things back in them Dragon Wars would scare the scales of a fully grown torradon, Boone ranted.

Solrac here. Ask about Vidya and the egg.

"Shut up," I said, realizing too late that I'd spoken aloud.

Lothar tilted his head quizzically.

At least the voices in my head went silent.

"Forgive me," Lothar said, looking at the ground. "It was foolish of me to think I was ready for such a secret now."

"Very foolish indeed," I confirmed.

"What can I do, oh great skymage, to one day be worthy of such a bestowal?"

"Uh..." I mumbled, then got quickly back into character. "If you wish to cleanse yourself of unworthiness, you must perform a special ritual."

Solrac caught on and fed me lines in my head as I said them out loud to Lothar.

"Each morning when you rise," I repeated, "Meditate in stages. Open your senses to feel the world around you—this will prepare you to receive the etherarchy of a Sentinel. Next, open your imagination to envision what is not, but could yet be—this will prepare you to receive the etherarchy of a Mystic. Finally, open your heart to connect with the truth about the world around you, what lies beyond, as well as your true, authentic self—this will prepare you to receive the etherarchy of an Archon. Meditate thus each day for two third parts of a year, then return to me to evaluate your preparedness to learn the ancient secrets of the skymage."

Lothar was nodding furiously by the time I finished delivering Solrac's speech.

"Thank you, thank you, great one." Lothar gave a deep bow.

I stifled a chuckle. Nobody had ever bowed to me before.

In my head, Solrac was laughing as well. *He's actually going to do it.*

Y'all are as odd as a seventh scale on a basilisk, Boone put in.

I've got an escape plan for you, Asher, Kai thought. *Whenever you're ready.*

Wait! Solrac thought. *Before you go, ask about Vidya's plans for the egg.*

"Now," I said regally. "I require one thing as payment for the great knowledge I have imparted to you this night."

"Anything," Lothar said.

"Anything, great one," I corrected.

"Of course, oh great one." Lothar took a knee before me.

Laying it on a little thick, aren't you? Kai said through the mindlink.

I can appreciate the instinct, Solrac thought back.

I went on. "You must tell me what your mistress, the Valkyrie of Black, wishes to do with the true dragon egg once she acquires it."

The Valkyrie of Black? Boone questioned.

Come on, Asher. I could feel Kai rolling his eyes.

That was pretty dumb, even for you, Solrac added.

I'm under a lot of pressure here, okay? I thought back, returning my attention to Lothar.

"I don't know of her specific plans for the egg," Lothar said. "But I know the egg is not her true prize. What is a true dragon egg to the ether well of the Farseer himself?"

"The Farseer's ether well?" I said.

Drak infinity, Solrac thought, and I could sense just how disturbed he was to hear that.

"Lothar?" Jaira's voice came from behind the hedge.

Okay, Kai thought. *You really need to get out of here.*

"Almost finished, Jaira," Lothar called over the hedge before whispering to me. "You must go. My partner does not comprehend the grandeur of what you are."

"Wise words," I said. "You are learning already."

Lothar beamed at me.

Ready? Kai asked.

Ready, I replied.

I felt a strong wiggle from the mirror gecko in my boot as Kai channeled his etherarchy through Glint Four. I raised one arm in a dramatic gesture and pretended to runetrace. Kai projected an illusion of gold etherlight trailing from my finger as a golden Mystic rune glowed softly from my forehead. I definitely traced it wrong, but I was certain Lothar wouldn't notice.

I saw Lothar's eyes widen again as a golden rift appeared in the air—or at least the illusion of one. The illusory portal ripped open and I nodded to Lothar once more as I stepped inside.

Of course, my foot landed on solid dirt rather than sending me teleporting through Etheria. But I quickly burned ether of my own and hover-dashed back toward the hedge, ducking underneath the bushy foliage. It wasn't very sophisticated, but from my hiding place I saw Lothar looking at the dying golden embers of Kai's illusory rift in amazement.

"Rifter," he whispered to himself in awe as the remains of the rift disappeared completely.

I tucked myself deeper under the hedge as Jaira crossed the threshold, striding up to Lothar. Accompanying her was Lothar's forlorn-looking green evren, walking with the claws at the corners of her four tucked wings. I couldn't hear Jaira from here, but her body language told me she was annoyed with her partner.

Jaira gestured toward the citadel, then pointed to the cord around Lothar's neck. He pulled out the green dragon's heartscale, rubbing it as he ordered the dragon to take them back quickly.

The evren let out a low growl, as if she didn't want to obey. But Lothar had the dragon's heartscale, and she had no choice. She crouched as Jaira and Lothar mounted her. Using her wing claws to gain a little momentum, the dragon took off into the air. It looked painful, taking off like that with two riders on her back, but the Mage Hunters didn't seem to care.

I frowned, feeling sorry for the green evren. This must've been why Elle was so against forced bonds with dragons.

Mission accomplished? I thought through the mindlink.

Well done, Asher, Solrac's thought came through.

Kai's thought came next. *Now, get back to the hideout before you think of any more stupid ideas to get yourself killed.*

I stared blankly at the needle and thread in my hands as if they were speaking to me in a foreign language. Looking around the circle at the members of our team, I wasn't the only one who appeared baffled by the sewing tools.

"I can kill a man with any weapon under the sun," Valla said. "Just don't ask me to sew on a button."

Kari gave a strained laughed as she passed out fabric and scissors.

"Sewing's not that hard," she said.

"Says the armorer and clothing-designer extraordinaire," muttered Valla.

Kari put her hands on her hips and glared. "Oh, I'm sorry. Would you like to be in charge of producing two noble-worthy, full-length ballgowns, one serving dress, one formal attendant's suit, a manservant's outfit, plus minor repairs to Asher and Jax's guard uniforms? Oh, and did I mention I have less than forty-eight hours to get it all done?"

That shut Valla and the rest of us up. We ducked our heads and let Kari boss us around as we painstakingly worked on completing our disguises for the heist.

After using my ascension bracers to heal myself from sticking my fingers with needles for the tenth time, Kari finally gave me a different job. She had me carefully use starglass to create a three-dimensional dress form for each disguise. She gave me a list of measurements for everyone on the team, and I had to layer starglass to make sure each torso mannequin matched them exactly.

When I finished, I couldn't help but laugh. A row of white, crystalline figures stood in a row. Boone's wiry frame stood tall and proud beside Solrac's surprisingly fit one. Kai didn't need one since he'd be outside running the group mindlink, and I didn't need to make figures of Jax and me either, since we already had our guard uniforms. If I was being honest, I was relieved. I wasn't interested in a direct comparison of Jax's muscular torso and mine. I was athletic and all, but working out was Jax's life.

Then came the women—Valla, Kari, and Shaya. I felt a little heat rush to my cheeks as I looked their forms over. I couldn't help but notice Shaya's curves.

"What are you staring at?" Shaya meandered over to where I stood surveying my work.

"Nothing," I said too quickly.

Shaya laughed and playfully shoved my chest. Out of nowhere, an image of Elle came to mind, and I automatically stepped away from her.

"What's up?" Shaya tilted her head, her brown eyes inquisitive.

"Uh..." I started.

"I'll tell you what's up," Kari materialized beside us, a swatch of royal blue fabric in her hands. "Our heist is basically two minutes from now, and you're wasting precious time flirting. Drak, guys."

Kari never swore. She must've really been at the end of her rope with this disguise-making project.

Just then, the sound of someone dropping a pile of cloth caught my attention. Looking over, I saw Jax leaving his work behind and heading for the hideout door. He shut the door loudly behind him.

Kari bared her teeth as she watched him go. Then she called out, "I guess some people aren't interested in making sure things get done."

The team looked at her, confused and concerned.

"Why are you all just sitting here gaping? These disguises won't sew themselves."

Everyone hurriedly returned to their work, doing their best to keep a low profile.

Hmm. I guessed Kari was upset about more than just the heist preparations.

"The mannequins are finished," I said to Kari. "You guys can start loading the clothes onto them whenever you're ready. In the meantime, I need to check in on Thorn."

Kari grumbled something about me being useless with a needle anyway, and I headed for the door.

Asher? I felt Thorn's spark of worry through the bond at the mention of his name. He'd been sleeping back in the dragon dens at the citadel.

I sent back a feeling that I was fine and that he should return to his rest. He sent back an image of warm embers as he drifted back into slumber.

Meanwhile, I climbed the stairs that led back to the tavern above the hideout. The Dreamy Drakalope was even busier than usual tonight, with patrons at all levels of sobriety gathered around tables. Many sat at regular tables while others drunkenly splashed water at each other from their places in the hot springs.

I found Jax sitting alone at the main bar, his head in his hands. I watched as a barmaid tapped him on the shoulder, striking a flirtatious pose as he looked up.

Jax's shockingly high kiss count came to mind, and I wondered if he'd drown his sorrows in the pretty barmaid. To my surprise, whatever he said to her next made her shrug her shoulders and walk away.

Stars, Jax must really be down.

I figured I was the last person he wanted to talk to right now. In fact, part of me wanted to let him wallow alone. But I appreciated the change I'd been seeing in him lately. He'd really surprised me with his genuine commitment to Kari, and I couldn't just leave him there alone. I strode over and took a seat beside him.

"Can I get a couple of sparkling dragonfruit spritzers?" I called to the barkeep, who gave me a nod.

Beside me, Jax grumbled. "Get lost, Dragon-boy."

"I just thought you could use a drink." I shrugged.

"You look like you could use another punch to the jaw."

"Spare us the bar fight," I held up both hands. "Look, I'll go if you really want me to. I just figured it might help if you talked about your breakup with Kari."

Jax looked at me, his eyebrows lowered over red-tinted eyes. "How'd you know?"

"I've known Kari for a while. Plus, you storming out of the hideout helped."

Jax groaned, running his fingers through his wild, steely gray hair. "What's wrong with me?" he mumbled. "I really thought she was into me."

"I know she was into you," I said, accepting the two tall, carbonated drinks from the bartender. "So what happened?"

"I've never cared about anyone like this before, I guess." Jax took his drink and began tracing the lip of the glass with his finger. "Kari... she's different. She saw my imperfections, but she liked me anyway. She didn't care that I wasn't as strong as I pretend to be."

Soot, I hadn't realized Jax was that self aware. I sipped my drink and kept listening.

"That's why it hurt so much when she ended it," Jax continued, staring at the tiny bubbles in his glass. "She saw the real me, but didn't want it. Or at least she wanted something else more."

"What's that?" I asked.

"Ambition, I guess. We argued last night, and she let me know that if it ever came down to it, she'd choose her inventions over her relationship with me. Then she broke it off." Jax lightly slammed his fist against the bar, squeezing his eyes shut.

"Soot, man," I said. "That's rough."

"I just don't get it. I thought I was doing everything right this time."

"Maybe that was part of her problem."

Jax looked at me like I was dumber than a drekling.

"Want to hear a Kari story?" I asked.

"Sure," Jax sighed.

"Once when we were kids, Kari, Kai, and I wanted to capture this horned lizard that had been living in their family's pantry. We laid all kinds of traps trying to get it, but that lizard was elusive."

"Okay," Jax said, not sure where I was going with this.

"Kari threw herself into finding this thing. She read every book in the town library about horned lizards, figured out what kind of food they liked, what their weaknesses were... literally everything she could about it. Then she built this crazy trap using an entire colony of rust ants as bait. It was the most elaborate, multi-step trap I've ever seen."

Jax chuckled. "That sounds like Kari."

"She caught the lizard and released it far away from the house. Then the next day, instead of relishing in her victory, she'd already gone back to the library and checked out all the books on water collection methods. See, the well near our houses had started drying up. As far as I know, she's never thought about horned lizards ever again."

"Makes sense," Jax said. "The water became a bigger priority."

"Exactly."

"Okay. Cute story I guess, but what does it have to do with anything?"

"Kari's the kind of girl who loves nothing more than the next big challenge. Maybe she saw you that way. Once she solved the problem of capturing your heart, she felt fulfilled and ready to move on."

"That's a terrible way to handle relationships."

"Maybe," I shrugged. "But that's something she needs to work through herself. Doesn't mean you should beat yourself up over her choice."

"But I hate her choice," Jax said, grabbing his drink and taking a massive gulp. He immediately put the glass down and coughed.

"Drak," he sputtered. "I don't do alcohol."

"Oh," I said. "Sorry, I forgot. Mystic."

"Keep your voice down about that," Jax said with a quick glance around the bar. "But even besides that, I don't do alcohol."

"Why not?"

"Just... reasons." Jax pushed the drink away, then laced his fingers around the back of his neck and rested his elbows on the bar. "Thanks for the insight, Dragon-boy. Maybe you're not as big a drakpat as I thought."

"Gee, thanks," I said, standing up. "I'm going to head back to the hideout. Want to come?"

"Not yet. But you go ahead. I'll be fine."

I cast one last look toward Jax as I headed back to the door behind the bar.

Despite Jax's assurances last night, the next morning, he was clearly not fine. As we walked down to Guard Square to report with the rest of Squad Nimble, he had dark circles under his slightly red eyes. From the looks of things, he hadn't gotten much sleep.

Guard Square was in a state of chaos when we arrived. It looked like every soldier in the Drakfell guard was here, dozens of squad captains doing their best to wrangle their squads into neat lines.

"There you two are." Squad Captain Sven hurried up to us, his face etched with stress. "I thought you were going to pick today of all days to be late."

"What's going on?" I asked.

"After that group of Drekai attacked us in the dens yesterday, the scouts from the northern border returned with news that a Drekai army was marching on Drakfell. They haven't attacked yet, but they're camped just outside the city. They're probably here for the duel between King Rodan and their champion."

"Soot," I cursed.

"They're tightening up security on the guard," Sven continued. "Have to make sure none of us are illusion-clad spies sent by the Drekai. Everyone's getting silver rod tested."

My heart dropped. Jax's jaw clenched.

"Is that a problem?" Sven looked between the two of us, his lower eyelids squinting up.

"Of course not," I said casually.

"Sven!" a voice barked.

Sven turned around and stood at attention. "Yes, Commander Vath!"

"Your squad's turn," the commander said, whacking a silver rod against his palm. The rod was a little thicker than my thumb and as long as my forearm.

Sven assembled Squad Nimble into a line, with me and Jax at the end. I wasn't too worried—Baron Eidan had forced me to get silver rod tested back in Steel Rim a dozen times, trying to expose me as a magi. I'd passed every time.

Still, I felt my palms growing sweaty. This was Keep Drakfell, not some backwater outlander town.

The commander slapped the rod into each of my squadmates' palms in turn. He held it there for several seconds as they gripped the silver. None of them had any reaction at all.

"Not magi," the commander said after Friga's turn. I was next.

The commander stood in front of me, beckoning me to hold out my hand.

He thumped the rod onto my open palm, and the silver sent icy pain shooting up my arm.

My instinct was to cry out, but years of practice had trained me to show no emotion. I gripped the rod, swallowing the freezing burn from the anti-ether silver.

I threw in a casual tilt of my head as I looked up at the commander.

"Not a magi," the commander said, and I breathed a silent sigh of relief. I don't know why I'd gotten so worked up over nothing. Maybe it was because I hadn't been tested in months since crossing the Scar and arriving in Keep Drakfell.

"Augh," I heard Jax's sharp, pained inhale next to me as the silver hit his hand.

I stared in horror as the commander's face hardened. Jax looked just as horrified as he looked up at the officer with exhausted, terrified eyes.

"Magi," the commander muttered bitterly. Then he called out louder. "Magi!"

"Wait," Jax protested. "Just let me—"

But at least two squads worth of guards already had crossbows, swords, and spears trained on him. Out of nowhere, two Mage Hunters appeared, wielding gleaming silver swords of their own. I relaxed a little—but not much—when I saw that they weren't any of the Mage Hunters we knew from the Black Valkyrie's entourage.

"What kind of magi are you?" one of the Mage Hunters barked.

"Didn't know I was one," Jax replied weakly.

"Demonstrate which type you are, or we'll mark you with all nine symbols." The other Mage Hunter sheathed his sword and took out a sharp, knife-like pen and a small bottle of silver ink.

Jax gulped.

The bulk of Drakfell's guard watched with bated breath as Jax slowly raised a finger. He traced a few lines in the air, the corresponding gold rune appearing over his forehead.

Then he made a raising motion with his hand, lifting a small group of pebbles from the ground. The pebbles shook a little, and Jax's hand trembled. With a grunt, Jax let the small rocks fall.

"Psion," the first Mage Hunter hissed.

"Not a very strong one," Jax said. "Didn't think it was worth reporting."

The Mage Hunters didn't reply. Instead, the second one walked forward, holding his knife-like pen at the ready.

"You're going to silvermark me? Here and now?" Panic colored Jax's tone.

It took everything I had not to run in there and start a fight. But I knew that would just get Jax and me both killed.

"You'll be imprisoned here in Drakfell for the time being," the first Mage Hunter said as her partner prepared to brand Jax. "Then shipped to Evyndara for the cure."

"No," Jax protested. "Please."

I rooted my feet to the ground.

"Hold still." The Mage Hunter pressed the pen into Jax's left cheek, and Jax cried out in pain as the silvered ink set in and blood began dripping down his chin.

FRAGMENT - ARADAN

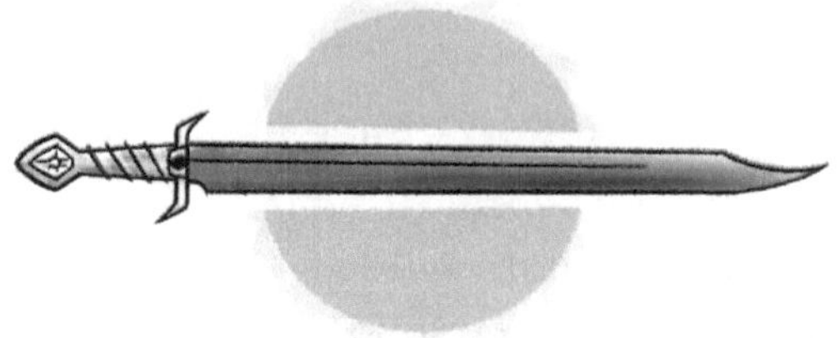

Aradan could smell the fruity scents of flowering cacti from the citadel's inner courtyard. Beautifully cultivated juniper trees and well-manicured desert succulents lined the stony castle walls. A sparring circle was the courtyard's centerpiece—Rodan had added it to the courtyard once he took the throne. Inside the circle, Rodan and Aradan's ascension blades clashed.

Four dragons watched from the sidelines, as did the royal high guard and a few scattered spectators milling about along the fringes of the courtyard. That was one of the many reasons Aradan was glad he wasn't king. No time to yourself.

A pair of beautiful courtiers wearing tightly-fitted gowns tittered and waved at Aradan from their place near the citadel wall. Aradan flashed them a smug grin before gesturing to the woven marriage bracelet on his wrist.

At that moment of brief distraction, Rodan's enormous dragonforged warsword carved through the air, slashing right through Aradan's neck.

Luckily, the white blade passed harmlessly through Aradan as if it was made from pure shadow. It had been Aradan's smokescale drake, Shade, who had the idea to empower their weapons with her shadowbinding ether-archy. The shadowsilk relics tied around the handguards of their swords allowed the weapons to phase shift right through the men's bodies. Aradan had tried to tell Shade she was being overly cautious, but after years of watching the king and his brother spar together, she insisted she knew what she was doing.

A smattering of weak applause rang through the courtyard, but when Rodan removed his brilliant, crowned white helmet, his face was anything but pleased about his victory.

"What was that?" Rodan asked, his eyes narrowing.

"Just had to break a few hearts," Aradan shrugged, removing his own, less flashy helmet and nodding to the courtiers. Already the women were walking away from the fight, disappointment etched on their pretty faces.

"You know they're only flirting with you because you're my brother. They think they can use you to improve their status."

"Perhaps they're hoping you'll die in your duel against the Drekai general."

Rodan set his jaw. "If you wouldn't mind getting your head back into the match, I'd like to prove them wrong. Let's go again. More weights this time."

Hearing the king's wish, Aradan's red starshard wyvern, Glass, began using his astromancy to breathe starglass onto Rodan's wrists and ankles. The white, crystalline structures clung to his pure white bracers and gauntlets. That would slow him down for sure.

"This is excessive, even for you, Rodan," Aradan sighed.

"If I practice under worse conditions than the actual duel, I'll be that much more prepared."

Without wasting another second, Rodan came at his brother again, his enormous blade held high.

Aradan raised his black warsword to block at the last second. Then he engaged his brother, allowing him to get a few good swings in as he got used to the new weights on his arms and legs.

"Don't go easy!" Rodan yelled.

"You're crazy," Aradan observed.

With a roar, Rodan spun his heavy sword around his head, hacking toward Aradan from the side. Aradan barely managed to block in time.

"Rex," the king called out to his white drake sitting on the sidelines. The king didn't let up from the fight for even a moment as he spoke. "The

Drekai general has explosive dragonfire. I need you to mimic that using lightwielding."

The alabaster dragon obediently got to his feet, stretching out his neck toward the sparring circle. He opened his jaws, sending out a tight, crackling ball of what appeared to be golden lightning. It sparked and flared as it hit the ground, making both Rodan and Aradan jump backward.

"Good. Now Lyra," Rodan addressed Aradan's beloved, pale violet dreamwatcher evren. "The Drekai general is a Rifter, which means he'll be able to use his etherarchy to attack me through portals. I need you to imitate this using illusions."

Aradan felt through his dragon bond that Lyra was up for the challenge. A golden rune appeared over her forehead as an illusory, gold-rimmed rift ripped to life alongside Rodan. The king slashed toward it briefly, as if blocking an enemy strike coming at him through the portal. Without missing a beat, he continued the fight with Aradan.

"Oh, so you're giving orders to my dragon now?" Aradan asked, an edge in his voice as sharp as his blade. "Is that what you're planning to do to the true dragon as well?" Aradan slashed at his brother with renewed ire.

"I want the true dragon to be motivated to serve Drakfell," Rodan answered, sweat beading across his forehead. "Why do you think I'm trying so hard to hatch it through a natural bond?"

"So what?" Aradan swung his blade. "The creature will still live in captivity, as will its rider. And what'll you do if it doesn't bond anyone at your sooty gala?"

Rex spat more crackling balls of lightning at the brothers' feet. Both Aradan and Rodan expertly dodged them before returning to the fight. The once-indifferent spectators now watched with interest.

Rodan spoke through gritted teeth. "Drakfell has my loyalty. I can't stand by and watch it suffer. Already we're falling behind on the High King's skyfall tribute, despite the more frequent skyfalls within our border. More refugees flock to the cities every day, seeking shelter from towns overrun with dreklings, or healing from the shadow wasting."

Rodan's heavy blade arced through the air, clashing against his brother's. The king spoke with ire and passion. "I'll do whatever it takes to preserve my keepdom. I put that responsibility above all others."

"Above your honor?" Aradan challenged, pressing in on Rodan's sword. "Above your family?"

"Even above High King Magnus himself." Rodan grunted, his eyes storming as he hacked at two of Lyra's illusory portals. He leaped over another of Rex's balls of lightning, spinning low and faking a strike toward Aradan's legs. Aradan moved to defend himself, but he was too late to stop Rodan's over-the-top blow right through Aradan's middle. If his brother's blade hadn't been infused with a Shadowbinder's phase shifting powers, Aradan would be lying dead in the dirt.

Enthusiastic applause met Rodan's grand victory. Aradan gave a subtle eye roll as he extended a congratulatory arm toward his brother.

Rodan took Aradan's arm at the elbow, and Aradan leaned in. "Was the big show really necessary?"

Rodan's voice was ragged and serious as he answered. "Yes. People don't care about intricacies or technicalities. What they need to see from their king is a show of strength."

Chapter 23: The Plan

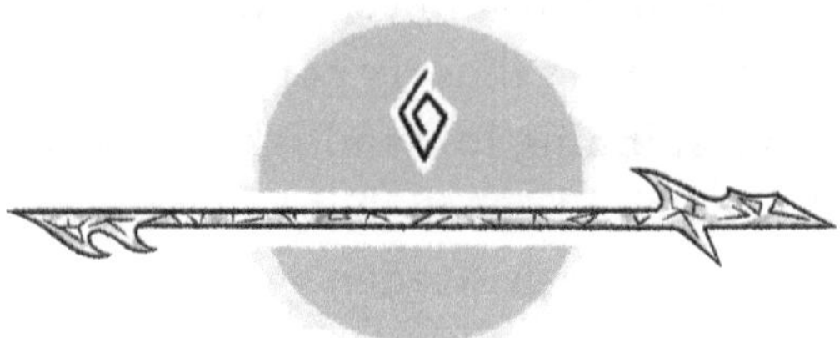

I wasn't able to sneak away from guard duties for hours. Squad Captain Sven kept an extra close eye on us until the Mage Hunters had finished setting Jax up in prison. Then the dusk blue-cloaked pair interviewed our squad.

Convincing the Mage Hunters that I knew nothing about Jax being a magi was hard, mostly because of my being a half-born. Then again, my being a half-born made it easier to convince the Mage Hunters that I was too stupid to really know anything. I played up the whole 'from-a-backwater-outlander-town' angle, and they moved on.

After the interviews, Sven made us report to Aradan at the dragon dens for our usual duties. Without Jax or Korvald, there were only five of us now.

Once I got set up to muck out stalls with Elle, I told her about Jax. I didn't tell her why, but she seemed to understand when I asked her to cover for me because I needed to go.

It was late afternoon when I finally got back to the hideout. I found everyone basically where I'd left them this morning—hard at work on the final preparations for the heist.

I told them about Jax, expecting some negative responses. Kari immediately looked upset, and the news clearly put Kai and Boone on edge, too. But nothing could've prepared me for the storm that burst from Shaya.

"And you just let them take him?" Shaya's eyes blazed.

"Jax is essential for the heist," Solrac muttered. "We'll have to rework the switch completely without him."

"I can't believe you just said that," Shaya turned on Solrac.

"What?"

"Jax is silvermarked and in custody, and all you can think about is how to replace him?"

"Of course Jax himself is the priority," Solrac said, giving Shaya a hurt look.

"It's not 'of course' to you. Your first response is to think of how this affects your goals."

The rest of us shrank back, looking between Shaya and Solrac as they argued.

"That's quite the accusation," Solrac crossed his arms.

"It's not an accusation, it's an observation. You've never given a flying scale about Jax's well being. You'd sacrifice any member of this team if it meant you succeeding in getting that stupid egg."

"How dare you," Valla stood, reaching for a knife strapped to her thigh.

"Stay out of this," Shaya snapped, not taking her eyes off of Solrac.

"What gives you the right to—" Valla started, and I automatically took a few more cautious steps backward.

"Back off, Valla," Shaya said. "I'm warning you."

"It's alright, Valla," Solrac said, his brow furrowing. "Shaya's right. We must make a plan to rescue Jax as well. We won't be able to breach the prison before the gala, but we might have a chance during it."

"But what about the egg?" Valla asked.

"We'll just have to multitask," Solrac said. "It'll be more complicated, but we can't leave Jax like this."

Everyone looked at Shaya to gauge her response. She still looked livid, but placated.

"We'll have to outline the plan very carefully," Solrac said, mostly to himself. "Not enough teammates for redundancies, no room for error."

"We should contact the Farseer," Shaya suggested. "We need insight on what's going to happen tomorrow night."

"No," Kai spoke up.

"Why not?" Shaya retorted. "You don't think Jax's safety is important enough—"

"That's not it," Kai said, casting meaningful looks toward Solrac, Boone, and me. "I just think we shouldn't call on the Farseer except as a last resort, because of—"

"Because we can handle Jax's rescue ourselves, right Boone?" Solrac said, glancing at Kai in a way that told me he didn't want Vidya's true goal of taking the Farseer to be common knowledge. I wondered why.

Shaya cocked her head, about to push back when Boone cut in.

"I've broken plenty a people out of worse. Now, this ain't worth our time arguin' 'bout no more. Best we make like beaverdrakes and prepare ourselves against what's a comin' tomorrow night."

"I agree," Solrac nodded. "Get some sleep. Tomorrow morning, we'll have our final dress rehearsal."

After a fitful night's rest, I discovered that Solrac's version of a 'dress rehearsal' meant watching the entire heist play out in illusory miniature.

With tonight's heist hanging over our heads, we gathered together in the common room of our hideout. Solrac and Kai, the team's Mystics, had teamed up to build a three-dimensional illusion of the southeast section of the Keep Drakfell citadel. Solrac had used the intel we'd gotten during our undercover mission as florists to make the map as accurate as possible.

Both of them had several Dreamweave runes activated across their foreheads like glowing gold crowns. They'd covered the hot spring in the center of the room with a large, round board. We all gathered around the board as the citadel took shape on top.

I wasn't sure if it was just because the room's torches were running low, or if Solrac or Kai had built dim, ambient lighting into their illusion. Either way, it honed our focus onto the soft glow of the illusory citadel before us.

"Kai, would you do the honors?" Solrac gestured to Kai.

Kai's face scrunched up like he was focusing really hard, then he raised a hand to trace one more intricate rune. The corresponding rune joined the others around his forehead just as eight pinkie finger-sized illusory people appeared on the grounds outside the citadel.

"Aww, look how cute and widdle we are!" Kari said, reaching a finger toward the pint-sized avatar of herself.

"Hey," Kai protested as the tiny Kari turned on her heels and ran from real Kari's giant finger. "Don't touch them or they might burst. They're visual illusions only."

"Sorry little brother," Kari laughed and rescinded her finger.

"What about Thorn, His Majesty, and Flint?" I said.

"Of course." A look of concentration crossed Kai's face as a miniature wyvern, evren, and bloodhusky materialized beside the rest of us.

"Oh! Thorn's teeny weeny antlers," Kari gushed.

"Control yourself, woman," Valla said.

Thorn must've been listening in, because I felt my wyvern snort in laughter through our bond. Meanwhile, Shaya reached across the board, her finger outstretched.

"What are you—" Kai started.

Shaya burst the tiny illusory Jax. "He'll be in prison on the other side of the citadel, remember?"

For a moment, the only sound was the soft bubbling of the hot spring beneath the board.

"Right," Solrac agreed gently. "But not for long. Ladies and gentle-man, let part one begin."

We leaned closer as Solrac used etherarchy to move the players around the board.

"Yesterday, Jax and His Majesty excavated an old servant's passage that hasn't been operational in over a decade," Solrac began, pointing to a broken section of wall on the map. "The passage leads through the wall adjacent to the ballroom, and makes for the perfect central location for Kai to run the group mindlink."

The illusory Kai ducked through the opening in the wall. The illusion went translucent for a moment so that we could see the little Kai run along the wall and set up a spot inside.

"Flint can be my bodyguard this time," Kai said as the illusory stonescale evren hovered near the passage entrance. The illusory Flint landed and used his stonescale etherarchy to camouflage himself as a statue of an evren.

"Exactly," Solrac agreed. "Next, it's up to Shaya and me to sneak in through the regular servants' entrance and join the staff. Kari, how are those disguises coming?"

Kari hurried over to one of the enormous armchairs in the corner, rummaging through her piles of fabric for a moment before whipping out two perfectly-accurate serving outfits. White aprons covered black and gray tunics, and the crest of Drakfell—a tan fang—was embroidered on the right just below the collar.

Kai squinted at the disguises. Then, with a motion from his hand, he swapped the clothing on the illusory versions of Solrac and Shaya for the servant's garb. Solrac's silvermark disappeared under makeup, and a ridiculous beard appeared over his goatee. Together, they walked into the castle, then split off as Solrac went to the ballroom while Shaya strode into the kitchens.

"Excellent." Solrac smiled. "Now, Shaya, you'll need to work quickly. You'll have the astralock solution hidden on you—be careful, you might need to use your invisibility. You'll need to spike the High Mage's drink before you serve it to him."

The small, illusory Shaya went invisible, which Kai and Solrac's illusion represented by making her turn translucent and tinted light purple. She pulled a tiny vial out from a pocket of her skirts, slipping a few drops into one of the five goblets on a serving tray.

She hid behind a corner, returned to normal visibility, then picked up the tray as if she were one of the many other serving girls at the gala. The little Shaya elegantly made her way down the hall and out into the main ballroom.

I saw Kai brush a bead of sweat off his forehead as he conjured more illusory figures. A Captain of the Guard and Royal High Mage faded into existence near the thrones.

"Is that really what they look like?" Kari asked.

"According to Solrac's memories of visions from the Farseer, yes," Kai responded.

That sounded complicated. Mystics.

Shaya served the nobility their drinks, taking extra care to ensure the High Mage took the astralock-laced goblet.

"Make sure he drinks the whole thing," Solrac instructed. "It's the only way to ensure he gets a concentrated enough dose for the drunken hallucinations to take effect."

The illusory High Mage guzzled his drink, then started laughing hysterically until he fell to the floor. I chuckled as I watched.

"Will he be okay?" Kari asked.

"The effects will wear off by the end of the night," Solrac assured her. "But it will keep him distracted enough that he shouldn't notice the egg swap."

Kari nodded as Solrac continued outlining the plan.

"Meanwhile, at precisely seven o'clock, the Captain of the Guard will usher in the true dragon egg."

The Captain of the Guard raised her glass to the ballroom as a squad of the king's high guard walked through the doors. They surrounded their squad captain, who carried the true dragon egg on a lush, ornately decorated pillow. He placed the egg on the pedestal that matched the one Solrac and I had seen when we scoped out the ballroom. Then he and the rest of his high guard squad took their places around the egg.

Solrac went on. "At that point we'll have fifteen minutes before they line up the guard and nobility to try their hands at bonding the egg. We'll have to act fast. Next, we'll have Jax come in with—"

"Ahem." Shaya pointedly folded her arms.

"Right," Solrac said. "Without Jax, that means Asher will have to run point on the swap. It's your job to convince the high guard squad that Squad Nimble is there to relieve them from watching the egg while they escort the royal family into the ballroom. Drak, I wish you had backup in Jax."

"It's no problem," I said, confidently tossing my hand. "Talking nonsense is my specialty."

"Hold on," Valla narrowed her eyes. "I doubt even Asher's fancy words could pull that off. Squad Nimble is down to five soldiers, anyway."

"It only has to work for a few minutes," Solrac said. "Asher?"

I tapped a finger to my chin. "Aradan, the head dragon keeper, is the king's brother. He trusts Sven. If the order came from him it would work. And Sven would be too busy glowing with pride to protest."

"Get me a sample of Aradan's handwriting," Solrac said. "I'll write up the order."

The illusory version of me hurried in, accompanied by four other tan-cloaked figures representing the rest of Squad Nimble. Kai didn't know them well, so their figures lacked details like facial features and distinct hair colors. We replaced the vague illusory figures of the high guard, standing in a protective circle around the shiny, white egg.

"Then we move into phase two," Solrac said grandly, ushering in the small illusory figures of Valla and Kari. "Care to show off your work, Kari?"

Kari proudly grabbed two bundles of fabric from the armchair. She turned to the group, a hopeful expression on her face. "Valla?"

Valla's face was stone as she stared Kari down. Then, with the most massive eye roll I'd ever seen, she got up and reached for one of the gowns in Kari's hands.

Kari squealed with delight as she and Valla retreated to the bedrooms to change. When they returned to the common room, I did a double take.

I'd never seen Kari wear anything but her work tunic, and I certainly hadn't seen Valla wear anything but what I could only describe as assassin's garb.

Both dresses fell to the floor in sweeping folds of fabric. Valla's was a sleek, velvety green, while Kari's was a rich shade of deep maroon, with sleeves long enough to touch the floor. It took me a minute, but it dawned on me that Kari's dress almost perfectly matched the color of the bandana Jax always wore. I wondered if that was an accident.

"Wow," I said. "You guys look fantastic."

Boone let out a low whistle. "Two of y'all look better'na fresh kilt ridgerat looks to a fangbuzzard."

"Uhh, thanks?" Kari swished her full skirt.

Solrac seemed to approve as well, based on the entranced way he was watching Valla. The illusory map of the citadel began partially melting away as he redirected his focus elsewhere.

"What?" Valla said as heat rushed to her cheeks.

Solrac grinned broadly, but before he could answer, Shaya cut in.

"So, phase two?"

"Right," Solrac said, tearing his eyes away from Valla and refocusing on the illusion. The walls rebuilt themselves before our eyes as detail returned to the ballroom.

"Kari and Valla will pose as noblewomen," Solrac said. "Your job is to distract the members of Squad Nimble. Do whatever you have to do, whether that's spill a drink, twist an ankle, or use your... feminine charm."

Solrac's eyes once again flashed to Valla. She looked embarrassed, but not upset.

"Meanwhile, I'll be wheeling a dirty dish cart past the pedestal," Solrac went on. The little illusion of Solrac pushed a dish laden cart toward the egg while the illusory Kari and Valla pulled the attention of my squad.

Well, almost the whole squad. My tiny illusory copy slunk toward the pedestal holding the egg. Just as Solrac's cart rode past, the little Asher smoothly ducked, grabbed the fake true dragon egg from off the cart, and swapped it with the real one.

The motion was so quick, I wouldn't have noticed it if I hadn't been watching for it specifically. I wondered if I'd be able to pull off a switch that smoothly tonight.

"Don't worry, Asher," Solrac said, reading my face. "I'll cover for you with an illusion that masks all motion immediately surrounding the egg."

At that point, Solrac invited Kai to show the group the egg replica he'd been working on.

I had to hand it to my friend. His replica looked incredible. Tiny white illusory scales formed what looked like a fist-sized egg. Using a skystone from Solrac, Kai had enchanted the rock in the replica to hold the illusion indefinitely. The skystone acted as an ether well all on its own, powering the illusion constantly.

The most impressive part was the way he'd incorporated how the illusion felt. When I got close to the fake egg and put a hand on it, I felt a surge of power, and what seemed like life.

It was remarkable. Kai's replica was nearly identical to the true dragon egg Elle had shown me that day in the hatchery, down to the gently pulsing light coming from within the egg.

It was perfect. Almost.

When I looked closely, I could tell the pulsing light was set to a pattern. It had a nice irregular, lifelike rhythm, but when I stared at it for a long time, I could tell that it repeated itself. But with Shaya drugging the High Mage and a little luck, nobody would notice.

"What about the Black Valkyrie and her Mage Hunters?" I asked. "Won't they be keeping a careful watch on things?"

"They'll be at the gala, alright," Solrac said. "But if there's one thing I know about Vidya, it's that she likes making a dramatic, fashionably late entrance. She won't show up until we're long gone with the egg."

Valla nodded in agreement, which was enough for the rest of us.

Next, Solrac moved on to explain phase three. We watched as the illusory Solrac pushed the cart across the ballroom and out the staff door toward the kitchens. The illusion shifted a little, pulling our focus to the kitchen outside the ballroom.

I laughed a little when I saw the avatar of Boone down there, dressed as an undercook. Even in illusion form, his white apron looked like it would fall off his thin frame.

The miniature Solrac parked his cart beside a dishwashing station, where Boone began unloading dishes from the cart into the sink. I felt myself growing nervous just watching the tiny Boone move the bowl from where the tiny me had stashed the real true dragon egg.

Just before the bowl hit the water, Boone slipped the egg onto a plate atop a nearby serving tray. The egg sat in a bed of greens, its smooth, white surface mimicking the look of the boiled chicken breasts atop the other plates.

A vague, unknown servant came for the tray, and my heart beat a little faster as he picked it up and carried it back to the ballroom. He set it down at a table surrounded by party guests and laden with all kinds of food.

"Hold up," Shaya said. "We're letting a stranger take the egg in plain sight?"

Boone chimed in. "And you're sayin' that lot of scalebrained nobles won't notice a glowin' dragon's egg amidst their white meat poultry feast?"

"I'll put a light illusion over the egg just to be safe. But I spent enough time doing sleight of hand to say this: You'd be surprised what people overlook when they aren't expecting it. Especially when it's right in front of them."

Shaya seemed to accept that, and Boone gave a slight nod as well. But next came Valla's turn on the skepticism caravan.

"Why not just take the egg from the kitchens and leave?"

"Because the High Mage isn't the only one who'll be keeping his eyes peeled," Solrac responded. "If Boone or I left with the egg right then, we'd have to go out through either the servant's entrance or the front gates. Both options would raise serious suspicion and get us caught."

He played out each scenario in the illusion, showing the tiny Boone getting caught by Mage Hunters at the kitchen's exit, then his own illusory self getting caught and run through by a mob of guards at the front gates.

Solrac went on. "Our best chance of not being discovered is to keep the egg moving until we can smuggle it out more subtly. In other words, we need to scramble the egg."

Solrac raised both hands to the side with his fingers splayed, shaking them rapidly like a showman. He looked around at our faces, his mouth wide open in a grin.

Shaya and Valla remained stone-faced, Kai and Boone raised eyebrows, and Kari and I burst into laughter.

"Meanwhile," Solrac said, "Boone will be on a special mission of his own to break Jax out of prison."

"How is he going to manage that?" Shaya asked. "The Mage Hunters are in the citadel, not to mention all of the guards there to try and bond the egg.

Plus, the prisons here will be covered in silver, so you won't be able to bust him out using etherarchy."

Boone cracked his knuckles. "I'mma do the same thing I did back in forty-three durin' the Dragon Wars."

We waited for him to elaborate, but Boone seemed to think that was more than enough information to share.

"Well, at least he won't go in empty-handed," Kari put in. She pulled out a small, silver coin from her pocket, as well as a vial of greenish-gold liquid.

She looked at Solrac, who nodded.

"Behold, silverbane," Kari smiled as she poured a few drops from the vial onto the coin.

We watched with amazement as the substance ate through the silver, dissolving it on contact. I got nervous when the mixture burned through the metal and onto Kari's hand, worried that it would hurt her. For a moment, it looked like it was burning her skin as well. But a moment later, her hand was fine.

We congratulated Kari on her success, and she immediately launched into a scientific explanation of what she'd done to make it work. The burning effect stopped on anything that wasn't silver because of a few drops of liquid light she'd borrowed from Valla's supply. Then Kari went on, saying something about needing an amplifier for the ether-based component in the spydra venom she'd used. She'd found that amplifier in none other than my own failure—the liquid ether I'd accidentally made while trying to shoot ether blasts with Boone. All together, she'd created the substance she called 'silverbane.'

Solrac applauded before returning to the plan. Swirling his hand, he brought the illusion back to the crowd reaching for plates of food. Among those guests was the illusion of Valla, who quickly chose the plate holding the softly glowing egg. In a fake moment of clumsiness, she nearly dropped her food.

The act garnered attention from a few servants and guests, but while their eyes were on Valla's spilled greens, she slipped the egg into a pocket sewn into the long, hanging sleeves of her ballgown.

That's when a tiny, regal illusion of King Rodan appeared beside the pedestal where the fake true dragon egg sat. Even in his illusory form, I could see the resemblance between him and his brother Aradan, down to the topaz-colored eyes and sleek, white hair around his temples. Beside the king stood a beautiful woman with a shiny, iron crown nestled in her flowing, dark hair. To the king's other side stood his bond, a proud, white stormscale drake on its third ascension.

"That drake gonna be a problem?" Boone asked.

"Already taken care of," Solrac replied. "Early this morning, Valla snuck into the dragon dens. She passed by the king's drake's feeding trough and sprinkled just a touch of dreamberry juice into his food. During the gala, he'll be very sleepy, but very happy."

Solrac continued narrating the events, explaining how at this point King Rodan would announce the opportunity of Drakfell's loyal guard and nobility to attempt to bond the greatest treasure their fair keepdom had ever seen. Starting with the king's own high guard, the bonding attempts began. One by one, the soldiers touched the egg with their bare hands.

While the party guests were distracted with the first attempted bonds, the illusory Valla excused herself to get some fresh air.

Once Valla was out on the balcony, she found a place to wildshape. A golden cloud engulfed the ballgown-clad Valla, and when it dispersed, in her place was a black dragonhawk. The true dragon egg glowed as Valla's talons carefully clutched around it.

"Why would Valla's clothes and weapons wildshape along with her, but the true dragon egg wouldn't?" Kai asked.

"You wouldn't wildshape along with me if I shifted while holding your hand," Valla said. "You're a living, breathing individual. You're not as easy to manipulate as clothing or inanimate objects." That seemed to both satisfy and intrigue Kai. I could almost see the wheels of his mind turning as he jotted down notes in his journal.

The illusory Valla-dragonhawk took off into the air, diving over the edge of the balcony. Solrac explained that while in dragonhawk form, Valla wouldn't be able to fly far while carrying the egg. That's why she'd need to meet Thorn in a secluded area behind the castle wall.

The illusion of Thorn met with Valla. Dragonhawk-Valla carefully dropped the egg into a padded pouch on Thorn's saddle, right next to the pouch where I kept my dad's rift anchors. Valla then flew back toward the party so her absence wouldn't raise suspicion. With the true dragon egg in tow, Thorn took to the skies.

Through the bond, I felt Thorn glow with pride. He was excited to have such an important role in the heist.

"Thorn will then fly the egg back to the alley outside the Dreamy Drakalope, where he and His Majesty will protect it," Solrac said. "The rest of us will get out one by one until we can all meet up back at the hideout and claim our prize."

With that, Solrac clapped his hands together and beamed.

I had to admit, it seemed like a pretty solid plan. Risky, but solid. Nerves and excitement jumbled around in my stomach as I thought about actually carrying it out tonight. Solrac's plan was good, but from where I stood, it was missing one important element.

But I was planning to take care of that last detail myself.

Solrac hoped that the Black Valkyrie wouldn't show up to the gala until after we'd taken the egg. But either way, I planned on sticking around, patiently awaiting her arrival.

Tonight was my chance to avenge my mother.

Solrac answered some questions from the rest of the team as I watched the illusory Asher hover obediently alongside the rest of Squad Nimble. The illusion of me may've been standing at attention, but if all went according to my own plan, that's not where I would be by the end of the night.

Solrac interrupted my thoughts with one last thing. "I've come up with the title of tonight's heist."

He waited until we were all paying attention, then announced in a grand voice:

A Summer Solstice Swindle: Torching the True Dragon Egg's Fate of Being Forced to Bond a Buffoon and Subsequently Saving Drakfell from War with the Drekai.

Silently, we all stared at him.

"A little long?" he said. "Fine. In that case, get ready for the opening and closing night of *The Dragon Egg's Deliverance.*"

Chapter 24: The Gala

ELLE

Elle stood in the dragon hatchery, holding her long skirt so its white hem wouldn't get dirty. Across from her, Aradan stiffly crossed his arms, a look of frustration on his face. But Elle wasn't about to back down.

"We can't just stand by and let it happen," Elle said forcefully.

"We don't have a choice," Aradan said. "I've known Rodan my whole life—long enough to know he won't change his mind. If none of the guard or selected nobility bond the egg tonight, my brother will force the true dragon egg to bond with someone from his high guard."

"The bond won't be as strong. It would be foolish, even if we weren't talking about a true dragon."

"I agree."

Elle wanted to bring up the fact that she suspected a group of rogues was planning on trying to steal the egg tonight anyway. But she knew telling Aradan would mean revealing Asher, and she couldn't do that to him.

Part of her might have even wanted him to succeed.

"Besides," Elle continued passionately, "what about the dragon herself? Are we not going to even consider how miserable a forced bond would make her?"

"You think it's a female?" Aradan tilted his head to the side.

Elle nodded. She wasn't sure why—the dragon within the egg simply...
felt female. Something about the energy it gave off.

"I can't stand by and watch her suffer through a bond with someone she
didn't choose," Elle said, feeling the truth of what she said deeply in her
bones.

"You know there's nothing we can do," Aradan said.

"Yes there is."

"You aren't still thinking of... Elle, no. It's a dangerous plan. I can't in
good conscience—"

"There you are," a woman's voice came from the hatchery's entrance
cavern, cutting Aradan off.

"Mom," Elle nodded as the woman gingerly approached. Elle's mother
wore a dress just as long as Elle's—though much more low cut, Elle noted—and getting dirty now wouldn't bode well for the rest of the evening.

"I've been looking everywhere for you," Elle's mom said. "I was about
to send out three squads to hunt you down."

"I'm fine," Elle harrumphed.

"I completely believe you," her mother replied, her voice laced with
sarcasm. "Let me guess. You're upset because your special someone can't
make it tonight?"

"My special someone?" Elle put a hand on her hip. "Is that what we're
calling him?"

"I mean, he's special and he's someone." Her mother gave a goofy shrug.

"He's someone alright. But as far as being special, I wouldn't know, as
I've only met him three times."

"That's three times more than I'd seen your father before we got married."

"That's not even true."

"That's fair." Elle's mother tapped a finger to her chin. "Either way, try
to pretend you're happy tonight, alright? We have to support your father."

"Whether he's wrong or not, right?"

"Right," her mother agreed with a wink.

Another figure appeared in the doorway, this one decked out in the
black trimmed tan cloak of Drakfell's high guard.

"There you two are," he said. "We've been scouring the citadel. The king is waiting."

Elle's mother quirked up her lip. "Tell the king we made him wait on purpose to build anticipation. He likes the anticipation almost as much as the main event, if you know what I mean."

With that, she gave the high guard a wink that made every inch of him turn beet red. Elle stifled a laugh. More often than not, her mother said the things she did just to get a reaction.

Elle's mother breezed past the guard, leading him down the hallway, and Elle got up to follow. It was time to stop being Elle, the girl who spent her days in the dragon dens, pretending she was a servant.

It was time to be Eliana, Princess of Drakfell.

She gave her Uncle Aradan one last significant look before she left. He still looked conflicted, but Elle relaxed just a little when she saw him give the slightest nod back.

Elle and her parents waited outside the large, double doors that led to the ballroom. To their left and right, the seven members of her father's high guard, Squad Eagle-eye, stood at attention.

"Ready, my king and queen?" the squad captain said, laying a hand on the door handle.

"Yes, yes," King Rodan answered with a creased brow. "We're already behind schedule. Nothing can go wrong tonight, do you understand?"

"Yes, King Rodan."

"Relax," Queen Liana said, slipping her hand into Rodan's. "This way we'll make a grander entrance."

Elle's father looked at her mother and seemed to calm down just a little. Then he frowned as he looked around at Squad Eagle-eye.

"I thought my high guard was supposed to be guarding the egg."

"We are," the squad captain answered. "Aradan sent another squad to take our place while we escorted the royal family into the ballroom, then we'll be right back to our posts."

"I see," King Rodan said. "Let's get this over with, then."

The doors opened, and Elle accompanied her parents into the splendor that was the Keep Drakfell ballroom.

The tan colored floors and walls had been polished to gleaming. Rich, velvety curtains hung from the windows, and ceremonial totem pillars carved with dragons dotted the room. The flowers looked particularly nice. The smells of wyvernhog ham, dragonbuffalo wings, and flaky pastry filled the air, and a hush fell over the room as the nobility and guards turned their attention to the royal family.

Elle spotted him immediately. He could never simply wear the proper guard uniform—he always had to add that bright, turquoise scarf around his neck.

Scarf aside, Asher stood out to Elle. Especially tonight—his usually wild black hair was smoothed into a sleek warrior's knot, and his clothes were freshly patched and pressed. But none of that gave Elle the same pleasure as the look on Asher's face as he noticed her walking in alongside her parents, the king and queen of Drakfell.

Elle knew she looked amazing in her long, white dress with silvery trim. It wasn't real silver, like many nobles wore to show off their wealth and superiority over magi. Not only did Keep Drakfell not have enough silver to waste on baubles, but Elle didn't want a certain secret Astromancer to be uncomfortable being close to her tonight.

Doing her best not to smile, Elle watched Asher pick his jaw up off the floor. He and his squad stood in formation around the true dragon egg's pedestal, and he couldn't take his eyes off of her. Good.

Elle had known she wouldn't be able to keep her rank a secret from Asher forever. But she'd dealt with so many guys who found out who she was and treated her differently because of it. It had been nice getting close to Asher without any of that getting in the way first.

Well, the big secret might as well come out in the most dramatic way possible at her parents' royal gala.

Once the high guard settled Elle and her parents around the thrones, the gala guests resumed their chatter, snacking, and dancing. Elle took her place to the side of Queen Liana's throne, standing regally as she oversaw the ballroom. Her father's Lightwielder drake, Rex, was already in his place beside the king's throne. He swayed gently to the music, eyes partly closed and looking perfectly content. He deserved a night off, after all the work he'd been doing to help her father monitor the Drekai camp.

Off to the side, Elle noticed the High Mage, deep into his drink. At least he looked like he'd be enjoying himself tonight.

Elle looked over the crowd, trying to observe objectively. But her gaze kept returning to Asher.

He still stood with the rest of Squad Nimble, guarding the pedestal. A pair of beautiful noblewomen chatted with the group, and Elle noticed one in particular was standing very close to Asher. She had thick, curly hair, and her tight-bodiced maroon dress showed off a stunning figure.

Elle didn't recognize the noblewoman, but then again, there were so many smaller keeps across Drakfell whose nobles were impossible to keep track of.

Her companion, another noblewoman in a green gown, fumbled the glass of punch in her hand. Red liquid spilled all over Nimble's squad captain, the uptight soldier named Sven.

Elle chuckled under her breath as Sven looked down at his clothing in horror. The rest of the squad rallied around him to see what was going on, and Elle almost missed Asher ducking behind the egg pedestal.

At the same moment, a heavily bearded servant on his way back to the kitchens pushed a cartful of dishes, blocking Asher from Elle's view. Elle took a step toward them.

Then the servant was rolling away, and Asher was standing at perfect attention again.

Elle frowned. Not a moment later, her father's high guard was back to replace Squad Nimble as the squad on duty guarding the true dragon egg.

Squad Captain Sven was grateful for the chance to go change out of his soiled uniform. Elle was sure that when he returned, he'd have plans for his squad—joining the rest of the guard as they waited for a chance to bond the egg.

For now, that left Asher meandering the ballroom.

Elle smiled.

She reached Asher in a few strides. He seemed a little nervous, which was unusual for him. But he still had that irresistible, classically crooked smile ready for her when she arrived.

"You would," he said.

"Would what?"

"Be a princess."

With a laugh, Elle took Asher by the hand and pulled him toward the dance floor.

It surprised Elle that Asher's dancing was passable. She figured he'd never danced at a noble gala before, and when she asked, he confirmed that this was, indeed, his first time. She liked how quickly Asher picked up on things.

"So," Asher began as he and Elle spun in time to the music. "Eliana."

"That's right." Elle liked the way shivers ran down her back when he said her full name.

"I'm guessing you don't want me to kiss you here?"

Elle tossed her hair over her shoulder and gave Asher a look. "You guess correct. That is, unless you want my parents sending word to my betrothed to let him know."

Asher looked dumbfounded for only a second before taking the news in stride.

"The surprises just keep coming, Princess Eliana. It looks like I'm not the only one whose heart may involve a fight."

Elle felt her heartbeat speed up. Elle didn't want to admit how much she'd been thinking about the words from her dear friend Lyra's prophecy.

Do not trust this one with your heart unless you wish for a fight, Lyra had said. So Asher had been thinking about that line, too.

"You're not intimidated by my being all but engaged to another man?" Elle asked.

"Nah," Asher said, his dragonfire green eyes dancing almost as much as the couples in the ballroom. "Stealing from nobles is kind of my specialty."

The song ended and the couples surrounding them clapped. Out of nowhere, a pretty serving girl with dark red hair brushed past them, accidentally hitting Asher in the shoulder as she walked.

"Excuse me," the girl bowed her head as she gave Asher an intense look. Then she lowered her voice so that Elle only caught a few words. "Silver... noblewoman's dress... lost my glint."

Elle frowned, unsure what any of that meant. The serving girl gave Elle a meek, apologetic look before hurrying away.

"What's wrong?" Elle asked.

"I have to go," Asher said, looking distracted and worried. He squeezed her hand once more before dropping it.

"You have to go?" Elle put a hand on her hip. "I'm the princess with all the obligations here. Bold move, abandoning me in the middle of the dance floor."

Asher gave her one last flirty, apologetic smile before melting into the crowd.

"At least she's pretty," Elle called after Asher. He stopped in his tracks and turned back to Elle.

He opened his mouth to speak, but ended up just awkwardly shrugging. He held up one finger as if to let Elle know he planned to be back in one moment. She smiled, and shook her head.

As she watched him go, the High Mage suddenly eclipsed him from view.

"Princess," he said, looking around as if he were being watched. "The starmoths have found us."

Elle raised an eyebrow.

"They hunger for my silvermark," he added, pointing at the Woodweaver's symbol on his cheek. Elle could smell the alcohol on his breath.

"Alrighty then," Elle said, trying to steer him toward the ballroom doors. "I think we should find someone who can get you to bed."

"Starmoths eat bedclothes," the High Mage whispered conspiratorially, raising a finger in the air. "Eat... yes. Good idea, Princess Eliana. I should eat something." He straightened up considerably.

"But—"

Elle didn't get to finish before the High Mage was marching off to the long buffet table across the room. He only staggered once, swatting at an imagined starmoth.

Elle shook her head. She really ought to tell someone that the High Mage had had too much to drink before he got the royal family into trouble.

Then a gleam of glowing white caught Elle's eye. There on the ornately carved pedestal, erected just for this occasion, sat the true dragon egg on a silky pillowcase.

Elle glided across the floor toward the egg. The high guard didn't think twice when Elle walked past them to get a better look.

Its scaly surface looked perfect, down the pulsing shine within. But Elle had expected that. Goosebumps popped up along her arm as she reached toward the egg.

She hesitated just for a moment before touching it.

It's okay, she reminded herself.

Elle closed the distance, gently grazing the egg's bumpy scales with her fingertip. A warm feeling seemed to emanate through her finger and into her core as she made contact with the egg.

She pulled her finger back, puzzled. Something was off. How did Aradan—

Crash!

A loud clanging made Elle and half the ballroom turn their heads toward the food table.

It was that noblewoman in the green dress again—the one who'd spilled her drink all over Sven earlier. She'd dropped an entire tray of meals onto the floor, and already two servants were trying to minimize the damage.

Stars, that noblewoman was having a clumsy night. Her face looked panicked, perhaps mortified by the negative attention she was bringing to herself.

Elle saw the High Mage there in the thick of things as well. He yelled drunkenly at the woman, pointing to her long sleeves. The woman shook her head in fear.

Suddenly, Asher was by the noblewoman's side. And… wasn't that the bearded servant who'd been pushing the cart near Asher earlier?

The three of them huddled together for a second, and Elle could've sworn she saw a pulse of some kind of purplish energy roll off of Asher. The High Mage was still yelling and pointing, but Asher walked away, carrying what looked like a platter of chicken in his hands.

What in the void was going on?

Asher was almost to the balcony when an unnaturally loud voice filled the ballroom.

"Stop, thief!"

Elle turned to see the Black Valkyrie herself, decked out in her charcoal colored armor and black, swan feathered cloak. A golden rune was alight over her forehead. Jaira and Lothar flanked her on one side, while on the other stood that burly Geomancer, Shaw, and Ilyan, the Mage Hunter with the creepy snake. Two other local Mage Hunters followed closely behind.

The Black Valkyrie was staring ice at the noblewoman in the green dress. The High Mage had finally gotten his way, and was searching the noblewoman's long, green sleeves. Both he and the Black Valkyrie looked surprised when he found nothing there. The servant with the bushy beard held tightly to the noblewoman's arm as he glared at the Black Valkyrie, something like a warning in his eyes.

Then Elle felt her stomach drop as the Black Valkyrie turned her murderous gaze on Asher's retreating back. He still held the plate of food in his hand.

"There," the Black Valkyrie said, again using some kind of auditory illusion to make her voice seem louder. She runetraced, a golden psionic rune appearing over her forehead alongside the first.

Suddenly, Asher's tan guard's cloak pulled tightly around his neck, stopping him in his tracks. With a strangled cough, Asher dropped the plate of food.

The Black Valkyrie's Mage Hunters gasped as the plate and its contents fell toward the ground. But the Black Valkyrie acted quickly, thrusting a hand out toward Asher's cloak and telekinetically using the fabric to catch the large, white meat chicken before it hit the floor.

Elle frowned. She was sure the chicken was delicious, but...

Then she realized why the Black Valkyrie had to save the meal.

Ilyan lit up a rune of his own, then with one flick of his wrist, the illusion over the poultry course vanished. The purple dream energy dissipated, revealing the true dragon egg.

The ballroom gasped. Jaira rushed toward the egg, scooping it up in her arms before returning to the Black Valkyrie's side.

"Impossible," King Rodan stood up from his throne. "Then what is—"

In one swift movement, the Black Valkyrie whipped out a silver dagger and threw it toward the egg on the pedestal. The hilt must've been made from something other than silver, because she psionically guided the dagger so that it stabbed straight into the egg.

Again, the crowd gasped as the egg dissipated into a cascade of golden etherdust. The illusion burst, leaving behind a heavily runemarked rock attached to a skystone with a band of steel.

"By the goddesses," the Captain of the Guard marveled.

"Etherarchy," someone from the high guard said.

"Magi," a few more from the crowd muttered.

The Black Valkyrie addressed the ballroom. "This is what happens when your king is weak and allows magi to roam freely throughout his keepdom."

Elle saw her father take an angry step toward the Black Valkyrie, but her mother put a firm hand on his shoulder before he could do anything stupid.

Then Elle's heart skipped as the Black Valkyrie used her telekinetic powers to wrench and drag Asher across the room by his scarf. He kicked and struggled, but her hold was strong. Once he was close enough, each of the Mage Hunters from the Black Valkyrie's entourage used their silver chain whips to tie off one of Asher's four limbs. He winced as the painful silver held him fast.

"Evgard will not tolerate such insubordination," the Black Valkyrie continued. "Let this magi stand as an example to you as we execute him for his crimes."

Elle felt panic rising in her throat. The Black Valkyrie was going to kill Asher, here and now. Asher struggled against the silver as if trying to get to the Black Valkyrie, but he was helpless against it.

Elle had to do something. It went against all of her political training, not to mention reason, but she had to stop this. She was about to step out and speak on Asher's behalf when her father, King Rodan, beat her to it.

"You will unhand the magi," Rodan's voice boomed. He wasn't using etherarchy to enhance his volume, but his presence was commanding nevertheless as he stood in front of his throne. "You may be the great Black Valkyrie, but Drakfell does not take orders from you. Unless you have direct orders from High King Magnus himself, you won't be executing any of my citizens tonight, magi or otherwise."

Elle hadn't realized she'd been holding her breath. She released it now, relief flooding her.

"Drakfell will execute him tomorrow," her father finished.

Stars.

"Tomorrow, I will fight the Drekai champion to win the rights to this egg, and win glory for Evgard," Rodan announced to the gala guests and servants. "We shall start with a show of loyalty by executing this traitorous magi. We will prove to Magnus that Drakfell serves only Evgard."

The crowd murmured. Elle noticed the girl in the maroon dress—the one who'd been talking with Asher earlier—had a look of fear on her face and tears in her eyes.

"Now," King Rodan commanded, "hand over the egg."

Silence stretched across the room as the Black Valkyrie and King Rodan glared at each other, neither backing down.

Gold lightning crackled over the top of King Rodan's white-scaled ascension gauntlets as he showed the Lightwielder etherarchy granted to him by his stormscale drake. Rex himself growled, joining her father at his side. A reminder that the Black Valkyrie was not the only one with power here.

The Black Valkyrie looked around the room as if she expected something to happen. When nothing did, she finally relented, nodding to Jaira. Jaira walked across the room and delivered the egg to Elle's father.

"I and mine will be watching you and yours closely, Rodan," the Black Valkyrie said, her voice icy and sharp.

The king's eyes narrowed. "Likewise."

Then Elle's father barked to his high guard.

"Take the magi to the dungeon."

Elle watched helplessly as Asher thrashed against his silver bonds, then disappeared from the ballroom.

A slight tug at the bottom of her dress drew her attention. Elle looked down, and found herself looking into the large, shiny eyes of a tiny mirror gecko.

Vision 4

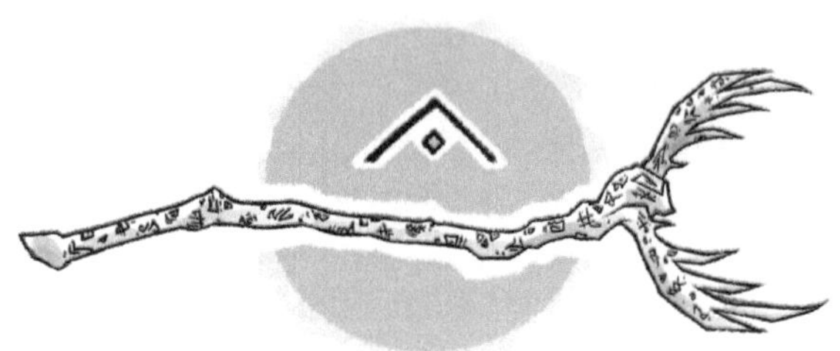

The team spilled back into the hideout one by one. His Majesty welcomed Solrac and Valla, though even the bloodhusky recognized that all had not gone according to plan at the gala tonight.

Kai and Kari returned as well, fear for Asher's life evident in their faces. Last to arrive was Boone, accompanied by Jax. His Majesty immediately tackled Jax to the floor, nuzzling up to him while Jax scratched him behind the ears.

"At least one thing went right tonight," Solrac said, helping Jax up and then wrapping his arms around him. He pulled back, still holding him around the shoulders as he examined Jax's new Psion's silvermark—the same one borne by Solrac himself.

"Now we match," Solrac said, reaching into a pocket and pulling out a crystal filled with ether. He handed it to Jax.

"Where's Shaya?" Jax asked, looking around the room.

"Probably still at the citadel," Kari said.

"She lost Glint Eight to some silver bauble on a noblewoman's dress," Kai muttered. "Stupid. I can't reach her."

"Should someone go back to check on her?" Jax asked.

"It might already be too late for Shaya," Kai said. "Not long after her Glint went down, some guards came for me at the servant's entrance. Flint barely got me out of there in time."

"We can't just leave her," Jax said.

"We don't have a choice," Valla replied harshly.

A moment of tense silence reigned over the group until finally Kai voiced the question they were all thinking.

"So... Asher?"

Solrac looked out over the team. "Vidya is using Asher's execution as bait. Her true prize is the Farseer—she thinks he'll come to save Asher tomorrow."

"Will he?" Kari asked, hope filling her wet eyes.

"I... I don't know." Solrac shook his head. "Perhaps if I go to Vidya tonight—"

"No." Valla still wore her ballgown, but that didn't make her dark glare any less menacing.

"No?"

Valla didn't take her eyes off of Solrac as she barked at the group. "Everyone, to their rooms."

A few protests sounded, but Valla's hiss sent everyone retreating from the common room. Now she and Solrac stood alone.

"I know you went to her chamber at the citadel," Valla said.

Solrac was taken aback. "How did you—the dragonhawk on the sill..."

"You have to stop letting her get under your skin. It's going to get you killed," Valla said.

"Even now, she wouldn't hurt me—"

"She'll kill all of us then! Solrac, you're blind when it comes to that woman. She's too strong with her psionics to fight without every one of us working together. And tomorrow, whether the Farseer comes or not, it may come to just that. I need to know I can count on you to help us stop her."

Solrac was silent. He looked away.

Suddenly, a splashing sound drew their attention. In a burst of purple light, a mythraven shot out of the still water of the hot spring.

The Farseer's mythraven.

The creature circled the room once, then perched on the edge of the pool.

Solrac and Valla hurried over, gazing into the water. Across the surface shone a reflection of the Farseer's shrouded face.

"Solrac, Duke of Glacia," the Farseer's voice rose from the spring. "I did as you requested and have sent my mythraven out to seek information on the skymages."

Valla and Solrac exchanged concerned looks.

"He found something."

The subtle scent of lavender reached their noses as the vision opened within the pool.

Dim, bluish light cutting through darkness. The sound of slowly dripping water. Two blurry, murky figures. Behind one sat a majestic, midnight blue dragon with four legs and a pair of wide wings tucked behind him.

A true dragon.

"Is that..." Solrac's voice sounded over the vision. "Noctus?"

"The true dragon of High King Magnus," Valla muttered. "Is one of those people the High King?"

"Silver enshrouds them," the Farseer explained. "You will not see their faces. Though, if you listen closely, you may hear them speak."

Another rune on the Farseer's staff glowed gold, and the voices in the vision grew louder.

Solrac and Valla leaned in.

A slick, echoey voice filled their ears, sounding almost as if it were two voices overlapping one another. "The experiments are working, my liege. The survival rate of the subjects has risen significantly, and of course, there is the case of the Black Valkyrie herself."

"The Black Valkyrie's soul has fully accepted the second ether well then?"

"Indeed. She can fully channel both her natural psionic well and the etherarchy of the transplant. She and your other chosen servants can use this power to administer the cure to all magi."

"I want the magi to come in voluntarily," Magnus replied forcefully.

"Of course," the other voice echoed.

"Will they not rebel and join the Farseer?"

"The omens say otherwise. Once the Black Valkyrie has retrieved the Farseer, rebellions will cease. We will use his potent well to save your son."

"How?" High King Magnus asked, desperation coloring his voice.

"Think of it like ascending a dragon," the layered voice responded. "When the high prince is given the power of the Farseer, his soul will be renewed. This is the power that will save your son, and your kingdom."

There was a long pause, and Noctus's dragonfire eyes narrowed with suspicion.

Finally, High King Magnus's voice broke the silence. "So be it."

Chapter 25: Betrayed

The magi prison of Keep Drakfell was by far the nicest one I'd ever been in.

The design was regal, with circular pillars rising from floor to ceiling at every corner. It was an old style, reminiscent of the time when our ancestors first landed here.

Everything was silver, from the bars on my cell to the crisscrossed inlays of silver in the walls. The ceiling had thin, silver netting stretched across it. Even the tray a guard had shoved in earlier with some food for me had been made of silver.

I shivered, both from the icy aura the silver gave off and the knowledge that accessing my etherarchy while in here would be impossible.

There were no windows down here, but low torchlight flickered against the gleaming, silvery surfaces. Looking through my bars, I counted eight other cells in the dim light. I didn't see any other magi locked up in there, so the plan to save Jax must've worked. In fact, as I looked more closely, I could tell that something had eaten away the silver from one cell. I felt the tiniest flicker of pride when I saw it. Boone must've used Kari's silverbane to break him out.

That meant Solrac and the team were capable of breaking someone out. Only this time, the guard would be on higher alert, so they were less likely to try something like that with me.

My hand absently went to my throat, searching for Thorn's heartscale. But, of course, they'd taken that when they took the rest of my guard's uniform, right down to my tunic. They'd left me with my pants after searching me, but that was it. Whitestone Hall had given me a scratchy burlap shirt to wear in their prison, but Keep Drakfell hadn't even given me that.

They may have taken the very shirt off my back, but that's not what left me feeling half-naked. It was the fact that they'd taken my mother's turquoise scarf.

How could I have gotten myself into this mess? I wanted to bang my head against the wall, but I knew the silver would give me a cold headache. Instead, I sat in the middle of the floor with my legs crossed, rethinking my life.

The Black Valkyrie had known we'd be at the gala. The heist had failed, and I feared it was all my fault.

I'd told the Princess of Drakfell that I'd been trying to steal the true dragon egg.

Elle—that is, Eliana—must've tipped the Mage Hunters off. It was the only explanation. I felt like such an idiot. Even at the gala when we'd danced and I'd found out she was a noble, I'd trusted her.

I only hoped she hadn't known who I was working with. I had to believe that Kai, Kari, Shaya, and the rest were all safe.

The fact that they weren't in the prison cells next to mine was comforting. But I had to face the reality that more than likely, nobody was coming for me.

I stood up. I had to get out of here.

I went to the lock on my cell door. Pure silver. Even if I somehow managed to channel etherarchy past the room's general silver presence, there was no way I could get starglass to hold inside that lock.

But I had to try.

I raised my hands toward the lock, making the motions I normally would in order to form starglass. I internally reached for my ether well, but felt the block as strongly as a beaverdrake's dam stopping a rushing river.

Click.

I jolted backward as the sound of the lock opening filled the quiet space. I looked through the bars, but there was nobody there.

The door swung open, and I jumped as I cocked my head. Still, I saw no one.

Then, as if melting into existence from the shadows, there stood a girl with long, red hair. Her sparkling eyes faded from glowing gold back to their natural brown with blue flecks as her invisibility stopped working from the silver inside the cell. She held a rusty iron key in one hand.

"Nice try," she said with a grin. "But a real key works better."

"Shaya!" I rushed toward her with my arms outstretched.

Before I got to her, she held up a hand to stop me.

"Wait, Asher," she said, her smile disappearing instantly. "I'm here to offer you one last chance."

"What do you mean?" I said, confused. "Shouldn't we be getting out of—"

"Join us."

I stared at her. Shaya went on.

"Join the Mage Hunters and I can get you out of here. Please. It's your only chance at surviving this."

"No." I shook my head. "I'd never join the Mage Hunters. You know that."

Shaya sighed. "Then I guess I'm not here to rescue you."

Before I could react, Shaya slipped back out of my cell and shut the door with a clang. I heard another click as she turned the key, locking me in once more.

"Hey," I protested, grabbing onto the bars after her. I gasped as the silver sent cold pain shooting through my palms and up my wrists.

Shaya cast her gaze down at the floor outside my cell. "I'm sorry, Asher."

Glowing gold patterns flowed across her face, from the bridge of her nose to her chin and across her forehead. Marks even appeared in her irises. Then gold mist swirled around Shaya, completely obscuring her. When it dissipated, my breath caught in my throat. She'd grown a few inches taller. Her red hair had turned steely gray, her brown eyes midnight blue. Her features had shifted as well, hardening into the cruel face of the woman I'd spent years despising.

"No," I said, my voice barely a whisper. "Shaya."

"It's the Black Valkyrie now," Vidya said, tossing her black swan feather cloak behind her. "Although, Shaya has been one of my favorite roles. She's quite the bubbly adventurer, isn't she?"

I felt like I was choking. As if my lungs had frozen up, and I couldn't get a full breath. My vision blurred, and I realized it was from a film of hot tears.

I could only speak one word.

"How?"

"Oh, that," Vidya said casually, clearly enjoying my reaction. "I assume Solrac has told you something of skymages by now? Although, he was rather withholding from all of us, wasn't he... All except Valla."

Vidya sneered as she said Valla's name.

"Anyway," she went on, "we skymages possess certain extra abilities. I was born with the ether well of a Psion. I've been gifted that of a Shadowbinder as well."

She reached under her collar and pulled out the Soleian sun locket Shaya always wore. She popped it open with a thumb to reveal a tiny clipping of dark red hair.

"This is from the real Shaya—a girl who lives in Evyndara. Had to pick someone none of you would recognize or ever see. I had it put into this locket and formed into a Wildshaper's relic. Combine that with my Mystic etherarchy and just a little bit of shadowbinding, and it allows me to access an ancient power the Guardians once had."

With another intricately flowing golden pattern on her face and a puff of gold smoke, Vidya's face shifted into Shaya's, then back again.

I breathed heavily, trying to take it in. My mind—no, my heart—refused to accept the reality before my eyes.

Vidya continued. "Drak, it got exhausting to keep up, though. It feels good not having to perform etherarchy all the time, not to mention running the Mage Hunters from afar without you people figuring it out."

She sighed, a faraway look crossing her face. "It'll be easier when I get my hands on a Wildshaper well of my own rather than using this weak relic. I have just the well in mind, but it'll take some work to get."

Vidya paced a short distance deeper along the row of cells. She craned her neck, looking inside each one.

"It seems Boone's plan to get Jax out worked well enough. Probably down to my order to keep my Mage Hunters busy elsewhere during the gala. I owe him thanks for that."

"Why do you care?" I said quietly.

"Oh, I needed Jax free. I plan for my son to join my skymages soon enough, though he must do so of his own free will. I know forced bonds are weak, even among humans. Jax will see how weak the Knights of the Torch are tomorrow, and this will start him on the right path, back to me."

She returned to my cell, leaning against it with her black, swan-adorned pauldron to keep the silver from touching her skin.

"Perhaps when he sees me capture the legendary Farseer, he'll see things my way." She looked at me, as if waiting for a response. I still couldn't speak as I fought the pain of betrayal ripping through me.

"I should thank you," Vidya continued when I didn't reply. "Rodan thinks he's so smart, executing you on his own terms. He doesn't realize he played right into my plan. See, I needed Drakfell to make a big show of executing one of you Knights as a way to lure the Farseer into my hands. Although I never wanted it to be you, sweet Asher."

She reached a hand through the bars, brushing the back of her fingers over my shoulder. Every muscle in my body tensed at the contact.

"Then again," she said, slowly looking me over, "my offer to join me still stands. I can always have Ilyan make an illusion of you to use as Farseer bait instead. Or use my great skill as the leader of the Mage Hunters to 'uncover' the Knights of the Torch's base at the tavern. Then I can take my pick from Valla, Boone, or even Kai—"

My rage mounted. With a yell, I threw myself at the bars, reaching through them to try and... I didn't know. Strangle her, punch her, twist her arm... anything.

"You kill magi!" I shouted. "You killed my mother."

She leaped backward gracefully. I cried out again, straining to get at her, ignoring the icy pain from the silver bars.

Vidya laughed. "You and your incessant quest for revenge. If only you'd swallow your pride and accept my offer. I offered Zerana the same opportunity, you know."

I stopped in my tracks, my blood running cold.

"How dare you speak her name!" I yelled, my voice breaking.

Vidya threw salt on the open wound in my heart. "Zerana chose wrong as well." She seemed like she wanted to say something more, then changed her mind. "Unless you've had a change of heart and wish to avoid execution tomorrow morning?"

I stared daggers at her, seeing red as I gave my answer.

"If my choice is death or death, I guess I choose death."

Silence fell between us. I held my chin high, refusing to cringe back as her cold, midnight blue eyes looked me over once more.

"Very well," she said, her voice tinged with frustration. "Still, I will grant you one last gift for your kindness to me these past months."

With that, she pulled out a sharp, knife-like pen. She twirled it between her fingers as she stepped closer to my cell. I held perfectly still as she reached through the bars with the pen, pressing the cold tip gently against my cheek. There was no point in fighting this now.

"I told them I'd silvermark you myself," she said. "But I'd hate to mar such a handsome face."

She pulled the pen back, then traced a rune in the air outside the silver cell. Purple dreamweave energy swirled around her pointer finger, settling onto the tip. Then she reached back through the bars and lightly dragged her finger against my left cheekbone.

"There," Vidya murmured. "The illusion of an Astromancer's mark will hold for three days. Take comfort, dear Asher. You'll be dead and buried before anyone notices it was a fake."

"Silvermarking is kinda low on my list of concerns right now," I said, keeping my voice even.

Vidya chuckled, a laugh painfully similar to the one I'd heard so many times from the girl I thought was Shaya. If hearts could bleed, mine would be pouring all over the floor.

Then Vidya walked away, heading toward the stairs that led back to the citadel. Just before she disappeared, she turned to me, her swan-feathered cape silhouetted against the silver wall.

"One last thing," she said, then retrieved something from her bag and tossed it through the bars.

My fingers closed around the familiar fabric of my mother's turquoise scarf.

When I looked up, Vidya was gone.

My hands trembled as they clutched the scarf, and I felt my knees buckle beneath me. With Vidya gone and no one else in the surrounding cells, I was completely alone.

Except for the memory of my mother held within that scarf.

I curled up on the stinging silver floor of my prison cell and gave in to the pain.

FRAGMENT - THORN

Thorn silently circled above the citadel for what must've been the seventh or eighth time by now. He flew high, avoiding the guards on patrol so he wouldn't attract suspicion. Why hadn't Valla shown up at the balcony when she was supposed to?

Thorn had nearly flown into the citadel on his own when he'd felt Asher panic through the bond, but it could have just been nerves from the heist. He hadn't been sure if trying to intervene would've just made things worse. So he'd held back, trusting the team.

Then Thorn had seen the others sneaking away from the gala and hurrying back to the hideout. But Asher wasn't with them—Thorn could feel it.

The worst was when Thorn had felt his bond with Asher dim, nearly going out altogether. That meant Asher no longer held Thorn's heartscale. What had once been a roaring bonfire now felt like dull embers. But it was enough that Thorn was certain his rider remained inside the citadel. Thorn could only hope he wasn't in prison—though based on Asher's history, that was a strong possibility.

Pain. Fear. Loneliness. Thorn thought he could sense these emotions from Asher through the bond. Thorn flew lower, wondering if somehow he could get inside the citadel now.

Suddenly, a cold, harsh feeling gripped Thorn's heart. He froze mid-flight, all at once compelled to fly downward. It was as if someone was forcing him to return to the dragon dens.

Thorn let out a small, low whimper. That meant someone—not Asher—was using his heartscale.

Thorn fought the feeling, but in the end couldn't help but return to his small, wooden pen. He wanted to fly away from here and continue waiting for Asher, or at least return to the Knights of the Torch hideout to see if any of the others had a plan to rescue him. But whoever held his heartscale was ordering him to stay put.

Suddenly, the tense grip on Thorn's heart eased. Thorn relaxed, as if a tender hand were stroking the back of his neck.

Someone else held his heartscale now. Someone who would protect him. A friend.

Chapter 26: Executed Again

Tiny, wet particles of mist cooled my face as a strong wind blew in from the geyser fields. The sun hadn't quite begun to stream over the mountains to the east, so the land was bathed in a grayish-violet wash.

They'd set up the gallows atop a platform at the edge of the geyser fields north of Keep Drakfell proper. They wouldn't be relying on wild dragons to finish me off this time. Not when a good ol' silvered rope would do.

Against my back, a tall, upside-down L-shaped post held the noose that would end my life. The heavy rope hung loosely draped over my shoulders and around my neck. They'd taken extra precautions, and I could feel the silver strands braided into it, like rivers of ice against my collarbone. I stood on a trap door, the lever just out of reach to my side.

Silver manacles trapped my hands and cut off my etherarchy. As if that weren't enough, the Black Valkyrie's four Mage Hunters—the Geomancer, the illusionist and his snake, Jaira, and Lothar—surrounded me at the four corners of the trapdoor. I could hear the humming sound from an evren's four beating wings, letting me know Lothar's green dragon hovered nearby.

The royal family stood on the opposite side of the platform. King Rodan, Queen Liana, and Princess Eliana stood regally, all in brilliant white armor to match Rodan's ascension armor. They were surrounded by the seven soldiers of the high guard squad. They must've been taking extra precautions with the royal family's safety, because two extra soldiers, one thin and one muscular, stood alongside the high guard in full armor with heavy helmets.

Elle wouldn't look at me. The whole time I'd been standing here, she hadn't so much as glanced in my direction.

I didn't like to admit just how much I wanted her to. One last look at her sparkling amber eyes. I still wasn't sure if she'd betrayed me, but what did it matter now? There was no chance of escape. Even if the team wanted to, to try and rescue me with all this security would be suicide.

Hundreds of spectators flooded the area surrounding the platform. In front were rows and rows of women and men in the tan cloaks of the Drakfell guard. Among them, I saw Sven, Friga, and the rest of Squad Nimble staring up at me in pity.

Behind the guard writhed a sea of citizen spectators, and off to the side nearest the geyser fields stood an army of Drekai. The draconic humans held gleaming weapons, ready to fight should the need arise. In the wooded area behind them, I could just make out the tents of their army's camp.

The crowd wasn't assembled just to see me die, of course. They'd come to watch King Rodan and the Drekai champion in their honor duel for the true dragon egg.

Near the platform, I caught the gleam of the egg itself. In a soft, downy bed of grass, King Rodan's Lightwielder drake, Rex, sat guarding it. I found myself wondering if the dragon would willingly let the egg go should King Rodan lose the duel.

I probably wouldn't live to find out.

"...Since our ancestors first arrived in Evgard on skyboats, we've been at odds with dragonkind. They consume our citizens, they burn our keeps. But why? The answer, of course, is magi. Drawn by their ether..."

The Black Valkyrie's speech droned on and on as she used her voice amplification illusion to address the crowd. She stood atop the platform too, her back to me.

Turn around, I thought as I stared at her. *Just turn toward me.*

They'd trapped my hands in silver manacles. They'd draped a silvered rope around my neck. But my feet remained free of silver.

I breathed deeply, silently. The silver cut off my ether flow to most of my body. But I was an Archon, so my ether well was in my heart.

I curled and uncurled my toes from within my boots. The ether flowed from my heart, through my gut, and down my legs. I'd spent the last few months practicing ether blasts with Boone. I knew I could do it now. But Vidya's back was armored. Her entire body had some kind of black armor on it. She was even wearing an open-faced black helmet, its cheekguards fashioned to look like swan wings.

But her face was exposed. If she would just look at me, I could take the shot.

Of course, they'd kill me. But they were going to do that anyway.

Just turn around.

"...Evgard has no need for weak queens and kings," Vidya said, her tone tipping me off that her speech was wrapping up. "Now, before we execute this thieving, traitorous magi—"

She gestured toward me, but kept her face on the crowd.

"King Rodan of Drakfell will say a few words."

Rodan replaced Vidya centerstage. But instead of backing up to a place where I could get a clean shot, Vidya stepped to the side, on the other side of Elle.

Soot.

Rodan cleared his throat. "People of Drakfell..."

He launched into a speech about showing strength in these uncertain times. Sweat beaded along his forehead, and he kept clenching his fists. He was nervous.

Seeing General Kheradok, the Drekai champion, standing at the head of the Drekai army, I couldn't blame him. Though he was young, he had obviously seen his fair share of battles and won. His red and black scales that grew in patches along his body were like built-in armor. On top of that, he wore overlapping plates of battleworn bronze armor and wielded a long-handled, ornately-marked scimitar. His large, red and black wings made him look like a legend.

"...so, without further ado, the execution of the prisoner."

All at once, King Rodan's speech ended. He turned toward me, hands clasped expectantly behind his back.

The crowd's attention was entirely on me. Every head turned, all except Vidya's.

Look, I thought again, willing her to give me a clear shot.

To my surprise, Elle stepped toward me. She kept her eyes focused on the ground as she reached for the lever connected to my trapdoor.

"You're going to be the one to finish me off, then?" I spoke quietly enough that only Elle could hear. "Was that your request, or is it just a poetic slap in the face from the goddesses?"

Elle didn't reply. She still wouldn't even look me in the eye.

Black, swan feather-lined fabric rustled in the breeze as I bored holes into the back of Vidya's cloak.

Turn around.

Elle's hand grasped the lever.

Vidya's face rotated ever so slightly so I could just see the tip of her nose. So close.

Turn.

Vidya's eyes met mine just as Elle pulled the lever.

I jumped at the last second, my feet tingling as I burned all the ether I could muster.

Chapter 27: Mutiny

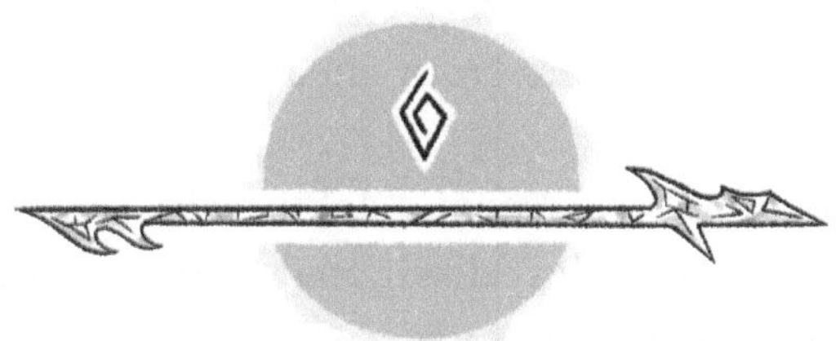

Just before the ether blast could leave my feet, I felt silver tighten around me.

But... it wasn't the silvered rope around my neck.

Silver flew at my torso, a chain with heavy twin spheres attached to the ends. The icy, silver bolas wrapped around my waist, cutting off the ether flow into my legs and choking off my ether blast.

It also strapped me to the post behind me so that the noose didn't snap my neck.

I looked up in shock, searching for the person who'd just saved my life.

There, in the front row of the crowd, holding some kind of crazy, crossbow-like bola launcher, was Kari.

The crowd gasped as chaos erupted on the platform.

"Kill the magi!" Vidya roared, but made no move toward me herself. Instead, she scanned the crowd, undoubtedly searching for the Farseer. Why would she waste her energy on me when he was her true prize?

Vidya's Mage Hunters sprang into action. Jaira and Lothar spun toward me, silver swords making a deadly *shing* sound as they drew them.

Jaira's face was pure fury, but Lothar's was apologetic.

"Forgive me, oh great one," he whispered as he and his partner went in for the kill.

Clang! A pair of axes blocked the blows as a soldier slid between the Mage Hunters and me.

With an insane amount of strength, the armor-clad soldier held off both Jaira and Lothar's weapons. With a grunt, he shoved them off, causing both Mage Hunters to stumble backward. The other armored soldier who'd been standing with the king's high guard jumped in, whipping a pair of pistol-gripped starglass daggers from sheaths behind his back that he'd hidden under his tan cloak.

"Dragonfire in the hole!" the second soldier shouted, firing off blasts of ether from his daggers. One blast dissipated against Jaira's silver sword as she blocked, but the other took Lothar in the arm, sending a painful jolt surging through it.

Both of the guards threw off their heavy helmets, and for the first time since the gala, I felt hope.

"Boone! Jax!" I said.

"Good to see you, Dragon-boy," Jax replied, lighting up a psionic rune as he prepared for Jaira's next strike.

"Hurry up with that there silverbane, little lady," Boone said with a nod to Elle.

Elle sprang into action. She pulled a small starglass vial from her sleeve and dropped it onto my silver manacles. The silver shattered the starglass, and the glowing substance began immediately eating away at the silver. When it got to my wrists, it burned for a split second before I felt my skin heal itself. In seconds, the silver had all melted away, leaving my hands free once more.

"Silverbane..." I said as Elle began working on the rope and the bolas. "But how did you... you're not..."

"Your friend Kari seems pretty cool." Elle nodded toward Kari, who had dropped her bolas launcher and was loading up a crossbow to join the fight.

"How do you know—"

"We met after the gala," Elle explained. "Long story involving a determined gecko, but I'm helping your friends rescue you now, so that's fun."

I couldn't even speak as she helped me down from the gallows. I just laughed.

"The Farseer is using his dark power to mind control the princess!" the Black Valkyrie bellowed from where she stood at the head of the platform. "Stop her!"

She impatiently scanned the crowd for the Farseer again while some of Drakfell's guard started to follow her orders.

Queen Liana and King Rodan didn't waste a second. The king drew his massive white warsword from the specialized scabbard on his back, as the queen drew her own sword from her side.

"You may be the Black Valkyrie," Liana retorted. "But you don't mess with my daughter."

With that, Liana and Rodan rushed toward the Black Valkyrie. At their side, the royal high guard joined them, as well as their High Mage, the Woodweaver. I guess he'd finally slept off his astralock hangover.

Instead of cowering in fear or fighting back herself, Vidya just smiled. From behind her, her Geomancer and illusionist Mage Hunters rushed up to the king and queen, swords drawn and snake poised to strike. Following them was the Captain of the Guard, and from their places at the foot of the platform, over half the Drakfell guard bore arms against their king and queen.

Rodan, Liana, and the high guard all stopped in their tracks.

Vidya smiled.

"What's this?" the king balked at the Captain of the Guard as she stood alongside the Black Valkyrie.

"The Black Valkyrie is right, Rodan," she said, gripping her sword. "You were never strong enough to do what it takes to protect Drakfell."

She swung at Rodan. The king raised his sword against the captain.

The members of the guard who'd sided with the Black Valkyrie turned on their counterparts. Many soldiers dropped their weapons and fell to their knees on the spot—Drakfell had been recruiting anyone off the street, after all.

A few brave soldiers bore arms against the traitors. Among those loyal to Drakfell, I saw Sven fighting with all his strength.

Above the commotion of the burgeoning battle, I heard a thunderous voice.

"King Rodan of Drakfell!" Kheradok boomed as he launched himself into the air, wings spreading wide. "I will not suffer you to die at anyone's hand but mine this day!"

With that, the Drekai general soared over the screaming, scattering spectators and toward the platform. He landed, swinging his vicious scimitar toward the king just as the Captain of the Guard came at Rodan with another strike.

Rodan's giant dragonforged blade halted Kheradok's while Liana's saber rose up to stop the captain's.

"You take care of your duel, honey," Liana grunted. "I'll take care of the mutiny."

Liana engaged the Captain of the Guard with a blade that matched Elle's. I could see where Elle got her skill with a sword from. The queen was fast and elegant as she fought in her gleaming white armor.

Vidya laughed from where she stood, thrilled with the division she'd caused in Drakfell.

Meanwhile, the duel for the true dragon egg between Rodan and Kheradok started with a bang. Meaning, Kheradok threw another ball of explosive green dragonfire like he'd done back at the dens.

Boom!

The blast sent Rodan flying backward off the platform. He landed hard in the grass below.

Rodan rolled quickly back to his feet, adjusting his grip on his white ascension blade. Kheradok slashed with his scimitar as he glided down to meet him.

They fought, inching their way toward the geyser fields to the north as the execution platform began to burn with green dragonfire.

The battle raged around me as Elle pulled me off the back of the now flaming platform and out of the fray.

"I'll be right back," she said. "Take this."

With that, she took off running toward the citadel. I was a little confused, but at the same time glad she'd be out of harm's way.

I looked down at what she'd placed in my hand just before running off, and found myself staring into the enormous, mirrored eyes of Glint.

Well, more likely Glint Six or Seven or something. Kai had color-coded them, and this one was indigo.

I slipped the mirror gecko into my boot and felt the group mindlink flood my brain.

...the Geomancer's coming up on your right, Boone, Kai was thinking.

On 'im, Boone thought back.

Hi guys, I chimed in as I joined.

Asher! several thoughts chorused in unison. Stars, it felt good to connect with the team again.

Asher, Kai's thought rang loud and clear, *never do that again, got it? Or I'll tell Flint to drop pellets on your head.*

I looked up and realized Kai's threat was valid. Hovering in the air far above the battlefield was a stony gray evren with Kai on his back. It was the perfect vantage point for Kai to both run the mindlink and direct us in the fight.

Hey Asher, Elle's voice played in my thoughts next, and my heart skipped a beat. I was glad my feelings didn't get sent through the link without my intent.

We missed you, Kari thought. *And Shaya, of course.*

Shaya, I thought somberly, looking back up onto the platform toward where Vidya stood, directing her soldiers. She seemed to be looking for someone again.

What is it? Solrac thought. *Nobody's seen Shaya since the gala—we assumed you may have an idea of where she's been.*

Did she get captured too? Valla put in.

Not exactly, I thought. *But I know where she is.*

Where? Boone thought.

I played back my memory from the prison. Everyone watched from my eyes as Vidya used Wildshaper, Shadowbinder, and Dreamweave etherarchy simultaneously to melt Shaya's appearance away and reveal her true identity.

There was silence over the mindlink.

No, Kari thought.

Impossible... Boone's voice sounded broken.

No, Jax thought. *Streya, please. No.*

I knew she was hiding something, Kai thought.

Gross. GROSS, Jax continued.

The whole time? Valla asked, and I confirmed.

The group continued processing this new information over the mindlink, and I couldn't help but notice how long it was before Solrac sent his own thoughts through.

This is... not the greatest thing that could've happened, Solrac's thought was uncharacteristically grim. *Do you realize what this means?*

We're all drakked fools is what it means, Boone thought.

That, Solrac replied, *and that Vidya really has discovered some sort of dark etherarchy. As Shaya, she truly was able to shadowbind. That means she can wield at least two types of etherarchy as some kind of corrupted skymage. Be careful.*

Another moment of silence stretched over the mindlink as we let that sink in.

We're doomed, Valla concluded.

Oh, almost certainly, Solrac agreed.

Vidya chose that moment to prove us all right. Guards fought one another all around her as she raised her black gauntleted hand to runetrace.

A golden rune glowed over her forehead as she held out her hands to either side. Beside the platform, I noticed pooling water with a mirror-like sheen as from the water, six black starswans formed from purple energy and took to the air.

Hands raised, Vidya called out. "Show yourselves, Knights of the Torch. Call upon your beloved Farseer to save you, or let him watch as I dispose of you one by one."

Vidya thrust her hands forward, and the swans zoomed through the air. Their wings were edged in some kind of purple energy dreamblades.

And they were heading straight toward Kari in the crowd at the front of the battle.

Kari, watch out! Kai sent the thought a little too late.

I hover-ran over the burning platform, channeling ether as I went. My starglass spear crystalized in my hands as I slashed at the nearest swan.

I hit, sending the swan back to the dream realm in a flurry of black feathers. But the other five swans swiped at Kari with their purple-bladed feathers, aggressive honking sounds filling the air.

Kari screamed and dropped her weapon as the birds sliced at her with their dream energy. They left no physical marks, but each cut drained her energy. Kari fell to her knees.

I whipped my spear toward the remaining swans, and rather than letting themselves get sent back to the dream realm, they scattered. Other fighters picked off some, while the rest joined the treasonous guard.

"Kari, are you alright?" I bent down to help her up.

"Fine," she murmured, clearly tired.

Kari, Kai's voice sounded through the mindlink. *Get out of there.*

I'm fine, okay? Kari snapped at her little brother as she leaned on me.

I'll get her somewhere safe, I thought.

"I have to help—" she protested out loud as I half dragged her away from the action.

"Come back once the dream damage wears off," I said.

I'd almost gotten her to a copse of trees behind the platform when the earth below my feet shook. Across the geyser fields, several geysers began to shoot boiling hot water into the air all at once, and some new geysers formed.

The earthquakes stopped, but the geysers continued. I looked behind me and found myself face to face with the source of the commotion.

The Geomancer Mage Hunter.

He raised his thick arm and backhanded me across the face.

I did my best to shield Kari from the ground as we went skidding across the dry surface.

I got to my feet just in time to strike back against the Geomancer's next blow. But my starglass spear shattered immediately against his silver sword.

Honestly, Asher, Kai's voice rolled through my head. *If you're going to go up against Mage Hunters so much, you really should get yourself a weapon that isn't so vulnerable to silver.*

Gee, great idea, I thought as I stumbled backward, searching for anything I could use as a weapon. I came up empty, but Kari didn't. She threw another starglass vial of silverbane at the Geomancer. He blocked it with his silver sword, but it shattered, melting his sword and starting to eat through his pauldron.

That works, Kai thought. *Nice job, Kari.*

I resummoned my starglass spear, darting forward and jabbing into the Geomancer's gut. His rock hard skin stopped my blow, golden Sentinel patterns appearing on him.

He held up a rock, and it grew into a massive club.

Soot.

We swung at each other back and forth for a moment, neither of us able to get the upper hand. As our weapons came together, I saw the glow of a skystone hanging around his neck underneath his dusk blue cloak. If I could just get to it, I might stand a chance.

Valla and Solrac coming in on your left, Kai thought.

Valla slid between me and the Geomancer, stopping the blow of his massive club with her seaxes. She fought him efficiently, pushing him further and further back until he had to leap up onto the platform in order to dodge her blows.

Solrac waited for him atop the flaming platform. He'd pulled the gallows lever back, resetting the trap door. He held the silvered noose ready. Once Valla pushed the Geomancer into range, Solrac threw the rope around his neck and psionically pulled the lever in the same motion.

I cringed backward as the Geomancer dangled from the noose that had been meant for me. He dropped his club, clawing at his neck for a moment before going limp.

But there wasn't time to dwell on his hanging.

Valla, Solrac, Kai ordered over the mindlink. *We need to take down the illusionist. He's messing with too much of Drakfell's guard.*

He sent us a mental image of the illusionist conjuring swirling starry patterns in front of the eyes of Drakfell's loyal guard, blinding them as they fought. His starspitter snake spat violet energy at anyone who got too close.

On it, Solrac replied, and he and Valla disengaged.

Kari, stay out of it until the dreamblade effect wears off, Kai ordered.

Kari sent back a mental grumble.

Soot, Kai swore. *Asher and Jax, cover Boone.*

I whipped my head around, searching for a shock of snowhead hair and a tan scarf. Boone stood nearby, engaging what looked like half of Drakfell's treasonous guard.

"Yee haw!" Boone shouted as he fired ether blast after ether blast, the rebel guard closing in on him. One particularly wide blast downed three guards at once.

Jax and I arrived on the scene at the same time. Jax's telekinetic rune glowed from his forehead as he prepared to throw his axe.

"Go low," he called to me.

I ducked low, sweeping the legs of the nearest guard with my spear while Jax chucked the axe over my head to hit another. Together, we stopped them from overpowering Boone.

"Much obliged, boys," Boone said.

We fought on, and I became aware of the Drekai watching the duel between Rodan and Kheradok with bated breath.

The two crossed blades deep in the geyser fields now. They were too evenly matched to tell who was winning. Kheradok used small rifts to aim precise stabs at Rodan where he was unprotected, but Rodan kept absorbing the blows with bursts of golden light that flashed across his armor wherever Kheradok struck. Lightwielding power, granted him by his ascension armor. Both fought like dragons.

Nearer the platform, King Rodan's drake, Rex, guarded the true dragon egg jealously. Any time a guard got too close, Rex sent out a quick warning blast of lightning from his mouth to ward them off.

Over the mindlink, Kai called out more orders, directing the members of our team to wherever they were most needed. There were so many guards, Mage Hunters, and their bonded dragons fighting for the Black Valkyrie. Our meager force of the loyal guard plus our little heist crew wasn't faring so well. Already, dozens of tan-cloaked soldiers lay motionless on the ground. We all kept checking in with the other members of our team to make sure we were okay. Kari was still hiding out, Valla had gained a new scar, and Jax was already running low on ether. Soot, I wished I had my ascension armor bracers right now in case I got hurt. But they'd taken those when they'd thrown me in prison.

Kai had just ordered me to join His Majesty in fighting off Lothar's green evren when an amplified voice pierced the air.

"Call upon the Farseer!" the Black Valkyrie raged again. She still hadn't really joined the fight herself. Rather, her Mage Hunters and starswans surrounded her, fighting every foe who dared come near.

As I looked at her, hatred filled my heart. Automatically, my feet began taking me toward her.

Asher? Kai thought over the mindlink. *His Majesty is the other direction... oh.*

My path was a straight line, like I had tunnel vision. I rushed forward, shoving the guards standing between me and Vidya away with the shaft of my double-bladed spear.

Blocking my way were Lothar and Jaira. And by the murderous look in the jailer's daughter's eyes, she wasn't about to let me by so easily.

Lothar, on the other hand, looked torn. Like he wasn't sure who to fear and who to follow—the Black Valkyrie, or me.

That gave me an idea.

If the Farseer wasn't showing up to save us himself, then he couldn't get mad at me for what I was about to do.

Kai, I directed my thoughts to my best friend. *Double trouble, Farseer style.*

Kai understood immediately. The illusion of a Mystic rune lit up over my forehead as I burned my own ether to levitate myself into the air. Kai's illusion took effect at the same moment, and two illusory versions of me split off to my left and right.

Illusory hoods of fur and raven feathers appeared over the heads of all three of me. Each of our starglass spears became gnarly, antlered staffs covered in Mystic runes. Flowing red cloaks streamed out behind us.

Both Lothar and Jaira's jaws hit the ground as they took in my appearance. In fact, Lothar's jaw wasn't the only thing to hit the ground as he dropped his sword and threw himself at my feet.

At least, at the feet of the illusion to my left.

"Of course," Lothar said as he bowed. "It all makes sense now. You are the great Farseer."

Kai added an auditory illusion to my voice so that when I spoke, it came out tripled.

"Indeed."

With that, I sprang into action. Using my starglass spear-turned-Farseer staff, I sent Lothar's sword flying across the battlefield, careful to hit it by its dragonleather-wrapped handle so I didn't disrupt the illusion or shatter my starglass. He watched it go, a look of resignation on his face.

Lothar may've been all but worshiping me, but Jaira knew whom she served. She got over her initial shock quickly, coming at me with her silver sword.

Unfortunately, she picked the right me to come at. I made what I hoped was a grand, Farseer-like gesture and thrust my hand toward her, and she naturally cringed backward in anticipation.

Nothing happened.

Uhh... Kai? I thought.

What? Oh, soot. Kai thought back. *We're really struggling out here and I'm doing a lot of different things, okay Asher? It's not like I can read your mind.*

Um, yes you can.

Ugh. You know what I mean.

Kai caught up, and Jaira got a somewhat delayed wave of purple dreamweave energy flying right at her face.

That much dream energy would've gotten her groggy at the very least, but she was a trained Mage Hunter. There was a reason the Black Valkyrie herself had picked her for her entourage.

Before the dream energy reached her, Jaira pulled out her silver whip, spinning it in front of her face like a lasso. As the silver hit the dream energy, it dissipated into nothing.

Next, Jaira snapped her whip at the illusory me to the right. He vanished on contact. Then she did the same to the copy of me that Lothar was groveling before. He looked surprised as Farseer-me burst into shimmering gold stars.

Jaira lashed toward the real me last. I jumped backward with a levitation-powered leap.

I didn't have time for this. Jaira wasn't my target.

I tried to sidestep her, but she swirled her whip into my path.

My hands went up a little too late. To my shock, at the last moment, a thick, wood-like bronze spike came flying through the air, catching the silver chain and pinning it harmlessly to the ground.

I looked up, my heart filling with unexpected joy.

Thorn.

Elle sat astride him. Flying in low behind Elle and Thorn were Lyra and Glass from the hatchery. The black, third ascension drake followed fast on the ground below, Aradan riding on her back in his tri-colored ascension armor.

Thought we could use some reinforcements, Elle thought over the mindlink.

Whoop! Boone whooped. *Shoulda picked up a princess on the ol' team ages ago!*

This is the greatest thing that could've possibly happened, Solrac agreed.

We might even stand a chance, Valla thought.

I had to admit, watching Elle ride in on my dragon, her dark hair streaming out behind her, sent shivers up my spine.

They landed directly on top of Jaira, smashing her into the soft ground of the geyser fields. I heard a muffled cry as Jaira protested from underneath Thorn's scaly body. With a proud smile, Thorn stayed put, leaving Jaira pinned.

"I'm digging the Farseer look," Elle said, reaching into Thorn's saddlebag. "Here, thought you might want these." She tossed me my jacket, ascension bracers, and...

"Thorn's heartscale." I wasted no time in slipping the cord around my neck. It made a satisfying thump against my collarbone, and I felt my bond with Thorn blaze to life like a brilliant bonfire. He roared with joy and relief.

Asher! I heard Thorn call my name through the bond. I still wasn't completely used to him communicating with words since his ascension.

He shielded me protectively as I hurriedly pulled my arms through my armored jacket sleeves and put on my climbing gloves. Even though they disappeared underneath the Farseer illusion, it felt right to be in my own clothes again.

"Let me," Elle said, reaching toward my forearms to help me buckle on my ascension bracers. Even amidst the chaos all around us, her touch set my heart racing.

It almost made me forget my real goal.

"Hello, Asher."

Vidya's cruel voice sent me crashing back to reality. I guess she'd noticed the wyvern landing on one of her star pupils. She stood mere yards away, her steely gray hair blowing across her face, her black armor shining in the newly risen sun.

She'd seen right through my disguise.

"Thought you'd try your hand at playing the Farseer, I see," she said, fingers flying as she runetraced. My illusion burst. Then she thrust her hand to the right, using her psionic powers to hold Elle to the ground by her armored dress. Vidya swiped the air with the other hand, pinning Thorn to the ground by his saddle.

Jaira crawled out from under him, and Vidya dismissed her with a wave.

"You're just like us, you know," Vidya said, ignoring Elle and Thorn's protests. "Solrac and me."

"I'm nothing like you," I retorted. My dragonfire green eyes flashed gold, and I burned ether, starglass armor forming over my legs, chest, and shoulders.

Vidya continued toward me, dropping her silver dragonhook spear carelessly to the ground. "Determined. Single-minded. A flair for the dramatic. You're one of us, alright."

Still keeping Elle and Thorn pinned, she runetraced again, and another golden rune appeared alongside the first over her forehead. Soot, she was good. She reached out toward the battlefield, telekinetically pulling a dragonhook spear from one of the fallen soldiers.

The spear flew to her open hand. She examined it—it was just a standard issue guard's spear, nothing silver about it. I guess she still had a shred of honor, choosing not to face me with the advantage of her silver.

Anger burned in my heart alongside my ether.

"I could never do what you do. Taking innocent magi's lives like that." I brandished my own starglass spear.

"Still haven't come to grips with reality, have you? No magi is innocent, Asher. Etherarchy corrupts us all to the core."

"If you believe that, then how can you live with yourself?" I spat.

"Because power breeds power, Asher. Some of us cursed with it bear the burden of keeping the rest from destroying all that we hold dear."

"That sounds nice and vague." I lowered my brows and widened my stance. "But I think we both know why I'm here. So if you don't mind, I have a mother to avenge."

Vidya's lips curled into a dark smile. "I suppose you do."

With a yell, I made the first swing.

Chapter 28: The Duel

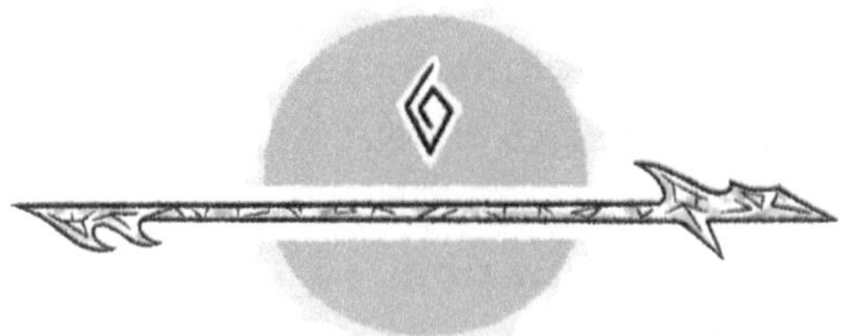

Battles raged all around the geyser fields.

Kai relayed key updates to the team through their shared mindlink. Rifter's portals and flashes of gold lightning punctuated King Rodan and Kheradok's honor duel, while Drakfell's guard engaged in a miniature civil war.

But I blocked it all out for now.

Vidya might've been willing to fight me without silver on her side, but she had zero reservations about using her powers as a skymage. Her eyes flashed with archonic etherarchy as she sent a line of black Shadowbinder fire along the edge of her spear.

We fought, shadowspear on starglass spear. Dread and pain filled my heart as I realized just how familiar this felt.

The difference was, Vidya was no longer playing the part of an upbeat, adventure-loving teenager. There was no going easy, no playful banter, and no holding back. Our dance had become reckless, and I was in trouble. My ascension bracers had Thorn's regenerative powers baked into them, but those lay in the dirt near where Elle still struggled to break free from Vidya's psionic hold.

Sweat flew off the ends of my hair as I pushed toward Vidya, slashing with my starglass blades. I nearly got close enough to land a strike, but Vidya calmly used her left hand to runetrace. Another psionic rune glowed from her forehead and she made a yanking motion, throwing me backward by my jacket, despite my starglass armor.

Once I was out of her range, Vidya swung her spear around her head like a windmill. I scrambled to my feet, trying to find an opening, but even one hit from the heavy, shadow-edged speartip would start burning away at my flesh.

I accessed more ether, launching myself into the air above her spear. Using my levitation powers to direct and accelerate my descent, I pointed my own spear down toward her from above.

She barely saw me coming in time, redirecting her spear to try and stab at me. I was already within her guard though, past the shadow-edged blade of her spear. She adjusted and whacked the shaft of her spear against my side. Her interference threw off my attack so my spear only grazed her arm instead of stabbing into her middle. Meanwhile, she'd definitely bruised my ribs through my starglass plate.

I whirled back through the air. I needed a moment to catch my breath, so I tried aiming a few ether blasts at her as I hovered, firing them from the tip of my spear. All that practicing with Boone was finally paying off.

She had to focus a lot of ether to cast up dream barriers to block each blast. Looking annoyed, she jumped into the air with a levitation-powered leap. I guess I wasn't the only one getting better with etherarchy.

She psionically pulled herself forward with her spear to meet me in the air. Her eyes narrowed at me as they glowed gold with archonic power. I raised my spear, and she did the same.

We clashed in the sky, neither of us able to find an opening in the other's defenses. Months of sparring came to a head as white ether and black shadowfire flashed.

Then, just as she had done so many times before, Vidya flourished her weapon, throwing in an impressive—but fatally unnecessary—twirl.

The momentary reprieve was the chance I needed. I undercut her maneuver, levitating into the perfect position. I jabbed for her heart, blasting her with raw ether from the point of my blade.

Her eyes went wide and she reeled backward, pulling herself psionically by her armor as she rolled to the side, her cloak getting caught on my spear and tearing on the hook.

She dropped to the ground, clutching at her heart. I landed beside her and positioned my spear for another strike.

I frowned as I realized Vidya's shoulders were shaking. Had my blow done more damage than I'd thought?

But Vidya wasn't trembling in pain or fear. Sharp, peeling laughter took me aback as she clutched her locket—the one she'd been using to wildshape into Shaya.

My spear must've struck the necklace, because jagged, white marks spiraled across its surface. The locket was open in her palm, and I could see that the lock of red hair from the real Shaya was charred, whitened and disintegrated by my ether blast. But there was something else inside the locket—A gleaming crystal that looked like a skystone.

Skystones usually glowed white with raw, ready ether. This one, however, gave off an eerie, almost otherworldly blue light. There was something scratched onto the surface of the stone, and when I squinted my eyes I could make out a single name.

Vidya.

My brows knit. The stone reminded me of the eyes of the umbral sandsharks we'd fought back in the Scar. Seeing the blue skystone with Vidya's name scrawled onto it filled me with a sinking feeling. My ether blast had left its jagged, white mark on the stone as well—right across Vidya's name.

That dark feeling only got worse when Vidya, still laughing, turned to face me.

The golden psionic rune over Vidya's forehead as well as the archonic light in her eyes had both changed to the same lightning blue. My heart all but stopped when I recognized it as the exact shade of sapphire as the flecks that had been in her eyes when she'd been playing Shaya.

All at once, Vidya stopped laughing. Her gaze darkened, lightning blue eyes flashing brighter right before she vanished.

I stumbled backward, whipping my head back and forth to try and catch sight of her. Scorch. I'd forgotten about that aspect of her shadowbinding.

Every muscle in my body tensed as I held my spear defensively, taking cautious footsteps forward. Suddenly, I heard the shuffle of boots behind me, and I whirled around.

Big mistake.

I found myself face to face with Vidya, her cold, blue eyes boring into mine as her shadowspear bored into my abdomen, just under the bottom edge of my starglass armor.

She yanked back her blade and I cried out in pain, falling to my knees and dropping my spear.

My vision blurred, and I felt all my senses go into shock. Nothing felt real. Through my bond with Thorn, I felt fiery fury. Elle's scream sounded distant and broken.

Through the haze, I looked up as Vidya's even face stared down at me. Her voice was silky and cold as she spoke.

"A shame. You'd have made such a strong skymage. Perhaps the omens were wrong about you." She shook her head. "Tell your half-born mother I say *kaiitya*."

I recognized the Drekai word for 'thank you' as Vidya stepped forward, raising her shadowspear for the killing blow.

Then she stepped on the locket, breaking it beneath her foot.

I wanted to cringe backward, close my eyes. But I stared boldly into the bright, lightning blue eyes of the Black Valkyrie as she held her shadowy weapon over my head.

For an instant, those eyes flashed back to their natural dark blue. A wave of hesitation washed over her face, as if she realized what she was doing and wanted to stop.

Then, just as quickly, the otherworldly blue blazed back to life across her irises. Her face hardened, and she thrust the spear toward my neck.

Whoosh!

With a shrieking caw, an enormous bird swooped through the air, its large talons clawing at Vidya's head as some form of psionics stopped her strike.

She roared, her eyes widening as she took in the sight of a black mythraven covered in gleaming golden runes. The raven spread its wings and cawed again, flying back up high.

The entire battle seemed to grind to a halt around us as a hooded figure in red emerged from the treeline. He held a gnarled, runemarked staff topped with antlers in his red gauntleted hand, and white eyes glowed from within his hood as golden runes floated over his forehead like a crown of stars.

Vidya began to laugh. A desperate, maniacal sound.

"Yes! Yes!"

"This has gone on long enough, Vidya," the Farseer said, his own voice amplified across the battlefield. The Black Valkyrie's name sounded like mockery as it rolled off his tongue.

Vidya continued laughing as she stooped to pick up her strange, blue skystone. She walked away from me, leaving me to bleed out in the dirt as shadowfire ate away at my body.

Overhead, the mythraven clashed with the two remaining starswans.

Then the Farseer raised his staff high in the air, and the real fight finally began.

With Vidya finally focused on her prize, Elle and Thorn were at my side in an instant.

"Oh," Elle said as my blood soaked into her skirt. She looked as much in shock as I felt.

My brain was muddled as well. I didn't even realize I'd been tuning out the mindlink's background chatter until I became vaguely aware of Kai giving orders.

Jax appeared beside Elle, asking if I could walk.

I nodded, then burned a little ether to assist Elle and Jax as they hoisted me up from either side. Thorn walked along behind us, shielding us from the battle's action with his diamondoak armored body.

He nervously nudged at my ascension bracers, and quietly spoke beyond my mind for the first time so everyone could hear.

Elle.

Elle understood immediately, and began tying my ascension bracers to my forearms.

Her fingers trembled as they worked, and she kept casting frantic glances toward my bleeding, shadowfire-scorched torso.

I reached toward her and placed a hand on her thigh as she knelt over me. She locked eyes with me and I saw the deeply etched worry behind her amber eyes.

We didn't speak, but I breathed in deeply, and she followed with her own breath. Together we exhaled, then inhaled again.

That seemed to relax her at least enough to finish buckling the ascension bracers to my arms. The copper pattern of scales glowed with Sentinel markings, and I could already feel them beginning to knit my wound back together.

"It'll probably take some time for it to work," Jax said, wincing and putting a hand to his forehead. As usual, he was getting an ether overuse headache.

He pulled a quartz crystal from his belt, quickly replenishing his ether supply. I really needed to get one of those.

The sound of crackling lightning made us all jump. Our heads turned, looking out toward the geyser fields where King Rodan and Kheradok still fought.

Lightning blasted from Rodan's ascension blade, arcing through the air toward Kheradok. The young Drekai champion rolled to avoid getting struck, coming back at the king with another one of his explosive dragonfire balls from his clawed gauntlet.

Green flame burst at Rodan's feet, throwing him backward and into the crater of a recently burst geyser. The super-heated water jetted all around the king, and Elle gasped as he scrambled to get out of there. A glowing lightwielding barrier flashed from his ascension armor, barely keeping him from getting boiled alive.

From the sidelines where he protected the true dragon egg, Rodan's drake, Rex, let out a roar. He must've been itching to join his bond and help him fight. A half-dozen Drekai from their ranks stood by, ready to hold back the dragon should he break free and interfere with the honor duel.

I could tell Elle wanted to jump in and help her father as well. I was sure she wouldn't, knowing it would bring the wrath of the Dragon Isles down on Drakfell, but I gripped her hand pretty tightly, just in case. The princess couldn't stop this without starting a full-blown war.

While the duel between Kheradok and Rodan raged on, most everyone on the field had their eyes on the spectacular battle between the Black Valkyrie and the Farseer. The Mage Hunters, guard, and dragons had all given them a wide berth as they fought on and around the brightly burning gallows platform.

Where Vidya had fought me with a regular spear, she wasn't showing any such restraint against the Farseer. She now wielded her long, black-bladed dragonhook spear, complete with the silver swan insignia on its blade. She'd activated a bright blue psionic rune, and was telepathically controlling a shield that hovered at her side. Her eyes still glowed with that strange blue light, and her spear's blade was ablaze with shadowy fire.

Guys, Kai's thought played over the mindlink. *Is it just me, or is the Black Valkyrie somehow channeling etherarchy over silver?*

I felt my stomach drop as I realized Kai was right. The shadowfire burned bright along the silvered edge of her spear.

Drakkin' drakefish, Boone thought. *It's the ghosts, I'm tellin' ya.*

Impossible, Kari's thought seemed both horrified, and a little intrigued. That must've meant she was recovering well from the dreamblades.

Solrac? Kai thought. *Any insight?*

Silence.

Solrac? Jax repeated. *Valla, where's Solrac?*

I've got him, Valla replied. *He... he's not doing great.*

What happened? we chorused.

Not sure. He was fighting one minute, then I turn my back for one second and he's passed out on the ground. Could be ether overuse. Might've been that soot-faced Geomancer.

I thought you took him out on the gallows, Kai thought.

So did I, Valla responded with annoyance. *But he's not hanging around anymore. I also thought we took him out with a blade to the chest, and an anchor through the middle.*

The sound of dozens of swords, spears, and axes clanging drew our attention back to the epic fight between Vidya and the Farseer. Vidya raised her arms as she psionically lifted the weapons of every fallen soldier within range.

She guided the weapons with her hands, training them all on the Farseer. Then, with a thrust, she sent them all racing toward him.

My breath caught in my throat. I'd never stood a chance against her.

But the Farseer stood as calmly as if it were a group of gentle dragonflies coming at him rather than an arsenal of deadly blades.

A few gold runes from his staff glowed, matching ones lighting up along his forehead from within his hood.

Then the Farseer walked straight into the storm of weapons, leaning and dodging as if he knew exactly where each one would fly. The Farseer psionically caught every weapon that got too close, turning them to block the other weapons under Vidya's control.

So he was a Psion too. Did that make him a skymage as well?

The Farseer swung his staff dramatically over his head, ending with it pointing toward Vidya. Darts of more violet dream energy went flying from each point of the antlers.

The energy blasted through the air like purple shooting stars. Vidya's silver shield darted in front of her, absorbing most of the comets. But a couple smaller ones changed direction mid-flight and hit her in the thigh. She wobbled ever so slightly.

They fought on, both showcasing an almost unreal mastery of etherarchy. Vidya's strange, blue eyes blazed as she used invisibility to appear and disappear all around the Farseer as she struck blow after blow. The Farseer always knew exactly where she'd be, using his ability to foresee the future to keep himself out of any real danger.

It was still impossible to tell who would win.

Meanwhile, the Black Valkyrie's Mage Hunters and traitorous guard had resumed their attack on Drakfell. Jaira and a few others had badly wounded the third ascension drake from the hatchery. More soldiers fell. An air of doom began to settle over our heads.

My wound was by no means healed, but the ascension bracers were doing their job well, and I was almost confident enough to stand up again.

Scenes of the action played out both where I could see as well as over the mindlink. Kari was back in the fight, and had used her crossbow to hit the Black Valkyrie's illusionist with silver bolos. He limped behind the burning platform, neutralized with silver as the ethereal snake slithered away beside him. Kai noted over the mindlink that the Black Valkyrie herself had stayed intact after Kari's shot, which meant this was really her whom the Farseer fought and not just a projection of her over a starswan made by the illusionist.

I saw Queen Liana disarm the Captain of the Guard with the help of the Royal High Mage. He used his woodweaving to grow bramblethorns to root the Captain of the Guard to the spot, trapping her in the plant. From there, the queen knocked away the captain's sword.

"No!" Elle suddenly shouted. I followed her gaze and saw Jaira had some soldiers with her and was fighting the evren, Lyra. Lyra was a strong, third ascension dragon, but Jaira was fast and she fought with silver. She'd landed a hit on one of Lyra's hindwings, and Elle wasn't about to take that sitting down.

Elle knew I'd be fine, especially with Jax and Thorn by my side. She ran into the action, her sword meeting Jaira's as Lyra nursed her injured wing.

Then Thorn roared, and I turned to see what was the matter. Lothar's green dragon had zoomed in toward him, probably trying to get at me. Thorn and the green evren took to the skies, jaws snapping and claws raking. Below them a short distance away, I saw Lothar cast me an apologetic look. I guess he'd decided he feared the Black Valkyrie's skymage powers more than he feared me, the injured fake Farseer.

Rude.

"Be right back," Jax said darkly, brandishing one of his axes as he stalked toward Lothar. Lothar's eyes widened as Jax lit up a psionic rune.

Jax's axe went zooming through the air. Lothar scrambled to get away, but Jax psionically flung his second axe as well. The two fanged axes came together, locking Lothar up from either side of his neck. The redheaded Mage Hunter gulped.

Jax glared menacingly down at Lothar, who squeezed his eyes shut. Jax's gaze flicked to Lothar's collar, then in one swift motion, Jax grabbed the cord around his neck and pulled hard.

The cord snapped, and Jax looked down at the emerald heartscale in his palm. We both looked up as the fight between Thorn and the green evren came to a halt. The evren disengaged.

Thorn watched the enemy dragon skeptically as she hovered, unsure. Then the evren looked down, her bright eyes fixed on Jax.

Jax looked up with equal surprise and… connection? Was that the right word? I recognized the look in Jax's eyes. It was something I felt all the time with my bond, Thorn.

Stars, had Jax just bonded Lothar's dragon?

I didn't have time to think about it long before the sound of exploding dragonfire drew my attention back to the geyser fields. This time, Kheradok's fireball must've hit too close, because it threw King Rodan far. He came to a limp stop at the base of another geyser crater.

My chest felt hollow as I waited for him to get up. His hand barely moved.

Soot, Valla swore over the mindlink. *Vidya's spotted us.*

I whipped my head back toward the battle between the Black Valkyrie and the Farseer. Sure enough, her vivid blue eyes flashed back to normal again for just a split second when she saw Solrac lying with his head in Valla's lap. Worry, fear, jealousy… they all etched themselves onto her face for only a moment before the umbral blue took over again.

In an excessive burst of anger and power, Vidya threw out both hands with a violent yell. With a strained series of splinters and cracks, the entire gallows platform lifted from the ground. The wooden construction flew toward the Farseer, knocking him back and landing on top of him.

A faint yelp from Elle sent my attention whipping back toward her. Jaira still had her locked in combat, blade against blade, but Elle was watching the action on the geyser fields.

Rodan still lay on the ground, as Kheradok stalked toward him, his black and red hair falling over one of his dragonfire green eyes.

The Black Valkyrie roared again as Kai sent anyone from the Knights of the Torch rushing onto the scene to back up the Farseer. Boone, Kari, and Jax came running, and even Valla left Solrac's side to join them.

I knew I should run in to help too. My wound still burned with pain, but I knew I could walk. I shuddered to think what Vidya would do if we didn't stop her now.

But back on the geyser fields, Kheradok was almost to King Rodan. The weary Drekai general gripped his scimitar tightly.

Just then, Vidya's hands flourished in front of her. Cries from my team sounded over the mindlink as she used her psionics to throw everyone back and away from her. Everyone, I noticed, but her son, Jax.

The Farseer emerged from the wreckage of the gallows platform, looking battered and drained. Even with a skystone, he would surely run out of ether eventually. I had no idea how Vidya was still channeling etherarchy—even with that strange, blue skystone.

The Farseer's staff glowed gold with runic power, and he reached out a gauntleted hand. Jets of violet dream energy shot from each of his five fingers and toward Vidya.

The energy shot toward her, each beam coming in at a different angle. One streaming for her neck, another for her heart, and still more toward her back, face, and legs.

There was no way she could avoid them all.

So she didn't.

Vidya cried out defiantly, adding a lightning blue rune to her crown of runes floating over her forehead. Her own blue tinted dream energy swirled around her, curving the beams from the Farseer and shielding her from them.

But the beams tightened in on her dream wall. She was trapped.

The Farseer's shards of purple energy crackled with power, and I had no doubt that to touch one would drain her completely. She must've known that too, because Vidya snarled at the Farseer, but didn't move.

They were both so spent.

The Farseer's hands shook. It was taking all his energy just to hold the beams in place.

Jax! Kai shouted over the mindlink. *Your axes will pass through the dream energy. Take her out!*

Jax's thoughts were a jumbled mess. He looked like he wanted to move, and though he was the only one who wasn't psionically rooted to the spot, he was the only one emotionally trapped.

Jax! Kai's thought came again, louder.

Mom... was Jax's muddled reply.

Soot, Kai swore again. *Asher! Take her down!*

I was on my feet in an instant. This was my chance for revenge, but I turned my head for one last look at Kheradok moving in on Rodan. He was almost upon the king, his scimitar raised to land the killing blow. The Drekai cheered.

Asher! Now!

The Farseer held the Black Valkyrie perfectly ready for my strike. She was weakened enough now that I could finally get my revenge. My window was closing fast.

But so was Rodan's.

TAKE HER DOWN!

Time seemed to freeze in that instant as a million different thoughts bombarded my head.

Suddenly, I wasn't standing on a battlefield beside the geyser fields of Keep Drakfell. I was in our valley—Mom's and mine. We sat on the sun-warmed grass, scents of wildflowers filling the air, and I could hear the lake lapping at the shore. A couple of lazy dragon buffalo grazed nearby.

Beside me, Mom laughed. A sweet sound, like bells.

Then Shaya's face took over the scene as I remembered her laughing in the rain atop Kaliiko Mountain. She spun, water flying off the ends of her hair.

Then Shaya's laugh twisted, morphing into the cruel laughter of the Black Valkyrie.

Next, I was hiking with Mom as we searched for the perfect cactus to add to our home garden.

Then I was hiking with Shaya, racing along the path toward the top of the mountains outside Keep Drakfell. All at once, Shaya was Vidya, her back to me as she led my mother out of Steel Rim and ultimately to her death.

Then I was just a child, lying in my bed back at our family's home. I'd just had a nightmare, and Mom was tucking me back in under my blankets. She sang her dragon lullaby to me before kissing me on the forehead.

I remembered Shaya's kiss in the alley near Guard Square when she'd asked for my help in keeping Jax at bay. When Shaya pulled away, it was Vidya's face I saw.

I remembered standing by, uselessly watching through the window as I saw my mother for the last time.

I could end it all now.

Don't let anyone else control your choices. Those are yours, Dad's words from the day I left with the Knights of the Torch played in my head.

You're as free as you choose to be.

Ether coursed through my entire body as I hover-dashed faster than I ever had before.

Toward Rodan.

With an immense boost from my levitation powers, I shot between Kheradok and the king. A jet of misty white ether trailed behind me like a comet. I didn't have time to fully form my usual starglass spear, so I redirected Kheradok's blow with a half-formed starglass pole.

Whack! Kheradok's scimitar embedded itself into the ground, mere inches from Rodan's head.

Kheradok looked at me, his dragonfire green eyes alight with utter shock and horror. Behind him, the Drekai army roared with rage. I couldn't understand all of what they said, but I translated the words 'cannot interfere,' and 'kill the half-born.'

Wonderful.

If I wanted to make it out of this alive, I needed a distraction.

My specialty, apparently.

Out of the corner of my eye, I saw King Rodan's white drake, Rex, lean forward onto his claws. He seemed to want so badly to save his bond.

"Uh," I began as Kheradok stared at me like he wanted to hack me to bits. "I just thought you ought to know it doesn't matter who wins this duel."

Kheradok looked incredulous as he growled. "And why is that, half-born?"

I swallowed. "Because... this."

With that, I hover-dashed as fast as lightning toward the king's dragon. The drake barely had time to register that I was there before I'd grabbed the true dragon egg from its nest of grass and hover-dashed back out of there.

Kheradok roared with fury, as did the rest of the Drekai. Rex dashed to Rodan's side, already beginning to heal him with a mist of liquid light from one of his clawed hands. I clutched at the heartscale at my neck as I ran, and felt a warm, protective sensation through the bond. Thorn was already on his way.

I hopped onto Thorn's back, clutching the true dragon egg under my arm as we took off over the geyser fields.

Thorn and I had to dodge a few jets of white hot water. The geysers went off sporadically, probably because of the Geomancer Mage Hunter's stunt earlier.

Boom! Boom!

Two of Kheradok's dragonfire bombs exploded just behind us in the air as we flew. Thorn roared as he soared out of the way.

I chanced a glance behind me and saw the army of Drekai still protesting. But where was—

Gold light pulled my focus back to the air in front of me. Thorn reared back as a black exit portal ripped to life.

Kheradok stepped through, his red and black wings spread wide behind him as the rift winked out.

"You dared to interrupt an honor duel," Kheradok's accented voice yelled as he brandished his scimitar at me.

"I did, yes, that was me," I responded.

"You have brought dishonor on all of Drakfell, and now my people must wage war with them," he said, enraged. It seemed like he really didn't want a war.

"Actually, I'm the guy they just executed... unsuccessfully," I clarified. "I'm not on their side."

Kheradok looked at me, confusion evident on his face.

"I'm not with Drakfell. They don't have the egg."

"Then by Drekai code," Kheradok continued, "my fight is now with you."

"Oh. Maybe we could schedule that for sometime next year?"

Kheradok began charging another emerald green explosive.

"Fine," I said. "Six months?"

"Return the egg, thief!" Kheradok yelled.

"Actually, I've gotten pretty attached to it," I said, looking at the glowing egg in my hand.

Kheradok's patience ran out, and he threw the bomb.

Thorn tried to dodge, but we weren't fast enough. The explosive went off, and my ears rang as I fell from Thorn's back. Panic welled inside me as the egg slipped from my grasp.

"No!" I heard Kheradok cry as the egg plummeted toward the dry, cracked earth below.

He dove to save the egg as I put on another burst of speed, using my archonic power to propel myself toward the egg as well.

He opened a portal, but was obviously tired from his fight with Rodan and missed catching the egg.

I could almost reach it... my fingertips just grazed the tiny scales of the shell...

But the ground was rising up too quickly. Neither Kheradok nor I was fast enough.

Crash!

The egg shattered on impact. But not in the way I'd expected an egg to crack. Instead of tiny bits of shell, tiny bits of starglass scattered in every direction. The starglass blew away into the wind, dissipating into etherdust until there was no evidence that there'd ever been an egg in the first place.

Kheradok's green eyes went wide. "*Ka varehnti.*"

I felt his sentiment, just as surprised.

Another fake true dragon egg? I'd watched the one Kai made dissolve at the gala. How was this possible?

Both Kheradok and I turned to King Rodan. Queen Liana was at his side, and he was slowly but surely regaining consciousness. He'd seen the egg break into shards of starglass as well, and he looked just as dumbfounded.

Several other Drekai converged around Kheradok, speaking to him in their native language. They were all talking at once, and so quickly I had a hard time keeping up, but I got the idea that without the egg here, they were trying to decide whether war with Drakfell was really necessary.

I needed that not to happen.

I staggered toward Kheradok, exhausted.

"Of course I wouldn't let you near the real egg now," I bluffed. "And if you kill or imprison me now, my allies will ensure you never find it."

Kheradok turned to me, clutching at his side. I hadn't noticed it before, but he had a gushing wound along his ribcage. Rodan must've struck a severe blow. He seemed to be considering his options. He didn't want war, and seemed to not know whether taking me might provoke that.

He also needed urgent medical attention.

One of the Drekai propped Kheradok up, speaking harshly to him. Reluctantly, Kheradok nodded, then addressed me again.

"My challenge stands. In one month's time, I shall fight you in an honor duel. Your name, half-born?"

"Uh, Asher of Steel Rim, but I'd rather—"

"*Ziiken aasti*, Asher of Steel Rim."

Before I could let him know definitively that I'd prefer not to have to fight the general of the Drekai army, he traced a rifting rune. Another portal ripped through the air, and Kheradok stepped through, disappearing into Etheria's whiteness.

Before I could relax for even one second, my brain stopped blocking out the mindlink, jolting me back to reality. In my mind's eye, I saw the fight with the Black Valkyrie.

She must've overpowered the Farseer's dream beams. The Farseer was exhausted, getting beaten back further and further. The rest of the team wasn't doing well either—Solrac was still down, His Majesty protectively perched over him. Jax was out now too, probably from ether overuse, but his new green evren remained at his side.

Boone had taken a hit to the leg and was limping as he fired weaker and weaker ether blasts from his daggers at the illusionist and his snake. Meanwhile, Valla had taken full polar wolf form and was locked in combat with the Geomancer who just wouldn't die. Kari was out of crossbow bolts and she was no good with a sword, so she was falling back to Solrac and

His Majesty's position. Elle was expertly fighting off Jaira and Lothar, while Aradan and his third ascension dragons were keeping the rest of Drakfell's treacherous guard away from the fight, but only barely.

The battlefield was too hectic. My chance for revenge on Vidya had passed, but that didn't bother me anymore. I just wanted my friends to be safe. But how?

We need backup... Kai thought groggily through the mindlink. Running the link for so long had been draining him, too. Having a team of mostly magi made us extra powerful, but also more vulnerable when we were low on ether.

And stars, was I low on ether. I could feel my heart starting to flutter, and it wouldn't be long before I joined Solrac and Jax.

Kai, I thought. *I'm here. What's the plan?*

I could almost feel the wheels of Kai's mind spinning through the mindlink. Then I sensed a bright flash of an idea from his end.

Your rift anchor from your dad. Do you still have it?

I rummaged for a moment through Thorn's saddlebag, and sure enough, the stones were there. I grabbed the white, runemarked entrance portal gem.

I have it, I replied. *But it's useless. My last pair of anchors are incomplete, remember? I dropped the other end back in the Dragonstorm Sea.*

Exactly.

I caught on to Kai's idea. *That's brilliant. But how do we get them to go through?*

Leave that to me. Just get near the Farseer, then open the rift.

You got it, I thought as I hopped onto Thorn's back and flew toward the fight.

The Farseer is the Black Valkyrie's true prize. He's going to lead them through the rift.

What? Alarms went off in my head. *But the Farseer will drown along with them.*

Trust me, Kai thought. *If I'm right about the Farseer, it won't matter.*

Thorn and I soared over the battlefield. Just as I was about to activate the rift anchor, my vision started going white. I wasn't going to be able to do it.

Kai, I don't think I have enough ether to get them all through, I thought to him.

Soot, Kai thought back.

I can, Thorn thought to me with a warm, reassuring flame through our bond. His ether well was certainly bigger than mine, and he hadn't had to use it much during the battle since Vidya'd had him pinned. I leaned forward, pressing the anchor to his forehead.

Thorn activated the rift anchor, and I dropped it behind the struggling Farseer.

The gold-rimmed portal tore open the air behind the Farseer, backlighting him in gold and white. In a grand movement, he dove through it, disappearing into the whiteness of Etheria.

"You can't escape me so easily!" Vidya raged, her eyes glowing even brighter lightning blue as she pursued the Farseer through the portal. Jaira followed without hesitation, as did the Black Valkyrie's Geomancer and Lothar. The snake-laden illusionist followed through last. His snake went wide eyed and hissed a futile warning as he leapt through the closing portal.

And just like that, the Black Valkyrie was gone. I had no doubt she and her followers were coming through the other end now, shocked to find themselves drowning in a cold, watery tomb.

Chapter 29: Thief

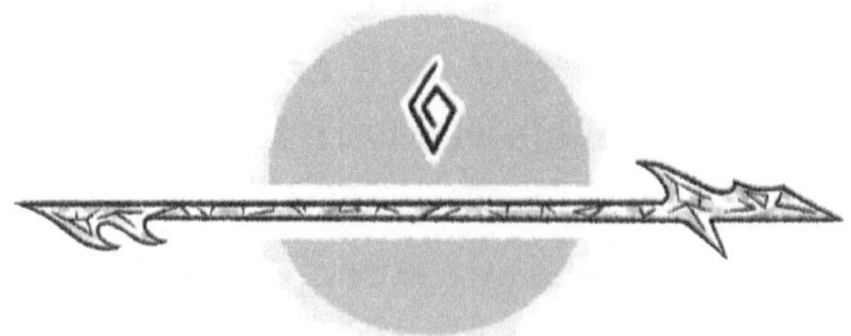

Without the Black Valkyrie and the Mage Hunters, and with the Captain of the Guard still trapped by the High Mage's bramblethorn bonds, the battle ended quickly. The undecided members of the guard joined those loyal to Drakfell in capturing their traitorous counterparts. I was glad to see that Sven had made it through the battle. He cradled an injured arm as he and Aradan took control in arresting the rebels.

The Drekai army packed up and left, following Kheradok's lead.

Elle and Queen Liana supported King Rodan as they hobbled back over from the geyser fields. The king still looked weary, but Rex's healing powers had kept him from death.

I breathed a sigh of relief when the healers were able to revive both Solrac and Jax. Neither looked great, but at least our team had survived. Valla and His Majesty hovered over Solrac, while Kari and the green evren sat beside Jax. She was careful not to touch him as they spoke, but it was good to see that she still cared about him.

My eyes were drawn to Elle. She'd left her father in her mother and the healer's care, hurrying over to Lyra, the dreamwatcher evren. Lyra's wing was injured, and while I couldn't hear her from so far away, I was sure she was softly singing to the dragon while Rex approached to heal her too.

I stroked Thorn's neck as I watched Elle. Her armored white dress was torn and stained from blood—probably mine. Her long, dark hair was tangled, but still fell in waves down her back. I admired the intense, caring light in her brilliant, amber eyes as she tended to her friend.

Maybe she felt me staring, I don't know. She looked up at me from across the field and quirked up an eyebrow.

I felt blood rush to my cheeks. I'd probably been making a dumb face or something.

But she gave me her mischievous smile and a little wink. I grinned back, and she waved me over. Thorn glowed with approval through our bond.

I'd only taken my first few steps when mottled gray scales filled my vision. Kai swooped down on his stonescale evren, Flint. My best friend had dark circles under his eyes, and a little bit of blood coming from his nose. The battle had really taken a lot out of him. But he was smiling as he hopped off his dragon's back and rushed up to Thorn and me.

"I can't believe we did it," he laughed, his voice a little ragged. "We only had about a six percent chance of success, but we did it."

"You did it," I replied.

"Despite you trying to give me a heart attack. I had a list of fifteen different backup plans, and backup plans for those backup plans. But you going rogue and saving King Rodan wasn't on the list. Thanks a lot for making me improvise."

"That's what I do."

He gave me a playful shove, and I shoved him right back. We both cringed, me from my still healing torso and him from his ether overuse headache.

"Speaking of your crazy plans," I started. "What did you mean about the—"

As if on cue, I noticed smoke billowing out over the ground. The din of voices around us stopped, and heads began to turn toward the copse of trees that stood behind what was once the gallows platform.

In a melodramatic puff of smoke, a figure in dark red robes emerged, holding his antlered staff high. A series of runes on his staff glowed, and gold flames leapt out from the antler points. The fire twisted in the air to form a giant floating symbol of the Knights of the Torch.

The crowd stood in stunned silence at the display.

Even I did a double take as the Farseer grandly strode up to the king.

"But..." I stuttered to Kai. "Didn't you send him through the rift?"

Kai's grin took up half his face. "I knew it. Why fight with your real self when you're the world's greatest illusionist?"

My eyes widened as I realized what Kai was saying. The Farseer was even more powerful than I'd thought. Kai looked at the Farseer with respect—and maybe just a little bit of jealousy—as he stood before King Rodan.

The crowd watched on as the Farseer waited for the king to get to his feet. King Rodan inclined his head toward the Farseer as he spoke.

"A deal is a deal," the king said. "You defeated the Black Valkyrie and defended Drakfell against the Mage Hunters. I believe you can protect us from the skyfalls as well."

The king turned out toward the crowd of onlookers, raising his great white ascension blade high over his head as his booming voice carried across the field.

"Let it be known throughout the keepdoms that I, King Rodan, pledge Drakfell to the service of the Knights of the Torch."

Gasps rippled throughout the crowd, along with a bit of an uproar. I myself had to keep my jaw from falling onto the ground below.

The Captain of the Guard struggled against her woodwoven bonds. "Drakfell would turn its back on Evgard?"

"No," King Rodan looked her dead in the eye. "It was Evgard who turned its back on us."

Rodan took another step out toward the crowd, wincing a little from his wounds. They hadn't all had a chance to fully heal yet.

"For too long, Drakfell has lived in fear of Evgard and High King Magnus' wrath. We've fought to meet their demands by paying their skystone tribute, and suffered at the hands of their anti-magi laws. We've struggled without support as more skyfalls ravaged our lands with more dragons, as well as suffered from the spread of the shadow-wasting. But today, the Farseer has proven that the Knights of the Torch can do more to protect Drakfell than Evgard ever has."

Rodan looked out over the people, his eyes coming to rest on me.

"Take this magi," Rodan gestured to me, and the crowd turned. "Despite being sentenced to death by my own hand, he showed me great mercy on the field of battle. This has shown me what the Farseer and the Knights have been trying to impress on my mind for many months: It is not magi who bring destruction to Evgard. It is the darkened hearts of its leaders."

Stars and soot. Was a nobleman actually being cool right now?

"I hereby pardon this magi of all his crimes. People of Drakfell, it is time for a new era. I know High King Magnus will not be pleased, and there will be ramifications for this choice. But today marks the day where Drakfell no longer takes orders from Evgard. Today, Drakfell declares freedom for all its citizens, magi or not."

His speech was so powerful, many people began to cheer. Many still seemed unsure, afraid even, and I couldn't blame them. But my heart swelled inside my chest as I felt like I was truly a part of something good.

Solrac appeared behind Kai and me, clapping a hand onto each of our shoulders. We turned, surprised to see him on his feet already.

"Isn't this the best way this could've ended?" he whispered. "Everything went precisely according to plan."

"What do you mean?" Kai asked. "Our heist for the true dragon egg failed. We don't even know where it is."

"Ah, but that wasn't our real heist. No, the true heist was a little something I like to call *The Ballad of Knights and Kings Part One*. Our real goal was to take the keepdom of Drakfell itself. And would you look at that, we pulled it off."

My mind was a little bit blown, but it all reminded me of another mystery.

"The true dragon egg..." I started. "It was a fake."

Solrac frowned. "What?"

"The egg the king's drake was guarding." I cocked my head. "Was that part of your plan too?"

"No," Solrac said, a deep look of confusion clouding his face.

"So, where's the real true dragon egg?"

"I can answer that," a deep voice drew our attention. I looked over and saw Aradan and Elle walking toward us. In Aradan's hands sat the shining, pearlescent egg, covered in miniature scales and pulsing with life.

A few in the crowd turned toward the egg, watching it in Aradan's hands.

"But... how?" Kai said.

"I couldn't let my father and his court force its bond," Elle said. "Aradan and I had Lyra and Glass from the hatchery build a replica out of starglass. We replaced it before the gala."

"You're kidding," Kai said. "We were trying to steal a fake the whole time?"

Elle shrugged.

"So what do we do with it now?" I asked.

"I mean," Solrac broke in, reaching toward the egg. "The Knights of the Torch will gladly find a use for it—"

"Nice try," Aradan said, holding the egg back from Solrac, "But the whole point in hiding the egg was to keep it from any forced bonds."

Solrac's usually jovial face took on a serious vibe. "I couldn't agree more." Then he gestured to the circle of people who'd gathered around—our Knights of the Torch team.

Solrac smiled. "This is a group of the finest freedom fighters I've ever met. I can't think of anyone more deserving of a chance to bond the true dragon than any one of these people here."

Aradan looked around the circle and into each of our faces. He looked at Elle, and she nodded with approval.

Before passing the egg off to Solrac, though, Aradan removed his ascension gauntlet. He placed his bare hand on the egg, and we all leaned forward with anticipation.

Aradan cursed when nothing happened. "Drak. Third time's not the charm, I guess."

He carefully handed the egg over to Solrac. Solrac's hands cradled the egg, the pulsing light within keeping its natural rhythm. Nothing.

Valla went next, holding the egg with reverence, but still not forging a bond with the true dragon inside.

Boone, Jax, Kari, then Kai each took a turn with the egg as well. Still, it didn't choose a bond.

I felt dragonbumps appear along my skin as Kai passed the egg to me. Thorn held his breath in anticipation. The scaly egg felt pleasantly warm against my palms as I held it gently. I could feel the true dragon's presence inside—playful and eager.

The light pulsed brightly once, and my heart leaped into my throat. I heard a couple of people's breath catch.

Then the egg went back to normal, the light pulsing just as evenly as before.

I heard a few disappointed sighs as I turned to hand off the egg to Elle.

She surprised me by taking a step backward and gesturing for Aradan to take it back.

Aradan didn't extend a hand, instead giving Elle a meaningful look.

Elle put her hands up. "No, thanks. I've never touched it before, and I couldn't now. My father..."

"Things are changing, Eliana. Don't worry. Take it," Aradan said.

"But—"

"Just try."

We waited with bated breath while Elle reached toward the egg in my hands with her long, slender fingers. Her fingertips rested on the scaly, white surface, and I handed it to her.

For a moment, everything was still. The pulsing light inside the egg went dim. Elle's brow furrowed.

Then the egg began to crack. The shell split, golden light forming along the cracks like a Rifter's portal. An exit rift.

The first thing to emerge was a tiny, snow white snout. A draconic face with intelligent, dragonfire green eyes came next. The little dragon had a pair of nubs on either side of its head where no doubt a pair of magnificent horns would one day grow.

The true dragon crawled out of the egg, already bigger than what the egg could feasibly have contained. Rifter etherarchy was definitely at play here.

More pieces of shell cracked and fell away as the little dragon stretched out its bright white wings. Four clawed legs came out next, stepping onto Elle's palm.

The little true dragon looked up at Elle's shining eyes. Then the creature reached toward its chest with its foreclaw and scratched until a white scale fell off into Elle's hand. The dragon's heartscale was larger than the rest of the dragon's scales, already full sized. It left a large area of bare hide on the dragon's chest exposed. It would need extra guarding to keep it safe as it grew.

Already, I noted a fierce protectiveness in Elle's features as she stared lovingly at her brilliant new bond, the true dragon.

The tiny true dragon shot a jet of emerald green dragonfire triumphantly into the sky.

Steam rose from the hot springs in the hideout. Solrac, Valla, Boone, Jax, and I relaxed in the pool while Kari sat on the side and dipped her bare feet in. Each of us had a celebratory glass of golden boltbrew from the Dreamy Drakalope in our hands. His Majesty sat just outside of the spring as Solrac stroked the back of his neck. Nearby, Kai scribbled in his notebook, surrounded by bundles and packs.

It had been just over two weeks since the battle at the geyser fields. So much had happened in that time that the battle itself almost felt like a dream. Solrac and Valla had been working with King Rodan and Queen Liana to reorganize Drakfell's leadership. A few additional members of the Knights of the Torch had come in from Skygard to assume permanent roles as royal advisors. After the king's announcement, several nobles and others had taken what they could and fled Drakfell, presumably heading for Rengard or the central keepdoms where the governments still supported anti-magi attitudes.

There had already been a few altercations in various regions across the Badlands Keepdom as word of Rodan's announcement spread. The guards had to work to keep riots from getting out of hand as a result of the change in policy. But they had help from an astonishing number of unregistered magi who were thrilled with the new direction. The Knights' assistance had already begun to turn the tide against the swarms of dreklings from the skyfalls, though there still weren't enough Lightwielders to effectively combat the shadow wasting. Solrac said people across Evgard were already referring to Drakfell as 'the Traitor Keepdom,' and things were sure to get worse before they got better.

Elle had been spending every free moment with her new dragon, Aurora. She'd been so afraid that whoever bonded the true dragon would be subject to King Rodan's every whim, forced to be another card in his deck. I knew she was still nervous about that sort of thing in the future, but at least for now, Rodan was too preoccupied to stop Elle from doing whatever she wanted.

Part of me was worried, though. I was sure that by now the Drekai had discovered that the egg had hatched. There was no way they were just going to let Drakfell get away with something like that with no response.

Thinking about Elle made a few dragonflies jump into my stomach. Amidst all the chaos, there hadn't been a good moment for us to really sit down and talk yet. I didn't want to admit it, but maybe part of me was afraid to see her alone. After all that had happened with Shaya—or, Vidya—something inside me felt raw and closed off. But still, my heart ached at the thought of going a whole week without seeing Elle. At least I knew she'd be there when we all met up again in Skygard.

"Alright." The sound of Kai shutting his notebook cut into the peaceful silence. "Well, I'm ready to go when you guys are."

"Aww," Kari whined. "Do we have to?"

"Yes," Kai replied. "If we leave now, we'll be back well before sunset, which will give us time to get settled before dark. That'll give us a few extra hours to get everything prepared for tomorrow. We have a lot to pack if we're going to get everything from your workshop ready to bring all the way to Skygard next week. Plus, we still need to check and make sure Akayto's on board with all of this. Although, I have prepared three backup plans in case he isn't. Maybe I should put together a fourth..."

Kai reopened his notebook and jotted down a few more lines. Kari and I exchanged looks, rolling our eyes.

"I do wish you didn't have to go," Solrac said, taking a sip from his drink. His Majesty growled in agreement. "Although Kai's right about one thing: The next week will go by quickly, then we'll reunite in Skygard for the Farseer to tell us what comes next."

I chugged the rest of my drink, then climbed out of the pool.

"No reason for prolonged goodbyes, then." I couldn't hide the excitement in my voice as I dried off. As I pulled my shirt over my torso, I startled at the fiery, black shadowscar that slanted just above my right hip. I was still getting used to the souvenir from my fight with the Black Valkyrie.

I finished changing and hurried to Kai's side, grabbing my satchel off the floor and slinging it across my back. I turned to Kai expectantly.

"Aren't you going to pack?" he asked.

I held up my satchel.

Kai gave a resigned sigh. "Right. Kari?"

"Coming," she sang, hurrying to put on her shoes as well. "I packed last night, so I'm good to go."

"Kari, wait," Jax said, setting down his drink and stepping out of the pool. He was shirtless and dripping wet, and I couldn't help but notice Kari's dark cheeks go even darker. She may've broken up with Jax, but she still wasn't immune to his muscles.

He went up to her, muttering something in a voice too low for me to hear. She gave him one last touch on the shoulder, her fingers lingering a little too long on his bicep, before she rushed to join Kai and me.

We said one last goodbye to the group before climbing the stairs up to the tavern and heading outside. Thorn and Flint were already waiting for us.

I pulled out the last rift anchor stone from Thorn's saddlebag—the white entrance portal. I knew my father had the other end with him.

I'd thought I'd need to find an ether vent or some other extreme source of ether for us to use it, but saving the keepdom of Drakfell had been... rewarding.

I activated the anchor using the huge chunk of skystone King Rodan had given us—we'd need a lot to make this big of a jump—and the portal ripped open before us. Together, we stepped through, leaving Keep Drakfell behind and stepping into Steel Rim.

CHAPTER 30: SKYGARD

The late summer air would've been scorching, but with the strong breeze and the lake nearby, it was perfect.

Thorn splashed in the water, half trying to catch a wingtrout and half playing around. I could tell through our bond how happy he was to be back in Mom's valley.

I stood on the shore, breathing in the scents of wildflowers and algae, as well as the earthy musk from the herd of dragon buffalo grazing in the field.

Against the natural beauty, a spark of gold light played at the edge of my vision. When I turned toward the cliffside, I saw a gold-rimmed black portal ripping through the air on *Kiivi Zariika*, Mom's favorite cozy rock.

Dad stepped through the portal moments later. I should've known he'd want to say goodbye to the valley too.

I gave one last look to Thorn as his strong, second ascension legs thrust down to finally catch the fish. He tossed it onto the shore and dug in while I climbed the cliffside to join my dad on the *zariika*.

We sat together in silence for a long time, like we'd done many times before since losing Mom. I observed the valley with natural eyes as he did so through Etheria, the rune for the Sight aglow over his forehead.

"So," I began gruffly. "This is it then. Today we leave for Skygard."

"That we do," Dad said, holding up a small metal hoop with gold threads crossing through the center to form a star. "Solrac and the others contacted

"

me this morning through this dreamweb thing you brought back. Said the messenger dragon just arrived with my rift anchor, so we can leave anytime now."

"You'll be able to rift all of us that far? Including Thorn, Flint, and all the tools from Kari's workshop?"

"Void no," Dad laughed. "I couldn't jump a quarter that far even if I drained my entire ether well. But I can do it with the help of the ether vents down in the caves, and of course, this generous gift from your old pal the King of Drakfell."

Dad flipped open the top of the satchel at his side to show off the gigantic, fist-sized skystone Rodan had sent with us. It had been enough to get Kai, Kari, Thorn, Flint, and me all the way back here. And now that it'd had more than enough time to refill, it was ready to assist with yet another jump.

Thorn looked at it hungrily, eyeing me as if asking for permission, yet again. I laughed and shook my head. My wyvern snorted, but he understood. He was already in desperate need of a new saddle after his first ascension. Besides, I couldn't let him eat our mode of transportation to Skygard.

Dad's gaze drifted to something behind me. I turned and saw nothing, but Dad smiled warmly.

"What?" I asked.

"Oh nothing," he sighed. "So, the Black Valkyrie really is dead then?"

"She has to be," I said. "Solrac still isn't sure, but I don't see how she or any of her Mage Hunters could've survived the Dragonstorm Sea."

"Mom hopes she survived."

I bristled at that. But to my surprise, Dad's claim didn't send me into a rage. Just a few months ago, I'd have been cursing and summoning my starglass spear.

Of course, I hoped the Black Valkyrie was dead. But it startled me to realize that even more than that, I hoped that Dad was right and that Mom really was around, still involved in our lives and sharing her opinions.

"Mom," I said. "She wants us to be happy, huh?"

Dad smiled again, first at me and then over my shoulder. "She really, really does."

I felt a warm glow in my heart. It was similar to the fiery feelings I got from Thorn through our bond, only this one resonated with the comfort of a lullaby.

"Speaking of happiness," Dad said with a sly sideways glance, "I'm excited to meet this Elle girl I keep hearing about. Kari says the two of you are... friends."

My pulse sped up just thinking about Elle. And the thought of her meeting my father was almost enough to get my palms sweating.

"Yeah," I confirmed. "She's supposed to be in Skygard tonight as well."

"Then what are we waiting for?" Dad got to his feet. "I say, let's get Kari and Kai and get out of this little old outlander town of ours."

The second we set foot in Skygard, it hit me that this was the first time I'd ever been outside of the Badlands Keepdom. Thorn sent me an excited flame of agreement.

They called Skygard the Cliffside Keepdom, and it was easy to see why. Skygard bordered the ocean, the edge of the land coming up against the water with high, rocky dropoffs. The stones were an odd mix of slate gray and a rich, rusty red.

The enormous trees were red as well, with ruddy, splintering bark. Each towering tree had a trunk almost as thick around as our house back in Steel Rim. I'd never felt so small as I did looking up at one.

The crown jewel of the landscape rose off the edge of one of the cliffs overlooking the ocean. An imposing castle built from mottled gray and red stone loomed proudly at Skygard's southern tip. Brilliant gold mortar held the stones together, catching the low sunlight behind the castle.

The castle's shape reminded me of the spines along a dragon's back. A series of increasingly tall spires rose from north to south, ending with the tallest tower at the southernmost point, nearest to the ocean. This last spire was flush with the cliff face, and jutted straight into the sky, then sloped backward into the rest of the castle. Each floor along the spire had a balcony with a stunning ocean view, and a golden dome crowned the top, bearing a bright light that shone out to sea. A small city spread all around the base of the castle's fortified walls.

"Orothion," Kai murmured, remembering what Solrac had told us was the fort's name. It didn't sound very Evgardian, and I remembered Kai mentioning something from his research about the Knights of the Torch headquarters being called after the ancient order of the Guardians. I wasn't really sure what that meant, and I suspected that if Kai was being honest, neither did he.

Other members of the Knights of the Torch greeted us and helped us bring all of our things into the castle. They took Thorn and Flint to the dragon caverns while the rest of us followed a man down a long, narrow hallway.

The man wore red robes that reminded me of the Farseer's. He stopped at a large, plain wooden door.

"Once you walk through this door," the man said. "You will not be the same as you are now. You will find yourself amidst the finest food, drink, and company."

"Great," I said, reaching for the door handle. "I'm starving."

I pulled, then leaped backward as a wall of golden flames erupted to life inside the doorframe.

"Stars," I shielded my eyes from the unexpected brilliant fire. The red robed man chuckled.

"As I was saying," he continued. "To pass through the flames will transform you into a true Knight of the Torch."

"You mean we weren't already Knights?" Kari asked.

"More like Knights in training. You served the light well, but now you have the chance to understand it more fully. To do this, I must impress upon your mind the four principles of the Knight's Code."

"The Knight's Code?" Kai repeated.

The man went on. "Choose light. Burn bright. Drive out darkness. Light the way."

As he spoke, a good feeling settled over me. I liked that code—it was simple, and felt somehow right to me. When I looked at my dad and my friends, I saw that they were smiling too. Kai was already scribbling the words in his black journal.

"These principles will serve you well as you serve them," the man said. "Now…"

He gestured toward the fiery doorway once more.

Kai shut his notebook, then narrowed his eyes at the flames. "I think I've read something about this." Kai's fingers brushed the heavy satchel of books at his side. "The Knights of the Torch anciently made their initiates walk through golden fire in order to cleanse them and prove their loyalty. Some stories say men and women died going through when their hearts weren't sufficiently pure."

"Well, doesn't that sound nice," Dad said with a nervous snort.

"Is it safe?" Kari asked warily.

"Being a Knight of the Torch is never safe," the red robed man said reassuringly.

Through the bond, I could feel Thorn's warm, calming presence as I stared into the golden flames. The way he spoke to me had always reminded me of fire burning in my heart.

Without thinking, I took a step toward the doorway.

"Asher," Kai warned. "Maybe we should think this through—"

I walked into the fire.

I expected to feel heat burning into my skin, or perhaps singing my clothes. Instead, a pleasantly cool calmness overwhelmed my senses. While the flames had appeared gold from the outside, from within them every-thing seemed white.

Bright flashes of color streaked across my vision, some lingering while others zipped by. Everything was misty and bright. I couldn't help but reach toward the lights as they passed.

When I held out my hand, I realized I was glowing with vibrant light as well. Playful turquoise clouds clung to my hand and arm. Around my wrist was a sort of translucent, black and copper cuff. It reminded me of the color of Thorn's hide.

I continued walking through the strange white fire. I could feel the flames thinning when another turquoise aura—this one several shades deeper than mine—appeared beside me. I got the strongest impression of love, almost as if someone were embracing my soul. A tear sprang to my eye, and I could swear I almost heard the sound of my mother's voice singing her dragon lullaby.

Then suddenly, the flames were gone. At my back, gold fire burned in a simple, rectangular doorway. I'd walked straight through to the other side.

Before me was one of the most welcoming, homey scenes I'd ever taken in. A large banquet table ran through the center of the room, and men and women laughed and drank as they feasted on the mountain of food heaped onto it. I felt my stomach growl at the sight of steaming meat, roasted vegetables, and golden-crusted breads.

Tall windows invited the fresh, salty breeze from the ocean, and behind some pillars I noted one of the balconies I'd seen from outside. The red, setting sun lit the room.

Wooden panels lined the red and gray stone walls, and each panel had been painted with life-sized depictions of the Knights' history in Evgard. They showed the Knights' hand in everything from the Dragon Wars to the Drekai's arrival to the way they resisted the recent Rifter Purge enacted by High King Magnus's mother. They even had a few panels dedicated to the formation of the Knights. In the background of those pieces were the ancient skyboats used by our ancestors to flee to safety in Evgard from their dying old land. It surprised me to see the Farseer's likeness, from his red robes to his antlered staff, painted alongside the Knights even so far back as that.

Among the guests at the feast I saw Boone and Valla pouring cider, Jax piling pork onto his plate, and Solrac sitting with two others at the table's head. One was a tight-jawed woman in her fifties, and the other was a peppy-looking man so old I wondered if he remembered when the ancients arrived himself. The man had bright green eyes and red scale-tipped ears—a half-born, like me. They both had silvermarks on their left cheeks, though I couldn't tell what types they were from here.

And then there was Elle.

Well, based on the tiara atop her head as she sat near the end of the table, tonight she was Eliana, Princess of Drakfell.

She gave a smile and a wink when she saw me. I waved, just about to join her when Solrac appeared in front of me.

"Asher," he grinned, clapping a hand onto my shoulder. "So glad you're here. I was worried you wouldn't make it through the flames."

He smiled to let me know he was teasing. Next, he reached into his pocket and pulled out a gold coin, which he dropped only somewhat melodramatically into my hand. On one side of the coin was a torch icon, on the other, a symbol I didn't recognize, surrounded by a circle of tiny lettering.

"A token given to every new Knight," Solrac explained. Then his gaze rose to something beyond my shoulder, and I turned to see my father emerging from the golden fire. Solrac greeted him as well. Kari and Kai followed close behind, and Solrac handed each of them a gold coin just like mine. Finally, Solrac eagerly guided us to our places at the feast.

After the meal, Solrac and the other two leaders retreated into a room adjacent to the banquet hall. In small groups, pairs, or sometimes one at a time, they invited the Knights present at the feast into the room.

"They're giving us all assignments," Valla explained as our team grouped together near the head of the table. Elle had gone to check on Aurora in Orothion's dragon caverns, but promised she'd be back soon.

Kai glanced toward the door. "So Solrac is one of the leaders of the Knights. But what about the other two?"

"First one's a nasty lil' drakpat called Vesta," Boone whispered so loudly I doubted he really cared if he was being subtle.

"*Lady* Vesta," Valla reminded him.

"She won't let anyone forget it, neither. She's the sister of the Queen of Skygard. A Geomancer more talented'na cindermoth weavin' a cocoon, but she ain't got a heart."

"And the man?" Kai asked, taking notes in his black leather book.

"Zel of Veil Falls," Valla said, narrowing her eyes. "Everyone loves him because he never forgets a birthday. But I have a policy not to trust anyone who never stops smiling."

"He's the Triarchy's Archon," Boone said. "Happiest drakkin' Shadow-binder I ever done met."

Solrac appeared in the doorway, calling Kari's name. Kari hurried into the room, eager to get her assignment from the heads of the Knights of the Torch.

She was only in there a couple of minutes before she emerged, beaming. We made our way toward her.

"So?" Kai said, prompting his sister.

"It's better than I ever could've dreamed," Kari squealed, clapping her hands together. "They're giving me an entire workshop here in Orothion in their ancient skyforge. I get to work on developing silverbane and other weapons the Knights can use. I'll have access to any equipment, any texts I want!"

Kai's eyes popped. Besides Kari, he was one of the only people I knew who could get that excited about books.

"And they're giving me some apprentices," Kari went on. "As well as a partner. They should be here to meet me any—"

"Are you Kari?" a deep, male voice rose from behind us. We all turned to see a tall, extremely muscular guy with thick, black hair, which he tossed out of one eye.

I didn't think much of him, but Kari looked like she was about to start drooling.

"Yes," she managed.

"Nice," the stranger replied. "I'm Daro. I guess we'll be working togeth-er."

"Guess so," Kari smiled and subconsciously tucked a lock of hair behind her ear.

I couldn't help but notice what this new guy's presence was doing to Jax. Jax's jaw tensed and relaxed in rapid succession, and I thought the vein in his forehead would explode.

"Hi there y'all," came another voice.

Speaking of things exploding.

"Enya?" Kari cocked her head. "You're not..."

"Oh, you *know* I'm here as one of your apprentices," Enya tipped her draccoonskin cap. "After escapin' those Mage Hunters at the Drowsy Drekling, I figured it was only a matter of time before the likes of y'all showed up. And I'm sure as the void glad you brought along this sweet piece of man cake."

Enya looked over at Kai, her eyelashes fluttering. "So what you think, hot scales? Have we got over an eighty-seven percent chance of kissin' under the stars tonight?"

Kai's cheeks deepened. "Still no, Enya."

Enya shrugged, then looked over Jax.

"What's got your craghopper, Muscles?"

Solrac swung open the door to the room and called Jax in, much to Jax's relief.

Jax spent a long time in there. When he finally emerged, Boone and Valla took his place, but Jax skirted around the edge of the room away from us. I followed him.

"You okay?" I said quietly so I wouldn't draw attention from the others.

"Fine," Jax grumbled, not looking my way.

"Sorry about Kari and that guy. She doesn't mean to—"

"Get out of my face, Dragon-boy." Jax stormed away, heading straight for a chair at the banquet table. He angrily propped his feet up onto it and started doing decline push-ups.

"Okay then, Swan-spawn," I grumbled, just loudly enough that I was sure he could hear. He tensed, but refrained from coming over and punching me in the nose. I'd have to warn him about his mother's plans for him later. He probably wouldn't take it well right now. Nor would I deliver it well.

Our blossoming friendship was off to a great start.

The leaders assigned Valla and Boone to some kind of mission to Behrfell in the North. Solrac would be joining them as they spoke with nobility and some magi groups about supporting the Knights' cause.

The Farseer had also asked Boone to continue training me. When Boone left the room, he slipped me one of two identical dreamwebs from under his dragonscale cloak. They were covered in runes. He said the Farseer made them for us so we'd be able to meet together for practice sessions in the dream realm. I wasn't quite sure how it would work, but I was looking forward to finding out.

My dad received a special mission that he wasn't supposed to tell anyone, but he whispered to me that he'd be staying here in Orothion, helping establish a portal network for the Knights of the Torch. That made me smile the same crooked smile as he did.

Elle returned just in time for Solrac to call her name. As she headed into the room, Solrac asked Kai and me to join her.

A jolt of excitement went through me. Did they want me working with Elle?

I mean, I wouldn't complain about that.

They'd set up three chairs behind an extra-wide redwood desk. The uptight woman with a Geomancer's silvermark and an angry scowl leaned back in her chair, arms crossed. The elderly man had a pleasant smile as he sat on the edge of his seat, hands primly clasped atop the desk. Solrac leaned casually against the side of the desk, ignoring his chair completely.

I startled a little when I saw the Farseer himself standing ominously in the corner of the room. His white eyes and bright skystone glowed from within his deep red hood.

"Have a seat," the old man, Zel, said kindly, gesturing to some wooden stools in front of the desk. I sat between Elle and Kai.

"You may have guessed what the Knights desire from you, Princess Eliana of Drakfell," the old man smiled formally, but there was an air of enthusiasm behind his tone.

"I presumed I'd be joining my father and mother as they work to stabilize Drakfell under the Knights," Elle said with confident grace.

"Wrong answer, Princess," the angry woman, Vesta, spoke as if she were bored to tears by our mere presence. "That's a job for someone who didn't just bond the most powerful creature in the whole drakked realm. With the Drekai about to eat your keepdom alive for snatching their true dragon egg, we need you as far away from Drakfell as we can get you. No way we'll calm those tensions with you flying around on your new pet. So we're sending you to meet Rhana."

"Rhana?" Elle tilted her head.

"Rhana is a special correspondent of ours," the old man said, completely unfazed by his fellow leader's rudeness. "She has a particular interest and skill in training true dragons and their riders."

Elle's face lit up. "When will she arrive? Is she here already?"

Solrac chuckled. "Rhana doesn't come to us. You go to her."

The old man explained. "Rhana lives deep in the Mirror Forest of Evyndara's Ridgeback Mountains. She hasn't left her hovel in over two decades."

I grinned. "Awesome."

"I'll tell you what's awesome, you precious little man-dragonmutt," Vesta glared at me with a condescending finger point. "It'll be awesome when you and your friend get the princess to that cursed Mirror Forest in one piece." She paused, sniffing the air. "Do you smell that?"

Taken aback, Kai and I looked at each other, then took a series of quick inhales through our noses. Nothing. We shook our heads.

"That's the smell of potential failure. You two reek of it. Problem is, we need the princess to learn how to use her dragon. So I'm only gonna say this once: You'd better get your sorry scales into a bath and wash off that stink, because the Knights of the Torch don't have a place for failures."

Kai and I nodded at her with wide eyes.

"Isn't Vesta delightful?" Solrac grinned.

Vesta turned on Solrac. "I'd like to rip that stupid goatee right off your pretty face, Solrac. I mean, what is it doing there? Are you a married man with a beard, or a simpering, baby-faced single loser?"

Solrac protectively stroked his goatee. "It's complicated."

"Don't worry," the old man's already wrinkly crows feet deepened as he smiled. "Rhana's at least a little nicer than Vesta, and much more stable than Solrac's love life."

Kai, Elle, and I exchanged glances. Elle shrugged.

"We particularly want you to meet with Rhana as well, Kai," Solrac put in. "She's not a Seer herself, but we think she can teach you one or two things that may come in handy should the Knights find themselves in need."

Next, Solrac extended a hand toward the Farseer, who ceremoniously passed something to him. "Additionally," Solrac went on, "he would like you to take this."

I watched Solrac hand Kai a small, roundish rock with intricately carved runes on it. Kai examined it with fascination.

"A Seer stone," Kai murmured. He clearly recognized the markings from his studies.

"It will help you as you practice more with omens," Solrac explained. Then he turned to me, a serious look in his eye. "Asher. You're going along as their primary bodyguard. The way to the Mirror Forest is riddled with dangers."

"In fact," Zel said, pulling out a small map of Evgard from a drawer in the desk. "The Mage Hunters have such a strong presence throughout all of the Capital Keepdom that you won't be able to use any of the direct routes to the Ridgebacks."

Elle, Kai, and I leaned in as Zel pointed a gnarled old finger to our location in Skygard, then traced it eastward toward the mountain range near the center of Evgard.

"Instead," Zel continued, "we're sending you all the way down here first. La dee dah, hop and a skip, and there we go."

His finger dipped deeply southward, dancing along the map until it came to rest on a little circle drawn in the middle of what looked like some kind of redrock canyon.

"That can't be the most efficient route," Kai said. "That must be hundreds of miles out of the way."

"That is accurate." Zel smiled.

"But it's also the most direct route to the small mission we need you to complete before seeing Rhana," Solrac said.

"What mission is that?" I asked.

"An important correspondence of ours was somehow intercepted recently," Solrac hung his head. "One of our agents, Cenrik of Keep Rengard, has been compromised."

"Poor fool's getting arrested by Mage Hunters as we speak," said Vesta, more amused than concerned.

I tried to remember where I'd heard the name Cenrik before. It dawned on me that I'd seen it in the note Shaya had read when we were picking up that parcel for Solrac. Only Shaya was never really Shaya.

A pit formed in my stomach.

"Cenrik left behind some important intelligence," Solrac said. "We need someone to retrieve a case he left behind in Keep Rengard. If that case were to fall into the wrong hands, it could put all of the Knights in danger."

"So that's where we're going?" Elle asked, looking at the map. "Keep Rengard?"

Solrac nodded. "That's right. I hope you all like canyon views. You leave tomorrow morning."

They gave us each our own room in the castle to stay that night, but I couldn't sleep. I wandered the castle, finding myself drawn to one of the balconies overlooking the Scarlet Strait. Tomorrow we'd take a ship across those waters toward the northern shores of Rengard.

Thorn found me quickly, flying around the outside of the castle to meet me. The balcony was wide, and there was plenty of room for a second ascension wyvern to perch beside his bond and enjoy the salty sea air.

As I leaned dangerously far over the edge, a little flash caught my eye. A small, white true dragon as long as my forearm clung to the balcony railing as she scooted along it toward me.

"Well, hello Aurora." I smiled as she struggled to keep her grip on the iron rail. "You've gotten bigger since the last time I saw you." She looked up at me with wide, dragonfire green eyes.

"She's growing up too fast," Elle's voice followed as she entered the balcony.

She joined me at the edge, staring out into the sea. At the same time, we looked up to see the millions of brilliant, white stars blanketing the night sky. I heard Thorn sneak away, taking Aurora with him to give Elle and me some privacy. He was a very good dragon.

I became extremely aware of everything around me as Elle leaned in a little closer, her upper arm brushing against mine. A slight breeze ruffled her hair and I could smell her sweet emberfern perfume.

"I missed you this past week," I said.

"Good," Elle replied, her bright amber eyes flashing. She turned to me and my body responded as we wrapped our arms around each other. Her hands slid around my back and she tilted her chin upward toward my face.

She leaned in to close the distance between our lips.

Just then, an inexplicable feeling of fear bubbled up inside me, and I froze. Every muscle in my body tensed.

"Stop," I heard myself say. I pulled back, feeling like a crazy person for ruining the moment.

Elle arced a perfect eyebrow. "What?"

"I... I don't know exactly."

I stepped backward from her, grabbing the rail of the balcony with both hands.

"Is it the whole princess thing?" Elle put a hand on her hip. "That really freaked you out, didn't it? I mean, I knew you didn't like nobles, but..." she trailed off, looking at me expectantly.

"No, it's not that. I just..."

Images flashed through my mind. Moments with Shaya. That is, Vidya posing as Shaya. I remembered being in prison at Keep Drakfell, then later, standing on the gallows awaiting my death. In those moments, I'd thought Elle had betrayed me too.

Of course, she hadn't. She'd done the opposite, really, joining the team of Knights to save me.

So why was I afraid?

"It's fine," Elle said with a little smirk.

"What's fine? The fact that I just turned down a kiss from the most beautiful, sword-wielding, true dragon-riding princess in all of Evgard? For no good reason, either, I might add."

"Yeah, that was pretty stupid," Elle agreed.

I shrugged.

"But now you know I'm ready whenever you are," she said.

Now it was my turn to raise an eyebrow. "What about your engagement?"

"An engagement isn't a marriage." Elle gave a mischievous smile as she put a hand to the white heartscale hanging around her neck. Aurora scampered out from the shadows and climbed up Elle's outstretched hand and into her arms. "Plus, with Drakfell being the traitor keepdom and all, I imagine I'll be more available in no time. Your move, Asher of Steel Rim," Elle said with one of her trademark winks as she retreated back into the castle.

I stood there, watching her go for as long as I could. She didn't look back, but I knew she was aware that I couldn't look away. She disappeared into the hallway beyond.

A low growl sounded behind me, and when I turned, I saw Thorn giving me a confused look. Through our bond, I felt a flash of heat like a wildfire as my dragon scolded me for screwing up my chance with Elle.

"I know, I know," I said. "I'm insane. I just need a little more time. Shaya... Vidya messed me up I think."

Thorn let out a draconic groan and tossed his head melodramatically.

I laughed, and I felt our bond glow to life like a comforting candle and the feeling of home.

Then Thorn's gaze darted toward the ocean. He looked back at me, flicking his tail with hopeful anticipation as he sent a single word to me through our bond.

Fun?

I grinned, knowing exactly what he was thinking.

"We really should get some sleep," I said, tapping a finger to my chin. "We're leaving in the morning, and it's the responsible thing to do. Just think of what Kai would say."

Thorn gave me a look, and I burst out laughing. I took a few steps backward, away from the balcony.

My eyes flashed gold as I burned ether. Then I rushed forward, hover-jumping to give me some extra height as I launched myself over the edge of the rail.

I fell toward the open ocean, the wind pulling my hair free from its knot. Thorn roared and dove after me. After a few more seconds of freefall, he swooped under me, catching me on his back.

I laughed as I grabbed hold of his saddle and, together, we zoomed upward, Thorn opening his wings wide to catch the wind. We soared as one through the open air, backlit by the moonlight as distant skyfalls streaked across the night sky.

VISION 5

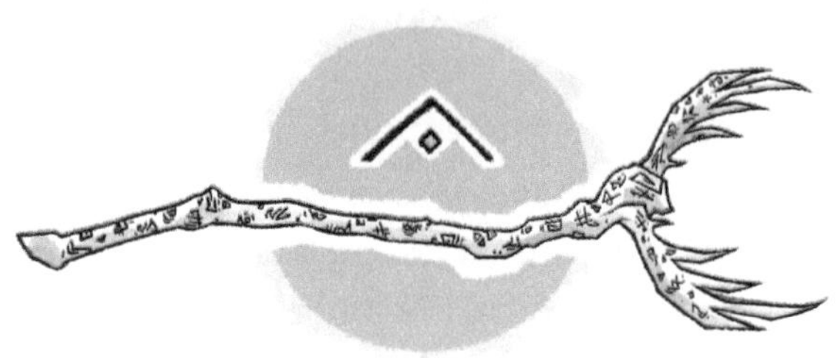

The Farseer stood silently at the edge of his cove near the base of Orothion's tower. The ocean waves crashed at his feet, threatening to spill over onto the rocky floor.

Crabs skittered into the safety of the tide pools scattered along the surface of the rock. Moonlight reflected into the pools from the open end of the cavern.

The Farseer looked out over the water. He could see Asher of Steel Rim and his bond flying over the cresting waves. The Farseer gave a low chuckle. It reminded him of himself in his younger years.

The Farseer looked up into the stars. The alignments were just right. Tomorrow, many journeys would be set in motion.

He retreated deeper into the cove, leaving the harsh sounds of the ocean behind.

He climbed the staircase carved into the cold, barnacle-encrusted rock. He traced a psionic rune, then used it to telekinetically pull open a heavy, weathered, hidden door. The Farseer slipped inside.

Whoever said the Farseer's cove couldn't be comfortable?

The Farseer entered a warm room that smelled of spiced cider. An ornate yet comfortable armchair sat on lush red carpet before a roaring hearth. The hearth burned bright with gold omenfire. Inside, the flames danced with flashes of the future of his team.

Valla and Boone would head North. The people of Behrfell would be difficult to convince, but the flames showed the possibility of bringing the Glacier Keepdom around to the Knights' side.

Next, the Farseer observed a vision of Jax saddling up his new bonded dragon, Jade, as he prepared to embark on his own journey. No longer forced to follow the Mage Hunter Lothar, the evren was finally happy with Jax. They would make a strong pair, though the Farseer worried. Jax's future was so uncertain, hinging on decisions Jax didn't yet know he would have to make. The Farseer reminded himself to ensure Jax brought extra ether crystals. It wouldn't matter if he hid them now that he was silvermarked.

The visions showed Kari hard at work in the smithing workshops here in Orothion. She would do well. Akayto, too, would stay in Orothion. The Farseer was glad to finally have a Rifter as part of the Knights. Evgard's Rifter purge had left them too vulnerable, and besides, the Farseer had special plans for Akayto's skill with rift anchors.

Kai would learn much from the woman in the Mirror Forest. His desire to learn would fuel his skill, and perhaps eventually provide him with a great destiny.

As uncertain as Jax's future appeared, Asher's was far worse. The Farseer gazed into the flames as flashes of gray mist rushed over the young Archon's face. Then Asher wore a dusky blue cloak and silvery pauldron. Next, the Farseer saw Asher's dark hair highlighted with eerie, blue light right before he screamed in terror.

He saw a sword trained on Asher's chest, wielded by a young woman with the white hair of a snowhead.

The Farseer frowned. He'd seen this girl in visions before, but had not yet found her. The stars told him that she, like Asher, would be crucial in the coming convergence of mythic stars. That was one of the reasons he'd been so glad to find Asher in Steel Rim, and why he'd been thrilled when Asher agreed to join the quest for the true dragon egg.

The Farseer smiled. Asher was already beginning to live more aspects of the code of the Knights of the Torch, whether he knew it or not. In saving King Rodan, he had found a way out of choosing death. He had chosen light.

Momentarily, the flames danced, their fiery tendrils morphing into the shape of a golden tree. The tree shrank into the background, and a tower made entirely from crystalline blue glass sprouted up from the hearth. Then the tower shattered as the flames showed a darkened, reddish moon.

The Farseer grimaced. He didn't yet comprehend any of that. Omens were terribly tricky.

Then the vision shifted again, and the Farseer saw a group of Mage Hunters, fighting like dragons as guards in orange cloaks lay dead at their feet. These Hunters wielded the same blue, netherworldly power as Vidya had at the geyser fields.

Voidarchy.

Among these Hunters the Farseer saw Jaira, the girl from Whitestone Hall. Shaw, that absurd Geomancer who just never seemed to stay dead, stood by her side as well, as did Lothar and Ilyan.

The Farseer closed his eyes. He'd felt certain they hadn't truly died in the Dragonstorm Sea. This vision confirmed it. Lines of worry appeared along the Farseer's forehead as he watched a cold, flameless torch appear in the fire, followed by flakes of rapidly swirling snow. Just after the snowstorm, the Farseer saw a single, black feather flicker before the whole vision vanished.

The runes along the Farseer's staff glowed brighter as he channeled more ether into the fire. He tried to guide the flames toward the future of the person he needed to see most.

First the flames burned black, then deep violet, then cool gray for just a moment before shrinking down to nothing and dying out completely. A second later, the flames burned gold again. Above them hung the blue-black darkness of a night sky filled with stars.

Vidya knew he'd be watching her. She must've been taking extra precautions to keep herself from appearing in his flames.

"Soot on a stick," the Farseer cursed, falling back into the fancy armchair.

Woof! a bloodhusky entered the room, whining in sympathy for his owner's plight. The large dog padded over toward the armchair, resting his head on the Farseer's lap.

The Farseer threw off his red hood and stroked his goatee before he ran his hand through the bloodhusky's red fur.

"Get some rest, His Majesty," the Farseer said. "Tomorrow we head to Behrfell with Valla and Boone."

The bloodhusky barked with approval.

"That's right," the Farseer laughed. "Tomorrow we head home to Glacia. Isn't this the greatest thing that could've possibly happened?"

The Farseer and bloodhusky turned once more toward the gold flames of the visions. The image of the night sky still hung in the air above the fire as the Farseer took one last look at the fading stars.

End of Book One

Now, check out a sneak peak of:

DRAGON GUARD

Book 2 in the Skystone Chronicles

Reflection I

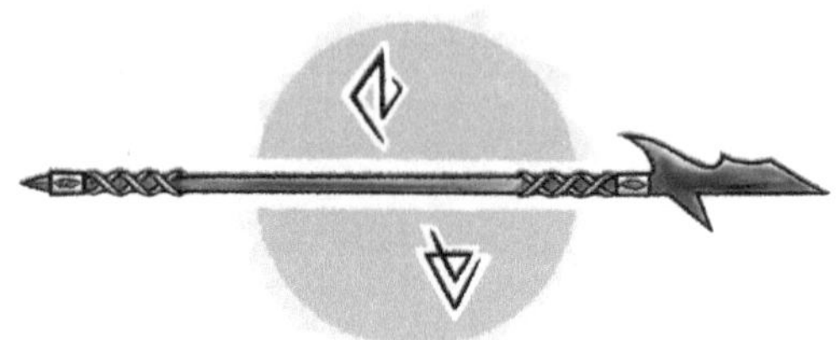

Icy stillness.

The frigid water rushed around Vidya's ears. It filled her nose and stung her eyes as it surrounded her.

She squeezed her mouth shut, swallowing the last bit of air she'd taken in before leaping through the portal. If only she'd taken a bigger breath.

Withering into nothingness in the salty water were the red robes of the Farseer. No, not the Farseer. An illusion.

A drakking illusion. Vidya couldn't believe she'd let herself fall for the Knights of the Torch's trick. She'd been so focused on obtaining her prize that she'd acted impulsively. Foolishly.

Now, she and her entourage would pay the price.

Her four Mage Hunters floated weightlessly to her left and right, their dusky blue cloaks flowing with the current while their heavy armor pulled them down toward the sea floor. The last embers of golden light from the portal winked out, leaving them in complete darkness to await their deaths.

No.

Vidya was not about to die at the bottom of the sea because of some trick from the Knights of the Torch. She wouldn't let Solrac win that easily.

Put me back in control, a soft, feminine voice echoed in her head. *I can save us.*

Vidya hated not being in command of her own actions. But she was running out of air.

She closed her eyes, letting go. She felt the other being slip into her soul, her presence filling her chest, arms, legs, and mind.

When Vidya opened her eyes again, her glowing, lightning blue irises lit the water. Power rushed through her, from her core to her fingertips.

She traced a psionic rune, more blue light trailing from her finger as the rune appeared over her forehead like a sapphire in a crown. Raising her dragonhook spear high above her head, she reached out with her other hand to telekinetically grab hold of her Mage Hunters' heavy armor.

Drawing her entourage close, Vidya's shadowbinding power surged first through her own body before flowing into those of her Hunters. They appeared as shadows of themselves, their bodies not quite solid. It was a form of etherarchy that Vidya herself didn't understand. But the being controlling her radiated confidence.

With a burst of otherworldly might, Vidya pushed her spear upward, clinging to it until her knuckles turned white. She accessed her archonic levitation ability as well, aiding the telekinetic push against the spear.

Vidya and her Mage Hunters shot upward, and it was as if their semi-incorporeal bodies weighed next to nothing. They flew through the water like a meteor cuts through the sky.

Finally, they broke the water's surface. Vidya gasped for breath as they launched into the air. She scanned her surroundings for somewhere to land, recognizing the salty scent and the outline of mountains along the distant horizon. They were in the dead center of the Dragonstorm Sea.

Drak, Vidya mentally swore.

The Soul Reaper's anchor, her companion reminded her.

Vidya strained to continue their ascension as she fumbled in her pocket for the white, runemarked stone. She felt more precious ether drain from her as she activated the stone, dropping it below them toward the water.

Just before falling back into the sea, the portal spun to life. Rather than the telltale gold rim of etherarchy, eerie blue light edged the rift.

Vidya felt her Mystic ether well run out as a headache split across her forehead, the rune there vanishing. Likewise, her chest felt so tight she thought it would burst. She was almost completely drained of power.

Vidya went limp, barely conscious as she felt the other being's presence leave her body. Both she and her four Mage Hunters fell through the air, disappearing into the portal below.

A hollow feeling filled Vidya as she and her Hunters came tumbling out the other end of the portal. Through blurred vision, she saw familiar black stone walls and a silver swan insignia adorning the large black door. They'd come through right where Vidya had left the exit anchor.

Swan Spire.

Vidya had turned the tower into her own personal sanctuary. It stood overlooking the Mage Hunter Academy, on a high cliffside in the heart of the Ridgeback Mountains.

Beside Vidya, her Mage Hunters breathed heavily as their waterlogged cloaks drenched the black, painted slats of the wooden floor.

Vidya gasped for air. Her lungs felt like lead.

But she was alive.

You're welcome, the voice purred inside her mind.

"Come in."

Vidya's voice was ragged as she spoke. The door creaked open to reveal the shadowy silhouette of a tall man with angular horns sprouting off the back of his scalp amidst his dark hair. A gleaming silver pauldron graced his shoulder, and the long, dusky blue cloak of a Mage Hunter swept off his back as he entered Swan Spire.

"The Ursadon," Vidya said as he stalked toward where she sat.

"The Black Valkyrie," he replied in an accented voice, using her title. Few knew her true name, which was the way Vidya liked it. At least, it was the way things had to be.

"Take a seat," she gestured toward a finely-carved, black wooden chair opposite her. A shudder ran through her body—a lingering effect from both her fight with the Farseer and subsequent escape from the Dragonstorm Sea earlier that day.

The Ursadon sat down, the dim sunlight from the window streaming onto his face through black curtains. It shone off of the deep violet scales along his hairline and cheekbones. A spiraling, white ether scar crept along one side of his jawline. The Drekai Mage Hunter stared at Vidya expectantly through his bright, dragonfire green eyes.

"Things did not go as planned in Keep Drakfell." Vidya coughed, a wet, hollow feeling aching inside her chest.

"Perhaps you need some time to recover," the Ursadon replied.

"No," Vidya snapped. "There's no time to waste. If I am to capture the Farseer and obtain his ether well, I need more power."

"What would you have me do?" the Ursadon asked, loyalty coloring his otherwise flat tone.

"I'm sending a group of enforcers to arrest the Captain of the Guard in the Canyon Keepdom. I've uncovered evidence that Captain Cenrik is in league with the Knights of the Torch."

The Ursadon's brow furrowed. "Well done. But what do you need from me?"

Vidya's lip curled into a smile. "You're my best Hunter. I need you to take Cenrik's place as Captain over Keep Rengard's army."

No sooner had the words left Vidya's mouth than the Ursadon was on his feet, his dragonfire green eyes flashing.

"No. I'll go anywhere across the realm other than there."

"Why ever not?" Vidya pouted, feigning ignorance.

"You know *she's* in Keep Rengard."

Vidya gave a light chuckle. "Exactly why I thought you'd want to go. To be close to her."

"Her daughter is about to join the guard there. I can't go."

Vidya's voice hardened suddenly. "You *will* go."

The Ursadon pressed his lips into a tight line.

"You will," Vidya repeated. "You said yourself that I need time to recover. Until then, I need you to do some digging—Have you heard of one called the Liberator who leads the Coven of the Gray Ones?"

"I've heard of them, yes." The Ursadon's jaw tensed.

"I need you to go to the Canyon Keepdom, where the Coven is based, and find out the identity of the Liberator."

"I told you, I can't go to Rengard."

"Then I have no choice," Vidya spoke with sweet sharpness. "Either you do as I say, or I send you to the Soul Reaper's laboratory and you become a skymage tonight."

The Ursadon growled in his throat. "You're no skymage. I'll never become what you are."

He's too weak-minded to wield our power anyway, the voice whispered in Vidya's mind.

Vidya smiled. "I thought not. In that case, congratulations on your appointment as leader of the Keep Rengard army, Captain Zoren."

Chapter I: The Dragon Chasm

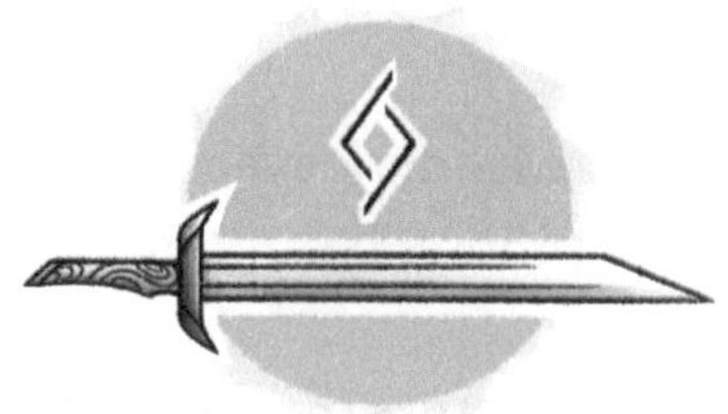

I squared my shoulders as I stared into the gaping redrock chasm, pretending that facing down a few dozen wild dragons was no big deal. But inside, my stomach was in knots.

Clanking sounds from long, seaxe-style swords mingled with creaks from recruits loading their scaleslayer crossbows. The blazing desert sun warmed the sandy red stone beneath our feet, the heat only adding to our anxious energy.

"Here you go, Solvai," I said, passing my best friend a long, newly-sharpened dragonhook spear. "The one you were sparring with yesterday had a splintering haft, so I brought a replacement."

"Oh," Solvai took the spear, weighing it in her hand. "Thanks, Meleya."

"And Brigan," I said, turning to my other best friend. "Your cloak isn't latched properly—There you go."

"Thanks, Meleya." Brigan's warm brown eyes sparkled at me as I smoothed his gray recruit's cloak.

I tucked a few flyaway locks of hair back into my long, white scaletail braid, racking my brain for anything else we might have missed.

"Did you both hydrate enough this morning?"

"Yes, Meleya," both Solvai and Brigan said in unison.

"Do you have your backup weapons?"

"Meleya." Brigan gave a dimpled grin. "I get the sense you're a little on edge."

"I'm just checking," I raised my hands defensively. Though he was absolutely right. We were about to head into a gigantic chasm to face our deaths—Of course I was on edge.

"Yes, we have our backup weapons," Solvai patted the tomahawk hanging from her belt.

"Are they sharpened?" I raised a dark eyebrow.

"You left whetstones on our pillows last night," Brigan reminded me. "So, that's a definite yes."

A commander's voice boomed across the mesa. "Recruits to the platform."

My friends and I exchanged glances. This was it.

Nine.

My heart dropped into my feet as the large, heavy platform jerked downward.

Eight.

The metal creaked as the commander spun the crank. We hugged the platform's center as it descended into the chasm. The harsh sunlight overhead dimmed, the striped, weather-worn orange walls rising up on our left and right.

Seven. Six.

Thud. The platform hit the sandy earth at the bottom of the chasm. We scrambled to get off, clouds of red dust puffing up around our boots.

Five, four, three...

The chains tightened as the commander pulled the platform back up to the top, removing any chance of escape. I'd heard lectures on the Dragon Chasm, how it was the best way to separate the strong soldiers from the weak. Keep Rengard's ultimate test that ensured it had the most powerful army in the realm.

Two.

But watching them unbolt the heavy gate at the other end of the chasm, it became very clear that this was no classroom.

One.

With feral roars, wild dragons spilled from the cave within the rock. Serpentine wyverns launched into the air, jets of lime green dragonfire spraying from their jaws. Four-winged evren shrieked like something from the void as they shot out of the cave. The ground shook as mighty wingless drakes bolted across the chasm toward us.

I lowered my eyebrows, gripping the handle of my seaxe. The long, single-edged sword felt familiar in my hands. The blade was sturdy, the angular tip sharp enough to cut through dragon hide.

For many of my fellow recruits, this would be their first time facing a wild dragon. But I'd spent my childhood roaming the canyons with the nomads. This wasn't my first dragon rodeo. Plus, these dragons were young, probably even less experienced than we were. But they were still wild dragons.

With a warrior's cry, I was the first to charge across the chasm. Then Brigan joined in, followed closely by Solvai and the rest of the recruits.

We screamed until we ran out of breath, but the dragons were still several yards away. It turned out the chasm was a little longer than we'd thought.

We inhaled deeply, then gave another battle cry.

This time we timed it right, clashing against the dragons with a discord of roars, shrieks, and clangs. I came up against a fierce, towering drake that reared up on its hind legs and raked its claws toward me.

I ducked, then rolled out of the way, red dust from the ground streaking across my pale gray recruit's cloak. I launched out of the maneuver and landed on my feet. Then I whacked the flat of my sword down on the base of the dragon's tail. It whirled on me, its fiery green eyes fixed on my dark brown ones.

It took a lot of willpower to not strike at its heart then and there. I could practically hear Dad's voice screaming at me in my head.

A wild dragon never hesitates, and neither should you.

That's what he told me the day he gave me my first dagger. The dagger was one of my fanciest possessions—Dad had stolen it from a nobleman before I was born. With a northern-style sloped blade and a handle carved from a dragonmoose antler, the dagger now served as my ever-present backup weapon, hidden inside my boot.

But today wasn't about killing as many wild dragons as we could in order to survive. Today, the commanders hoped for as many new soldiers as possible to bond a dragon of their own. Not all of us would, of course. Most squads had at least three or four non-riders. But bonding a dragon made a soldier a lot more effective when it came to defending the keep.

A bonded dragon was different from a wild one. Dad always said that the bonding process changed something in the dragon's soul, advancing it beyond a savage animal.

Never kill a bonded dragon, Meleya, he used to say. *They have souls as refined as yours and mine.*

I stared up at the narrowed eyes of the drake, my heart thumping wildly. Every drill instructor who'd ever tried to explain the bonding process had used words like 'connection,' 'sharing,' or the ever-helpful phrase, 'you just kind of feel it.' That didn't seem to be doing a lot for me now.

The dragon let out a low, throaty growl, looking confused as to why the tasty human wasn't fighting back. The veins in my forehead would've burst had I focused any harder on trying to forge a connection.

I didn't feel anything, but then again, I wasn't sure what I was supposed to feel. Hesitantly, I raised one eyebrow.

Big mistake.

That seemed to snap the dragon out of whatever befuddled trance it'd been in. It flared its nostrils, vertical pupils shrinking as it breathed in my scent.

Drak. One look told me that not only had I failed to bond the dragon, but it had just caught a whiff of my ether well. As much as wild dragons enjoyed the taste of regular people, it was the ether inside us magi that drew them to the keeps.

The drake sucked in, jaws wide. In the back of its throat, I saw the sparks of green dragonfire ready to roast me on the spot.

Experience kept me from running away—that would only get me scorched from behind. Instead, I dove toward the space between the drake's forelegs.

When the dragonfire blast came, I was already scrambling underneath the drake's scaly underbelly. It was the perfect spot to take a stab at it, but just because the drake hadn't wanted to bond me didn't mean it wouldn't want to bond another recruit.

I got to my feet and rushed back toward the thick of the action, where the other recruits were busy trying to bond dragons of their own. It looked like a few had already succeeded. One gray-cloaked recruit sat astride a pale blue wyvern, already flying out of the chasm toward safety. Another held on for dear life as his wingless drake crawled straight up the canyon walls like an enormous lizard.

Circling the air above the chasm was a group of soldiers on wyvernback. They allowed the newly bonded pairs to pass over the high edge, but each time one of the wild dragons tried to escape alone, the soldiers used their dragonhook spears to redirect them. For the dragons, there was no getting out without a rider.

I scanned my surroundings, looking for another potential bond. I had to get out of here too, before any of the commanders watching from the ledges above noticed that the dragons wanted to get to me more than the others.

A scream from Solvai made my heart drop. I spun around, gaze honing in on my friend as she looked upward with wide eyes.

I was at her side in a second, seaxe ready to take a swing at whatever dragon was daring to threaten her.

"What is it?" I frowned, seeing no dragon asking for me to hack it to pieces.

"Did you see that?" Solvai shrilled.

"Where?" I demanded, knuckles whitening around the hilt of my sword.

"It was just there," Solvai said, pointing at absolutely nothing. "A violet-scaled hummingbird. I've never seen one this far west before."

My adrenaline rush vanished in an instant. "Drak, you bird nerd."

"Sorry," she blushed. "Their beaks are so interesting, though. I hope I can remember so I can carve it later."

"There will be no carving later unless we make it out of here alive," I warned.

Behind her, I caught sight of a four-winged evren rocketing toward us in a blur of sapphire-colored wings. At the same moment, a white wyvern jumped at us from the side, teeth exposed. I gulped. Both clearly wanted a taste of ether.

Violet-scaled hummingbirds forgotten, Solvai and I maneuvered as one. Time seemed to slow as Solvai bent low to jab at the wyvern. At the same moment, I went high, rolling over Solvai's back with my seaxe arcing to slash at the evren.

I hit the evren right across the belly, and bronze dragon blood sprayed across my face and hair, standing out against the snow white strands. By the sound of the wyvern's pained screech, Solvai's dragonhook spear had struck true as well. Both creatures retreated to nurse their wounds, neither of them interested in forming a bond.

"The commanders *have* to put us on the same squad after that," Solvai said with a grin.

"They'd better," I smiled back. "Now go get yourself a bond."

Solvai nodded, then hurried back into the fray. I felt my muscles relax as she left. I didn't want any of my friends near me and my dragon-attracting ether well.

Come on, Meleya, I thought to myself. *Bond a dragon and get out of here before the commanders realize what you are.*

I could picture the distress on Mom's face if anyone were to find out I was a magi. Already, more dragons were looking my way, eyeing me with barbaric hunger.

I had to find a bond, and fast. My gaze flashed back and forth as I looked for a nice, calm-looking dragon.

I almost missed her, with her rusty orange scales that blended into the chasm walls. A regal, majestic drake oversaw the action with intelligent, green eyes.

She stretched her neck upward and opened her jaws wide. Instead of dragonfire, she breathed out crackling, gold lightning. My breath caught—she was a mythic dragon with etherarchy. A Lightwielding stormscale drake.

I darted toward her, praying to any of the three goddesses willing to listen that the other hungry dragons wouldn't follow me.

The drake watched my approach with curiosity. I tried to calm my soul, preparing to attempt another bond.

But before I got the chance, another recruit eclipsed the dragon from my view. Edrea sneered, stabbing toward me with her dragonhook spear.

I leaped backward to avoid getting skewered.

"What in the void?" I protested. "We're only supposed to be fighting dragons today, not each other."

Apparently, Edrea didn't care. She came at me again, and this time I blocked with my seaxe.

"Stay away from that stormscale drake." Edrea's black eyebrows lowered into her usual scowl. "She's mine."

"If you want her that bad, then try to bond her yourself," I said, blocking another blow from Edrea.

"You don't think I already tried that?"

"Then let me—"

"If I can't have her, neither can you," Edrea snapped.

I ground my teeth in frustration. Edrea was honestly wasting time guarding the drake when she could be out trying to bond another dragon? I wished I could say that surprised me, but throughout boot camp Edrea had always been one to scratch my scales. If the commanders assigned us to squads on opposite sides of the keepdom, it would be too close for me.

"That's ridiculous." I glared, losing my cool. I pushed back her spear with my seaxe, then with a grunt, I swung back.

"Find your own dragon, snowhead," Edrea said, spinning to block my blow. "Or better yet, go back to the dirty nomads."

I leaped toward Edrea, sword raised. She held the haft of her spear between her hands to block me, and my blade hacked into the wood, leaving a notch. My cheeks flushed with frustration.

"At least the nomads taught me manners," I barked.

Suddenly, a flash of lemon yellow came careening toward us from the heavens like a shooting star.

The brightly colored dragon plummeted, knocking straight into both Edrea and me. We screamed as we went rolling across the sandy floor. I managed to hold onto my seaxe, but Edrea's spear went clattering in the opposite direction.

Soot. I'd let myself get distracted. No doubt the evren was here for me and my ether well. The yellow dragon shrieked, pulling upward as it violently flapped its four wings. It was already circling back to take another snap at us.

"Drak, snowhead," Edrea swore as she caught sight of her spear. It had snapped in half right where I'd been whacking at it. "Look what you did."

"Maybe if you hadn't been gatekeeping dragons, we wouldn't be in this situation," I responded.

The evren must've noticed that Edrea was defenseless, because it raced toward her, jaws open wide.

Edrea cried out again, scrambling to get away. But she was going about it all wrong, running straight ahead, in line with the dragon's flight path. Any second, it would either roast her alive with a jet of dragonfire, or simply catch up and sink its teeth into her flesh.

I ground my teeth in frustration and let out an annoyed growl before jumping between her and the evren.

I maniacally swung my sword in warning toward its legless underside. Rather than get stuck with a blade, the evren pulled back at the last second, opening its four wings to catch air and halt its momentum. I leaped toward it, still slashing.

The evren backed up, flapping its wings rapidly. I kept coming at it, and out of the corner of my eye I saw Edrea scuttle toward the bladed end of her broken dragonhook spear. She grabbed it, then turned toward me.

We locked eyes for a split second before she grimaced. Then she dashed away, probably to try and bond another dragon and let me take care of the yellow evren myself.

Thanks a lot, Edrea.

The evren lashed its long, scaly tail toward me. It snapped against the back of my hand, knocking my seaxe to the ground. I inhaled sharply, cradling my hand.

But the evren wasn't finished. It reared back its head, preparing to blast me. I crouched, ready to duck under its belly and run.

At the last moment, the evren went cross-eyed. Instead of spraying me with dragonfire, it let out a massive sneeze.

That caught me off guard, especially when along with the sneeze came a white blast of energy. Pure ether—this dragon was an Astromancer, a starshot evren. The ether shot toward me like a dart, and I leaped backward, falling back into the dirt. The white ether blast hit the earth between my legs, a jagged, white mark spiraling across the red chasm floor.

The evren sneezed again and again, each outburst sending another blast of ether shooting at me from its mouth. I scrambled backward on my hands to avoid getting hit.

Sneeze after sneeze, the ridiculous evren got closer and closer. Before long, my back hit against the chasm wall. The evren had me trapped in a somewhat concealed alcove in the rock. I realized with a degree of horror that the commanders watching us wouldn't be able to see me here, which meant I was on my own, even if things got bad. I cringed, covering my face with my hands as the creature reared back for one final blast.

But the Astromancy-powered sneeze never came.

I dared to open one eye, peeking at the dragon. Its dragonfire green eyes were no longer narrowed to slits. Rather, they were round and shining as they caught the rays of sunlight streaming into the chasm.

Then it hit me like a strong gust of wind.

Not the evren, but the feeling.

Calm filled my heart, despite the tension and chaos surrounding me. My anxiety about the Dragon Chasm and the worry about Solvai and Brigan getting through it melted away. Even the darkness that always plagued the back of my mind—the fear that I'd fail my parents—vanished for that one beautiful instant.

As I stared at the bright yellow evren, it was like I was hearing music, too—A spirited melody, like a flute rising and falling. It captivated me.

Before I knew it, I was runetracing.

Tiny threads of golden light trailed from my finger, and the mystic rune for the Sight appeared, hovering over the center of my forehead.

Then I blinked.

All at once, a set of brilliant new colors bloomed to life before my eyes. Glowing, rust-colored clouds danced along the horizontal lines in the canyon rock. I could see the uniquely colored auras of every creature and person in the chasm—the action of the battle like a clashing of rainbows.

But the aura that drew my attention was the one right in front of me. As I watched, the evren's soul went from a muted yellow to a vibrant, lemony gold. It exploded with beams of light like the sun.

One of the beams seemed to reach toward me. I reached back, holding out a hand toward the dragon's aura. I watched with wonder as the light encompassed my hand, forming a golden cuff around my wrist—an ethereal symbol of our newly-formed bond.

In turn, I saw a coil of fiery indigo light slip from off the tip of my finger and float toward the evren. The piece of my aura formed into a shiny, blue-violet triangle right over the evren's heart.

The dragon landed on the ground, folding up his wings and standing on the claws at his wing-joints. Using the claw at the hinge of his right forewing, the evren scratched vigorously at the scales over his chest. A bright yellow scale fell to the ground in front of me.

The evren's heartscale.

I watched as the indigo piece of my soul filled the void left by the dragon's heartscale, then picked up the yellow scale the evren had dropped before me. The moment it touched my skin, I felt the bond solidify as a flash of white-gold light bloomed from my hand.

The smooth, triangular scale fit perfectly in my palm. I felt a series of musical notes play in my heart, and I smiled as I realized that it was the evren communicating to me through our bond.

The evren seemed to smile back, his tongue hanging out of his mouth as he panted gleefully. As I studied the evren's face, I realized that the panting wasn't the only thing that reminded me of a puppy. His short snout and erect ears brought to mind the wolf-like snow dogs that lived in the northern keeps. Sharp horns curved backward off the top of the dragon's head, and ridges ran down his neck and tail.

Gold light played at the edge of my vision, and I realized I was still using the Sight.

Instantly, I stopped focusing on the etherarchy. The rune hanging over my forehead went out and dissolved into gold etherdust. The brilliant colors and lights of the spirit plane vanished, giving way to the relative dullness of the physical world.

My head was buzzing, my pulse out of control. What was I thinking? Using etherarchy out in the open? Not just in the open, but while the commanders observed us?

My eyes flew to the chasm ledge high above where I sat. The yellow evren had backed me into a tight corner of the redrock. It would've been pretty hard for anyone to catch sight of the golden rune over my forehead from so far away.

Nobody was screaming the word 'magi' or mounting their dragons to swoop in and arrest me. I'd gotten away with it—for now.

Still, I was furious with myself. I needed to be more careful.

A growl pulled my focus. While the commanders and my fellow re-cruits hadn't noticed, another handful of dragons must've picked up on my ether well. A whole group of them stalked toward me.

I felt a tug from whatever ethereal string tied my heart to that of the sneeze-happy evren. He nudged me excitedly, enormous eyes bouncing between me and his back.

In theory, I knew exactly how to ride a dragon. I'd studied for three years at Keep Rengard, the finest boot camp in the Canyon Keepdom, and probably all of Evgard.

I cautiously grabbed hold of the spine at the base of the evren's neck and swung one leg over his scaled back.

"Are you sure about this?" I asked the evren, aware that the ether-hun-gry wild dragons were getting closer.

Ping! My new evren's reply played in my heart like music as he crouched.

One of the wild drakes leaped toward us, and at the same moment, my dragon launched us into the air. I yelped as the drake's claw just missed my leg.

My evren gave an enthusiastic shriek as we soared upward and out of the chasm.

The rich orange fabric of my brand new cloak, made to match the redrock of our land, fell over my shoulders and down to my calves. I was an official soldier of Rengard now.

We stood in the front row of a huge stone amphitheater not far from the Dragon Chasm. A few juniper trees shot up at odd angles from gaps between the stones and small, bristled spineweeds filled in most of the cracks in the rocky seats.

In the seats behind us sat the army of Rengard. Not all of it, of course. Many squads were on duty at the main keep or posted in neighboring towns or outposts. But a couple hundred orange-cloaked soldiers had come to welcome us into their ranks. I even spotted a few members of the nobility's high guards back there, their cloaks of black with orange trim setting them apart.

A flat, stone surface at the base of the amphitheater's seats served as a stage. Beyond the stage, assistants to the dragon keeper helped round up our new bonds. While we went through our induction ceremony, they'd take our dragons back to Keep Rengard's stables.

Beside me, Brigan and Solvai held their heads high. Solvai hadn't bonded a dragon in the chasm, but Brigan stood with shoulders back, his new rusty orange heartscale hanging from a cord around his neck. It perfectly matched his new cloak. It was somehow fitting that despite Edrea's best efforts, Brigan had bonded that regal stormscale drake from the chasm.

He looked like the perfect soldier, his thick, black hair cropped short on the sides with the top pulled into a smooth ridgeknot style. Despite all we'd gone through in the Dragon Chasm less than an hour ago, not a hair was out of place, except for that little corkscrew curl he always pretended just happened to fall perfectly over his forehead.

Brigan turned my way, a dimpled smile playing at his lips.

"I'd ask which dragon was yours, but with a heartscale that bright, he's hard to miss."

Brigan nodded toward where a couple of assistant dragon keepers were struggling to get a certain yellow evren to stay still. My dragon hovered a few feet in the air, his four spastic wings beating fast. He flew in tiny circles, chasing his own tail.

I gave Brigan a shrug. He chuckled.

"I put in a good word with a couple of commanders," he said. "I'm almost positive they're gonna put you, me, and Solvai on a squad together."

"Glad to see you putting your title to good use," I replied.

"No point in being the Heir Duke of Keep Solhelm if you can't swing a few favors for your best friends."

"So you'd consider being your squadmate a favor? Sure it's not a curse?"

"Whoa," Brigan folded his arms across his broad chest. "Curse? Don't go accusing me of being a magi now."

He gave another winning smile, but my jaw tensed at the joke. I turned away.

Brigan frowned. "Meleya—"

The sound of marching cut him off. We both stood at attention as Keep Rengard's nine commanders took the stage. They all wore their full uniforms, from the oversized pauldrons on their right shoulders to the gleaming ravenhelms on their heads. Six of them had ascension armor incorporated into their uniforms—pieces forged using the shed scales from their own bonded dragons.

After the commanders came the Captain of the Guard. Captain Cenrik's ascension armor chestplate and gauntlets were a vibrant shade of sage green to match the heartscale he no doubt wore around his neck under the uniform. He took a step forward, and golden lightning crackled across his scaled ascension armor in a display of power—lightwielding etherarchy granted to him through his dragon's shed scales. The crowd watched on with respect as Captain Cenrik raised his right fist to the left side of his chest.

"For Evgard, unite," he shouted in a deep, resounding voice.

Every member of the guard, including our row of new soldiers, raised our fists to our chests in the same gesture.

In booming chorus, we answered with the Guard's Salute.

"For Evgard, we serve. For her flag, we fight. For her people, we protect. For Evgard, unite."

The last word echoed across the stony amphitheater and out into the rugged desert terrain beyond. A few dragonbirds—Solvai would probably know exactly what species—fled their perches among the junipers at the sound.

"Be seated," Captain Cenrik ordered, and we obliged, settling in for what would no doubt be a long welcome speech. "Before we announce squads, I'd like to thank you all for your service. What an honor to serve alongside you all these years. And to you new soldiers…" Cenrik gestured toward those of us sitting in the front row. "I only wish I'd have had the chance to work with you."

Murmurs ripped throughout the crowd. Brigan, Solvai and I looked at each other. What was Captain Cenrik saying?

Captain Cenrik went on, confirming our suspicions. "But the time has come for me to step down. I wish you the best of luck. May the goddesses favor you and our great keepdom."

There was a small uproar as Captain Cenrik, his face a neutral mask, began to walk off the stage the same way he'd come. A pair of armored men met him at the edge of the amphitheater, one subtly taking hold of the back of his arm as if they were worried he'd try to run or something. It took me a second to realize what uniforms the armored men were wearing.

Silver pauldrons with the symbol of a sword through a triangle on them. Silver swords sheathed at their belts beside hanging silver chain whips. Long, dusk blue cloaks.

My heart sank. Years on the run, hiding among the nomad caravans made it so I knew that uniform all too well.

Those were Mage Hunters.

I was so focused on the action surrounding Captain Cenrik that I almost missed the new arrival taking center stage. But when he spoke, I felt my blood run cold.

"Soldiers of Rengard," his accented voice was commanding, yet somehow flat and emotionless.

He too wore the dusky blue cloak and silver armor of a Mage Hunter, though his was adorned with pieces of black and amethyst ascension armor. His helmet had been modified to accommodate a pair of black horns curving off the top of his head, and a long, dark purple tail coiled around his legs. Patches of black scales grew along his knuckles. The symbol of the Captain of the Guard had been set above the Mage Hunter mark on his oversized pauldron.

I heard a single word uttered over and over in the whispered conversations of the guards behind me:

Drekai.

Please, I prayed to the goddesses. *Let it not be him.* But I knew of only one Drekai Mage Hunter throughout all of Evgard.

He removed his helmet, revealing an ether-scarred face. The white scar crept along his jawline, across the patch of scales growing along his right cheekbone and into his hair. The jagged, spiraling scar sent a shock of white through his dark hair as well.

I remembered the day he got that scar.

"That's the Ursadon," Brigan muttered beside me, using the name the realm had given the famous Mage Hunter. They called him the Ursadon after the dragon bear, because he always tracked down his magi targets, never missing even one.

None, except for me.

My hands balled into fists as the man just stood there, perfectly still. He stared out over the crowd for a full minute as he waited for us to go silent.

Then, just to prove who had the authority here, he waited another minute while the last embers of conversation went dead, had funerals, then completely decayed.

Finally, he resumed speaking, his cold, monotonous voice filling the amphitheater.

"My name is Zoren," he said. "I am your new Captain of the Guard."

A Brief Guide to EVGARD

By Blake & Raven Penn

the skystone chronicles

mystic
Mind

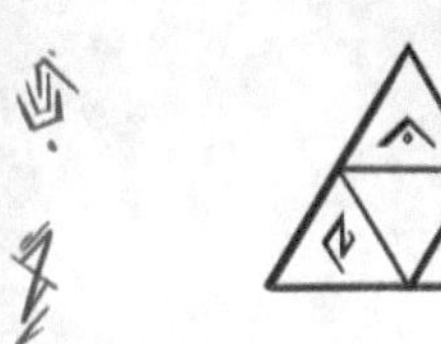

Seer

Seers are Mystics that can access telepathic runes. Some of the more basic runes enable them, to read minds or see omens of the future, while more advanced runes can enable mind control, precognition, and memory wiping.

Mystic ether wells are located in their minds. They trace runes of golden etherlight in the air to achieve mythic effects. Mystics must know the correct runes and have the right intention behind them, and each rune requires a certain amount of ether. Once the rune is completed, it appears over the Mystic's forehead.

Runes can also be carved onto objects to save time. This is most commonly seen with runemarked wands or staffs. We once met a certain Mystic who'd even carved psionic runes onto a whisk. The meringue was delicious.

SHARED POWER: DREAMWEAVE

All Mystics can access the Dreamweave. In the most basic terms, the Dreamweave deals with illusions.

This can manifest through simple runes to trick the eyes, or more advanced runes to trick the other senses. Some runes enable the use of dreamblades—weapons made of focused, purple dream energy that passes through physical objects, but drains the soul's vitality and the victim's stamina. Quite inconvenient when someone blasts you midway through a meeting about the end of the world.

Additionally, the Dreamweave can be used to make illusory bodies for ethereal familiars, which, for lack of a better term, are almost like a solidified imaginary pet.

Psion

Psions are Mysitcs that can access telekinetic runes. More basic runes enable pushing, pulling, or holding objects in place. Psionics only work on non living things (like rocks or metal), and they require more ether to move things that were once living (like wood or leather.)

Rifter

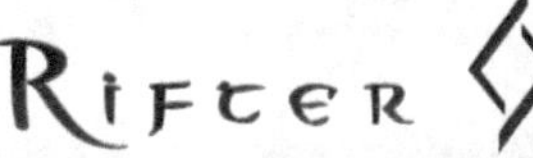

Rifters are Mysitcs that can access teleportation runes. The most basic runes involve making portals through Etheria (the spirit plane), while more advanced runes allow them to make anchors, rift holds, and access the Sight to see into Etheria itself. Rifters can only open portals to places they can see or to an anchor.

the skystone chronicles

Sentinel
Body

Method of Accessing Ether

Sentinel ether wells are located in their core, near the belly button. Their mythic powers are more instinctually driven, and generally require a physical totem of some kind for use. A Geomancer's totem might be a volcanic stone or granite, while a Wildshaper's might be a wolf's fang or a dragonhawk's feather. A Woodweaver's totem could be a leaf or a piece of amber.

When Sentinels access their ether, golden patterns appear on their bodies around whatever area is being affected.

Wildshaper

Wildshapers are fauna-based Sentinels. They can take on aspects of and transform into animals for which they have a totem. This is commonly used to enhance senses or gain a creature's strength or agility. Full transformations are typically accompanied by a cloud of golden ethermist. Careful—that desert finch perched on your sill might not be what she seems.

Geomancer

Geomancers are earth-based Sentinels. Using a totem take from a certain environment can grant them aspects of power related to that environment. A totem of sandstone might be used to make sandstorms, while a stalactites totem could grow into a large club. A common use we've seen is to make one's skin hard as stone, so try not to make any Geomancer enemies. Trust us, they know how to take a hit.

Woodweaver

Woodweavers are flora-based Sentinels. They can use their ether to manipulate and even generate plants based on what totems they have. Some use this power to keep an endless supply of freshly-grown arrows in their quiver or grow diamondoak armor. Others maintain their crops even throughout the winter months. Some have even discovered the secret to making plant servants, called Folians.

Shared Power: Regeneration

All Sentinels share the power of regeneration. This enables them to use their ether to heal wounds. They can train to heal themselves more quickly or learn to heal others. Sentinel regeneration does not work on wounds caused by the anti-ether metal, silver.

The Skystone Chronicles

Archon
Spirit

Lightwielder

Lightwielders are Archons that manipulate light. Different forms of light carry different properties. Commonly, lightwielders use lightning for raw power or liquid light to heal. Lightwielding can reveal things hidden using etherarchy. Less commonly, these Archons can concentrate light into blades or barriers of a weightless, solid material called Luxite.

Method of Accessing Ether

Archon ether wells are located in their hearts. They achieve mythic effects through the will of their spirits. When they command ether, their eyes glow gold. When an Archon learns a new way to use their ether, it is typically through a "breakthrough" during a moment of intense emotion.

Shadowbinder

Shadowbinders are Archons that manipulate darkness. Solid darkness forms shadowsilk, while darkness in its plasmic form makes shadowfire that slowly disintegrates anything it touches. It's actually quite useful in sewer systems. Shadowbinders can even use their affinity for darkness to turn invisible and pass through objects.

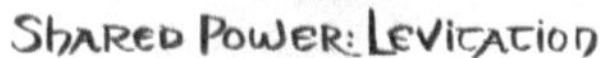

Shared Power: Levitation

All Archons share the power of levitation. This entails Archons using their ether to manipulate how they move. It's most commonly used to make themselves lighter and faster, through hover-jumps and hover-dashes. Levitation has its limits, and in the past thousand years, we've only met one who learned how to use this ability to fly. An Archon manipulating their movement in this way leaves a faint trail of warped golden light behind them as they go.

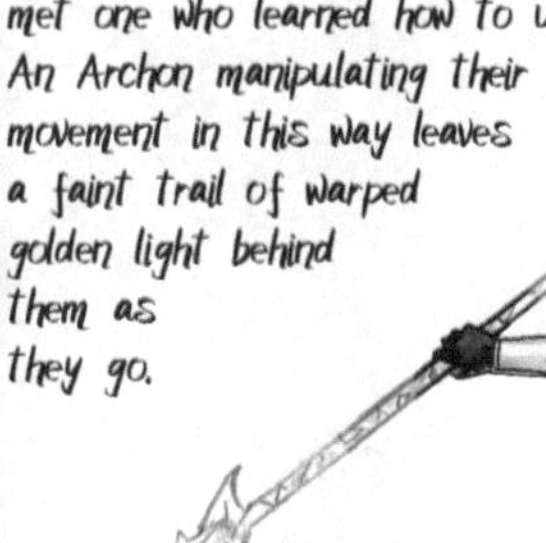

Astromancer

Astromancers use ether to manipulate ether itself. They can condense ether into starglass objects that will last a day, or blast ether directly. Ether leaves a white mark, and hurts both physical and ethereal creatures. It can stop dream energy as well. Some Astromancers can even sense where ether is, and what type is being used. Very few can give their ether away, and even fewer can take it from others. We think it's a latent astromantic sense in dragons that enables them to hunt magi by sensing their ether wells.

the skystone chronicles 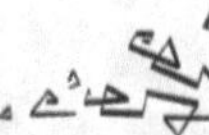

True Dragons

True dragons are what your world generally thinks of as simply... dragons. They are great, intelligent, flying beasts with armored scales, four legs, two wings, and a tail. They vary in color, length, size, and style of horns. Every true dragons can command all nine types of etherarchy as well as breathe dragonfire, which produces an ultra-hot, emerald-green flame.

Since the Dragon Wars, true dragons are incredibly rare in Evgard.

Dragon Eyes

The eyes of dragons are a burning emerald green, just like their dragonfire. All dragons (as far as we know), even lesser dragons, share this trait.

A Note On True Dragon Eggs

Usually no larger than a fist, True Dragon eggs harbor immense power. Their shell tends to be scaly, with a color matching the scales that the hatchling will have. Hatchlings are always bigger than the space the egg could have contained, which implies they must have some form of rift hold within them. The shell ought to be saved for its mythic properties.

Dragon Blood

While true dragons have gold blood, the blood of drakes, wyverns, and evren is more bronze or copper in color. Some like a few drops in their draquila, but it was a little acrid for our taste.

DRAGONS

DRAKES

Drakes are dragons with four legs and no wings. They're commonly built like this worlds panthers or tigers, but more serpentine. They vary greatly in appearance, though most are large enough to carry two human riders on their first ascension.

DRAGON BONDS

All dragons have a heartscale. It's found on their chest, near the heart. Dragons and humans can forge a bond if the dragon gives the human their heartscale. This grants the human power over the dragon, while enhancing the dragon's own cognitive abilities.

EVREN

Evren are dragons with four wings and no legs. They have small claws on the joint of each wing which they can use to crawl, but evren are much more suited to the air. They tend to have more canine features, almost like this world's flying foxes. Evren prefer to sleep hanging upside down from trees or cliffsides, and are usually only large enough to carry one human rider at a time until their second or even third ascension.

WYVERNS

Wyverns are dragons with two wings and two legs. Their wings have well-developed claws at the wing joint, allowing them to navigate the ground far better than evren, though not as well as drakes. They are the most snakelike of the dragons, and tend to have longer necks and tails. When it comes to size, they're generally larger than evren, but smaller than drakes.

Ascension

Evgardian nobility jealously guard the secret to dragon ascension. Still, we suspect the trigger to a dragon's ascension has something to do with their hunger for ether. When a dragon ascends, their ability to communicate grows, and they advance in mythic power, if they have any. Third ascension is the highest level of dragon ascension that we currently know of.

ETHER HUNGRY

Dragons love ether. They will take it from any source they can find, even human magi. It is for this reason that magi are outlawed in Evgard—their ether is what draws wild dragons to the Keeps.

THE SKYSTONE CHRONICLES

Evgardian Creatures

Draconic Animals

There are countless draconic animals in Evgard. From draccoons to wyvernhogs to aldraka, the draconic lifeforms have supplanted most non-mythic animals. Some of our favorites are kirin, which are draconic horses, and lutradons, which are large, scaly otters. There's nothing more fun than splashing around and riding a lutradon in the riverbank.

Ethereal Familiars

Ethereal familiars are not well understood. Born of etharchy, these creatures act as an extension of the magi who created them. They develop their own distinct—and often strong—personalities as well (we once had rather an interesting encounter with a passive aggressive shrew). While all magi types technically have the capacity to create one, Mystics tend to do it most, using a complicated set of runes that manifest on the skin of their familiar.

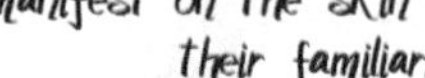

Umbrals

Umbrals are creatures corrupted by the shadow wasting. They fade until they become a smoky gray version of what they once were. They have lightning blue eyes. The bite of an umbral spreads the shadow wasting, though it will not turn humans or dragons fully umbral.

the skystone chronicles

Drekai

Half-Dragon People

The DreKai arrived in Evgard sometime after the Evgardians themselves, though no one is quite sure from where. They mostly resemble humans, though they have draconic horns, tails, dragonfire green eyes, and colorful scales that grow on different parts of their skin (usually the hairline, tips of the ears, cheekbones, shoulders, forearms, Knuckles, Knees, and back of the feet). Though they seem very draconic, they still bleed red as humans do.

Honorable Raiders

A secretive people that live on the Dragon Isles, most Evgardians only Know about the DreKai from their frequent raiding parties along the coasts. They often raid with boomerangs, but not aiming to Kill. They hold honor in high esteem and honor duels among them are frequent. Though they speak their own language, most have learned some amount of Evgardian, though they speak it with an accent you might find similar to this world's Australian.

Half-Borns

The offspring of humans and DreKai are called half-borns. Half-borns do not have tails, and have far fewer scales than their DreKai ancestry. Still, they almost always have dragonfire green eyes and colorfully scale-tipped ears. They are scorned throughout most of Evgard.

✳ note— The man featured here sports an ether scar along his jawline. This is not typical of DreKai, he just had a rather dramatic mishap with a portal

The Skystone Chronicles

ACKNOWLEDGMENTS

Saddle up, dragon riders. Our list of acknowledgements is gonna be LONG.

First off, a HUGE thanks to our parents for all the help and support they gave along the way, including, but not limited to: believing in us, watching our kids, occasionally feeding us, and helping with everything from writing advice (and training) to marketing. Beyond giving us life, you also gave us imaginations, and encouraged them, and we can't thank you for that enough.

A special thanks to Blake's mom for so much help and specific guidance in the world of writing.

A special thanks to Blake's dad for pretending to be a villain for marketing purposes.

A special thanks to Raven's dad for all of the help and understanding of the world of audiobooks and fantasy.

A special thanks to Raven's mom for the most candid reactions ever during beta reading.

Speaking of beta readers, a big thanks to our beta readers, particularly Kimball, Alex, Michael James, Michaela, Ella, Elissa, Ed, Amy, Brenden, Auriana, Bjorn, Sydney, and Cathy.

Oh, and a special thanks to Alex specifically for being the offical Skystone Chronicles character mood song consultant, along with Amy and Kimball for being unofficial love triangle consultants. Also, thanks to everyone who let Blake pester them about the intricacies of the magic system for years.

A massive special thanks to our mad genius editor, Nadav Laemmle, for being a wonder to work with.

Yet another special thanks to J. Scott Savage and Brandon Sanderson for your courses on writing. Outside of our own reading, the two of you have taught us literally everything we know about writing novels. Also, a big thanks to Shad Brooks, for answering all of our ridiculous questions with his YouTube videos, and for making the Shabbard, a slightly modified version of which appears in our world as a "Brookborne scabbard."

And thanks to George Nelson, who gave us such a strong foundation in understanding character, scenes, and good story structure. Your playwriting mentorship has paid off and made learning novelwriting a breeze.

Finally, thanks to you, for reading this. If you've read (or listened) this far, please accept a special thanks from us. We hope you've enjoyed Evgard, and that you'll have even more fun with the Skystone Chronicles as they continue.

If you liked the book, please let us know with a review. It will really help us get more people to give the book a chance, especially since this is our first book! Again, thank you so much for taking the time to read it.

Oh, and you can keep up with everything Evgard related at skystonechronicles.com.

(Direct Amazon Review Link)

About the Authors

BLAKE & RAVEN PENN

Blake and Raven Penn fought through epic battles and twisted love triangles to finally find each other. They both studied script writing in college, and now deign to turn their film and comedy experience into novel writing. Through sunshine or the dreaded Utah Valley inversion, they spend their days tending their wild offspring and dreaming of dragons. Aiming to write fantasy adventures that would keep their former teenage selves up reading long past midnight, Blake and Raven hope to brighten a world in desperate need of light.

To contact them, you can reach out via skystonechronicles.com or follow them on social media @skystonechronicles. Also, be sure to join their mailing list and get a free short story set in the world of Evgard!

461